P9-BIH-728

1949, a momentous year! A year that saw the publication of George Orwell's monumental classic *1984*. A year that saw the birth of the magazine which would become *The Magazine of Fantasy and Science Fiction*. A year during which the first of the 'Best Of' anthologies hit the market. What better way to go back in time and experience the excitement of the burgeoning new Science Fiction genre than with some of the greats as they saw it themselves:

Arthur C. Clarke, Edmond Hamilton, Clifford D. Simak, C.M. Kornbluth, Theodore Sturgeon, Ray Bradbury, James H. Schmitz, our own Isaac Asimov and more!

We offer you your own little time machine . . .
Bon Voyage!

Anthologies from DAW
include

ASIMOV PRESENTS THE GREAT SF STORIES
The best stories of the last four decades.
Edited by Isaac Asimov and Martin H. Greenberg.

THE ANNUAL WORLD'S BEST SF
The best of the current year.
Edited by Donald A. Wollheim with Arthur W. Saha.

THE YEAR'S BEST HORROR STORIES
An annual of gooseflesh tales.
Edited by Karl Edward Wagner.

THE YEAR'S BEST FANTASY STORIES
An annual of high imagination.
Edited by Arthur W. Saha.

TERRA SF
The best SF from Western Europe.
Edited by Richard D. Nolane.

ISAAC ASIMOV
— PRESENTS —
THE GREAT SCIENCE FICTION STORIES

Volume 11, 1949

Edited by
Isaac Asimov and Martin H. Greenberg

DAW BOOKS, INC.
DONALD A. WOLLHEIM, PUBLISHER

1633 Broadway, New York, NY 10019

Copyright ©, 1984, by Isaac Asimov and Martin H. Greenberg.
All Rights Reserved.

Complete list of copyright acknowledgements for the contents will be
found on the following page.

Cover design by One Plus One Studios.

Cover art by Michelangelo Miani.

First Printing, March 1984

1 2 3 4 5 6 7 8 9

DAW TRADEMARK REGISTERED
U.S. PAT. OFF. MARCA
REGISTRADA. HECHO EN U.S.A.

PRINTED IN U.S.A

ACKNOWLEDGMENTS

Asimov—Copyright © 1949 by Street & Smith Publications, Inc.; copyright renewed © 1976 by Isaac Asimov. Reprinted by permission of the author.

MacDonald—Copyright © 1976 by John D. MacDonald Publishing, Inc. Reprinted by permission of the author.

Padgett—Copyright © 1949, Renewed by Catherine Moore Kuttner. Reprinted by permission of Don Congdon Associates, Inc.

Phillips—Copyright © 1949 by Street & Smith Publications, Inc. Reprinted by permission of the author and his agents, the Scott Meredith Literary Agency, Inc., 845 Third Ave., New York, NY 10022.

Padgett (Prisoner in the Skull)—Copyright © 1949, Renewed 1977 by Catherine Moore Kuttner. Reprinted by permission of Don Congdon Associates, Inc.

Hamilton—Copyright © 1949 by Standard Magazines. Reprinted by permission of the agents for the author's estate, the Scott Meredith Literary Agency, Inc., 845 Third Ave., New York, NY 10022.

Clarke—Copyright © 1949 by Standard Magazines; copyright renewed. Reprinted by permission of the author and his agents, the Scott Meredith Literary Agency, Inc., 845 Third Ave., New York, NY 10022.

Simak—Copyright © 1949 by Street & Smith Publications, Inc; copyright renewed by the author. Reprinted by permission of Kirby McCauley, Ltd.

Kornbluth—Copyright © 1949 by Standard Magazines. Reprinted by permission of Robert P. Mills, Ltd.

MacDonald, Philip—Copyright © 1949, Mercury Press, Inc.

Sturgeon—Copyright © 1949 by Mercury Press, Inc; copyright renewed. Reprinted by permission of the author and Kirby McCauley, Ltd.

Bradbury—Copyright © 1949, Renewed 1977 by Ray Bradbury. Reprinted by permission of Don Congdon Associates, Inc.

MacLean—Copyright © 1949 by Street & Smith Publications, Inc., 1962 by Katherine MacLean; reprinted by permission of the author and the author's agent, Virginia Kidd.

Kuttner—Copyright © 1949, Renewed 1977 by Catherine Moore Kuttner. Reprinted by permission of Don Congdon Associates, Inc.

Schmitz—Copyright © 1949 by Street & Smith Publications, Inc. Reprinted by permission of the agents for the author's estate, the Scott Meredith Literary Agency, Inc., 845 Third Ave., New York, NY 10022.

Contents

1949 INTRODUCTION

In the world outside reality it was a most important year, one that saw the Soviet Union detonate a nuclear weapon and the victory of the Communists in China. On January 20 President Truman urged in "Point Four" of his inaugural address that the United States share its technological and scientific knowledge with "underprivileged areas." NATO (the North Atlantic Treaty Organization) came into being formally on April 4 and would soon be a major factor in American foreign policy. The Republic of Eire officially came into existence on April 18. In a relatively rare state name-change, Siam became Thailand on May 11, one day before the Berlin blockade was ended by the Soviets. West (the German Federal Republic) and East (the German Democratic Republic) Germany were established on May 23 and October 7.

The defeated Chinese Nationalists under Chiang Kai-shek began to evacuate their remaining forces to Formosa on July 16; the People's Republic of China, ruled by Mao Tse-tung and Chou En-lai, was proclaimed on October 1.

President Truman announces on September 23 that the Soviets have successfully tested a nuclear weapon.

The American domestic economy undergoes a series of major strikes, including a bitter dispute in the coal fields. Congress raises the minimum wage from 40 cents to 75 cents an hour.

During 1949 Simone de Beauvoir published *The Second Sex*, a work that greatly influenced the postwar feminist movement. The great Selman Waksman isolated neomycin, giving yet another important antibiotic to the world. Jackie Robinson was the Most Valuable Player in the National League, batting an impressive .342, while Ralph Kiner led the majors in home runs with 54. Hit songs included "Dear Hearts and Gentle People," "I

Don't Care if the Sun Don't Shine," " Scarlet Ribbons," and
"Rudolph the Red-Nosed Reindeer."

The Volkswagen automobile was introduced in the American
market but it got off to a very slow start—only two were sold in
1949. A gallon of gas cost 25 cents. Marc Chagall painted "Red
Sun," while *The Goldbergs*, sometimes called American TV's
first situation comedy, became a hit. Joe Louis retired as heavy-
weight boxing champion and Ezzard Charles became the new
champ by defeating Jersey Joe Walcott. Nelson Algren published
his powerful *The Man with the Golden Arm*, while important and
popular films included *Adam's Rib*, the tremendous *White Heat*,
All the King's Men, *Sands of Iwo Jima*, *Twelve O'Clock High*
(war pictures were particularly popular), and *She Wore a Yellow
Ribbon*.

Pancho Gonzales was U.S. Tennis Champion. Anaïs Nin pub-
lished *The House of Incest*. Top Broadway musicals included
South Pacific starring Ezio Pinza and Mary Martin, and *Gentlemen
Prefer Blondes*, with the wonderful Carol Channing. Ponder won
the Kentucky Derby. Jacob Epstein produced his sculpture of
"Lazarus." Silly Putty was introduced and became a big success.
The New York Yankees won the World Series by beating the
Brooklyn Dodgers (sorry again, Isaac) four games to one. A pack
of cigarettes cost 21 cents. The legitimate stage was graced by
Death of a Salesman by Arthur Miller and *Detective Story* by
Sidney Kingsley. Graham Greene published *The Third Man*.
Amos 'n Andy came to television.

A loaf of bread cost 15 cents. The National Football League
and the All-America Conference merged, bringing the Cleveland
Browns into the NFL, which they were to dominate for the next
decade. Alger Hiss was convicted of spying against the United
States for the Soviet Union.

The record for the mile run was still the 4:01.4 set by Gunder
Haegg of Sweden in 1945.

Mel Brooks was (probably) still Melvin Kaminsky.

In the real world it was another outstanding year as a large
number of excellent (along with a few not so excellent) science
fiction and fantasy novels and collections were published (again,
many of these had been serialized years earlier in the magazines),
including the titanic *1984* by George Orwell, *Lords of Creation*
by Eando Binder, *A Martian Odyssey* by Stanley G. Weinbaum,
Exiles of Time by Nelson Bond, *Skylark of Valeron* by E. E.
(Doc) Smith, *What Mad Universe* by Fredric Brown, *The Fox
Woman* by A. Merritt, *The Incredible Planet* by John W.

Campbell, Jr., *Sixth Column* by Robert A. Heinlein, *The Sunken World* by Stanton A. Coblentz, and *The Star Kings* by Edmond Hamilton. Two important anthologies were *The Best Science Fiction Stories, 1949*, the first annual "Best of" anthology, edited by E. F. Bleiler and T. E. Dikty, and *The Girl with the Hungry Eyes and Other Stories*, one of the first "original anthologies," edited by our own Donald A. Wollheim.

Important novels that appeared in magazines in 1949 included *Seetee Shock* by Jack Williamson, *Flight into Yesterday* by Charles L. Harness, and *Needle* by Hal Clement.

Super Science Fiction reappeared on the newsstands, this time edited by Eijer Jacobsson. Other sf magazines that began publication in 1949 were *Other Worlds Science Stories*, edited by Raymond A. Palmer, and *A. Merritt's Fantasy Magazine*. However, all these paled beside the launching in October of *The Magazine of Fantasy*, published by Mercury Press and edited by Anthony Boucher and J. Francis McComas—with its name changed to *The Magazine of Fantasy and Science Fiction*, it would soon become a major rival to *Astounding* and certainly one of the most important sf magazines of all time.

More wondrous things were happening in the real world as five writers made their maiden voyages into reality: in February, John Christopher (Christopher Youd) with "Christmas Tree"; in July, Kris Neville with "The Hand From the Stars"; in the Fall issue of *Planet Stories*, Roger Dee with "The Wheel is Death"; in October, Katherine MacLean with "Defense Mechanism"; and in the Winter issue of *Planet Stories*, Jerome Bixby, with "Tubemonkey."

Gnome Press, under the leadership of David Kyle and Martin Greenberg (the *other* Marty Greenberg) began publication during 1949. The *Captain Video* TV series took to the airways.

The real people gathered together for the seventh time as the World Science Fiction Convention (Cinvention) was held in Cincinnati. Notable sf films of the year were *Mighty Joe Young* and *The Perfect Woman*, the latter based on a play by Wallace Geoffrey and Basil Mitchell.

Death took Arthur Leo Zagat at the age of 54.

But distant wings were beating as Malcolm Edwards was born.

Let us travel back to that honored year of 1949 and enjoy the best stories that the real world bequeathed to us.

THE RED QUEEN'S RACE

By Isaac Asimov (1920–   )

Astounding Science Fiction, **January**

Marty Greenberg does have a tendency to pick my stories for this series. Not all of them, of course, but more than I think he ought to. Unfortunately, he insists on having the sole vote in this matter. He says I am too prejudiced to vote, which is ridiculous on the face of it. However, I don't dare do anything to offend him, for he does all the skutwork in this series (Xeroxing stories, getting permissions, paying out checks, etc.) and does it most efficiently. If he quit on me, there would be no chance whatever of an adequate replacement.

And then having picked a story, he refuses to write a headnote for it. He insists that I do the job alone.

Well, what can I say about "The Red Queen's Race"?

1. I wrote it after nearly a year's layoff from writing because I was working very hard to get my Ph.D. Once I got it, I went back to writing at once (with RQR as a result) and since then I have never had a sizable writing hiatus (or even a minor one) in my life.

2. Someone once said to me, "I didn't know you ever wrote a tough-guy detective story." I said, "I never have." He said, "How about 'The Red Queen's Race'?"—so I read it and it certainly sounds tough-guy detective. I've never been able to explain that.

3. If you were planning to write anyway (I wouldn't ask you if you weren't) do write to Marty to the effect that you loved this story. I want him to think highly of himself and of his expertise, and not even dream of quitting the team.—I.A.

Here's a puzzle for you, if you like. Is it a crime to translate a chemistry textbook into Greek?

Or let's put it another way. If one of the country's largest atomic power plants is completely ruined in an unauthorized experiment, is an admitted accessory to that act a criminal?

These problems only developed with time, of course. We started with the atomic power plant—drained. I really mean *drained*. I don't know exactly how large the fissionable power source was—but in two flashing microseconds, it had all fissioned.

No explosion. No undue gamma ray density. It was merely that every moving part in the entire structure was fused. The entire main building was mildly hot. The atmosphere for two miles in every direction was gently warm. Just a dead, useless building which later on took a hundred million dollars to replace.

It happened about three in the morning, and they found Elmer Tywood alone in the central source chamber. The findings of twenty-four close-packed hours can be summarized quickly.

1. Elmer Tywood—Ph.D., Sc.D., Fellow of This and Honorary That, one-time youthful participant of the original Manhattan Project, and now full Professor of Nuclear Physics—was no interloper. He had a Class-A Pass—Unlimited. But no record could be found as to his purpose in being there just then. A table on casters contained equipment which had not been made on any recorded requisition. It, too, was a single fused mass—not quite too hot to touch.

2. Elmer Tywood was dead. He lay next to the table; his face congested, nearly black. No radiation effect. No external force of any sort. The doctor said apoplexy.

3. In Elmer Tywood's office safe were found two puzzling items: *i.e.* twenty foolscap sheets of apparent mathematics, and a bound folio in a foreign language which turned out to be Greek, the subject matter, on translation, turning out to be chemistry.

The secrecy which poured over the whole mess was something so terrific as to make everything that touched it, *dead*. It's the only word that can describe it. Twenty-seven men and women, all told, including the Secretary of Defense, the Secretary of Science, and two or three others so top-notch that they were completely unknown to the public entered the power plant during the period of investigation. Any man who had been in the plant that night, the physicist who had identified Tywood, the doctor who had examined him, were retired into virtual home arrest.

No newspaper ever got the story. No inside dopester got it. A few members of Congress got part of it.

And naturally so! Anyone or any group or any country that could suck all the available energy out of the equivalent of perhaps fifty to a hundred pounds of plutonium without exploding it, had America's industry and America's defense so snugly in the palm of the hand that the light and life of one hundred sixty million people could be turned off between yawns.

Was it Tywood? Or Tywood and others? Or just others, through Tywood?

And my job? I was a decoy; or front man, if you like. Someone has to hang around the university and ask questions about Tywood. After all, he was missing. It could be amnesia, a hold-up, a kidnapping, a killing, a runaway, insanity, accident—I could busy myself with that for five years and collect black looks, and maybe divert attention. To be sure, it didn't work out that way.

But don't think I was in on the whole case at the start. I wasn't one of the twenty-seven men I mentioned a while back, though my boss was. But I knew a little—enough to get started.

Professor John Keyser was also in Physics. I didn't get to him right away. There was a good deal of routine to cover first in as conscientious a way as I could. Quite meaningless. Quite necessary. But I was in Keyser's office now.

Professors' offices are distinctive. Nobody dusts them except some tired cleaning woman who hobbles in and out at eight in the morning, and the professor never notices the dust anyway. Lots of books without much arrangement. The ones close to the desk are used a lot—lectures are copied out of them. The ones out of reach are wherever a student put them back after borrowing them. Then there are professional journals that look cheap and are darned expensive, which are waiting about and which may some day be read. And plenty of paper on the desk; some of it scribbled on.

Keyser was an elderly man—one of Tywood's generation. His nose was big and rather red, and he smoked a pipe. He had that easy-going and nonpredatory look in his eyes that goes with an academic job—either because that kind of job attracts that kind of man or because that kind of job makes that kind of man.

I said: "What kind of work is Professor Tywood doing?"

"Research physics."

Answers like that bounce off me. Some years ago they used to get me mad. Now, I just said: "We know that, professor. It's the details I'm after."

And he twinkled at me tolerantly: "Surely the details can't help much unless you're a research physicist yourself. Does it matter—under the circumstances?"

"Maybe not. But he's gone. If anything's happened to him in the way of"—I gestured, and deliberately clinched—"foul play, his work may have something to do with it—unless he's rich and the motive is money."

Keyser chuckled dryly: "College professors are never rich. The commodity we peddle is but lightly considered, seeing how large the supply is."

I ignored that, too, because I know my looks are against me. Actually, I finished college with a "very good" translated into Latin so that the college president could understand it, and never played in a football game in my life. But I look rather the reverse.

I said: "Then we're left with his work to consider."

"You mean spies? International intrigue?"

"Why not? It's happened before! After all, he's a nuclear physicist, isn't he?"

"He is. But so are others. So am I."

"Ah, but perhaps he knows something you don't."

There was a stiffening to the jaw. When caught off-guard, professors can act just like people. He said, stiffly: "As I recall off-hand, Tywood has published papers on the effect of liquid viscosity on the wings of the Rayleigh line, on higher-orbit field equation, and on spin-orbit coupling of two nucleons, but his main work is on quadrupole moments. I am quite competent in these matters."

"Is he working on quadrupole moments now?" I tried not to bat an eye, and I think I succeeded.

"Yes—in a way." He almost sneered, "He may be getting to the experimental stage finally. He's spent most of his life, it seems, working out the mathematical consequences of a special theory of his own."

"Like this," and I tossed a sheet of foolscap at him.

That sheet was one of those in the safe in Tywood's office. The chances, of course, were that the bundle meant nothing, if only because it was a professor's safe. That is, things are sometimes put in at the spur of the moment because the logical drawer was filled with unmarked exam papers. And, of course, nothing is ever taken out. We had found in that safe dusty little vials of yellowish crystals with scarcely legible labels, some mimeographed booklets dating back to World War II and marked "Restricted," a copy of an old college yearbook, and some correspondence concerning a possible position as Director of Research for American Electric, dated ten years back, and, of course, chemistry in Greek.

The foolscap was there, too. It was rolled up like a college diploma with a rubber band about it and had no label or descriptive title. Some twenty sheets were covered with ink marks, meticulous and small—

I had one sheet of that foolscap. I don't think any one man in the world had more than one sheet. And I'm sure that no man in the world but one knew that the loss of his particular sheet and of his particular life would be as nearly simultaneous as the government could make it.

So I tossed the sheet at Keyser, as if it were something I'd found blowing about the campus.

He stared at it and then looked at the back side, which was blank. His eyes moved down from the top to the bottom, then jumped back to the top.

"I don't know what this is about," he said, and the words seemed sour to his own taste.

I didn't say anything. Just folded the paper and shoved it back into the inside jacket pocket.

Keyser added petulantly: "It's a fallacy you laymen have that scientists can look at an equation and say, 'Ah, yes—' and go on to write a book about it. Mathematics has no existence of its own. It is merely an arbitrary code devised to describe physical observations or philosophical concepts. Every man can adapt it to his own particular needs. For instance no one can look at a symbol and be sure of what it means. So far, science has used every letter in the alphabet, large, small and italic, each symbolizing many different things. They have used bold-faced letters, Gothic-type letters, Greek letters, both capital and small, subscripts, superscripts, asterisks, even Hebrew letters. Different scientists use different symbols for the same concept and the same symbol for different concepts. So if you show a disconnected page like this to any man, without information as to the subject being investigated or the particular symbology used, he could absolutely not make sense out of it."

I interrupted: "But you said he was working on quadrupole moments. Does that make this sensible?" and I tapped the spot on my chest where the foolscap had been slowly scorching a hole in my jacket for two days.

"I can't tell. I saw none of the standard relationships that I'd expect to be involved. At least I recognized none. But I obviously can't commit myself."

There was a short silence, then he said: "I'll tell you. Why don't you check with his students?"

I lifted my eyebrows: "You mean in his classes?"

He seemed annoyed: "No, for Heaven's sake. His research students! His doctoral candidates! They've been working with him. They'll know the details of that work better than I, or anyone in the faculty, could possibly know it."

"It's an idea," I said, casually. It was, too. I don't know why, but I wouldn't have thought of it myself. I guess it's because it's only natural to think that any professor knows more than any student.

Keyser latched on to a lapel as I rose to leave. "And, besides," he said, "I think you're on the wrong track. This is in confidence, you understand, and I wouldn't say it except for the unusual circumstances, but Tywood is not thought of too highly in the profession. Oh, he's an adequate teacher, I'll admit, but his research papers have never commanded respect. There has always been a tendency towards vague theorizing, unsupported by experimental evidence. That paper of yours is probably more of it. No one could possibly want to . . . er, kidnap him because of it."

"Is that so? I see. Any ideas, yourself, as to why he's gone, or where he's gone?"

"Nothing concrete," he said pursing his lips, "but everyone knows he is a sick man. He had a stroke two years ago that kept him out of classes for a semester. He never did get well. His left side was paralyzed for a while and he still limps. Another stroke would kill him. It could come any time."

"You think he's dead, then?"

"It's not impossible."

"But where's the body, then?"

"Well, really— That is *your* job, I think."

It was, and I left.

I interviewed each one of Tywood's four research students in a volume of chaos called a research laboratory. These student research laboratories usually have two hopefuls working therein, said two constituting a floating population, since every year or so they are alternately replaced.

Consequently, the laboratory has its equipment stack in tiers. On the laboratory benches is the equipment immediately being used, and in three or four of the handiest drawers are replacements or supplements which are likely to be used. In the farther drawers, in the shelves reaching up to the ceiling, in odd corners, are fading remnants of the past student generations—oddments never used and never discarded. It is claimed, in fact, that no research student ever knew all the contents of his laboratory.

All four of Tywood's students were worried. But three were worried mainly by their own status. That is, by the possible effect the absence of Tywood might have on the status of their "problem." I dismissed those three—who all have their degrees now, I hope—and called back the fourth.

He had the most haggard look of all, and had been least communicative—which I considered a hopeful sign.

He now sat stiffly in the straight-backed chair at the right of the desk, while I leaned back in a creaky old swivel-chair and pushed my hat off my forehead. His name was Edwin Howe and *he* did get his degree later on. I know that for sure, because he's a big wheel in the Department of Science now.

I said: "You do the same work the other boys do, I suppose?"

"It's all nuclear work in a way."

"But it's not all exactly the same?"

He shook his head slowly. "We take different angles. You have to have something clear-cut, you know, or you won't be able to publish. We've got to get our degrees."

He said it exactly the way you or I might say, "We've got to make a living." At that, maybe it's the same thing for them.

I said: "All right. What's *your* angle?"

He said: "I do the math. I mean, with Professor Tywood."

"What kind of math?"

And he smiled a little, getting the same sort of atmosphere about him that I had noticed in Professor Keyser's case that morning. A sort of, "Do-you-really-think-I-can-explain-all-my-profound-thoughts-to-stupid-little-you?" sort of atmosphere.

All he said aloud, however, was: "That would be rather complicated to explain."

"I'll help you," I said. "Is that anything like it?" And I tossed the foolscap sheet at him.

He didn't give it any once over. He just snatched it up and let out a thin wail: "Where'd you get this?"

"From Tywood's safe."

"Do you have the rest of it, too?"

"It's safe," I hedged.

He relaxed a little—just a little: "You didn't show it to anybody, did you?"

"I showed it to Professor Keyser."

Howe made an impolite sound with his lower lip and front teeth, "*That* jackass. What did he say?"

I turned the palms of my hands upward and Howe laughed. Then he said, in an offhand manner: "Well, that's the sort of stuff I do."

"And what's it all about? Put it so I can understand it."

There was distinct hesitation. He said: "Now look. This is

confidential stuff. Even Pop's other students don't know anything about it. I don't even think *I* know *all* about it. This isn't just a degree I'm after, you know. It's Pop Tywood's Nobel Prize, and it's going to be an Assistant Professorship for me at Cal Tech. This has got to be published before it's talked about."

And I shook my head slowly and made my words very soft: "No, son. You have it twisted. You'll have to talk about it before it's published, because Tywood's gone and maybe he's dead and maybe he isn't. And if he's dead, maybe he's murdered. And when the department has a suspicion of murder, everybody talks. Now it will look bad for you, kid, if you try to keep some secrets."

It worked. I knew it would, because everyone reads murder mysteries and knows all the clichés. He jumped out of his chair and rattled the words off as if he had a script in front of him.

"Surely," he said, "you can't suspect *me* of . . . of anything like that. Why . . . why, my career—"

I shoved him back into his chair with the beginnings of a sweat on his forehead. I went into the next line: "I don't suspect anybody of anything *yet*. And you won't be in any trouble, if you talk, chum."

He was ready to talk. "Now this is all in strict confidence."

Poor guy. He didn't know the meaning of the word "strict." He was never out of eyeshot of an operator from that moment till the government decided to bury the whole case with the one final comment of "?." Quote, Unquote. (I'm not kidding. To this day, the case is neither opened nor closed. It's just "?.")

He said, dubiously; "You know what time travel is, I suppose?"

Sure I knew what time travel was. My oldest kid is twelve and he listens to the afternoon video programs till he swells up visibly with the junk he absorbs at the ears and eyes.

"What about time travel?" I said.

"In a sense, we can do it. Actually, it's only what you might call micro-temporal-translation—"

I almost lost my temper. In fact, I think I did. It seemed obvious that the squirt was trying to diddle me; and without subtlety. I'm used to having people think I look dumb; but not *that* dumb.

I said through the back of my throat: "Are you going to tell me that Tywood is out somewhere in time—like Ace Rogers, the Lone Time Ranger?" (That was junior's favorite program—Ace Rogers was stopping Genghis Khan single-handed that week.)

But he looked as disgusted as I must have. "No," he yelled. "I don't know where Pop is. If you'd *listen* to me—I said micro-temporal-translation. Now this isn't a video show and it isn't magic; this happens to be science. For instance, you know about matter-energy equivalence, I suppose."

I nodded sourly. Everyone knows about that since Hiroshima in the last war but one.

"All right, then," he went on, "that's good for a start. Now if you take a known mass of matter and apply temporal translation to it—you know, send it back in time—you are, in effect, creating matter at the point in time to which you are sending it. To do that, you must use an amount of energy equivalent to the amount of matter you have created. In other words, to send a gram—or, say, an ounce—of anything back in time, you have to disintegrate an ounce of matter completely, to furnish the energy required."

"Hm-m-m," I said, "that's to create the ounce of matter in the past. But aren't you destroying an ounce of matter by removing it from the present? Doesn't that *create* the equivalent amount of energy?"

And he looked just about as annoyed as a fellow sitting on a bumblebee that wasn't quite dead. Apparently laymen are never supposed to question scientists.

He said: "I was trying to simplify it so you would understand it. Actually, it's more complicated. It would be very nice if we could use the energy of disappearance to cause it to disappear but that would be working in a circle, believe me. The requirements of entropy would forbid it. To put it more rigorously, the energy is required to overcome temporal inertia and it just works out so that the energy in ergs required to send back a mass, in grams, is equal to that mass times the square of the speed of light in centimeters per second. Which just happens to be the Einstein Mass-Energy Equivalence Equation. I can give you the mathematics, you know."

"I know," I waxed some of that misplaced eagerness back. "But was all this worked out experimentally. Or is it just on paper?"

Obviously, the thing was to keep him talking.

He had that queer light in his eye that every research student gets, I am told, when he is asked to discuss his problem. He'll discuss it with anyone, even with a "dumb flatfoot"—which was convenient at the moment.

"You see," he said like a man slipping you the inside dope on a shady business deal, "what started the whole thing was this neutrino business. They've been trying to find that neutrino since the late thirties and they haven't succeeded. It's a subatomic particle which has no charge and has a mass much less than even an electron. Naturally, it's next to impossible to spot, and hasn't been spotted yet. But they keep looking because without assuming that a neutrino exists, the energetics of some nuclear reactions can't be balanced. So Pop Tywood got the idea about twenty years ago that some energy was disappearing, in the form of matter, back into time. We got working on that—or he did—and I'm the first student he's ever had tackle it along with him.

"Obviously, we had to work with tiny amounts of material and . . . well, it was just a stroke of genius on Pop's part to think of using traces of artificial radioactive isotopes. You could work with just a few micrograms of it, you know, by following its activity with counters. The variation of activity with time should follow a very definite and simple law which has never been altered by any laboratory condition known.

"Well, we'd send a speck back fifteen minutes, say, and fifteen minutes before we did that—everything was arranged automatically, you see—the count jumped to nearly double what it should be, fell off normally, and then dropped sharply at the moment it was sent back below where it would have been normally. The material overlapped itself in time, you see, and for fifteen minutes we counted the doubled material—"

I interrupted: "You mean you had the same atoms existing in two places at the same time."

"Yes," he said, with mild surprise, "why not. That's why we use so much energy—the equivalent of creating those atoms." And then he rushed on, "Now I'll tell you what my particular job is. If you send back the material fifteen minutes, it is apparently sent back to the same spot relative to the Earth despite the fact that in fifteen minutes, the Earth moved sixteen thouand miles around the Sun, and the Sun itself moves more thousand miles and so on. But there are certain tiny discrepancies which I've analyzed and which turn out to be due, possibly to two causes.

"First, there is a frictional effect—if you can use such a term—so that matter does drift a little with respect to the Earth, depending on how far back in time it is sent, and on the nature of material. Then, too, some of the discrepancy can only be explained by the assumption that passage through time itself takes time."

"How's that?" I said.

"What I mean is that some of the radioactivity is evenly spread throughout the time of translation as if the material tested had been reacting during backward passage through time by a constant amount. My figures show that—well, if you were to be moved backward in time, you would age one day for every hundred years. Or, to put it another way, if you could watch a time dial which recorded the time outside a 'time-machine', your watch would move forward twenty-four hours while the time dial moved back a hundred years. That's a universal constant, I think, because the speed of light is a universal constant. Anyway, that's my work.''

After a few minutes, in which I chewed all this, I asked: "Where did you get the energy needed for your experiments?"

"They ran out a special line from the power plant. Pop's a big shot there, and swung the deal.''

"Hm-m-m. What was the heaviest amount of material you sent into the past?"

"Oh''—he sent his eyes upwards—''I think we shot back one hundredth of a milligram once. That's ten micrograms.''

"Ever try sending anything into the future?"

"That won't work," he put in quickly. "Impossible. You can't change signs like that because the energy required becomes more than infinite. It's a one-way proposition.''

I looked hard at my fingernails: "How much material could you send back in time if you fissioned about . . . oh, say, one hundred pounds of plutonium.'' Things I thought, were becoming, if anything too obvious.

The answer came quickly: "In plutonium fission," he said, "not more than one or two percent of the mass is converted into energy. Therefore, one hundred pounds of plutonium when completely used up would send a pound or two back into time.''

"Is that all? But could you handle all that energy? I mean a hundred pounds of plutonium can make quite an explosion.''

"All relative," he said, a bit pompously. "If you took all that energy and let it loose a little at a time, you could handle it. If you released it all at once, but used it just as fast as you released it, you could still handle it. In sending back material through time, energy can be used much faster than it can possibly be released even through fission. Theoretically, anyway.''

"But how do you get rid of it?"

"It's spread through time, naturally. Of course, the minimum time through which material could be transferred would, therefore, depend on the mass of the material. Otherwise, you're liable to have the energy density with time too high.''

"All right, kid," I said. "I'm calling up headquarters, and they'll send a man here to take you home. You'll stay there awhile.''

"But— What for?"

"It won't be for long."

It wasn't—and it was made up to him afterwards.

I spent the evening at Headquarters. We had a library there—a very special kind of library. The very morning after the explosion two or three operators had drifted quietly into the chemistry and physics libraries of the University. Experts in their way. They located every article Tywood had ever published in any scientific journal and had snapped each page. Nothing was disturbed otherwise.

Other men went through magazine files and through book lists. It ended with a room at Headquarters that represented a complete Tywoodania. Nor was there a definite purpose in doing this. It merely represented part of the thoroughness with which a problem of this sort is met.

I went through that library. Not the scientific papers. I knew there'd be nothing there that I wanted. But he had written a series of articles for a magazine twenty years back, and I read those. And I grabbed at every piece of private correspondence they had available.

After that I just sat and thought—and got scared.

I got to bed about four in the morning and had nightmares.

But I was in the Boss' private office at nine in the morning just the same.

He's a big man, the Boss, with iron-gray hair slicked down tight. He doesn't smoke, but he keeps a box of cigars on his desk and when he doesn't want to say anything for a few seconds, he picks one up, rolls it about a little, smells it, then sticks it right into the middle of his mouth and lights it in a very careful way. By that time, he either has something to say or doesn't have to say anything at all. Then he puts the cigar down and lets it burn to death.

He used up a box in about three weeks, and every Christmas, half his gift-wraps held boxes of cigars.

He wasn't reaching for any cigars now, though. He just folded his big fists together on the desk and looked up at me from under a creased forehead. "What's boiling?"

I told him. Slowly, because micro-temporal-translation doesn't sit well with anybody, especially when you call it time travel, which I did. It's a sign of how serious things were that he only asked me once if I were crazy.

Then I was finished and we stared at each other.

He said, "And you think he tried to send something back in

time—something weighing a pound or two and blew an entire plant doing it?"

"It fits in," I said.

I let him go for a while. He was thinking and I wanted him to keep on thinking. I wanted him, if possible, to think of the same thing I was thinking, so that I wouldn't have to tell him—

Because I hated to *have* to tell him—

Because it was nuts, for one thing. And too horrible, for another.

So I kept quiet and he kept on thinking and every once in a while some of his thoughts came to the surface.

After a while, he said: "Assuming the student, Howe, to have told the truth—and you'd better check his notebooks, by the way, which I hope you've impounded—"

"The entire wing of that floor is out of bounds, sir. Edwards has the notebooks."

He went on: "All right. Assuming he told us all the truth he knows, why did Tywood jump from less than a miligram to a pound?"

His eyes came down and they were hard: "Now you're concentrating on the time-travel angle. To you, I gather, that is the crucial point, with the energy involved as incidental—purely incidental."

"Yes, sir," I said grimly. "I think exactly that."

"Have you considered that you might be wrong? That you might have matters inverted?"

"I don't quite get that."

"Well, look. You say you've read up on Tywood. All right. He was one of that bunch of scientists after World War II that fought the atom bomb; wanted a world state—You know about that, don't you?"

I nodded.

"He had a guilt complex," the Boss said with energy. "He'd helped work out the bomb, and he couldn't sleep nights thinking of what he'd done. He lived with that fear for years. And even though the bomb wasn't used in World War III, can you imagine what every day of uncertainty must have meant to him? Can you imagine the shriveling horror in his soul as he waited for others to make the decision at every crucial moment till the final Compromise of Sixty-Five?

"We have a complete psychiatric analysis of Tywood and several others just like him, taken during the last war. Did you know that?"

"No, sir."

"It's true. We let up after Sixty-Five, of course, because with the establishment of world control of atomic power, the scrapping of the atomic bomb stockpile in all countries, and the establishment of research liaison among the various spheres of influence on the planet, most of the ethical conflict in the scientific mind was removed.

"But the findings at the time were serious. In 1964, Tywood had a morbid subconscious hatred for the very concept of atomic power. He began to make mistakes, serious ones. Eventually, we were forced to take him off research of any kind. And several others as well, even though things were pretty bad at the time. We had just lost India, if you remember."

Considering that I was in India at the time, I remembered. But I still wasn't seeing his point.

"Now what," he continued, "if dregs of that attitude remained buried in Tywood to the very end. Don't you see that this time-travel is a double-edged sword? Why throw a pound of anything into the past, anyway? For the sake of proving a point? He had proved his case just as much when he sent back a fraction of a milligram. That was good enough for the Nobel Prize, I suppose.

"But there was *one* thing he could do with a pound of matter that he couldn't do with a milligram, and that was *to drain a power plant*. So that was what he must have been after. He had discovered a way of consuming inconceivable quantities of energy. By sending back eighty pounds of dirt, he could remove all the existing plutonium in the world. End atomic power for an indefinite period."

I was completely unimpressed, but I tried not to make that too plain. I just said: "Do you think he could possibly have thought he could get away with it more than once?"

"This is all based on the fact that he wasn't a normal man. How do I know what he could imagine he could do? Besides, there may be men behind him—with less science and more brains—who are quite ready to continue onwards from this point."

"Have any of these men been found yet? Any evidence of such men?"

A little wait, and his hand reached for the cigar box. He stared at the cigar and turned it end for end. Just a little wait more. I was patient.

Then he put it down decisively without lighting it.

"No," he said.

He looked at me, and clear though me, and said: "Then you still don't go for that?"

I shrugged, "Well—It doesn't sound right."

"Do you have a notion of your own?"

"Yes. But I can't bring myself to talk about it. If I'm wrong, I'm the wrongest man that ever was; but if I'm right, I'm the rightest."

"I'll listen," he said, and he put his hand under the desk.

That was the pay-off. The room was armored, soundproof, and radiation-proof to anything short of a nuclear explosion. And with that little signal showing on his secretary's desk, the President of the United States couldn't have interrupted us.

I leaned back and said: "Chief, do you happen to remember how you met your wife? Was it a little thing?"

He must have thought it a *non sequitur*. What else could he have thought? But he was giving me my head now; having his own reasons, I suppose.

He just smiled and said: "I sneezed and she turned around. It was at a street corner."

"What made you be on that street corner just then? What made her be? Do you remember just why you sneezed? Where you caught the cold? Or where the speck of dust came from? Imagine how many factors had to intersect in just the right place at just the right time for you to meet your wife."

"I suppose we would have met some other time, if not then?"

"But you can't *know* that. How do you know whom you *didn't* meet, because once when you might have turned around, you didn't; because once when you might have been late, you weren't. Your life forks at every instant, and you go down one of the forks, almost at random and so does everyone else. Start twenty years ago, and the forks diverge further and further with time.

"You sneezed, and met a girl, and not another. As a consequence, you made certain decisions, and so did the girl, and so did the girl you didn't meet, and the man who did meet her, and the people you all met thereafter. And your family, her family, their family—and your children.

"Because you sneezed twenty years ago, five people, or fifty, or five hundred, might be dead now who would have been alive or might be alive, who would have been dead. Move it two hundred years ago: two thousand years ago, and a sneeze—even by someone no history ever heard of—might have meant that no one now alive would have been alive."

The Boss rubbed the back of his head: "Widening ripples. I read a story once—"

"So did I. It's not a new idea—but I want you to think about it for a while, because I want to read to you from an article by Professor Elmer Tywood in a magazine twenty years ago. It was just before the last war.''

I had copies of the film in my pocket and the white wall made a beautiful screen which was what it was meant to do. The Boss made a motion to turn about, but I waved him back.

"No, sir," I said. "I want to read this to you. And I want you to listen to it.''

He leaned back.

"The article," I went on, "is entitled: 'Man's First Great Failure!' Remember, this was just before the war, when the bitter disappointment at the final failure of the United Nations was at its height. What I will read are some excerpts from the first part of the article. It goes like this:

" '. . . That Man, with his technical perfection has failed to solve the great sociological problems of today is only the second immense tragedy that has come to the race. The first, and perhaps the greater, was that once these same great sociological problems *were* solved; and yet these solutions were not permanent because the technical perfection we have today did not then exist.

" 'It was a case of having bread without butter, or butter without bread. Never both together . . .

" 'Consider the Hellenic world from which our philosophy, our mathematics, our ethics, our art, our literature—our entire culture, in fact—stem . . . In the days of Pericles, Greece, like our own world, in microcosm, was a surprisingly modern potpourri of conflicting ideologies and ways of life. But then Rome came, adopting the culture, but bestowing, and enforcing, peace. To be sure, the *Pax Romana* lasted only two hundred years, but no like period has existed since . . .

" 'War was abolished. Nationalism did not exist. The Roman citizen was Empire-wide. Saul of Tarsus and Flavius Josephus were Roman citizens. Spaniards, North Africans, Illyrians assumed the purple. Slavery existed, but it was an indiscriminate slavery, imposed as a punishment, incurred as the price of economic failure, brought on by the fortunes of war. No man was a *natural* slave, because of the color of his skin, or the place of his birth.

" 'Religious toleration was complete. If an exception was made early in the case of the Christians, it was because they refused to accept the principle of toleration; because they insisted that only they themselves knew truth—a principle abhorrent to the civilized Roman . . .

" 'With all of Western culture under a single *polis*, with the cancer of religious and national particularism and exclusivism absent; with a high civilization in existence—why could not Man hold his gains?

" 'It was because technologically, ancient Hellenism remained backward. It was because without a machine civilization, the price of leisure—and hence civilization and culture—for the few, was slavery for the many. Because the civilization could not find the means to bring comfort and ease to *all* the population.

" 'Therefore, the depressed classes turned to the other world, and to religions which spurned the material benefits of this world—so that science was made impossible in any true sense for over a millennium. And further, as the initial impetus of Hellenism waned, the Empire lacked the technological powers to beat back the barbarians. In fact, it was not till after 1500 A.D. that war became sufficiently a function of the industrial resources of a nation to enable the settled people to defeat invading tribesmen and nomads with ease . . .

" 'Imagine then, if somehow the ancient Greeks had learned just a hint of modern chemistry and physics. Imagine if the growth of the Empire had been accompanied by the growth of science, technology and industry. Imagine an Empire, in which machinery replaced slaves; in which all men had a decent share of the world's goods; in which the legion became the armored column, against which no barbarians could stand. Imagine an Empire which would therefore spread all over the world, *without* religious or national prejudices.

" 'An Empire of all men—all brothers—eventually all free . . .

" 'If history could be changed. If that first great failure could have been prevented—' "

And I stopped at that point.

"Well?" said the Boss.

"Well," I said, "I think it isn't difficult to connect all that with the fact that Tywood blew an entire power plant in his anxiety to send something back to the past, while in his office safe we found sections of a chemistry textbook translated into Greek."

His face changed, while he considered.

Then, he said heavily: "But nothing's happened."

"I know. But then I've been told by Tywood's student that it takes a day to move back a century in time. Assuming that ancient Greece was the target area, we have twenty centuries, hence twenty days."

"But can it be stopped?"

"*I* wouldn't know. Tywood might, but he's dead."

The enormity of it all hit me at once, deeper than it had the night before—

All humanity was virtually under sentence of death. And while that was merely horrible abstraction, the fact that reduced it to a thoroughly unbearably reality, was that I was, too. And my wife, and my kid.

Further, it was a death without precedence. A ceasing to exist, and no more. The passing of a breath. The vanishing of a dream. The drift into eternal non-space and non-time of a shadow. I would not be dead at all, in fact. I would merely never have been born.

Or would I? Would I exist—my individuality—my ego—my soul, if you like? Another life? Other circumstances?

I thought none of that in words, then. But if a cold knot in the stomach could ever speak under the circumstances it would sound like that, I think.

The Boss moved in on my thoughts—hard.

"Then we have about two and a half weeks. No time to lose. Come on."

I grinned with one side of my mouth: "What do we do? Chase the book?"

"No," he replied coldly, "but there are two courses of action we must follow. First, you may be wrong—altogether. All of this circumstantial reasoning may still represent a false lead, perhaps deliberately thrown before us, to cover up the real truth. That must be checked.

"Secondly, you may be right—but there may be some way of stopping the book: other than chasing it in a time machine, I mean. If so, we must find out how."

"I would just like to say, sir, if this is a false lead, only a madman would consider it a believable one. So suppose I'm right, and suppose there's no way of stopping it?"

"Then, young fellow, I'm going to keep pretty busy for two and a half weeks, and I'd advise you to do the same. The time will pass more quickly that way."

Of course he was right.

"Where do we start?" I asked.

"The first thing we need is a list of all men and women on the government payroll under Tywood."

"Why?"

"Reasoning. Your specialty, you know. Tywood doesn't know Greek, I think we can assume with fair safety, so someone else must have done the translating. It isn't likely that anyone would do a job like that for nothing, and it isn't likely that Tywood would pay out of his personal funds—not on a professor's salary."

"He might," I pointed out, "have been interested in more secrecy than a government payroll affords."

"Why? Where was the danger? Is it a crime to translate a chemistry textbook into Greek? Who would ever deduce from that a plot such as you've described."

It took us half an hour to turn up the name of Mycroft James Boulder, listed as "Consultant" and to find out that he was mentioned in the University Catalogue as Assistant Professor of Philosophy and to check by telephone that among his many accomplishments was a thorough knowledge of Attic Greek.

Which was a coincidence—because with the Boss reaching for his hat, the interoffice teletype clicked away and it turned out that Mycroft James Boulder was in the anteroom, at the end of a two-hour continuing insistence that he see the Boss.

The Boss put his hat back and opened his office door.

Professor Mycroft James Boulder was a gray man. His hair was gray and his eyes were gray. His suit was gray, too.

But most of all, his expression was gray; gray with a tension that seemed to twist at the lines in his thin face.

Boulder said, softly: "I've been trying for three days to get a hearing, sir, with a responsible man. I can get no higher than yourself."

"I may be high enough," said the Boss. "What's on your mind?"

"It is quite important that I be granted an interview with Professor Tywood."

"Do you know where he is?"

"I am quite certain that he is in government custody."

"Why?"

"Because I know that he was planning an experiment which would entail the breaking of security regulations. Events since, as nearly as I can make them out, flow naturally from the supposition that security regulations have indeed been broken. I can presume then that the experiment has at least been attempted. I must discover whether it has been successfully concluded."

"Professor Boulder," said the Boss, "I believe you can read Greek."

"Yes, I can,"—coolly.

"And have translated chemical texts for Professor Tywood on government money."

"Yes—as a legally employed consultant."

"Yet such translation, under the circumstances, constitutes a crime, since it makes you an accessory to Tywood's crime."

"You can establish a connection?"

"Can't you? Or haven't you heard of Tywood's notions on time travel, or . . . what do you call it . . . micro-temporal-translation?"

"Ah?" and Boulder smiled a little. "He's told you, then."

"No he hasn't," said the Boss, harshly. "Professor Tywood is dead."

"What?" Then—"I don't believe you."

"He died of apoplexy. Look at this."

He had one of the photographs taken that first night in his wall safe. Tywood's face was distorted but recognizable—sprawled and dead.

Boulder's breath went in and out as if the gears were clogged. He stared at the picture for three full minutes by the electric clock on the wall. "Where is this place?" he asked.

"The Atomic Power Plant."

"Had he finished his experiment?"

The Boss shrugged: "There's no way of telling. He was dead when we found him."

Boulder's lips were pinched and colorless. "That must be determined somehow. A commission of scientists must be established, and, if necessary, the experiment must be repeated—"

But the Boss just looked at him, and reached for a cigar. I've never seen him take longer—and when he put it down, curled in its unused smoke, he said: "Tywood wrote an article for a magazine, twenty years ago—"

"Oh," and the professor's lips twisted, "is *that* what gave you your clue. You may ignore that. The man is only a physical scientist and knows nothing of either history or sociology. A schoolboy's dreams and nothing more."

"Then you don't think sending your translation back will inaugurate a Golden Age, do you?"

"Of course not. Do you think you can graft the developments of two thousand years of slow labor on to a child society not ready for it? Do you think a great invention or a great scientific principle is born full-grown in the mind of a genius divorced from his cultural milieu? Newton's enunciation of the Law of Gravity was delayed for twenty years because the then-current figure for the Earth's diameter was wrong by ten percent. Archimedes almost discovered calculus, but failed because Arabic numerals, invented by some nameless Hindu or group of Hindus, were unknown to him.

"For that matter, the mere existence of a slave society in ancient Greece and Rome meant that machines could scarcely attract much attention—slaves being so much cheaper and more adaptable. And men of true intellect could scarcely be expected to spend their energies on devices intended for manual labor. Even Archimedes, the greatest engineer of antiquity, refused to publish any of his practical inventions—only mathematic abstractions. And when a young man asked Plato of what use geometry was, he was forthwith expelled from the Academy as a man with a mean, unphilosophic soul.

"Science does not plunge forward—it inches along in the directions permitted by the greater forces that mold society and which are in turn molded by society. And no great man advances but on the shoulders of the society that surrounds him—"

The Boss interrupted him at that point "Suppose you tell us what your part in Tywood's work was, then. We'll take your word for it that history cannot be changed."

"Oh it can, but not purposefully—You see, when Tywood first requested my services in the matter of translating certain textbook passages into Greek, I agreed for the money involved. But he wanted the translation on parchment; he insisted on the use of ancient Greek terminology—the language of Plato, to use his words—regardless of how I had to twist the literal significance of passages, and he wanted it hand-written in rolls.

"I was curious. I, too, found his magazine article. It was difficult for me to jump to the obvious conclusion since the achievements of modern science transcend the imaginings of philosophy in so many ways. But I learned the truth eventually, and it was at once obvious that Tywood's theory of changing history was infantile. There are twenty million variables for every instant of time, and no system of mathematics—no mathematic psychohistory, to coin a phrase—has yet been developed to handle that ocean of varying functions.

"In short, any variation of events two thousand years ago would change all subsequent history but in *no predictable way*."

The Boss suggested, with a false quietness: "Like the pebble that starts the avalanche, right?"

"Exactly. You have some understanding of the situation, I see. I thought deeply for weeks before I proceeded, and then I realized how I must act—*must* act."

There was a low roar. The Boss stood up and his chair went over backward. He swung around his desk, and he had a hand on Boulder's throat. I was stepping out to stop him, but he waved me back—

He was only tightening the necktie a little. Boulder could still breathe. He had gone very white, and for all the time that the Boss talked, he restricted himself to just that—breathing.

And the Boss said: "Sure, I can see how you decided you must act. I know that some of you brain-sick philosophers think the world needs fixing. You want to throw the dice again and see what turns up. Maybe you don't even care if you're alive in the new setup—or that no one can possibly know what you've done. But you're going to create just the same. You're going to give God another chance so to speak.

"Maybe I just want to live—but the world could be worse. In twenty million different ways, it could be worse. A fellow named Wilder once wrote a play called *The Skin of Our Teeth*. Maybe you've read it. Its thesis was that Mankind survived by just that skin of their teeth. No, I'm not going to give you a speech about the Ice Age nearly wiping us out. I don't know enough. I'm not even going to talk about the Greeks winning at Marathon; the Arabs being defeated at Tours; the Mongols turning back at the last minute without even being defeated—because I'm no historian.

"But take the Twentieth Century. The Germans were stopped at the Marne twice in World War I. Dunkirk happened in World War II, and somehow the Germans were stopped at Moscow and Stalingrad. We could have used the atom bomb in the last war and we didn't, and just when it looked as if both sides would have to, the Great Compromise happened—just because General Bruce was delayed in taking off from the Ceylon airfield long enough to receive the message directly. One after the other, just like that, all through history—lucky breaks. For every 'if' that didn't come true, that would have made wonder-men of all of us, if it had, there were twenty 'ifs' that didn't come true, that would have brought disaster to all of us, if they had.

"You're gambling on that one-in-twenty chance—gambling every life on Earth. And you've succeeded, too, because Tywood *did* send that text back."

He ground out that last sentence, and opened his fist, so that Boulder could fall out and back into his chair.

And Boulder laughed.

"You fool," he gasped, bitterly, "How close you can be and yet how widely you can miss the mark. Tywood *did* send his book back, then? You are sure of that?"

"No chemical textbook in Greek was found on the scene," said the Boss, grimly, "and millions of calories of energy had disappeared. Which doesn't change the fact, however, that we

have two and a half weeks in which to—make things interesting
for you.''

"Oh, nonsense. No foolish dramatics, please. Just listen to
me, and try to understand. There were Greek philosophers once,
named Leucippus and Democritus who evolved an atomic theory.
All matter, they said was composed of atoms. Varieties of atoms
were distinct and changeless and by their different combinations
with each other formed the various substances found in nature.
That theory was not the result of experiment or observation. It
came into being, somehow, full-grown.

"The didactic Roman poet, Lucretius, in his 'De Rerum
Natura,'—'On the Nature of Things'—elaborated on that theory
and throughout manages to sound startlingly modern.

"In Hellenistic times, Hero built a steam engine and weapons
of war became almost mechanized. The period has been referred
to as an abortive mechanical age, which came to nothing because
somehow, it neither grew out of nor fitted into its social and
economic milieu. Alexandrian science was a queer and rather
inexplicable phenomenon.

"Then one might mention the old Roman legend about the
books of the Sibyl that contained mysterious information direct
from the gods—

"In other words, gentlemen, while you are right that any
change in the course of past events, however trifling, would have
incalculable consequences, and while I also believe that you are
right in supposing that any random change is much more likely
to be for the worst than for the better, I must point out that you
are nevertheless wrong in your final conclusions.

"*Because* THIS *is the world in which the Greek chemistry text
WAS sent back.*

"This has been a Red Queen's race, if you remember your
Through the Looking Glass. In the Red Queen's country, one
had to run as fast as one could merely to stay in the same place.
And so it was in this case! Tywood may have thought he was
creating a new world, but it was *I* who prepared the translations,
and I took care that only such passages as would account for the
queer scraps of knowledge the ancients apparently got from
nowhere would be included.

"And my only intention, for all my racing, was to stay in the
same place.''

Three weeks passed; three months; three years. Nothing
happened. When nothing happens, you have no proof. We gave
up trying to explain, and we ended, the Boss and I, by doubting
it ourselves.

The case never ended. Boulder could not be considered a criminal without being considered a world savior as well, and vice versa. He was ignored. And in the end, the case was neither solved, nor closed out; merely put in a file all by itself, under the designation "?" and buried in the deepest vault in Washington.

The Boss is in Washington now; a big wheel. And I'm Regional Head of the Bureau.

Boulder is still assistant professor, though. Promotions are slow at the University.

FLAW

John D. MacDonald (1916–　　)

Startling Stories, January

John D. MacDonald returns (see his two excellent stories in our 1948 volume) with this interesting and unusual piece of speculative fiction. MacDonald was tremendously prolific in the late 1940s, working in almost every genre that still had magazine markets available, in what was the twilight of the pulp era. He got published because he was a wonderful storyteller, but also because he developed an excellent working knowledge of genres and their conventions. However, like all great writers, he could successfully defy genre conventions and get away with it, as in this story, which is blatantly pessimistic and questions the very possibility of going to the stars—an attitude and point of view that most late 1940s science fiction writers and their readers certainly did not share.—M.H.G.

(Science fiction can be at its most amusing [and most useful, perhaps] when it challenges our assumptions. And that is true of straightforward scientific speculation, also.

Even when the challenge is doomed to failure [and in my opinion the one in this story is so doomed] or when scientific advance actually demonstrates, within a few years, the challenge to be doomed, the story is likely to remain interesting.

—Thus, I once wrote a story in which I speculated that the Moon was only a false front and that on the other side were merely wooden supports. Within a few years the other side of the Moon was photographed and our satellite proved not to be a false front after all. But who cares? Anyone who reads the story is not likely to forget the speculation.

Read "Flaw," then, and ask yourself: With the rockets and probes of the last three decades, has the thesis of this story yet been demonstrated to be false? If so, how?—I.A.)

I rather imagine that I am quite mad. Nothing spectacular, you understand. Nothing calling for restraint, or shock therapy. I can live on, dangerous to no one but myself.

This beach house at La Jolla is comfortable. At night I sit on the rocks and watch the distant stars and think of Johnny. He probably wouldn't like the way I look now. My fingernails are cracked and broken and there are streaks of gray in my blonde hair. I no longer use makeup. Last night I looked at myself in the mirror and my eyes were dead.

It was then that I decided that it might help me to write all this down. I have no idea what I'll do with it.

You see, I shared Johnny's dreams.

And now I know that those dreams are no longer possible. I wonder if he learned how impossible they were in the few seconds before his flaming death.

There have always been people like Johnny and me. For a thousand years mankind has looked at the stars and thought of reaching them. The stars were to be the new frontier, the new worlds on which mankind could expand and find the full promise of the human soul.

I never thought much about it until I met Johnny. Five years ago. My name is Carol Adlar. At that time I was a government clerk working in the offices at the rocket station in Arizona. It was 1959. The year before the atomic drive was perfected.

Johnny Pritchard. I figured him out, I thought. A good-looking boy with dark hair and a careless grin and a swagger. That's all I saw in the beginning. The hot sun blazed down on the rocks and the evenings were cool and clear.

There were a lot of boys like Johnny at the rocket station— transferred from Air Corps work. Volunteers. You couldn't order a man off the surface of the earth in a rocket.

The heart is ever cautious. Johnny Pritchard began to hang around my desk, a warm look in his eyes. I was as cool as I could be. You don't give your heart to a man who soars up at the tip of a comet plume. But I did.

I told myself that I would go out with him one evening and I would be so cool to him that it would cure him and he would stop bothering me. I expected him to drive me to the city in his little car. Instead we drove only five miles from the compound, parked on the brow of a hill looking across the moon-silvered rock and sand.

At first I was defensive, until I found that all he wanted to do was talk. He talked about the stars. He talked in a low voice that was somehow tense with his visions. I found out that first evening that he wasn't like the others. He wasn't merely one of those young men with perfect coordination and high courage. Johnny had in him the blood of pioneers. And his frontier was the stars.

"You see, Carol," he said, "I didn't know a darn thing about the upstairs at the time of my transfer. I guess I don't know much right now. Less, probably than the youngest astronomer or physicist on the base. But I'm learning. I spend every minute I can spare studying about it. Carol, I'm going upstairs some day. Right out into space. And I want to know about it. I want to know all about it.

"We've made a pretty general mess of this planet. I sort of figure that the powers-that-be planned it that way. They said, 'We'll give this puny little fella called man a chance to mess up one planet and mess it up good. But we'll let him slowly learn how to travel to another. Then, by the time he can migrate, he will be smart enough to turn the next planet into the sort of a deal we wanted him to have in the beginning. A happy world with no wars, no disease, no starvation.' "

I should have said something flip at that point, but the words weren't in me. Like a fool, I asked him questions about the galaxies, about the distant stars. We drove slowly back. The next day he loaned me two of his books. Within a week I had caught his fervor, his sense of dedication.

After that it was, of course, too late.

All persons in love have dreams. This was ours. Johnny would be at the controls of one of the first interplanetary rockets. He would return to me and then we would become one of the first couples to become colonists for the new world.

Silly, wasn't it?

He told me of the problems that would be solved with that first interplanetary flight. They would take instruments far enough out into space so that triangulation could solve that tiresome bickering among the physicists and astronomers about the theory of the exploding universe as against the theory of "tired light" from the distant galaxies.

And now I am the only person in the world who can solve that problem. Oh, the others will find the answer soon enough. And then they, too, can go quietly mad.

They will find out that for years they have been in the position of the man at the table with his fingers almost touching the sugar bowl and who asks why there isn't any sugar on the table.

That year was the most perfect year of my life.

"When are you going to marry me, Johnny?" I asked him.

"This is so sudden," he said, laughing. Then he sobered. "Just as soon as I come back from the first one, honey. It isn't fair any other way. Don't you see?"

I saw with my mind, but not with my heart. We exchanged rings. All very sentimental. He gave me a diamond and I gave him my father's ring, the one that was sent home to my mother and me when Dad was killed in Burma in World War II. It fit him and he liked it. It was a star ruby in a heavy silver setting. The star was perfect, but by looking closely into the stone you could see the flaws. Two dark little dots and a tiny curved line which together gave the look of a small and smiling face.

With his arm around me, with the cool night air of Arizona touching our faces, we looked up at the sky and talked of the home we would make millions of miles away.

Childish, wasn't it?

Last night after looking in the mirror, I walked down to the rocks. The Government money was given to me when Johnny didn't come back. It is enough. It will last until I die and I hope it will not be too long before I die.

The sea, washing the rocks, asked me the soft, constant question. "Why? Why? Why?" I looked at the sky. The answer was not there.

Fourteen months after I met Johnny, a crew of two in the *Destiny I* made the famous circuit of the moon and landed safely. Johnny was not one of them. He had hoped to be.

"A test run," he called it. The first step up the long flight of stairs.

You certainly remember the headlines given that flight of *Destiny I*. Even the New York *Times* broke out a new and larger type face for the headlines. Korby and Sweeny became the heroes of the entire world.

The world was confident then. The intervening years have shaken that confidence. But the world does not know yet. I think some suspect, but they do not know. Only I know for a certainty. And I, of course, am quite mad. I know that now.

Call it a broken heart—or broken dreams.

*   *   *

Johnny was selected for *Destiny II*. After he told me and after the tears came, partly from fear, partly from the threat of loneliness, he held me tightly and kissed my eyes. I had not known that the flight of *Destiny II*, if successful, would take fourteen months. The fourteen months were to include a circuit of Mars and a return to the takeoff point. Fourteen months before I would see him again. Fourteen months before I would feel his arms around me.

A crew of four. The famous Korby and Sweeny, plus Anthony Marinetta and my Johnny. Each morning when I went to work I could see the vast silver ship on the horizon, the early sun glinting on the blunt nose. Johnny's ship.

Those last five months before takeoff were like the five months of life ahead of a prisoner facing execution. And Johnny's training was so intensified after his selection that I couldn't see him as often as before.

We were young and we were in love and we made our inevitable mistake. At least we called it a mistake. Now I know that it wasn't, because Johnny didn't come back.

With the usual sense of guilt we planned to be married, and then reverted to our original plan. I would wait for him. Nothing could go wrong.

Takeoff was in the cold dawn of a February morning. I stood in the crowd beside a girl who worked in the same office. I held her arm. She carried the bruises for over a week.

The silver hull seemed to merge with the gray of the dawn. The crowd was silent. At last there was the blinding, blue-white flare of the jets, the stately lift into the air, the moment when *Destiny II* seemed to hang motionless fifty feet in the air, and then the accelerating blast that arrowed it up and up into the dark-gray sky where a few stars still shone. I walked on leaden legs back to the administration building and sat slumped at my desk, my mouth dry, my eyes hot and burning.

The last faint radio signal came in three hours later.

"All well. See you next year."

From then on there would be fourteen months of silence.

I suppose that in a way I became accustomed to it.

I was numb, apathetic, stupefied. They would probably have got rid of me had they not known how it was between Johnny and me. I wouldn't have blamed them. Each morning I saw the silver form of *Destiny III* taking shape near where *Destiny II* had taken off. The brash young men made the same jokes, gave the office girls the same line of chatter.

But they didn't bother me. Word had got around.

I found a friend. The young wife of Tony Marienetta. We spent hours telling each other in subtle ways that everything would come out all right.

I remember one night when Marge grinned and said:

"Well anyway, Carol, nobody has ever had their men go quite so far away."

There is something helpless about thinking of the distance between two people in the form of millions of miles.

After I listened to the sea last night, I walked slowly back up the steep path to this beach house. When I clicked the lights on Johnny looked at me out of the silver frame on my writing desk. His eyes are on me as I write this. They are happy and confident eyes. I am almost glad that he didn't live to find out.

The fourteen months were like one single revolution of a gigantic Ferris wheel. You start at the top of the wheel, and through seven months the wheel carries you slowly down into the darkness and the fear. Then, after you are at your lowest point, the wheel slowly starts to carry you back up into the light.

Somewhere in space I knew that Johnny looked at the small screen built into the control panel and saw the small bright sphere of earth and thought of me. I knew all during that fourteen months that he wasn't dead. If he had died, no matter how many million miles away from me, I would have known it in the instant of his dying.

The world forgets quickly. The world had pushed *Destiny II* off the surface of consciousness a few months after takeoff. Two months before the estimated date of return, it began to creep back into the papers and onto the telescreens of the world.

Work had stopped on *Destiny III*. The report of the four crewmen might give a clue to alterations in the interior.

It was odd the way I felt. As though I had been frozen under the transparent ice of a small lake. Spring was coming and the ice grew thinner.

Each night I went to sleep thinking of Johnny driving down through the sky toward me at almost incalculable speed. Closer, closer, ever closer.

It was five weeks before the date when they were due to return. I was asleep in the barracks-like building assigned to the unmarried women of the base.

The great thud and jar woke me up and through the window I saw the night sky darkening in the afterglow of some brilliant light.

*   *   *

We gathered by the windows and talked for a long time about what it could have been. It was in all of our minds that it could have been the return of *Destiny II*, but we didn't put it into words, because no safe landing could have resulted in that deathly thud.

With the lights out again, I tried to sleep. I reached out into the night sky with my heart, trying to contact Johnny.

And the sky was empty.

I sat up suddenly, my lips numb, my eyes staring. No. It was imagination. It was illusion. Johnny was still alive. Of course. But when I composed myself for sleep it was as though dirges were softly playing. In all the universe there was no living entity called Johnny Pritchard. Nowhere.

The telescreens were busy the next morning and I saw the shape of fear. An alert operator had caught the fast shape as it had slammed flaming down through the atmosphere to land forty miles from the base in deserted country making a crater a half-mile across.

"It is believed that the object was a meteor," the voice of the announcer said. "Radar screens picked up the image and it is now known that it was far too large to be the *Destiny II* arriving ahead of a schedule."

It was then that I took a deep breath. But the relief was not real. I was only kidding myself. It was as though I was in the midst of a dream of terror and could not think of magic words to cause the spell to cease.

After breakfast I was ill.

The meteor had hit with such impact that the heat generated had fused the sand. Scientific instruments proved that the mass of the meteor itself, nine hundred feet under the surface was largely metallic. The telescreens began to prattle about invaders from an alien planet. And the big telescopes scanned the heavens for the first signs of the returning *Destiny II*.

The thought began as a small spot, glowing in some deep part of my mind. I knew that I had to cross the forty miles between the base and the crater. But I did not know why I had to cross it. I did not know why I had to stand at the lip of the crater and watch the recovery operations. I felt like a subject under post-hypnotic influence—compelled to do something without knowing the reason. But compelled, nevertheless.

One of the physicists took me to the crater in one of the base helicopters after I had made the request of him in such a way that he could not refuse.

Eleven days after the meteor had fallen, I stood on the lip of the crater and looked down into the heart of it to where the vast shaft had been sunk to the meteor itself. Dr. Rawlins handed me his binoculars and I watched the mouth of the shaft.

Men working down in the shaft had cut away large pieces of the body of the meteor and some of them had been hauled out and trucked away. They were blackened and misshapen masses of fused metal.

I watched the mouth of the shaft until my eyes ached and until the young physicist shifted restlessly and kept glancing at his watch and at the sun sinking toward the west. When he asked to borrow the binoculars, I gave them up reluctantly. I could hear the distant throb of the hoist motors. Something was coming up the shaft.

Dr. Rawlins made a sudden exclamation. I looked at the mouth of the shaft. The sun shone with red fire on something large. It dwarfed the men who stood near it.

Rudely I snatched the binoculars from Dr. Rawlins and looked, knowing even as I lifted them to my eyes what I would see.

Because at that moment I knew the answer to something that the astronomers and physicists had been bickering about for many years. There is no expanding universe. There is no tired light.

As I sit here at my writing desk, I can imagine how it was during those last few seconds. The earth looming up in the screen on the instrument panel, but not nearly large enough. Not large enough at all. Incredulity, then because of the error in size, the sudden application of the nose jets. Too late. Fire and oblivion and a thud that shook the earth for hundreds of miles.

No one else knows what I know. Maybe soon they will guess. And then there will be an end to the proud dreams of migration to other worlds. We are trapped here. There will be no other worlds for us. We have made a mess of this planet, and it is something that we cannot leave behind us. We must stay here and clean it up as best we can.

Maybe a few of them already know. Maybe they have guessed. Maybe they guessed, as I did, on the basis of the single object that was brought up out of that shaft on that bright, cold afternoon.

Yes, I saw the sun shining on the six-pointed star. With the binoculars I looked into the heart of it and saw the two dots and a curved line that made the flaws look like a smiling face. A ruby the size of a bungalow.

There is no expanding universe. There is no "tired light."

There is only a Solar system that, due to an unknown influence, is constantly shrinking.

For a little time the *Destiny II* avoided that influence. That is why they arrived too soon, why they couldn't avoid the crash, and why I am quite mad.

The ruby was the size of a bungalow, but it was, of course, quite unchanged. It was I and my world that had shrunk.

If Johnny had landed safely, I would be able to walk about on the palm of his hand.

It is a good thing that he died.

And it will not be long before I die also.

The sea whispers softly against the rocks a hundred yards from the steps of my beach house.

And *Destiny III* has not yet returned.

It is due in three months.

PRIVATE EYE

by "Lewis Padgett" (Henry Kuttner, 1914—1958 and C.L. Moore, 1911—   ; this story is generally believed to have been written by Kuttner)

Astounding Science Fiction, **January**

The Kuttners were so prolific that they made extensive use of pen names—in addition to Kuttner and Moore, singly and listed together, they wrote as "Lewis Padgett" and as "Lawrence O'Donnell," producing important stories under both of these pseudonyms. The present selection is the first of three in this book—the late 1940s were tremendously productive for this wonderful writing team.

As Isaac points out, "Private Eye" is a classic blend of mystery and science fiction and fully deserves the title of "classic." It is not now unusual for such combinations to see print; indeed, in the last twenty years dozens of stories incorporating a murder mystery with sf have appeared, and many have been collected in such anthologies as Miriam Allen deFord's Space, Time & Crime *(1964), Barry N. Malzberg and Bill Pronzini's wonderful* Dark Sins, Dark Crimes *(1978), and our own (along with Charles G. Waugh)* The 13 Crimes of Science Fiction *(1979).—M.H.G.*

(John Campbell, the greatest of all science fiction editors, was one of the most prescient people I have ever met—and yet he was given to peculiar blind spots. For instance, during the 1940's he frequently maintained that science fiction mysteries were impossible, because it was so easy to use futuristic gimmicks to help the detective crack his case.

I eventually showed, in 1953, that a classic mystery could be combined with science fiction if one simply set up the boundary conditions at the start and stuck to them. I resolutely allowed no futuristic gimmicks to appear suddenly and give the detective an unfair advantage.

In "Private Eye" however, Henry Kuttner [preceding me by four years] took the harder task of allowing a futuristic gimmick—one that would seem to make it impossible to get away with murder—and then labored to produce an honest murder mystery anyway. The result was an undoubted classic—I.A.)

The forensic sociologist looked closely at the image on the wall screen. Two figures were frozen there, one in the act of stabbing the other through the heart with an antique letter cutter, once used at Johns Hopkins for surgery. That was before the ultra-microtome, of course.

"As tricky a case as I've ever seen," the sociologist remarked. "If we can make a homicide charge stick on Sam Clay, I'll be a little surprised."

The tracer engineer twirled a dial and watched the figures on the screen repeat their actions. One—Sam Clay—snatched the letter cutter from a desk and plunged it into the other man's heart. The victim fell down dead. Clay started back in apparent horror. Then he dropped to his knees beside the twitching body and said wildly that he didn't mean it. The body drummed its heels upon the rug and was still.

"That last touch was nice," the engineer said.

"Well, I've got to make the preliminary survey," the sociologist sighed, settling in his dictachair and placing his fingers on the keyboard. "I doubt if I'll find any evidence. However, the analysis can come later. Where's Clay now?"

"His mouthpiece put in a *habeas mens.*"

"I didn't think we'd be able to hold him. But it was worth trying. Imagine, just one shot of scop and he'd have told the truth. Ah, well. We'll do it the hard way, as usual. Start the tracer, will you? It won't make sense till we run it chronologically, but one must start somewhere. Good old Blackstone," the sociologist said, as, on the screen, Clay stood up, watching the corpse revive and arise, and then pulled the miraculously clean paper cutter out of its heart, all in reverse.

"Good old Blackstone," he repeated. "On the other hand, sometimes I wish I'd lived in Jeffreys' time. In those days, homicide was homicide."

Telepathy never came to much. Perhaps the developing faculty went underground in response to a familiar natural law after the new science appeared—omniscience. It wasn't really that, of course. It was a device for looking into the past. And it was limited to a fifty-year span; no chance of seeing the arrows at Agincourt or the homunculi of Bacon. It was sensitive enough to pick up the "fingerprints" of light and sound waves imprinted on matter, descramble and screen them, and reproduce the image of what had happened. After all, a man's shadow can be photographed on concrete, if he's unlucky enough to be caught in an atomic blast. Which is something. The shadow's about all here is left.

However, opening the past like a book didn't solve all problems. It took generations for the maze of complixties to iron itself out, though finally a tentative check-and-balance was reached. The right to kill has been sturdily defended by mankind since Cain rose up against Abel. A good many idealists quoted, "The voice of thy brother's blood crieth unto me from the ground," but that didn't stop the lobbyists and the pressure groups. Magna Carta was quoted in reply. The right to privacy was defended desperately.

And the curious upshot of this imbalance came when the act of homicide was declared nonpunishable, unless intent and forethought could be proved. Of course, it was considered at least naughty to fly in a rage and murder someone on impulse, and there was a nominal punishment—imprisonment, for example— but in practice this never worked, because so many defenses were possible. Temporary insanity. Undue provocation. Self-defense. Manslaughter, second-degree homicide, third degree, fourth degree—it went on like that. It was up to the State to prove that the killer had planned his killing in advance; only then would a jury convict. And the jury, of course, had to waive immunity and take a scop test, to prove the box hadn't been packed. But no defendant ever waived immunity.

A man's home wasn't his castle—not with the Eye able to enter it at will and scan his past. The device couldn't interpret, and it couldn't read his mind; it could only see and listen. Consequently the sole remaining fortress of privacy was defended to the last ditch. No truth-serum, no hypnoanalysis, no third-degree, no leading questions.

If, by viewing the prisoner's past actions, the prosecution could prove forethought and intent, O.K.

Otherwise, Sam Clay would go scot-free. Superficially, it appeared as though Andrew Vanderman had, during a quarrel, struck Clay across the face with a stingaree whip. Anyone who has been stung by a Portuguese man-of-war can understand that, at this point, Clay could plead temporary insanity and self-defense, as well as undue provocation and possible justification.

Only the curious cult of the Alaskan Flagellantes, who make the stingaree whips for their ceremonials, know how to endure the pain. The Flagellantes even like it, the pre-ritual drug they swallow transmutes pain into pleasure. Not having swallowed this drug, Sam Clay very naturally took steps to protect himself—irrational steps, perhaps, but quite logical and defensible ones.

Nobody but Clay knew that he had intended to kill Vanderman all along. That was the trouble. Clay couldn't understand why he felt so let down.

The screen flickered. It went dark. The engineer chuckled.

"My, my. Locked up in a dark closet at the age of four. What one of those old-time psychiatrists would have made of that. Or do I mean obimen? Shamans? I forget. They interpreted dreams, anyway."

"You're confused. It—"

"Astrologers! No, it wasn't either. The ones I mean went in for symbolism. They used to spin prayer wheels and say 'A rose is a rose is a rose,' didn't they? To free the unconscious mind?"

"You've got the typical layman's attitude toward antique psychiatric treatments."

"Well, maybe they had something, at that. Look at quinine and digitalis. The United Amazon natives used those long before science discovered them. But why use eye of newt and toe of frog? To impress the patient?"

"No, to convince themselves," the Sociologist said. "In those days the study of mental aberrations drew potential psychotics, so naturally there was unnecessary mumbo-jumbo. Those medicos were trying to fix their own mental imbalance while they treated their patients. But it's a science today, not a religion. We've found out how to allow for individual psychotic deviation in the psychiatrist himself, so we've got a better chance of finding true north. However, let's get on with this. Try ultraviolet. Oh, never mind. Somebody's letting him out of that closet. The devil with it. I think we've cut back far enough. Even if he was frightened by a thunderstorm at the age of three months, that can be filed under Gestalt and ignored. Let's run through this chronologically. Give it the screening for . . . let's see. Incidents involving these persons: Vanderman, Mrs. Vanderman, Josephine Wells—and these places: the office, Vanderman's apartment, Clay's place—"

"Got it."

"Later we can recheck for complicating factors. Right now

we'll run the superficial survey. Verdict first, evidence later," he added, with a grin. "All we need is a motive—"

"What about this?"

A girl was talking to Sam Clay. The background was an apartment, grade B-2.

"I'm sorry, Sam. It's just that . . . well, these things happen."

"Yeah. Vanderman's got something I haven't got, apparently."

"I'm in love with him."

"Funny. I thought all along you were in love with me."

"So did I . . . for a while."

"Well, forget it. No, I'm not angry, Bea. I'll even wish you luck. But you must have been pretty certain how I'd react to this."

"I'm sorry—"

"Come to think of it, I've always let you call the shots. Always."

Secretly—and this the screen could not show—he thought: Let her? I wanted it that way. It was so much easier to leave the decisions up to her. Sure, she's dominant, but I guess I'm just the opposite. And now it's happened again.

It always happens. I was loaded with weight-cloths from the start. And I always felt I had to toe the line, or else. Vanderman—that cocky, arrogant air of his. Reminds me of somebody. I was locked up in a dark place, I couldn't breathe. I forget. What . . . who . . . my father. No, I don't remember. But my life's been like that. He always watched me, and I always thought some day I'd do what I wanted—but I never did. Too late now. He's been dead quite a while.

He was always so sure I'd knuckle under. If I'd only defied him once—

Somebody's always pushing me in and closing the door. So I can't use my abilities. I can't prove I'm competent. Prove it to myself, to my father, to Bea, to the whole world. If only I could—I'd like to push Vanderman into a dark place and lock the door. A dark place, like a coffin. It would be satisfying to surprise him that way. It would be fine if I killed Andrew Vanderman.

"Well, that's the beginning of a motive," the sociologist said. "Still, lots of people get jilted and don't turn homicidal. Carry on."

"In my opinion, Bea attracted him because he wanted to be bossed," the engineer remarked. "He'd given up."

"Protective passivity."

The wire taps spun through the screening apparatus. A new scene showed on the oblong panel. It was the Paradise Bar.

Anywhere you sat in the Paradise Bar, a competent robot analyzer instantly studied your complexion and facial angles, and switched on lights, in varying tints and intensities, that showed you off to best advantage. The joint was popular for business deals. A swindler could look like an honest man there. It was also popular with women and slightly passé teleo talent. Sam Clay looked rather like an ascetic young saint. Andrew Vanderman looked noble, in a grim way, like Richard Coeur-de-Lion offering Saladin his freedom, though he knew it wasn't really a bright thing to do. *Noblesse oblige*, his firm jaw seemed to say, as he picked up the silver decanter and poured. In ordinary light, Vanderman looked slightly more like a handsome bulldog. Also, away from the Paradise Bar, he was redder around the chops, a choleric man.

"As to that deal we were discussing," Clay said, "you can go to—"

The censoring juke box blared out a covering bar or two.

Vanderman's reply was unheard as the music got briefly louder, and the lights shifted rapidly to keep pace with his sudden flush.

"It's perfectly easy to outwit these censors," Clay said. "They're keyed to familiar terms of profane abuse, not to circumlocutions. If I said that the arrangement of your chromosomes would have surprised your father . . . you see?" He was right. The music stayed soft.

Vanderman swallowed nothing. "Take it easy," he said. "I can see why you're upset. Let me say first of all—"

"Hijo—"

But the censor was proficient in Spanish dialects. Vanderman was spared hearing another insult.

"—that I offered you a job because I think you're a very capable man. You have potentialities. It's not a bribe. Our personal affairs should be kept out of this."

All the same, Bea was engaged to me."

"Clay, are you drunk?"

"Yes," Clay said, and threw his drink into Vanderman's face. The music began to play Wagner very, very loudly. A few minutes later, when the waiters interfered, Clay was supine and bloody, with a mashed nose and a bruised cheek. Vanderman had skinned his knuckles.

*   *   *

"That's a motive," the engineer said.

"Yes, it is, isn't it? But why did Clay wait a year and a half? And remember what happened later. I wonder if the murder itself was just a symbol? If Vanderman represented, say, what Clay considered the tyrannical and oppressive force of society in general—synthesized in the representative image . . . oh, nonsense. Obviously Clay was trying to prove something to himself though. Suppose you cut forward now. I want to see this in normal chronology, not backwards. What's the next selection?"

"Very suspicious. Clay got his nose fixed up and then went to a murder trial."

He thought: I can't breathe. Too crowded in here. Shut up in a box, a closet, a coffin, ignored by the spectators and the vested authority on the bench. What would I do if I were in the dock, like that chap? Suppose they convicted? That would spoil it all. Another dark place— If I'd inherited the right genes, I'd have been strong enough to beat up Vanderman. But I've been pushed around too long.

I keep remembering that song.

Stray in the herd and the boss said kill it,
So I shot him in the rump with the handle of a skillet.

A deadly weapon that's in normal usage wouldn't appear dangerous. But if it could be used homicidally—No, the Eye could check on that. All you can conceal these days is motive. But couldn't the trick be reversed. Suppose I got Vanderman to attack me with what he thought was the handle of a skillet, but which I knew was a deadly weapon—

The trial Sam Clay was watching was fairly routine. One man had killed another. Counsel for the defense contended that the homicide had been a matter of impulse, and that, as a matter of fact, only assault and battery plus culpable negligence, at worst, could be proved, and the latter was canceled by an Act of God. The fact that the defendant inherited the decedent's fortune, in Martial oil, made no difference. Temporary insanity was the plea.

The prosecuting attorney showed films of what had happened before the fact. True, the victim hadn't been killed by the blow, merely stunned. But the affair had occurred on an isolated beach, and when the tide came in—

Act of God, the defense repeated hastily.

The screen showed the defendant, some days before his crime, looking up the tide-table in a news tape. He also, it appeared, visited the site and asked a passing stranger if the beach was often crowded. "Nope," the stranger said, "it ain't crowded after sundown. Gits too cold. Won't do you no good, though. Too cold to swim then."

One side matched *Actus non facit reum, nisi mens sit rea*— "The act does not make a man guilty, unless the mind be also guilty"—against *Acta exteriora indicant interiora secreta*—"By the outward acts we are to judge of the inward thoughts." Latin legal basics were still valid, up to a point. A man's past remained sacrosanct, provided—and here was the joker—that he possessed the right of citizenship. And anyone accused of a capital crime was automatically suspended from citizenship until his innocence had been established.

Also, no past-tracing evidence could be introduced into a trial unless it could be proved that it had direct connection with the crime. The average citizen did have a right of privacy against tracing. Only if accused of a serious crime was that forfeit, and even then evidence uncovered could be used only in correlation with the immediate charge. There were various loopholes, of course, but theoretically a man was safe from espionage as long as he stayed within the law.

Now a defendant stood in the dock, his past opened. The prosecution showed recordings of a ginger blonde blackmailing him, and that clinched the motive and the verdict—guilty. The condemned man was led off in tears. Clay got up and walked out of the court. From his appearance, he seemed to be thinking.

He was. He had decided that there was only one possible way in which he could kill Vanderman and get away with it. He couldn't conceal the deed itself, nor the actions leading up to it, nor any written or spoken word. All he could hide were his own thoughts. And, without otherwise betraying himself, he'd have to kill Vanderman so that his act would appear justified. Which meant covering his tracks for yesterday as well as for tomorrow and tomorrow.

Now, thought Clay, this much can be assumed: If I stand to lose by Vanderman's death instead of gaining, that will help considerably. I must juggle that somehow. But I mustn't forget that at present I have an obvious motive. First, he stole Bea. Second, he beat me up.

So I must make it seem as though he's done me a favor—somehow.

I must have an opportunity to study Vanderman carefully, and

it must be a normal, logical, waterproof opportunity. Private
secretary. Something like that. The Eye's in the future now, after
the fact, but it's watching me—

I must remember that. *It's watching me now!*

All right. Normally, I'd have thought of murder, at this point.
That can't and shouldn't be disguised. I must work out of the
mood gradually, but meanwhile—

He smiled.

Going off to buy a gun, he felt uncomfortable, as though that
prescient Eye, years in the future, could with a wink summon the
police. But it was separated from him by a barrier of time that
only the natural processes could shorten. And, in fact, it had
been watching him since his birth. You could look at it that
way—

He could defy it. The Eye couldn't read thoughts.

He bought the gun and lay in wait for Vanderman in a dark
alley. But first he got thoroughly drunk. Drunk enough to satisfy
the Eye.

After that—

"Feel better now?" Vanderman asked, pouring another coffee.

Clay buried his face in his hands.

"I was crazy," he said, his voice muffled. "I must have
been. You'd better t-turn me over to the police."

"We can forget about that end of it, Clay. You were drunk,
that's all. And I . . . well, I—"

"I pull a gun on you . . . try to kill you . . . and you bring me
up to your place and—"

"You didn't use that gun, Clay. Remember that. You're no
killer. All this has been my fault. I needn't have been so blasted
tough with you," Vanderman said, looking like Coeur-de-Lion
in spite of uncalculated amber fluorescence.

"I'm no good. I'm a failure. Every time I try to do something,
a man like you comes along and does it better. I'm a second-rater."

"Clay, stop talking like that. You're just upset, that's all.
Listen to me. You're going to straighten up. I'm going to see
that you do. Starting tomorrow, we'll work something out. Now
drink your coffee."

"You know," Clay said, "you're quite a guy."

So the magnanimous idiot's fallen for it, Clay thought, as he
was drifting happily off to sleep. Fine. That begins to take care
of the Eye. Moreover, it starts the ball rolling with Vanderman.
Let a man do you a favor and he's your pal. Well, Vanderman's

going to do me a lot more favors. In fact, before I'm through, I'll have every motive for wanting to keep him alive.

Every motive visible to the naked Eye.

Probably Clay had not heretofore applied his talents in the right direction, for there was nothing second-rate about the way he executed his homicide plan. In that, he proved very capable. He needed a suitable channel for his ability, and perhaps he needed a patron. Vanderman fulfilled that function; probably it salved his conscience for stealing Bea. Being the man he was, Vanderman needed to avoid even the appearance of ignobility. Naturally strong and ruthless, he told himself he was sentimental. His sentimentality never reached the point of actually inconveniencing him, and Clay knew enough to stay within the limits.

Nevertheless it is nerve-racking to know you're living under the scrutiny of an extratemporal Eye. As he walked into the lobby of the V Building a month later, Clay realized that light-vibrations reflected from his own body were driving irretrievably into the polished onyx walls and floor, photographing themselves there, waiting for a machine to unlock them, some day, some time, for some man perhaps in this very city, who as yet didn't know even the name of Sam Clay. Then, sitting in his relaxer in the spiral lift moving swiftly up inside the walls, he knew that those walls were capturing his image, stealing it, like some superstition he remembered . . . ah?

Vanderman's private secretary greeted him. Clay let his gaze wander freely across that young person's neatly dressed figure and mildly attractive face. She said that Mr. Vanderman was out, and the appointment was for three, not two, wasn't it? Clay referred to a notebook. He snapped his fingers.

"Three—you're right, Miss Wells. I was so sure it was two I didn't even bother to check up. Do you think he might be back sooner? I mean, is he out, or in conference?"

"He's out, all right, Mr. Clay," Miss Wells said. "I don't think he'll be back much sooner than three. I'm sorry."

"Well, may I wait in here?"

She smiled at him efficiently. "Of course. There's a stereo and the magazine spools are in that case."

She went back to her work, and Clay skimmed through an article about the care and handling of lunar filchards. It gave him an opportunity to start a conversation by asking Miss Wells if she liked filchards. It turned out that she had no opinion whatsoever of filchards but the ice had been broken.

This is the cocktail acquaintance, Clay thought. I may have a broken heart, but, naturally, I'm lonesome.

The trick wasn't to get engaged to Miss Wells so much as to fall in love with her convincingly. The Eye never slept. Clay was beginning to wake at night with a nervous start, and lie there looking up at the ceiling. But darkness was no shield.

"The question is," said the sociologist at this point, "whether or not Clay was acting for an audience."

"You mean us?"

"Exactly. It just occurred to me. Do you think he's been behaving perfectly naturally?"

The engineer pondered.

"I'd say yes. A man doesn't marry a girl only to carry out some other plan, does he? After all, he'd get himself involved in a whole new batch of responsibilities."

"Clay hasn't married Josephine Wells yet, however," the sociologist countered. "Besides, that responsibility angle might have applied a few hundred years ago, but not now." He went off at random. "Imagine a society where, after divorce, a man was forced to support a perfectly healthy, competent woman! It was vestigial, I know—a throwback to the days when only males could earn a living—but imagine the sort of women who were willing to accept such support. That was reversion to infancy if I ever—"

The engineer coughed.

"Oh," the sociologist said. "Oh . . . yes. The question is, would Clay have got himself engaged to a woman unless he really—"

"Engagements can be broken."

"This one hasn't been broken yet, as far as we know. And *we know*."

A normal man wouldn't plan on marrying a girl he didn't care anything about, unless he had some stronger motive—I'll go along that far."

"But how normal is Clay?" the sociologist wondered. "Did he know in advance we'd check back on his past? Did you notice that he cheated at solitaire?"

"Proving?"

"There are all kinds of trivial things you don't do if you think people are looking. Picking up a penny in the street, drinking soup out of the bowl, posing before a mirror—the sort of foolish or petty things everyone does when alone. Either Clay's innocent, or he's a very clever man—"

* * *

He was a very clever man. He never intended the engagement to get as far as marriage, though he knew that in one respect marriage would be a precaution. If a man talks in his sleep, his wife will certainly mention the fact. Clay considered gagging himself at night if the necessity should arise. Then he realized that if he talked in his sleep at all, there was no insurance against talking too much the very first time he had an auditor. He couldn't risk such a break. But there was no necessity, after all. Clay's problem, when he thought it over, was simply: How can I be sure I don't talk in my sleep?

He solved that easily enough by renting a narcohypnotic supplementary course in common trade dialects. This involved studying while awake and getting the information repeated in his ear during slumber. As a necessary preparation for the course, he was instructed to set up a recorder and chart the depth of his sleep, so the narcohypnosis could be keyed to his individual rhythms. He did this several times, rechecked once a month thereafter, and was satisfied. There was no need to gag himself at night.

He was glad to sleep provided he didn't dream. He had to take sedatives after a while. At night, there was relief from the knowledge that an Eye watched him always, an Eye that could bring him to justice, an Eye whose omnipotence he could not challenge in the open. But he dreamed about the Eye.

Vanderman had given him a job in the organization, which was enormous. Clay was merely a cog, which suited him well enough, for the moment. He didn't want any more favors yet. Not till he had found out the extent of Miss Wells' duties—Josephine, her Christian name was. That took several months, but by that time friendship was ripening into affection. So Clay asked Vanderman for another job. He specified. It wasn't obvious, but he was asking for work that would, presently, fit him for Miss Wells' duties.

Vanderman probably still felt guilty about Bea; he'd married her and she was in Antarctica now, at the Casino. Vanderman was due to join her, so he scribbled a memorandum, wished Clay good luck, and went to Antarctica, bothered by no stray pangs of conscience. Clay improved the hour by courting Josephine ardently.

From what he had heard about the new Mrs. Vanderman, he felt secretly relieved. Not long ago, when he had been content to remain passive, the increasing dominance of Bea would have satisfied him, but no more. He was learning self-reliance, and liked it. These days, Bea was behaving rather badly. Given all the money and freedom she could use, she had too much time on her hands. Once in a while Clay heard rumors that made him smile secretly. Vanderman wasn't having an easy time of it. A dominant character, Bea—but Vanderman was no weakling himself.

After a while Clay told his employer he wanted to marry Josephine Wells. "I guess that makes us square," he said. "You took Bea away from me and I'm taking Josie away from you."

"Now wait a minute," Vanderman said. "I hope you don't—"

"My fiancée, your secretary. That's all. The thing is, Josie and I are in love." He poured it on, but carefully. It was easier to deceive Vanderman than the Eye, with its trained technicians and forensic sociologists looking through it. He thought, sometime, of those medieval pictures of an immense eye, and that reminded him of something vague and distressing, though he couldn't isolate the memory.

After all, what could Vanderman do? He arranged to have Clay given a raise. Josphine, always conscientious, offered to keep on working for a while, till office routine was straightened out, but it never did get straightened out, somehow. Clay deftly saw to that by keeping Josephine busy. She didn't have to bring work home to her apartment, but she brought it, and Clay gradually began to help her when he dropped by. His job, plus the narcohypnotic courses, had already trained him for this sort of tricky organizational work. Vanderman's business was highly specialized—planet-wide exports and imports, and what with keeping track of specific groups, seasonal trends, sectarian holidays, and so forth, Josephine, as a sort of animated memorandum book for Vanderman, had a more than full-time job.

She and Clay postponed marriage for a time. Clay—naturally enough—began to appear mildly jealous of Josephine's work, and she said she'd quit soon. But one night she stayed on at the office, and he went out in a pet and got drunk. It just happened to be raining that night, Clay got tight enough to walk unprotected through the drizzle, and to fall asleep at home in his wet clothes. He came down with influenza. As he was recovering, Josephine got it.

Under the circumstances, Clay stepped in—purely a temporary job—and took over his fiancée's duties. Office routine was extremely complicated that week, and only Clay knew the ins and outs of it. The arrangement saved Vanderman a certain amount of inconvenience, and, when the situation resolved itself, Josephine had a subsidiary job and Clay was Vanderman's private secretary.

"I'd better know more about him," Clay said to Josephine. "After all, there must be a lot of habits and foibles he's got that need to be catered to. If he wants lunch ordered up, I don't want to get smoked tongue and find out he's allergic to it. What about his hobbies?"

But he was careful not to pump Josephine too hard, because of the Eye. He still needed sedatives to sleep.

The sociologist rubbed his forehead.

"Let's take a break," he suggested. "Why does a guy want to commit murder anyway?"

"For profit, one sort or another."

"Only partly, I'd say. The other part is an unconscious desire to be punished—usually for something else. That's why you get accident prones. Ever think about what happens to murderers who feel guilty and yet who aren't punished by the Law? They must live a rotten sort of life—always stepping in front of speedsters, cutting themselves with an ax—accidentally; accidentally touching wires full of juice—"

"Conscience, eh?"

"A long time ago, people thought God sat in the sky with a telescope and watched everything they did. They really lived pretty carefully, in the Middle Ages—the first Middle Ages, I mean. Then there was the era of disbelief, where people had nothing to believe in very strongly—and finally we get this." He nodded toward the screen. "A universal memory. By extension, it's a universal social conscience, an externalized one. It's exactly the same as the medieval concept of God—omniscience."

"But not omnipotence."

"Mm."

All in all, Clay kept the Eye in mind for a year and a half. Before he said or did anything whatsoever, he reminded himself of the Eye, and made certain that he wasn't revealing his motive to the judging future. Of course, there was—would be—an Ear, too, but that was a little too absurd. One couldn't visualize a large, disembodied Ear decorating the wall like a plate in a plate holder. All the same, whatever he said would be as important evidence—some time—as what he did. So Sam Clay was very careful indeed, and behaved like Caesar's wife. He wasn't exactly defying authority, but he was certainly circumventing it.

Superficially Vanderman was more like Caesar, and his wife was not above reproach, these days. She had too much money to play with. And she was finding her husband too strong-willed a

person to be completely satisfactory. There was enough of the
matriarch in Bea to make her feel rebellion against Andrew
Vanderman, and there was a certain lack of romance. Vanderman
had little time for her. He was busy these days, involved with a
whole string of deals which demanded much of his time. Clay,
of course, had something to do with that. His interest in his new
work was most laudable. He stayed up nights plotting and planning as though expecting Vanderman to make him a full partner.
In fact, he even suggested this possibility to Josephine. He
wanted it on the record. The marriage date had been set, and
Clay wanted to move before then; he had no intention of being
drawn into a marriage of convenience after the necessity had
been removed.

One thing he did, which had to be handled carefully, was to
get the whip. Now Vanderman was a fingerer. He liked to have
something in his hands while he talked. Usually it was a crystalline paper weight, with a miniature thunderstorm in it, complete
with lightning, when it was shaken. Clay put this where Vanderman
would be sure to knock it off and break it. Meanwhile, he had
plugged one deal with Callisto Ranches for the sole purpose of
getting a whip for Vanderman's desk. The natives were proud of
their leatherwork and their silversmithing, and a nominal make-
weight always went with every deal they closed. Thus, presently,
a handsome miniature whip, with Vanderman's initials on it, lay
on the desk, coiled into a loop, acting as a paperweight except
when he picked it up and played with it while he talked.

The other weapon Clay wanted was already there—an antique
paper knife, once called a surgical scalpel. He never let his gaze
rest on it too long, because of the Eye.

The other whip came. He absentmindedly put it in his desk
and pretended to forget it. It was a sample of the whips made by
the Alaskan Flagellantes for use in their ceremonies, and was
wanted because of some research being made into the pain-neut-
alizing drugs the Flagellantes used. Clay, of course, had engineered this deal, too. There was nothing suspicious about that;
the firm stood to make a sound profit. In fact, Vanderman had
promised him a percentage bonus at the end of the year on every
deal he triggered. It would be quite a lot. It was December, a
year and a half had passed since Clay first recognized that the
Eye would seek him out.

He felt fine. He was careful about the sedatives, and his
nerves, though jangled, were nowhere near the snapping point. It
had been a strain, but he had trained himself so that he would
make no slips. He visualized the Eye in the walls, in the ceiling,

in the sky, everywhere he went. It was the only way to play completely safe. And very soon now it would pay off. But he would have to do it soon; such a nervous strain could not be continued indefinitely.

A few details remained. He carefully arranged matters—under the Eye's very nose, so to speak—so that he was offered a well-paying position with another firm. He turned it down.

And one night an emergency happened to arise so that Clay, very logically, had to go to Vanderman's apartment.

Vanderman wasn't there; Bea was. She had quarreled violently with her husband. Moreover, she had been drinking. (This, too, he had expected.) If the situation had not worked out exactly as he wanted, he would have tried again—and again—but there was no need.

Clay was a little politer than necessary. Perhaps too polite, certainly Bea, that incipient matriarch, was led down the garden path, a direction she was not unwilling to take. After all, she had married Vanderman for his money, found him as dominant as herself, and now saw Clay as an exaggerated symbol of both romance and masculine submissiveness.

The camera eye hidden in the wall, in a decorative bas-relief, was grinding away busily, spooling up its wiretape in a way that indicated Vanderman was a suspicious as well as a jealous husband. But Clay knew about this gadget, too. At the suitable moment he stumbled against the wall in such a fashion that the device broke. Then, with only that other eye spying on him, he suddenly became so virtuous that it was a pity Vanderman couldn't witness his *volte face*.

"Listen, Bea," he said, "I'm sorry, but I didn't understand. It's no good. I'm not in love with you anymore. I was once, sure, but that was quite a while ago. There's somebody else, and you ought to know it by now."

"You still love me," Bea said with intoxicated firmness. "We belong together."

"Bea. Please. I hate to have to say this, but I'm grateful to Andrew Vanderman for marrying you. I . . . well, you got what you wanted, and I'm getting what I want. Let's leave it at that."

"I'm used to getting what I want, Sam. Opposition is something I don't like. Especially when I know you really—"

She said a good deal more, and so did Clay—he was perhaps unnecessarily harsh. But he had to make the point, for the Eye, that he was no longer jealous of Vanderman.

He made the point.

*　　　*　　　*

The next morning he got to the office before Vanderman, cleaned up his desk, and discovered the stingaree whip still in its box. "Oops," he said, snapping his fingers—the Eye watched, and this was the crucial period. Perhaps it would all be over within the hour. Every move from now on would have to be specially calculated in advance, and there could be no slightest deviation. The Eye was everywhere—literally everywhere.

He opened the box, took out the whip, and went into the inner sanctum. He tossed the whip on Vanderman's desk, so carelessly that a stylus rack toppled. Clay rearranged everything, leaving the stingaree whip near the edge of the desk, and placing the Callistan silver-leather whip at the back, half concealed behind the interoffice visor-box. He didn't allow himself more than a casual sweeping glance to make sure the paper knife was still there.

Then he went out for coffee.

Half an hour later he got back, picked up a few letters for signature from the rack, and walked into Vanderman's office. Vanderman looked up from behind his desk. He had changed a little in a year and a half; he was looking older, less noble, more like an aging bulldog. Once, Clay thought coldly, this man stole my fiancée and beat me up.

Careful. Remember the Eye.

There was no need to do anything but follow the plan and let events take their course. Vanderman had seen the spy films, all right, up to the point where they had gone blank, when Clay fell against the wall. Obviously he hadn't really expected Clay to show up this morning. But to see the louse grinning hello, walking across the room, putting some letters down on his desk—

Clay was counting on Vanderman's short temper, which had not improved over the months. Obviously the man had been simply sitting there, thinking unpleasant thoughts, and just as Clay had known would happen, he'd picked up the whip and begun to finger it. But it was the stingaree whip this time.

"Morning," Clay said cheerfully to his stunned employer. His smile became one-sided. "I've been waiting for you to check this letter to the Kirghiz kovar-breeders. Can we find a market for two thousand of those ornamental horns?"

It was at this point that Vanderman, bellowing, jumped to his feet, swung the whip, and sloshed Clay across the face. There is probably nothing more painful than the bite of a stingaree whip.

Clay staggered back. He had not known it would hurt so

much. For an instant the shock of the blow knocked every other consideration out of his head, and blind anger was all that remained.

Remember the Eye!

He remembered it. There were dozens of trained men watching everything he did just now. Literally he stood on an open stage surrounded by intent observers who made notes on every expression of his face, every muscular flection, every breath he drew.

In a moment Vanderman would be dead—but Sam Clay would not be alone. An invisible audience from the future was fixing him with cold, calculating eyes. He had one more thing to do and the job would be over. Do it—carefully, carefully!—while they watched.

Time stopped for him. *The job would be over.*

It was very curious. He had rehearsed this series of actions so often in the privacy of his mind that his body was going through with it now, without further instructions. His body staggered back from the blow, recovered balance, glared at Vanderman in shocked fury, poised for a dive at that paper knife in plain sight on the desk.

That was what the outward and visible Sam Clay was doing. But the inward and spiritual Sam Clay went through quite a different series of actions.

The job would be over.

And what was he going to do after that?

The inward and spiritual murderer stood fixed with dismay and surprise, staring at a perfectly empty future. He had never looked beyond this moment. He had made no plans for his life beyond the death of Vanderman. But now—he had no enemy but Vanderman. When Vanderman was dead, what would he fix upon to orient his life? What would he work at then? His job would be gone, too. And he liked his job.

Suddenly he knew how much he liked it. He was good at it. For the first time in his life, he had found a job he could do really well.

You can't live a year and a half in a new environment without acquiring new goals. The change had come imperceptibly. He was a good operator; he'd discovered that he could be successful. He didn't have to kill Vanderman to prove that to himself. He'd proved it already without committing murder.

In that time-stasis which had brought everything to a full stop he looked at Vanderman's red face and he thought of Bea, and of

Vanderman as he had come to know him—and he didn't want to be a murderer.

He didn't want Vanderman dead. He didn't want Bea. The thought of her made him feel a little sick. Perhaps that was because he himself had changed from passive to active. He no longer wanted or needed a dominant woman. He could make his own decisions. If he were choosing now, it would be someone more like Josephine—

Josephine. That image before his mind's stilled eye was suddenly very pleasant. Josephine with her mild, calm prettiness, her admiration for Sam Clay the successful businessman, the rising young importer in Vanderman, Inc. Josephine whom he was going to marry—Of course he was going to marry her. He loved Josephine. He loved his job. All he wanted was the status quo, exactly as he had achieved it. Everything was perfect right now—as of maybe thirty seconds ago.

But that was a long time ago—thirty seconds. A lot can happen in a half a minute. A lot had happened. Vanderman was coming at him again, the whip raised. Clay's nerves crawled at the anticipation of its burning impact across his face a second time. If he could get hold of Vanderman's wrist before he struck again—if he could talk fast enough—

The crooked smile was still on his face. It was part of the pattern, in some dim way he did not quite understand. He was acting in response to conditioned reflexes set up over a period of many months of rigid self-training. His body was already in action. All that had taken place in his mind had happened so fast there was no physical hiatus at all. His body knew its job and it was doing the job. It was lunging forward toward the desk and the knife, and he could not stop it.

All this had happened before. It had happened in his mind, the only place where Sam Clay had known real freedom in the past year and a half. In all that time he had forced himself to realize that the Eye was watching every outward move he made. He had planned each action in advance and schooled himself to carry it through. Scarcely once had he let himself act purely on impulse. Only in following the plan exactly was there safety. He had indoctrinated himself too successfully.

Something was wrong. This wasn't what he'd wanted. He was still afraid, weak, failing—

He lurched against the desk, clawed at the paper knife, and, knowing failure, drove it into Vanderman's heart.

*   *   *

"It's a tricky case," the forensic sociologist said to the engineer. "Very tricky."

"Want me to run it again?"

"No, not right now. I'd like to think it over. Clay . . . that firm that offered him another job. The offer's withdrawn now, isn't it? Yes, I remember—they're fussy about the morals of their employees. It's insurance or something, I don't know. Motive. Motive, now."

The sociologist looked at the engineer.

The engineer said: "A year and a half ago he had a motive. But a week ago he had everything to lose and nothing to gain. He's lost his job and that bonus, he doesn't want Mrs. Vanderman anymore, and as for that beating Vanderman once gave him . . . ah?"

"Well, he did try to shoot Vanderman once, and he couldn't, remember? Even though he was full of Dutch courage. But—something's wrong. Clay's been avoiding even the appearance of evil a little too carefully. Only I can't put my finger on anything, blast it."

"What about tracing back his life further? We only got to his fourth year."

"There couldn't be anything useful that long ago. It's obvious he was afraid of his father and hated him, too. Typical stuff, basic psych. The father symbolizes judgment to him. I'm very much afraid Sam Clay is going to get off scot-free."

"But if you think there's something haywire—"

"The burden of proof is up to us," the sociologist said.

The visor sang. A voice spoke softly.

"No, I haven't got the answer yet. Now? All right. I'll drop over."

He stood up.

"The D.A. wants a consultation. I'm not hopeful, though. I'm afraid the State's going to lose this case. That's the trouble with the externalized conscience—"

He didn't amplify. He went out, shaking his head, leaving the engineer staring speculatively at the screen. But within five minutes he was assigned to another job—the bureau was understaffed—and he didn't have a chance to investigate on his own until a week later. Then it didn't matter anymore.

For, a week later, Sam Clay was walking out of the court an acquitted man. Bea Vanderman was waiting for him at the foot of the ramp. She wore black, but obviously her heart wasn't in it.

"Sam," she said.

He looked at her.

He felt a little dazed. It was all over. Everything had worked out exactly according to plan. And nobody was watching him now. The Eye had closed. The invisible audience had put on its hats and coats and left the theater of Sam Clay's private life. From now on he could do and say precisely what he liked, with no censoring watcher's omnipresence to check him. He could act on impulse again.

He had outwitted society. He had outwitted the Eye and all its minions in all their technological glory. He, Sam Clay, private citizen. It was a wonderful thing, and he could not understand why it left him feeling so flat.

That had been a nonsensical moment, just before the murder. The moment of relenting. They say you get the same instant's frantic rejection on the verge of a good many important decisions— just before you marry, for instance. Or—what was it? Some other common instance he'd often heard of. For a second it eluded him. Then he had it. The hour before marriage—and the instant after suicide. After you've pulled the trigger, or jumped off the bridge. The instant of wild revulsion when you'd give anything to undo the irrevocable. Only, you can't. It's too late. The thing is done.

Well, he'd been a fool. Luckily, it *had* been too late. His body took over and forced him to success he'd trained it for. About the job—it didn't matter. He'd get another. He'd proved himself capable. If he could outwit the Eye itself, what job existed he couldn't lick if he tried? Except—nobody knew exactly how good he was. How could he prove his capabilities? It was infuriating to achieve such phenomenal success after a lifetime of failures, and never to get the credit for it. How many men must have tried and failed where he had tried and succeeded? Rich men, successful men, brilliant men who had yet failed in the final test of all—the contest with the Eye, their own lives at stake. Only Sam Clay had passed that most important test in the world—and he could never claim credit for it.

". . . knew they wouldn't convict," Bea's complacent voice was saying.

Clay blinked at her. "What?"

"I said I'm so glad you're free, darling. I knew they wouldn't convict you. I knew that from the very beginning." She smiled at him, and for the first time it occurred to him that Bea looked a little like a bulldog. It was something about her lower jaw. He thought that when her teeth were closed together the lower set probably rested just outside the upper. He had an instant's impulse to ask her about it. Then he decided he had better not.

"You knew, did you?" he said.

She squeezed his arm. What an ugly lower jaw that was. How odd he'd never noticed it before. And behind the heavy lashes, how small her eyes were. How mean.

"Let's go where we can be alone," Bea said, clinging to him. "There's such a lot to talk about."

"We *are* alone," Clay said, diverted for an instant to his original thoughts. "Nobody's watching," He glanced up at the sky and down at the mosaic pavement. He drew a long breath and let it out slowly. "Nobody," he said.

"My speeder's parked right over here. We can—"

"Sorry, Bea."

"What do you mean?"

"I've got business to attend to."

"Forget business. Don't you understand that we're free now, both of us?"

He had a horrible feeling he knew what she meant.

"Wait a minute," he said, because this seemed the quickest way to end it. "I killed your husband, Bea. Don't forget that."

"You were acquitted. It was self-defense. The court said so."

"It—" He paused, glanced up quickly at the high wall of the Justice Building, and began a one-sided, mirthless smile. It was all right; there was no Eye now. There never would be, again. He was unwatched.

"You mustn't feel guilty, even within yourself," Bea said firmly. "It wasn't your fault. It simply wasn't. You've got to remember that. You *couldn't* have killed Andrew except by accident, Sam, so—"

"What? What do you mean by that?"

"Well, after all. I know the prosecution kept trying to prove you'd planned to kill Andrew all along, but you mustn't let what they said put any ideas in your head. I know you, Sam. I knew Andrew. You couldn't have planned a thing like that, and even if you had, it wouldn't have worked."

The half-smile died.

"It wouldn't?"

She looked at him steadily.

"Why, you couldn't have managed it," she said. "Andrew was the better man, and we both know it. He'd have been too clever to fall for anything—"

"Anything a second-rater like me could dream up?" Clay swallowed. His lips tightened. "Even you— What's the idea?

What's your angle now—that we second-raters ought to get together?''

"Come on,'' she said, and slipped her arm through his. Clay hung back for a second. Then he scowled, looked back at the Justice Building, and followed Bea toward her speeder.

The engineer had a free period. He was finally able to investigate Sam Clay's early childhood. It was purely academic now, but he liked to indulge his curiosity. He traced Clay back to the dark closet, when the boy was four, and used ultraviolet. Sam was huddled in a corner, crying silently, staring up with frightened eyes at a top shelf.

What was on that shelf the engineer could not see.

He kept the beam focused on the closet and cast back rapidly through time. The closet often opened and closed, and sometimes Sam Clay was locked in it as punishment, but the upper shelf held its mystery until—

It was in reverse. A woman reached to that shelf, took down an object, walked backward out of the closet to Sam Clay's bedroom, and went to the wall by the door. This was unusual, for generally it was Sam's father who was warden of the closet.

She hung up a framed picture of a single huge staring eye floating in space. There was a legend under it. The letters spelled out: THOU GOD SEEST ME.

The engineer kept on tracing. After a while it was night. The child was in bed, sitting up wide-eyed, afraid. A man's footsteps sounded on the stair. The scanner told all secrets but those of the inner mind. The man was Sam's father, coming up to punish him for some childish crime committed earlier. Moonlight fell upon the wall beyond which the footsteps approached showing how the wall quivered a little to the vibrations of the feet, and the Eye in its frame quivered, too. The boy seemed to brace himself. A defiant half-smile showed on his mouth, crooked, unsteady.

This time he'd keep that smile, no matter what happened. When it was over he'd still have it, so his father could see it, and the Eye could see it and they'd know he hadn't given in. He hadn't . . . he—

The door opened.

He couldn't help it. The smile faded and was gone.

"Well, what was eating him?'' the engineer demanded.

The sociologist shrugged. "You could say he never did really grow up. It's axiomatic that boys go through a phase of rivalry with their fathers. Usually that's sublimated; the child grows up and wins, in one way or another. But Sam Clay didn't. I suspect he developed an externalized conscience very early. Symbolizing partly his father, partly God, an Eye and society—which fulfills the role of protective, punishing parent, you know.''

''It still isn't evidence.''

''We aren't going to get any evidence on Sam Clay. But that doesn't mean he's got away with anything, you know. He's always been afraid to assume the responsibilities of maturity. He never took on an optimum challenge. He was afraid to succeed at anything because that symbolic Eye of his might smack him down. When he was a kid, he might have solved his entire problem by kicking his old man in the shins. Sure, he'd have got a harder whaling, but he'd have made some move to assert his individuality. As it is, he waited too long. And then he defied the wrong thing, and it wasn't really defiance, basically. Too late now. His formative years are past. The thing that might really solve Clay's problem would be his conviction for murder— but he's been acquitted. If he'd been convicted, then he could prove to the world that he'd hit back. He'd kicked his father in the shins, kept that defiant smile on his face, killed Andrew Vanderman. I think that's what he actually has wanted all along—recognition. Proof of his own ability to assert himself. He had to work hard to cover his tracks—if he made any—but that was part of the game. By winning it he's lost. The normal ways of escape are closed to him. He always had an Eye looking down at him.''

''Then the acquittal stands?''

''There's still no evidence. The State's lost its case. But I . . . I don't think Sam Clay has won his. Something will happen.'' He sighed. ''It's inevitable, I'm afraid. Sentence first, you see. Verdict afterward. The sentence was passed on Clay a long time ago.''

Sitting across from him in the Paradise Bar, behind a silver decanter of brandy in the center of the table, Bea looked lovely and hateful. It was the lights that made her lovely. They even managed to cast their shadows over that bulldog chin, and under her thick lashes the small, mean eyes acquired an illusion of beauty. But she still looked hateful. The lights could do nothing about that. They couldn't cast shadows into Sam Clay's private mind or distort the images there.

He thought of Josephine. He hadn't made up his mind fully yet about that. But if he didn't quite know what he wanted, there was no shadow of doubt about what he *didn't* want—no possible doubt whatever.

"You need me, Sam," Bea told him over her brimming glass.
"I can stand on my own feet. I don't need anybody."

It was the indulgent way she looked at him. It was the smile
that showed her teeth. He could see as clearly as if he had X-ray
vision how the upper teeth would close down inside the lower
when she shut her mouth. There would be a lot of strength in a
jaw like that. He looked at her neck and saw the thickness of it,
and thought how firmly she was getting her grip upon him, how
she maneuvered for position and waited to lock her bulldog
clamp deep into the fabric of his life again.

"I'm going to marry Josephine, you know," he said.

"No, you're not. You aren't the man for Josephine. I know
that girl, Sam. For a while you may have had her convinced you
were a go-getter. But she's bound to find out the truth. You'd be
miserable together. You need me, Sam darling. You don't know
what you want. Look at the mess you got into when you tried to
act on your own. Oh, Sam, why don't you stop pretending? You
know you never were a planner. You . . . what's the matter,
Sam?"

His sudden burst of laughter had startled both of them. He
tried to answer her, but the laughter wouldn't let him. He lay
back in his chair and shook with it until he almost strangled. He
had come so close, so desperately close to bursting out with a
boast that would have been confession. Just to convince the
woman. Just to shut her up. He must care more about her good
opinion than he had realized until now. But that last absurdity
was too much. It was only ridiculous now. Sam Clay, not a
planner.

How good it was to let himself laugh, now. To let himself go,
without having to think ahead. Acting on impulse again, after
those long months of rigid repression. No audience from the
future was clustering around this table, analyzing the quality of
his laughter, observing that it verged on hysteria. Who cared? He
deserved a little blow-off like this, after all he'd been through.
He'd risked so much, and achieved so much—and in the end
gained nothing, not even glory except in his own mind. He'd
gained nothing, really, except the freedom to be hysterical if he
felt like it. He laughed and laughed and laughed, hearing the
shrill note of lost control in his own voice and not caring.

People were turning to stare. The bartender looked over at him
uneasily, getting ready to move if this went on. Bea stood up,
leaned across the table, shook him by the shoulder.

"Sam, what's the matter? Sam, do get hold of yourself!

You're making a spectacle of me, Sam! What *are* you laughing at?''

With a tremendous effort he forced the laughter back in his throat. His breath still came heavily and little bursts of merriment kept bubbling up so that he could hardly speak, but he got the words out somehow. They were probably the first words he had spoken without rigid consorship since he first put his plan into operation. And the words were these.

''I'm laughing at the way I fooled you. I fooled everybody! You think I didn't know what I was doing every minute of the time? You think I wasn't planning, every step of the way? It took me eighteen months to do it, but I killed Andrew Vanderman with malice aforethought, and nobody can ever prove I did it.'' He giggled foolishly. ''I just wanted you to know,'' he added in a mild voice.

And it wasn't until he got his breath back and began to experience that feeling of incredible, delightful, incomparable relief that he knew what he had done.

She was looking at him without a flicker of expression on her face. Total blank was all that showed. There was a dead silence for a quarter of a minute. Clay had the feeling that his words must have rung from the roof, that in a moment the police would come in to hale him away. But the words had been quietly spoken. No one had heard but Bea.

And now, at last, Bea moved. She answered him, but not in words. The bulldog face convulsed suddenly and overflowed with laughter.

As he listened, Clay felt all that flood of glorious relief ebbing away. For he saw that she did not believe him. And there was no way he could prove the truth.

''Oh, you silly little man,'' Bea gasped when words came back to her. ''You had me almost convinced for a minute. I almost believed you. I—'' Laughter silenced her again, consciously silvery laughter that made heads turn. That conscious note in it warned him that she was up to something. Bea had had an idea. His own thoughts outran hers and he knew in an instant before she spoke exactly what the idea was and how she would apply it. He said: ''I *am* going to marry Josephine,'' in the very instant that Bea spoke.

''You're going to marry me,'' she said flatly. ''You've got to. You don't know your own mind, Sam. I know what's best for you and I'll see you do it. Do you understand me, Sam?''

''The police won't realize that was only a silly boast,'' she told him. "They'll believe you. You wouldn't want me to tell them what you just said, would you, Sam?"

He looked at her in silence, seeing no way out. This dilemma had sharper horns than anything he could have imagined. For Bea did not and would not believe him, no matter how he yearned to convince her, while the police undoubtedly would believe him, to the undoing of his whole investment in time, effort, and murder. He had said it. It was engraved upon the walls and in the echoing air, waiting for that invisible audience in the future to observe. No one was listening now, but a word from Bea could make them reopen the case.

A word from Bea.

He looked at her, still in silence, but with a certain cool calculation beginning to dawn in the back of his mind.

For a moment Sam Clay felt very tired indeed. In that moment he encompassed a good deal of tentative future time. In his mind he said yes to Bea, married her, lived an indefinite period as her husband. And he saw what that life would be like. He saw the mean small eyes watching him, the relentlessly gripping jaw set, the tyranny that would emerge slowly or not slowly, depending on the degree of his subservience, until he was utterly at the mercy of the woman who had been Andrew Vanderman's widow.

Sooner or later, he thought clearly to himself, *I'd kill her.*

He'd have to kill. That sort of life, with that sort of woman, wasn't a life Sam Clay could live, indefinitely. And he'd proved his ability to kill and go free.

But what about Andrew Vanderman's death?

Because they'd have another case against him then. This time it had been qualitative; the next time, the balance would shift toward quantitative. If Sam Clay's wife died, Sam Clay would be investigated no matter how she died. Once a suspect, always a suspect in the eyes of the law. The Eye of the law. They'd check back. They'd return to this moment, while he sat here revolving thoughts of death in his mind. And they'd return to five minutes ago, and listen to him boast that he had killed Vanderman.

A good lawyer might get him off. He could claim it wasn't the truth. He could say he had been goaded to an idle boast by the things Bea said. He might get away with that, and he might not. Scop would be the only proof, and he couldn't be compelled to take scop.

But—no. That wasn't the answer. That wasn't the way out. He could tell by the sick, sinking feeling inside him. There had been just one glorious moment of release, after he'd made his confession to Bea, and from then on everything seemed to run downhill again.

But that moment had been the goal he'd worked toward all this time. He didn't know what it was, or why he wanted it. But he recognized the feeling when it came. He wanted it back.

This helpless feeling, this impotence—was this the total sum of what he had achieved? Then he'd failed, after all. Somehow, in some strange way he could only partly understand, he had failed; killing Vanderman hadn't been the answer at all. He wasn't a success. He was a second-rater, a passive, helpless worm whom Bea would manage and control and drive, eventually, to—

"What's the matter, Sam?" Bea asked solicitously.

"You think I'm a second-rater, don't you?" he said. "You'll never believe I'm not. You think I couldn't have killed Vanderman except by accident. You'll never believe I could possibly have defied—"

"What?" she asked, when he did not go on.

There was a new note of surprise in his voice.

"But it wasn't defiance," he said slowly. "I just hid and dodged. Circumvented. I hung dark glasses on an Eye, because I was afraid of it. But—that wasn't defiance. So—what I really was trying to prove—"

She gave him a startled, incredulous stare as he stood up.

"Sam! What are you doing?" Her voice cracked a little.

"Proving something," Clay said, smiling crookedly, and glancing up from Bea to the ceiling. "Take a good look," he said to the Eye as he smashed her skull with the decanter.

MANNA

by Peter Phillips (1921–   )

Astounding Science Fiction, February

British newspaperman Peter Phillips (not to be confused with Rog Phillips, another good writer) returns—his incredible "Dreams are Sacred" is a very tough act to follow—with this fine story about other dimensions and religious beliefs. We know far less about Peter Phillips than we should, except that at his best he was very good indeed, and that like many (too many) other writers he seems to have only had one solid productive decade in his career, in this case 1948 to 1958. It is interesting to speculate on what kind of sf he would be writing if he began his career in 1978 instead of thirty years earlier.—M.H.G.

(It seems to me that science fiction writers tend to avoid religion. Surely, religion has permeated many societies at all times; all Western societies from ancient Sumeria on have had strong religious components. And yet—

Societies depicted in science fiction and fantasy often ignore religion. While the great Manichean battle of good and evil—God and Satan—seems to permeate Tolkien's "Lord of the Rings," there is no religious ritual anywhere mentioned. In my own "Foundation" series, the only religious element found is a purely secular fake—and that was put in only at the insistence of John Campbell, to my own enormous unease.

Still, there are exceptions. Religion does appear sometimes, usually in forms that appear [to me] to be somewhat Catholic in atmosphere, or else Fundamentalist. "Manna" by Peter Phillips is an example.—I.A.)

* * *

Take best-quality synthetic protein. Bake it, break it up, steam it, steep in in sucrose, ferment it, add nut oil, piquant spices from the Indies, fruit juices, new flavors from the laboratory, homogenize it, hydrolize it, soak it in brine; pump in glutamic acid, balanced proportions of A, B_1, B_2, C, D, traces of calcium, copper and iron salts, an unadvertised drop of benzedrine; dehydrate, peptonize, irradiate, reheat in malt vapor under pressure compress, cut into mouth-sized chunks, pack in liquor from an earlier stage of process—

Miracle Meal.

Everything the Body Needs to Sustain Life and Bounding Vitality, in the Most DEEE LISHUSSS *Food Ever Devised. It will Invigorate You, Build Muscle, Brain, Nerve. Better than the Banquets of Imperial Rome, Renaissance Italy, Eighteenth Century France—All in One Can. The Most Heavenly Taste Thrills You Have Ever Experienced. Gourmets' Dream and Housewives' Delight. You Can Live On It. Eat it for Breakfast, Lunch, Dinner. You'll Never Get Tired of MIRACLE MEAL.*

Ad cuts of Zeus contemptuously tossing a bowl of ambrosia over the edge of Mount Olympus and making a goggle-eyed grab for a can of Miracle Meal.

Studio fake-ups of Lucretia Borgia dropping a phial of poison and crying piously: "It Would Be a Sin to Spoil Miracle Meal."

Posters and night-signs of John Doe—or Bill Smith, or Henri Brun, or Hans Schmitt or Wei Lung—balancing precariously on a pyramided pile of empty M.M. cans, eyes closed, mouth pursed in slightly inane ecstasy as he finished the last mouthful of his hundred-thousandth can.

You could live on it, certainly.

The publicity co-ordinator of the Miracle Meal Corporation chose the victim himself—a young man named Arthur Adelaide from Greenwich Village.

For a year, under the closest medical supervision and observation, Arthur ate nothing but Miracle Meal.

From this Miracle Meal Marathon, as it was tagged by videoprint newssheets, he emerged smiling, twice the weight—publicity omitted to mention that he'd been half-starved to begin with—he'd been trying to live off pure art and was a bad artist—perfectly fit, and ten thousand dollars richer.

He was also given a commercial art job with M.M., designing new labels for the cans.

His abrupt death at the end of an eighty-story drop from his office window a week or two later received little attention.

It would be unreasonable to blame the cumulative effect of M.M., for Arthur was probably a little unbalanced to begin with, whereas M.M. was Perfectly Balanced—a Kitchen in a Can.

Maybe you could get tired of it. But not very quickly. The flavor was the secret. It was delicious yet strangely and tantalizingly indefinable. It seemed to react progressively on the taste-buds so that the tastes subtly changed with each mouthful.

One moment it might be *omelette au fine herbes*, the next, turkey and cranberry, then buckwheat and maple. You'd be through the can before you could make up your mind. So you'd buy another.

Even the can was an improvement on the usual plastic self-heater—shape of a small, shallow pie-dish, with a pre-impressed crystalline fracture in the plastic lid.

Press the inset button on the preheating unit at one side, and when the food was good and hot, a secondary chemical reaction in the unit released a fierce little plunger just inside the perimeter fracture. Slight steam pressure finished the job. The lip flipped off.

Come and get it. You eat right out of the can it comes in. Keep your fingers out, Johnny. Don't you see the hygiplast spoon in its moisture- and heat-repellent wrapper fixed under the lid?

The Rev. Malachi Pennyhorse did not eat Miracle Meal. Nor was he impressed when Mr. Stephen Samson, Site Advisor to the Corporation, spoke in large dollar signs of the indirect bene-fits a factory would bring to the district.

"Why here? You already have one factory in England. Why not extend it?"

"It's our policy, Reverend—"

"Not 'Reverend' young man. Call me Vicar. Or Mr. Penny-horse. Or merely Pennyhorse— Go on."

"It's our policy, sir, to keep our factories comparatively small, site them in the countryside for the health of employees, and modify the buildings to harmonize with the prevailing architecture of the district. There is no interference with local amenities. All transport of employees, raw materials, finished product is by silent copter."

Samson laid a triphoto on the vicar's desk. "What would you say that was?"

Mr. Pennyhorse adjusted his pince-nez, looked closely. "Byzantine. Very fine. Around 500 A.D."

"And this—"

"Moorish. Quite typical. Fifteenth century."

Samson said: "They're our factories at Istanbul and Tunis respectively. At Allahabad, India, we had to put up big notices saying: 'This is not a temple or place of worship' because natives kept wandering in and offering-up prayers to the processing machines."

Mr. Pennyhorse glanced up quickly. Samson kept his face straight, added: "The report may have been exaggerated, but—you get the idea?"

The vicar said: "I do. What shape do you intend your factory to take in this village?"

"That's why I came to you. The rural district council suggested that you might advise us."

"My inclination, of course, is to advise you to go away and not return."

The vicar looked out of his study window at the sleepy, sun-washed village street, gables of the ancient Corn Exchange, paved market-place, lichened spire of his own time-kissed church; and, beyond, rolling Wiltshire pastures cradling the peaceful community.

The vicar sighed: "We've held out here so long—I hoped we would remain inviolate in my time, at least. However, I suppose we must consider ourselves fortunate that your corporation has some respect for tradition and the feelings of the . . . uh . . . 'natives.' "

He pulled out a drawer in his desk. "It might help you to understand those feelings if I show you a passage from the very full diary of my predecessor here, who died fifty years ago at the age of ninety-five—we're a long-lived tribe, we clergy. It's an entry he made one hundred years ago—sitting at this very desk."

Stephen Samson took the opened volume.

The century-old handwriting was as readable as typescript.

"*May 3, 1943. Long, interesting discussion with young American soldier, one of those who are billeted in the village. They term themselves G.I.'s. Told me countryside near his home in Pennsylvania not unlike our Wiltshire downs. Showed him round church. Said he was leaving soon, and added: 'I love this place. Nothing like my home town in looks, but the atmosphere's the same—old, and kind of comfortable. And I guess if I came back here a hundred years from now, it wouldn't have changed one bit.' An engaging young man. I trust he is right.*"

Samson looked up. Mr. Pennyhorse said: "That young man may have been one of your ancestors."

Samson gently replaced the old diary on the desk. "He wasn't.

My family's Ohioan. But I see what you mean, and respect it. That's why I want you to help us. You will?''

"Do you fish?" asked the vicar, suddenly and irrelevantly.

"Yes, sir. Very fond of the sport."

"Thought so. You're the type. That's why I like you. Take a look at these flies. Seen anything like them? Make 'em myself. One of the finest trout streams in the country just outside the village. Help you? Of course I will."

"Presumption," said Brother James. He eased himself through a graystone wall by twisting his subexistential plane slightly, and leaned reflectively against a moonbeam that slanted through the branches of an oak.

A second habited and cowled figure materialized beside him. "Perhaps so. But it does my age-wearied heart a strange good to see those familiar walls again casting their shadows over the field."

"A mockery, Brother Gregory. A mere shell that simulates the outlines of our beloved Priory. Think you that even the stones are of that good, gray granite that we built with? Nay! As this cursed simulacrum was a-building, I warped two hands into the solid, laid hold of a mossy block, and by the saints, 'twas of such inconsequential weight I might have hurled it skyward with a finger. And within, is there aught which we may recognize? No chapel, no cloisters, no refectory—only long, geometrical rooms. And what devilries and unholy rites may not be centered about those strange mechanisms, with which the rooms are filled?"

At the tirade, Brother Gregory sighed and thrust back his cowl to let the gracious moonbeams play on his tonsured head. "For an Untranslated One of some thousand years' standing," he said, "you exhibit a mulish ignorance, Brother James. You would deny men all advancement. I remember well your curses when first we saw horseless carriages and flying machines."

"Idols!" James snapped. "Men worship them. Therefore are they evil."

"You are so good, Brother James," Gregory said, with the heaviest sarcasm. "So good, it is my constant wonderment that you have had to wait so long for Translation Upwards. Do you think that Dom Pennyhorse, the present incumbent of Selcor—a worthy man, with reverence for the past—would permit evil rites within his parish? You are a befuddled old anachronism, brother."

"That," said James, "is quite beyond sufferance. For you to speak thus of Translation, when it was your own self-indulgent pursuit of carnal pleasures that caused us to be bound here through the centuries!''

Brother Gregory said coldly: "It was not I who inveigled the daughter of Ronald the Wry-Neck into the kitchen garden, thus exposing the weak flesh of a brother to grievous temptation."

There was silence for a while, save for the whisper of a midnight breeze through the branches of the oak, and the muted call of a nightbird from the far woods.

Gregory extended a tentative hand and lightly touched the sleeve of James's habit. "The argument might proceed for yet another century and bring us no nearer Translation. Besides it is not such unbearable penance, my brother. Were we not both lovers of the earth, of this fair countryside?''

James shrugged. Another silence. Then he fingered his gaunt white cheeks. "What we do, Brother Gregory? Shall we—appear to them?''

Gregory said: "I doubt whether common warp manifestation would be efficacious. As dusk fell tonight, I overheard a conversation between Dom Pennyhorse and a tall, young-featured man who has been concerned in the building of this simulacrum. The latter spoke in one of the dialects of the Americas; and it was mentioned that several of the men who will superintend the working of the machines within will also be from the United States—for a time at least. It is not prudent to haunt Americans in the normal fashion. Their attitude towards such matters is notoriously—unseemly.''

"We could polter," suggested Brother James.

Gregory replaced his cowl. "Let us review the possibilities, then," he said, "remembering that our subetheric energy is limited.''

They walked slowly together over the meadow towards the resuscitated gray walls of the Selcor Prior. Blades of grass, positively charged by their passage, sprang suddenly upright, relaxed slowly into limpness as the charge leaked away.

They halted at the walls to adjust their planes of incidence and degree of tenuity, and passed inside.

The new Miracle Meal machines had had their first test run. The bearings on the dehydrator pumps were still warm as two black figures, who seemed to carry with them an air of vast and wistful loneliness, paced silently between rows of upright cylinders which shone dully in moonlight diffused through narrow windows.

"Here," said Gregory, the taller of the two, softly, "did we once walk the cloisters in evening meditation."

Brother James's broad features showed signs of unease. He felt more than mere nostalgia.

"Power—what are they using? Something upsets my bones. I am queasy, as when a thunderstorn is about to break. Yet there is no static."

Gregory stopped, looked at his hand. There was a faint blue aura at his fingertips. "Slight neutron escape," he said. "They have a small thorium-into-233 pile somewhere. It needs better shielding."

"You speak riddles."

Gregory said, with a little impatience: "You have the entire science section of the village library at your disposal at nightfall for the effort of a trifling polter, yet for centuries you have read nothing but the *Lives of the Saints*. So, of course, I speak riddles—to you. You are even content to remain in ignorance of the basic principles of your own structure and functioning, doing everything by traditional thought-rote and rule of thumb. But I am not so content; and of my knowledge, I can assure you that the radiation will not harm you unless you warp to solid and sit atop the pile when it is in full operation." Gregory smiled. "And then, dear brother, you would doubtless be so uncomfortable that you would dewarp before any harm could be done beyond the loss of a little energy that would be replaced in time. Let us proceed."

They went through three departments before Brother Gregory divined the integrated purpose of the vats, driers, conveyor-tubes, belts and containers.

"The end product, I'm sure, is a food of sorts," he said, "and by some quirk of fate, it is stored in approximately the position that was once occupied by our kitchen store—if my sense of orientation has not been bemused by these strange internal surroundings."

The test run of the assembly had produced a few score cans of Miracle Food. They were stacked on metal shelves which would tilt and gravity-feed them into the shaft leading up to the crating machine. Crated, they would go from there to the copter-loading bay on the roof.

Brother James reached out to pick up a loose can. His hand went through it twice.

"Polt, you dolt!" said Brother Gregory. "Or are you trying to be miserly with your confounded energy? Here, let me do it."

The telekineticized can sprang into his solid hands. He turned it about slightly increasing his infrared receptivity to read the label, since the storeroom was in darkness.

"Miracle Meal. Press here."

He pressed, pressed again, and was closely examining the can when, after thirty seconds, the lid flipped off, narrowly missing his chin.

Born, and living, in more enlightened times, Brother Gregory's inquiring mind and insatiable appetite for facts would have made him a research worker. He did not drop the can. His hands were quite steady. He chuckled. He said: "Ingenious, very ingenious. See—the food is hot."

He warped his nose and back-palate into solid and delicately inhaled vapors. His eyes widened. He frowned, inhaled again. A beatific smile spread over his thin face.

"Brother James—warp your nose!"

The injunction, in other circumstances, might have been considered both impolite and unnecessary. Brother James was no beauty, and his big, blunt, snoutlike nose, which had been a flaring red in life, was the least prepossessing of his features.

But he warped it, and sniffed.

M.M. Sales Leaflet Number 14: It Will Sell By Its Smell Alone.

Gregory said hesitantly: "Do you think Brother James, that we might—"

James licked his lips, from side to side, slowly. "It would surely take a day's accumulation of energy to hold digestive and alimentary in solid for a sufficient period. But—"

"Don't be a miser," said Gregory. "There's a spoon beneath the lid. Get a can for yourself. And don't bother with digestive. Teeth, palate and throat are sufficient. It would not digest in any case. It remains virtually unchanged. But going down—ah, bliss!"

It went down. Two cans.

"Do you remember, brother," said James, in a weak, reminiscing voice, "what joy it was to eat and be strengthened. And now to eat is to be weakened."

Brother Gregory's voice was faint but happy. "Had there been food of this character available before our First Translation, I doubt whether other desires of the flesh would have appealed to me. But what was our daily fare set on the refectory table: peas; lentils; cabbage soup; hard, tasteless cheese. Year after year—*ugh!*"

"Health-giving foods," murmured Brother James, striving to be righteous even in his exhaustion. "Remember when we bribed the kitchener to get extra portions. Good trenchermen, we. Had we not died of the plague before our Priory became rich and powerful, then, by the Faith, our present bodies would be of greater girth.''

"Forms, not bodies," said Gregory, insisting even in *his* exhaustion on scientific exactitudes. "Variable fields, consisting of open lattices of energy foci resolvable into charged particles—and thus solid matter—when they absorb energy beyond a certain stage. In other words, my dear ignorant brother, when we polt. The foci themselves—or rather the spaces between them—act as a limited-capacity storage battery for the slow accretion of this energy from cosmic sources, which may be controlled and concentrated in the foci by certain thought-patterns."

Talking was an increasing effort in his energy-low state.

"When we polt," he went on slowly, "we take up heat, air cools, live people get cold shivers; de-polt, give up heat, live people get clammy, cold-hot feeling; set up 'lectrostatic field, live peoples' hair stan's on end''—his voice was trailing into deep, blurred inaudibility, like a mechanical phonograph running down, but James wasn't listening anyway—''an' then when we get Translated Up'ards by The Power That Is, all the energy goes back where it came from an' we jus' become thought. Thassall. Thought. Thought, thought, thought, thought—''

The phonograph ran down, stopped. There was silence in the transit storeroom of the Selcor Priory Factory branch of the Miracle Meal Corporation.

For a while.

Then—

"THOUGHT!"

The shout brought Brother James from his uneasy, uncontrolled repose at the nadir of an energy balance.

"What is it?" he grumbled. "I'm too weak to listen to any of your theorizing."

"Theorizing! I have it!"

"Conserve your energies, brother, else will you be too weak even to twist yourself from this place."

Both monks had permitted their forms to relax into a corner of the storeroom, supine, replete in disrepletion.

Brother Gregory sat up with an effort.

"Listen, you attenuated conserve of very nothingness, I have a way to thwart, bemuse, mystify and irritate these crass philistines—and nothing so simple that a psychic investigator could put a thumb on us. What are we, Brother James?"

It was a rhetorical question, and Brother James had barely formulated his brief repy—''Ghosts''—before Brother Gregory, energized in a way beyond his own understanding by his own enthusiasm, went on: "Fields, in effect. Mere lines of force, in our un-polted state. What happens if we whirl? A star whirls. It has mass, rate of angular rotation, degree of compactness—therefore, gravity. Why? Because it has a field to start with. But we are our own fields. We need neither mass nor an excessive rate of rotation to achieve the same effect. Last week I grounded a high-flying wood-pigeon by whirling. It shot down to me through the air, and I'd have been buffeted by its pinions had I not stood aside. It hit the ground—not too heavily, by the grace of St. Barbara—recovered and flew away."

The great nose of Brother James glowed pinkly for a moment. "You fuddle and further weaken me by your prating. Get to your point, if you have such. And explain how we may do anything in our present unenergized state, beyond removing ourselves to a nexus point for recuperation."

Brother Gregory warped his own nose into solid in order to scratch its tip. He felt the need of this reversion to a life habit, which had once aided him in marshaling his thoughts.

"You think only of personal energy," he said scornfully. "We do need that, to whirl. It is an accumulative process, yet we gain nothing, lose nothing. Matter is not the only thing we can warp. If you will only listen, you woof of unregenerate and forgotten flesh, I will try to explain without mathematics."

He talked.

After a while, Brother James's puzzled frown gave way to a faint smile. "Perhaps I understand," he said.

"Then forgive me for implying you were a moron," said Gregory. "Stand up, Brother James."

Calls on transatlantic tight-beam cost heavy. Anson Dewberry, Miracle Meal Overseas Division head, pointed this out to Mr. Stephen Samson three times during their conversation.

"Listen," said Samson at last, desperately, "I'll take no more delegation of authority. In my contract, it says I'm site adviser. That means I'm architect and negotiator, not detective or scientist or occulist. I offered to stay on here to supervise building because I happen to like the place. I like the pubs. I like the people. I like the fishing. But it wasn't in my contract. And I'm now standing on that contract. Building is finished to schedule, plant installed—your tech men, incidentally, jetted out of here without waiting to catch snags after the first runoff—and now I'm through. The machines are running, the cans are coming off—and if the copters don't collect, that's for you and the

London office to bat your brains out over. And the Lord forgive that mess of terminal propositions," he added in lower voice. Samson was a purist in the matter of grammar.

Anson Dewberry jerked his chair nearer the scanner in his New York office. His pink, round face loomed in Samson's screen like that of an avenging cherub.

"Don't you have no gendarmes around that place?" Mr. Dewberry was no purist, in moments of stress. "Get guards on, hire some militia, check employees. Ten thousand cans of M.M. don't just evaporate."

"They do," Samson replied sadly. "Maybe it's the climate. And for the seventh time, I tell you I've done all that. I've had men packed so tightly around the place that even an orphan neutron couldn't get by. This morning I had two men from Scotland Yard gumming around. They looked at the machines, followed the assembly through to the transit storeroom, examined the electrolocks and mauled their toe-caps trying to boot a dent in the door. Then the top one—that is, the one who only looked half-asleep—said, 'Mr. Samson, sir, do you think it's . . . uh . . . possible . . . that . . . uh . . . this machine of yours . . . uh . . . goes into reverse when your . . . uh . . . backs are turned and . . . uh . . . sucks the cans back again?' "

Grating noises that might have been an incipient death rattle slid over the tight-beam from New York.

Samson nodded, a smirk of mock sympathy on his tanned, humor-wrinkled young face.

The noises ended with a gulp. The image of Dewberry thrust up a hesitant forefinger in interrogation. "Hey! Maybe there's something to that, at that—would it be possible?"

Samson groaned a little. "I wouldn't really know or overmuch care. But I have doubts. Meantime—"

"Right." Dewberry receded on the screen. "I'll jet a man over tonight. The best. From Research. Full powers. Hand over to him. Take some of your vacation. Design some more blamed mosques or tabernacles. Go fishing."

"A sensible suggestion," Samson said. "Just what I was about to do. It's a glorious afternoon here, sun a little misted, grass green, stream flowing cool and deep, fish lazing in the pools where the willow-shadows fall—"

The screen blanked. Dewberry was no purist, and no poet either.

Samson made a schoolkid face. He switched off the fluor lamps that supplemented the illumination from a narrow window in the supervisor's office—which, after studying the ground-plan

of the original Selcor Priory, he had sited in the space that was
occupied centuries before by the business sanctum of the Prior—
got up from his desk and walked through a Norman archway into
the sunlight.

He breathed the meadow-sweet air deeply, with appreciation.

The Rev. Malachi Pennyhorse was squatting with loose-jointed
ease against the wall. Two fishing rods in brown canvas covers
lay across his lap. He was studying one of the trout-flies nicked
into the band of his ancient hat. His balding, brown pate was
bared to the sun. He looked up.

"What fortune, my dear Stephen?"

"I convinced him at last. He's jetting a man over tonight. He
told me to go fishing."

"Injunction unnecessary, I should imagine. Let's go. We
shan't touch a trout with the sky as clear as this, but I have some
float tackle for lazier sport." They set off across a field. "Are
you running the plant today?"

Samson nodded his head towards a faint hum. "Quarter-
speed. That will give one copter-load for the seventeen hundred
hours collection, and leave enough over to go in the transit store
for the night and provide Dewberry's man with some data. Or
rather, lack of it."

"Where do you think it's going?"

"I've given up guessing."

Mr. Pennyhorse paused astride a stile and looked back at the
gray bulk of the Priory. "I could guess who's responsible," he
said, and chuckled.

"Uh? Who?"

Mr. Pennyhorse shook his head. "Leave that to your investigator."

A few moments later he murmured as if to himself: "What a
haunt! Ingenious devils."

But when Stephen Samson looked at him inquiringly, he
added: "But I can't guess where your cans have been put."

And he would say nothing more on the subject.

Who would deny that the pure of heart are often simple-
minded? (The obverse of the proposition need not be argued.)
And that cause-effect relations are sometimes divined more readily by the intuition of simpletons than the logic of scholars?

Brother Simon Simplex—Simple Simon to later legends—looked
open-mouthed at the array of strange objects on the stone shelves
of the kitchen storeroom. He was not surprised—his mouth was
always open, even in sleep.

He took down one of the objects and examined it with mild curiosity. He shook it, turned it round, thrust a forefinger into a small depression. Something gave slightly, but there was no other aperture. He replaced it on the shelf.

When his fellow-kitchener returned, he would ask him the purpose of the objects—if he could remember to do so. Simon's memory was poor. Each time the rota brought him onto kitchen duty for a week, he had to be instructed afresh in the business of serving meals in the refectory: platter so, napkin thus, spoon here, finger bowls half-filled, three water pitchers, one before the Prior, one in the center, one at the foot of the table—"and when you serve, tread softly and do not breathe down the necks of the brothers."

Even now could he hear the slight scrape of benches on stone as the monks, with bowed heads, freshly washed hands in the sleeves of their habits, filed slowly into the refectory and took their seats at the long, oak table. And still his fellow-kitchener had not returned from the errand. Food was prepared—dared he begin to serve alone?

It was a great problem for Simon, brother in the small House of Selcor, otherwise Selcor Priory, poor cell-relation to the rich monastery of the Cluniac Order at Battle, in the year 1139 A.D.

Steam pressure in the triggered can of Miracle Meal did its work. The lid flipped. The aroma issued.

Simon's mouth nearly shut as he sniffed.

The calm and unquestioning acceptance of the impossible is another concommitant of simplicity and purity of heart. To the good and simple Simon the rising of the sun each morning and the singing of birds were recurrent miracles. Compared with these, a laboratory miracle of the year 2143 A.D. was as nothing.

Here was a new style of platter, filled with hot food, ready to serve. Wiser minds than his had undoubtedly arranged matters. His fellow-kitchener, knowing the task was thus simplified, had left him to serve alone.

He had merely to remove the covers from these platters and carry them into the refectory. To remove the covers—cause—effect—the intuition of a simple mind.

Simon carried fourteen of the platters to the kitchen table, pressed buttons and waited.

He was gravely tempted to sample the food himself, but all-inclusive Benedictine rules forbade kitcheners to eat until their brothers had been served.

He carried a loaded tray into the refectory where the monks sat in patient silence except for the one voice of the Reader who stood at a raised lectern and intoned from the *Lives of the Saints*.

Pride that he had been thought fit to carry out the duty alone made Simon less clumsy than usual. He served the Prior, Dom Holland, first, almost deftly; then the other brothers, in two trips to the kitchen.

A spicy, rich, titillating fragrance filled the refectory. The intoning of the *Lives of the Saints* faltered for a moment as the mouth of the Reader filled with saliva, then he grimly continued.

At Dom Holland's signal, the monks ate.

The Prior spooned the last drops of gravy into his mouth. He sat back. A murmur arose. He raised a hand. The monks became quiet. The Reader closed his book.

Dom Holland was a man of faith; but he did not accept miracles or even the smallest departures from routine existence without questioning. He had sternly debated with himself whether he should question the new platters and the new food before or after eating. The aroma decided him. He ate first.

Now he got up, beckoned to a senior monk to follow him, and paced with unhurried calmness to the kitchen.

Simon had succumbed. He was halfway through his second tin.

He stood up, licking his fingers.

"Whence comes this food, my son?" asked Dom Holland, in sonorous Latin.

Simon's mouth opened wider. His knowledge of the tongue was confined to prayers.

Impatiently the Prior repeated the question in the English dialect of the district.

Simon pointed, and led them to the storeroom.

"I looked, and it was here," he said simply. The words were to become famed.

His fellow-kitchener was sought—he was found dozing in a warm corner of the kitchen garden—and questioned. He shook his head. The provisioner rather reluctantly disclaimed credit.

Dom Holland thought deeply, then gave instructions for a general assembly. The plastic "platters" and the hygiplast spoons were carefully examined. There were murmurs of wonderment at the workmanship. The discussion lasted two hours.

Simon's only contribution was to repeat with pathetic insistence: "I looked and it was there."

He realized dimly that he had become a person of some importance.

His face became a mask of puzzlement when the Prior summed up:

"Our simple but blessed brother, Simon Simplex, it seems to me, has become an instrument or vessel of some thaumaturgical manifestation. It would be wise, however, to await further demonstration before the matter is referred to higher authorities."

The storeroom was sealed and two monks were deputed as nightguards.

Even with the possibility of a miracle on his hands, Dom Holland was not prepared to abrogate the Benedictine rule of only one main meal a day. The storeroom wasn't opened until early afternoon of the following day.

It was opened by Simon, in the presence of the Prior, a scribe, the provisioner, and two senior monks.

Released, a pile of Miracle Meal cans toppled forward like a crumbling cliff, slithering and clattering in noisy profusion around Simon's legs, sliding over the floor of the kitchen.

Simon didn't move. He was either too surprised or cunningly aware of the effectiveness of the scene. He stood calf-deep in cans, pointed at the jumbled stack inside the storeroom, sloping up nearly to the stone roof, and said his little piece:

"I look, and it is here."

"Kneel, my sons," said Dom Holland gravely, and knelt.

Manna.

And at a time when the Priory was hard-pressed to maintain even its own low standard of subsistence, without helping the scores of dispossessed refugees encamped in wattle shacks near its protecting walls.

The countryside was scourged by a combination of civil and foreign war. Stephen of Normandy against Matilda of Anjou for the British throne. Neither could control his own followers. When the Flemish mercenaries of King Stephen were not chasing Queen Matilda's Angevins back over the borders of Wiltshire, they were plundering the lands and possessions of nominal supporters of Stephen. The Angevins and the barons who supported Matilda's cause quite impartially did the same, then pillaged each other's property, castle against castle, baron against baron.

It was anarchy and free-for-all—but nothing for the ignored serfs, bondmen, villeins and general peasantry, who fled from stricken homes and roamed the countryside in bands of starving thousands. Some built shacks in the inviolate shadow of churches and monasteries.

Selcor Priory had its quota of barefoot, raggedly men, women and children—twelfth century Displaced Persons.

They were a headache to the Prior, kindly Dom Holland—until Simple Simon's Miracle.

There were seventy recipients of the first hand-out of Miracle Meal cans from the small door in the Priory's walled kitchen garden.

The next day there were three hundred, and the day after that, four thousand. Good news doesn't need radio to get around fast.

Fourteen monks worked eight-hour shifts for twenty-four hours, hauling stocks from the capacious storeroom, pressing buttons, handing out steaming platters to orderly lines of refugees.

Two monks, shifting the last few cans from the store, were suddenly buried almost to their necks by the arrival of a fresh consignment, which piled up out of thin air.

Providence, it seemed, did not depend solely upon the intervention of Simon Simplex. The Priory itself and all its inhabitants were evidently blessed.

The Abbot of Battle, Dom Holland's superior, a man of great girth and great learning visited the Priory. He confirmed the miracle—by studying the label on the can.

After several hours' work in the Prior's office, he announced to Dom Holland:

"The script presented the greatest difficulty. It is an extreme simplification of letter-forms at present in use by Anglo-Saxon scholars. The pertinent text is a corruption—if I may be pardoned the use of such a term in the circumstances—of the Latin '*miraculum*' compounded with the word '*maél*' from our own barbarous tongue—so, clearly, Miracle Meal!"

Dom Holland murmured his awe of this learning.

The Abbot added, half to himself: "Although why the nature of the manifestation should be thus advertised in repetitive engraving, when it is self-evident—" He shrugged. "The ways of Providence are passing strange."

Brother Gregory, reclining in the starlight near his favorite oak, said:

"My only regret is that we cannot see the effect of our gift—the theoretical impact of a modern product—usually a weapon—on past ages is a well-tried topic of discussion and speculation among historians, scientists, economists and writers of fantasy."

Brother James, hunched in vague adumbration on a wall behind, said: "You are none of those things, else might you explain why it is that, if these cans have reached the period for which, according to your obtuse calculations, they were destined—an age in which we were both alive—we cannot remember such an event, or why it is not recorded in histories of the period."

"It was a time of anarchy, dear brother. Many records were destroyed. And as for your memories—well, great paradoxes of time are involved. One might as profitably ask how many angels may dance on the point of a pin. Now if you should wish to know how many atoms might be accommodated in a like position—"

Brother Gregory was adroit at changing the subject. He didn't wish to speculate aloud until he'd figured out all the paradox possibilities. He'd already discarded an infinity of time-streams as intellectually unsatisfying, and was toying with the concept of recurrent worlds—

"Dom Pennyhorse has guessed that it is our doing."

"What's that?"

Brother James repeated the information smugly.

Gregory said slowly: "Well, he is not—unsympathetic—to us."

"Assuredly, brother, we have naught to fear from him, nor from the pleasant young man with whom he goes fishing. But this young man was today in consultation with his superior, and an investigator is being sent from America."

"Psychic investigator, eh? Phooey. We'll tie him in knots," and Gregory complacently.

"I assume," said Brother James, with a touch of self-righteousness, "that these vulgar colloquialisms to which you sometimes have recourse are another result of your nocturnal reading. They offend my ear. 'Phooey,' indeed—No, this investigator is one with whom you will undoubtedly find an affinity. I gather that he is from a laboratory—a scientist of sorts."

Brother Gregory sat up and rubbed his tonsure thoughtfully. "That," he admitted, "is different." There was a curious mixture of alarm and eagerness in his voice. "There are means of detecting the field we employ."

An elementary electroscope was one of the means. An ionization indicator and a thermometer were others. They were all bolted firmly on a bench just inside the storeroom. Wires led from them under the door to a jury-rigged panel outside.

Sandy-haired Sidney Meredith of M.M. Research sat in front of the panel on a folding stool, watching dials with intense blue eyes, chin propped in hands.

Guards had been cleared from the factory. He was alone, on the advice of Mr. Pennyhorse, who had told him: "If, as I suspect, it's the work of two of my . . . uh . . . flock . . . two very ancient parishioners . . . they are more likely to play their tricks in the absence of a crowd."

"I get it," Meredith had said. "Should be interesting."

It was.

He poured coffee from a thermos without taking his eyes from the panel. The thermometer reading was dropping slowly. Ionization was rising. From inside the store came the faint rasp of moving objects.

Meredith smiled, sighted a thumb-size camera, recorded the panel readings. "This," he said softly, "will make a top feature in the *Journal*: 'The most intensive psychic and poltergeist phenomena ever recorded. M.M.'s top tech trouble-shooter spikes spooks.' "

There was a faint snap beyond the door. Dials swooped back to Zero. Meredith quit smiling and daydreaming.

"Hey—play fair!" he called.

The whisper of a laugh answered him, and a soft, hollow whine, as of a wind cycloning into outer space.

He grabbed the door, pulled. It resisted. It was like trying to break a vacuum. He knelt, lit a cigarette, held it near the bottom of the nearly flush-fitting door. A thin streamer of smoke curled down and was drawn swiftly through the barely perceptible crack.

The soft whine continued for a few seconds, began to die away.

Meredith yanked at the door again. It gave, to a slight ingush of air. He thrust his foot in the opening, said calmly into the empty blackness: "When you fellers have quite finished—I'm coming in. Don't go away. Let's talk."

He slipped inside, closed the door, stood silent for a moment. He sniffed. Ozone. His scalp prickled. He scratched his head, felt the hairs standing upright. And it was cold.

He said: "Right. No point in playing dumb or covering-up, boys." He felt curiously ashamed of the platitudes as he uttered them. "I must apologize for breaking in," he added—and meant it. "But this has got to finish. And if you're not willing to—co-operate—I think I know now how to finish it."

Another whisper of a laugh. And two words, faint, gently mocking: "Do you?"

Meredith strained his eyes against the darkness. He saw only the nerve-patterns in his own eyes. He shrugged.

"If you won't play—" He switched on a blaze of fluor lamps. The long steel shelves were empty. There was only one can of Miracle Meal left in the store.

He felt it before he saw it. It dropped on his head, clattered to the plastocrete floor. When he'd retrieved his breath, he kicked it savagely to the far end of the store and turned to his instruments.

The main input lead had been pulled away. The terminal had been loosened first.

He unclamped a wide-angle infrared camera, waited impatiently for the developrinter to act, pulled out the print.

And laughed. It wasn't a good line-caricature of himself, but it was recognizable, chiefly by the shock of unruly hair.

The lines were slightly blurred, as though written by a needle-point of light directly on the film. There was a jumble of writing over and under it.

"Old English, I suppose," he murmured. He looked closer. The writing above the caricature was a de Sitter version of the Reimann-Christoffel tensor, followed in crabbed but readable modern English by the words: "Why reverse the sign? Do we act like anti-particles?"

Underneath the drawing was an energy tensor and a comment: "You will notice that magnetic momenta contribute a negative density and pressure."

A string of symbols followed, ending with an equals sign and a query mark. And another comment: "You'll need to take time out to balance this one."

Meredith read the symbols, then sat down heavily on the edge of the instrument bench and groaned. Time *out*. But Time was already out, and there was neither matter nor radiation in a de Sitter universe.

Unless—

He pulled out a notebook, started to scribble.

An hour later Mr. Pennyhorse and Stephen Samson came in.

Mr. Pennyhorse said: "My dear young fellow, we were quite concerned. We thought—"

He stopped. Meredith's blue eyes were slightly out of focus. There were beads of sweat on his brow despite the coolness of the storeroom. Leaves from his notebook and cigarette stubs littered the floor around his feet.

He jumped like a pricked frog when the vicar gently tapped his shoulder, and uttered a vehement cuss-word that startled even the broad-minded cleric.

Samson tutted.

Meredith muttered: "Sorry, sir. But I think I nearly had it."

"What, my son?"

Meredith looked like a ruffle-haired schoolboy. His eyes came back into focus. "A crossword puzzle clue," he said. "Set by a spook with a super-I.Q. Two quite irreconcilable systems of mathematics lumped together, the signs in an extended energy tensor reversed, merry hell played with a temporal factor—and yet it was beginning to make sense."

He smiled wryly. "A ghost who unscrews terminals before he breaks connections and who can make my brain boil is a ghost worth meeting."

Mr. Pennyhorse eased his pince-nez. "Uh . . : yes. Now, don't you think it's time you came to bed? It's four A.M. My housekeeper has made up a comfortable place on the divan in the sitting room." He took Meredith's arm and steered him from the store.

As they walked across the dewy meadows towards the vicarage, with the first pale streaks of dawn showing in the sky, Samson said: "How about the cans?"

"Time," replied Meredith vaguely, "will tell."

"And the guards?"

"Pay them off. Send them away. Keep the plant rolling. Fill the transit store tonight. And I want a freighter copter to take me to London University this afternoon."

Back in the transit store, the discarded leaves from Meredith's notebook fluttered gently upwards in the still air and disappeared.

Brother James said: "He is alone again."

They looked down on the sandy head of Sidney Meredith from the vantage point of a dehydrating tower.

"So I perceive. And I fear this may be our last uh . . . consignment to our erstwhile brothers," said Gregory thoughtfully.

"Why?"

"You will see. In giving him the clue to what we were doing, I gave him the clue to what we are, essentially."

They drifted down towards the transit store.

"After you, Brother James," said Brother Gregory with excessive politeness.

James adjusted his plane of incidence, started through the wall, and—

Shot backwards with a voiceless scream of agony.

Brother Gregory laughed. "I'm sorry. But that's why it will be our last consignment. Heterodyning is painful. He is a very intelligent fellow. The next time, he will take care to screen both his ultra-short generator and controls so that I cannot touch them."

Brother James recovered. "You . . . you use me as a confounded guinea pig! By the saints, you appear to have more sympathy with the man than with me!"

"Not more sympathy, my beloved brother, but certainly much more in common," Brother Gregory replied frankly. "Wait."

He drifted behind Meredith's back and poltered the tip of one finger to flick a lightly soldered wire from a terminal behind a switch. Meredith felt his scalp tingle. A pilot light on his panel blinked out.

Meredith got up from his stool, stretched lazily, grinned into the empty air. He said aloud: "Right. Help yourselves. But I warn you—once you're in, you don't come out until you agree to talk. I have a duplicate set and a built-in circuit-tester. The only way you can spike them is by busting tubes. And I've a hunch you wouldn't do that."

"No," James muttered. "You wouldn't. Let us go."

"No," Gregory answered. "Inside quickly—and whirl. Afterwards I shall speak with him. He is a youth of acute sensibilities and gentleness, whose word is his bond."

Gregory urged his fellow-monk to the wall. They passed within.

Meredith heard nothing, until a faint whine began in the store. He waited until it died away, then knocked on the door. It seemed, crazily, the correct thing to do.

He went into the darkness. "You there?"

A low and pleasant voice, directionless: "Yes. Why didn't you switch on your duplicate generator?"

Meredith breathed deep. "I didn't think it would be necessary. I feel we understand each other. My name is Sidney Meredith."

"Mine is Gregory of Ramsbury."

"And your—friend?"

"James Brasenose. I may say that he disapproves highly of this conversation."

"I can understand that. It is unusual. But then, you're a very unusual . . . um—"

" 'Ghost' is the common term, Mr. Meredith. Rather inadequate, I think, for supranormal phenomena which are, nevertheless, subject to known laws. Most Untranslated spirits remain quite ignorant of their own powers before final Translation. It was only by intensive reading and thought that I determined the principles and potentialities of my construction."

"Anti-particles?"

"According to de Sitter," said Brother Gregory, "that is what we should be. But we are not mere mathematical experessions. I prefer the term 'energy foci.' From a perusal of the notes you left behind yesterday morning—and, of course, from your use of ultra-short waves tonight—it seems you struck the correct train of deduction immediately. Incidentally, where did you obtain the apparatus at such short notice?''

"London University."

Brother Gregory sighed. "I should like to visit their laboratories. But we are bound to this area by a form of moral compulsion that I cannot define or overcome. Only vicariously, through the achievements of others, may I experience the thrill of research."

"You don't do so badly," Meredith said. He was mildly surprised that he felt quite so sane and at ease, except for the darkness. "Would you mind if we had a light?"

"I must be semipolted—or warped—to speak with you. It's not a pleasant sight—floating lungs, larynx, palate, tongue and lips. I'd feel uncomfortable for you. We might appear for you later, if you wish."

"Right. But keep talking. Give me the how and the why. I want this for my professional journal."

"Will you see that the issue containing your paper is placed in the local library?"

"Surely," Meredith said. "Two copies."

"Brother James is not interested. Brother James, will you kindly stop whispering nonsense and remove yourself to a nexus point for a while. I intend to converse with Mr. Meredith. Thank you."

The voice of Brother Gregory came nearer, took on a slightly professorial tone. "Any massive and rotating body assumes the qualities of magnetism—or rather, gravitic, one-way flux—by virtue of its rotation, and the two quantities of magnetic momentum and angular momentum are always proportional to one another, as you doubtless know."

Meredith smiled inwardly. A lecture on elementary physics from a ghost. Well—maybe not so elementary. He remembered the figures that he'd sweated over. But he could almost envisage the voice of Brother Gregory emananting from a black-gowned instructor in front of a classroom board.

"Take a star," the voice continued. "Say 78 Virginis—from whose flaming promontories the effect was first deduced a hundred years ago—and put her against a counter-whirling star of similar mass. What happens? Energy warp, of the kind we use every time we polt. But something else happens—did you infer it from my incomplete expression?"

Meredith grinned. He said: "Yes. Temporal warp."

"Oh." There was a trace of disappointment in the voice.

Meredith added quickly: "But it certainly gave me a headache figuring it out."

Gregory was evidently mollified by the admission. "Solids through time," he went on. "Some weeks ago, calculating that my inherent field was as great in certain respects as that of 78 Virginis, I whirled against a longitudinal line, and forced a stone back a few days—the nearest I could get to laboratory confirmation. Knowing there would be a logical extension of the effect if I whirled against a field as strong as my own, I persuaded Brother James to co-operate with me—and you know the result."

"How far back?"

"According to my mathematics, the twelfth century, at a time when we were—alive. I would appreciate your views on the paradoxes involved."

Meredith said: "Certainly. Let's go over your math together first. If it fits in with what I've already figured, perhaps I'll have a suggestion to make. You appreciate, of course, that I can't let you have any more cans?"

"Quite. I must congratulate your company on manufacturing a most delicious comestible. If you will hand me the roll of infrared film from your camera, I can make my calculations visible to you on the emulsion in the darkness. Thank you. It is a pity," Gregory murmured, "that we could not see with our own eyes what disposal they made of your product in the days of our Priory."

When, on the morning of a certain bright summer day in 1139, the daily consignment of Miracle Meal failed to arrive at Selcor Priory, thousands of disappointed refugees went hungry.

The Prior, Dom Holland—who, fortunately for his sanity or at least his peace of mind, was not in a position to separate cause from effect—attributed the failure of supply to the lamentable departure from grace and moral standards of two of the monks.

By disgracing themselves in the kitchen garden with a female refugee, he said, they had obviously rendered the Priory unfit to receive any further miraculous bounty.

The abject monks, Brother Gregory and Brother James, were severely chastised and warned in drastic theological terms that it would probably be many centuries before they had sufficiently expiated their sins to attain blessedness.

On the morning of another bright summer day, the Rev. Malachi Pennyhorse and Stephen Samson were waiting for Sidney Meredith in the vicar's comfortable study.

Meredith came in, sank into a century-old leather easy-chair, stretched his shoes, damp with dew from the meadow grass, towards the flames. He accepted a glass of whiskey gratefully, sipped it.

He said: "The cans are there. And from now on, they stay in the transit store until the copters collect."

There was an odd note of regret in his voice.

Samson said: "Fine. Now maybe you'll tell us what happened yesterday."

Mr. Pennyhorse said: "You . . . uh . . . liked my parishioners, then?"

Meredith combined a smile and a sigh. "I surely did. That Brother Gregory had the most intense and dispassionate intellectual curiosity of anyone I ever met. He nearly grounded me on some aspects of energy mathematics. I could have used him in my department. He'd have made a great research man. Brother James wasn't a bad old guy, either. They appeared for me—"

"How did you get rid of them?" Samson interrupted.

"They got rid of themselves. Gregory told me how, by whirling against each other with gravitic fields cutting, they drew the cans into a vortex of negated time that threw them way back to the twelfth century. After we'd been through his math, I suggested they whirl together."

"What—and throw the cans ahead?"

"No. Themselves, in a sense, since they precipitated a future, hoped-for state. Gregory had an idea what would happen. So did I. He'd only discovered the effect recently. Curiosity got the better of him. He had to try it out straight away. They whirled together. The fields reinforced, instead of negated. Enough ingoing energy was generated to whoop their own charges well above capacity and equilibrium. They just—went. As Gregory would put it—they were Translated."

"Upwards, I trust," said Mr. Pennyhorse gently.

"Amen to that," said Samson.

Upwards—

Pure thought, unbound, Earth-rid, roaming free amid the wild bright stars—

Thought to Thought, over galactic vastness, wordless, yet swift and clear, before egos faded—

"Why didn't I think of this before? We might have Translated ourselves centuries ago."

"But then we would never have tasted Miracle Meal."

"That is a consideration," agreed the Thought that had been Brother Gregory.

"Remember our third can?" came the Thought that had been Brother James.

But there was no reply. Something of far greater urgency and interest than memories of Miracle Meal had occurred to the Thought that had been Brother Gregory.

With eager curiosity, it was spiraling down into the heart of a star to observe the integration of helium at first hand.

THE PRISONER IN THE SKULL

by "Lewis Padgett" (Henry Kuttner, 1914—1958 and C.L. Moore, 1911—   )

Astounding Science Fiction, **February**

The dream of every anthologist is to discover a major story that has never been reprinted. This is particularly difficult in science fiction because there have been more than 800 sf reprint anthologies published to date, the majority edited by men and women who were themselves central to the field and tremendously knowledgeable. We would therefore love to take credit for finding "The Prisoner in the Skull" and bringing it to your attention but alas, we cannot. Barry N. Malzberg (himself an excellent anthologist) brought it to us and deserves the honor. Thanks, Barry.—M.H.G.

(There are certain irrepressible yearnings in the human heart which are universal and which are, therefore, obvious material for stories that will hit home. Don't we all long, in the midst of confusion and frustration, for someone supremely competent to come in and take over?

Is not this why the typical "woman's romance" so often features the Prince Charming figure, the knight on the white horse; and why Westerns so often feature the tall, silent stranger who rides into town, defeats the desperados and then rides away? Or, for that matter, is it not why Bertie Wooster has Jeeves?

It is in fantasy that this reaches its peak, and that peak is surely "Aladdin and His Wonderful Lamp." Who of us has not at some time in his life longed for the services of just such an all-powerful and utterly subservient genie, whose response to all requests, however unreasonable, is a calm, "I hear and obey"?

If science fiction is too disciplined to allow itself the utter

98

*chaos of omnipotence, neither is it forced to restrict itself to
something as dull and straightforward as a man with a gun
and a fast draw. In "The Prisoner in the Skull," then, we have
a science fictional Lamp, with its limits, its pity, and its
irony.—I.A.)*

He felt cold and weak, strangely, intolerably, inhumanly weak
with a weakness of the blood and bone, of the mind and soul. He
saw his surroundings dimly, but he saw—other things—with a
swimming clarity that had no meaning to him. He saw causes
and effects as tangible before him as he had once seen trees and
grass. But remote, indifferent, part of another world.
     Somehow there was a door before him. He reached vaguely—
     It was almost wholly a reflex gesture that moved his finger
toward the doorbell.

The chimes played three soft notes.
John Fowler was staring at a toggle switch. He felt baffled.
The thing had suddenly spat at him and died. Ten minutes ago he
had thrown the main switch, unscrewed the wall plate and made
hopeful gestures with a screwdriver, but the only result was a
growing suspicion that this switch would never work again. Like
the house itself, it was architecturally extreme, and the wires
were sealed in so that the whole unit had to be replaced if it went
bad.
Minor irritations bothered Fowler unreasonably today. He wanted
the house in perfect running order for the guest he was expecting.
He had been chasing Veronica Wood for a long time, and he had
an idea this particular argument might tip the balance in the right
direction.
He made a note to keep a supply of spare toggle switches
handy. The chimes were still echoing softly as Fowler went into
the hall and opened the front door, preparing a smile. But it
wasn't Veronica Wood on the doorstep. It was a blank man.
That was Fowler's curious impression, and it was to recur to
him often in the year to come. Now he stood staring at the
strange emptiness of the face that returned his stare without
really seeming to see him. The man's features were so typical
they might have been a matrix, without the variations that com-
bine to make up the recognizable individual. But Fowler thought
that even if he had known those features, it would be hard to
recognize a man behind such utter emptiness. You can't recognize a man who isn't there. And there was nothing here. Some

erasure, some expunging, had wiped out all trace of character
and personality. *Empty.*

And empty of strength, too—for the visitant lurched forward
and fell into Fowler's arms.

Fowler caught him automatically, rather horrified at the light-
ness of the body he found himself supporting. "Hey," he said,
and, realizing the inadequacy of that remark, added a few pertinent questions. But there was no answer. Syncope had taken
over.

Fowler grimaced and looked hopefully up and down the road.
He saw nobody. So he lifted his guest across the threshold and
carried him easily to a couch. *Fine,* he thought. *Veronica due
any minute,* and this paperweight barging in.

Brandy seemed to help. It brought no color to the pale cheeks,
but it pried the eyelids open to show a blank, wondering look.

"O.K. now?" Fowler asked, wanting to add, "Then go home."

There was only the questioning stare. Fowler stood up with
some vague intention of calling a doctor, and then remembered
that the televisor instrument hadn't yet been delivered. For this
was a day when artificial shortages had begun to supplant real
ones, when raw material was plentiful but consumers were wary,
and were, therefore, put on a starvation diet to build their
appetites and loosen their purse strings. The televisor would be
delivered when the company thought Fowler had waited long
enough.

Luckily he was versatile. As long as the electricity was on he
could jury-rig anything else he needed, including facilities for
first aid. He gave his patient the routine treatment, with satisfying results. Until, that is, the brandy suddenly hit certain nerve
centers and emesis resulted.

Fowler lugged his guest back from the bathroom and left him
on the bed in the room with the broken light switch to recuperate.
Convalescence was rapid. Soon the man sat up, but all he did
was look at Fowler hopefully. Questions brought no answers.

Ten minutes later the blank man was still sitting there, looking
blank.

The door chimes sang again. Fowler, assured that his guest
wasn't *in articulo mortis,* began to feel irritation. Why the devil
did the guy have to barge in now, at this particular crucial
moment? In fact, where had he come from? It was a mile to the
nearest highway, along a dirt road, and there was no dust on the
man's shoes. Moreover, there was something indefinably disturbing about the—*lack* in his appearance. There was no other word

that fitted so neatly. Village idiots are popularly termed "wanting," and, while there was no question of idiocy here, the man did seem—

What?

For no reason at all Fowler shivered. The door chimes reminded him of Veronica. He said: "Wait here. You'll be all right. Just wait. I'll be back—"

There was a question in the soulless eyes.

Fowler looked around. "There're some books on the shelf. Or fix this—" He pointed to the wall switch. "If you want anything, call me." On that note of haphazard solicitude he went out, carefully closing the door. After all, he wasn't his brother's keeper. And he hadn't spent days getting the new house in shape to have his demonstration go haywire because of an unforseen interruption.

Veronica was waiting on the threshold. "Hello," Fowler said. "Have any trouble finding the place? Come in."

"It sticks up like a sore thumb," she informed him. "Hello. So this is the dream house, is it?"

"Right. After I figure out the right method of dream-analysis, it'll be perfect." He took her coat, led her into the livingroom, which was shaped like a fat comma and walled with triple-seal glass, and decided not to kiss her. Veronica seemed withdrawn. That was regrettable. He suggested a drink.

"Perhaps I'd better have one," she said, "before I look the joint over."

Fowler began battling with a functional bar. It should have poured and mixed drinks at the spin of a dial, but instead there came a tinkle of breaking glass. Fowler finally gave up and went back to the old-fashioned method. "Highball? Well, theoretically, this is a perfect machine for living. But the architect wasn't as perfect as his theoretical ideas. Methods of construction have to catch up with ideas, you know."

"This room's nice," Veronica acknowledged, relaxing on airfoam. With a glass in her hand, she seemed more cheerful. "Almost everything's curved, isn't it? And I like the windows."

"It's the little things that go wrong. If a fuse blows, a whole unit goes out. The windows—I insisted on those."

"Not much of a view."

"Unimproved. Building restrictions, you know. I wanted to build on the top of a hill a few miles away, but the township laws wouldn't allow it. This house is unorthodox. Not very, but enough. I might as well have tried to put up a Wright house in Williamsburg. This place is functional and convenient—"

"Except when you want a drink?"

"Trivia," Fowler said airily. "A house is complicated. You expect a few things to go wrong at first. I'll fix 'em as they come up. I'm a jerk of all trades. Want to look around?"

"Why not?" Veronica said. It wasn't quite the enthusiastic reaction for which Fowler had hoped, but he made the best of it. He showed her the house. It was larger than it had seemed from the outside. There was nothing super about it, but it was—theoretically—a functional unit, breaking away completely from the hidebound traditions that had made attics, cellars, and conventional bathrooms and kitchens as vestigially unfunctional as the vermiform appendix. "Anyway," Fowler said, "statistics show most accidents happen in kitchens and bathrooms. They can't happen here."

"What's this?" Veronica asked, opening a door. Fowler grimaced.

"The guest room," he said. "That was the single mistake. I'll use it for storage or something. The room hasn't any windows."

"The light doesn't work—"

"Oh, I forgot. I turned off the main switch. Be right back." He hurried to the closet that held the house controls, flipped the switch, and returned. Veronica was looking into a room that was pleasantly furnished as a bedroom, and, with tinted, concealed fluorescents, seemed light and airy despite the lack of windows.

"I called you," she said. "Didn't you hear me?"

Fowler smiled and touched a wall. "Sound-absorbent. The whole house is that way. The architect did a good job, but this room—"

"What's wrong with it?"

"Nothing—unless you're inside and the door should get stuck. I've a touch of claustrophobia."

"You should face these fears," said Veronica, who had read it somewhere. Fowler repressed a slight irritation. There were times when he had felt an impulse to slap Veronica across the chops, but her gorgeousness entirely outweighted any weakness she might have in other directions.

"Air conditioning, too," he said, touching another switch. "Fresh as spring breeze. Which reminds me. Does your drink want freshening?"

"Yes," Veronica said, and they turned to the comma-shaped room. It was appreciably darker. The girl went to the window and stared through the immense, wall-long pane.

"Storm coming up," she said. "The car radio said it'll be a bad one. I'd better go, Johnny."

"Must you? You just got here."

"I have a date. Anyway, I've got to work early tomorrow." She was a Korys model, much in demand.

Fowler turned from the recalcitrant bar and reached for her hand.

"I wanted to ask you to marry me," he said.

There was silence, while leaden grayness pressed down beyond the window, and yellow hills rippled under the gusts of unfelt wind. Veronica met his gaze steadily.

"I know you did. I mean—I've been expecting you to."

"Well?"

She moved her shoulders uneasily.

"Not now."

"But—Veronica. Why not? We've known each other for a couple of years—"

"The truth is—I'm not sure about you, Johnny. Sometimes I think I love you. But sometimes I'm not sure I even like you."

He frowned. "I don't get that."

"Well, I can't explain it. It's just that I think you could be either a very nice guy or a very nasty one. And I'd like to be quite certain first. Now I've got to go. It's starting to rain."

On that note she went out, leaving Fowler with a sour taste in his mouth. He mixed himself another drink and wandered over to his drawing board, where some sketches were sheafed up on a disorderly fashion. Nuts. He was making good dough at commercial art, he'd even got himself a rather special house—

One of the drawings caught his eye. It was a background detail, intended for incorporation later in a larger picture. It showed a gargoyle, drawn with painstaking care, and a certain quality of vivid precision that was very faintly unpleasant. Veronica—

Fowler suddenly remembered his guest and hastily set down his drink. He had avoided that room during the tour of inspection, managing to put the man completely out of his mind. That was too bad. He could have asked Veronica to send out a doctor from the village.

But the guest didn't seem to need a doctor. He was working on the wall-switch, at some danger, Fowler thought, of electrocuting himself. "Look out!" Fowler said sharply. "It's hot!" But the man merely gave him a mild, blank stare and passed his hand downward before the panel.

The light went out.

It came on again, to show the man finishing an upward gesture.

No toggle switch stub protruded from the slot in the center of the plate. Fowler blinked. "What—?" he said.

Gesture. Blackout. Another gesture.

"What did you do to that?" Fowler asked, but there was no audible reply.

Fowler drove south through the storm, muttering about ham electricians. Beside him the guest sat, smiling vacantly. The one thing Fowler wanted was to get the guy off his hands. A doctor, or a cop, in the village, would solve that particular problem. Or, rather, that would have been the solution, if a minor landslide hadn't covered the road at a crucial point.

With difficulty Fowler turned the car around and drove back home, cursing gently.

The blank man sat obediently at his side.

They were marooned for three days. Luckily the larder was well-stocked, and the power lines, which ran underground, weren't cut by the storm. The water-purifying unit turned the muddy stream from outside into crystalline nectar, the FM set wasn't much bothered by atmospheric disturbances, and Fowler had plenty of assignments to keep him busy at his drawing board. But he did no drawing. He was exploring a fascinating, though unbelievable, development.

The light switch his guest had rigged was unique. Fowler discovered that when he took the gadget apart. The sealed plastic had been broken open, and a couple of wires had been rewound in an odd fashion. The wiring didn't make much sense to Fowler. There was no photo-electric hookup that would have explained it. But the fact remained that he could turn on the lights in that room by moving his hand upward in front of the switch plate, and reverse the process with a downward gesture.

He made tests. It seemed as though an invisible fourteen-inch beam extended directly outward from the switch. At any rate, gestures, no matter how emphatic, made beyond that fourteen-inch distance had no effect on the lights at all.

Curious, he asked his guest to rig up another switch in the same fashion. Presently all the switches in the house were converted, but Fowler was no wiser. He could duplicate the hookup, but he didn't understand the principle. He felt a little frightened.

Locked in the house for three days, he had time to wonder and worry. He fed his guest—who had forgotten the use of knife and fork, if he had ever known it—and he tried to make the man talk. Not too successfully.

Once the man said: "Forgotten . . . forgotten—"

"You haven't forgotten how to be an electrician. Where did you come from?"

The blank face turned to him. "Where?" A pause. And then—

"When? Time . . . time—"

Once he picked up a newspaper and pointed questioningly at the date line—the year.

"That's right," Fowler said, his stomach crawling. "What year did you think it was?"

"Wrong—" the man said. "Forgotten—"

Fowler stared. On impulse, he got up to search his guest's pockets. But there were no pockets. The suit was ordinary, though slightly strange in cut, but it had no pockets.

"What's your name?"

"No answer.

"Where did you come from? Another—*time?*"

Still no answer.

Fowler thought of robots. He thought of a soulless world of the future peopled by automatons. But he knew neither was the right answer. The man sitting before him was horribly normal. And empty, somehow—drained. Normal?

The norm? That non-existant, figurative symbol which would be monstrous if it actually appeared? The closer an individual approaches the norm, the more colorless he is. Just as a contracting line becomes a point, which has few, if any, distinguishing characteristics. One point is exactly like another point. As though humans, in some unpleasant age to come, had been reduced to the lowest common denominator.

The norm.

"All right," Fowler said. "I'll call you Norman, till you remember your right name. But you can't be a . . . point. You're no moron. You've got a talent for electricity, anyhow."

Norman had other talents, too, as Fowler was to discover soon. He grew tired of looking through the window at the gray, pouring rain, pounding down over a drenched and dreary landscape, and when he tried to close the built-in Venetian shutters, of course they failed to work. "May that architect be forced to live in one of his own houses," Fowler said, and, noticing Norman made explanatory gestures toward the window.

Norman smiled blankly.

"The view," Fowler said. "I don't like to see all that rain. The shutters won't work. See if you can fix them. The view—"

He explained patiently, and presently Norman went out to the unit nominally called a kitchen, though it was far more efficient. Fowler shrugged and sat down at his drawing board. He looked up, some while later, in time to see Norman finish up with a few swabs of cloth. Apparently he had been painting the window with water.

Fowler snorted. "I didn't ask you to wash it," he remarked. "It was the shutters—"

Norman laid a nearly empty basin on a table and smiled expectantly. Fowler suffered a slight reorientation. "Time-traveling, ha," he said. "You probably crashed out of some booby hatch. The sooner I can get you back there the better I'll like it. If it'd only stop raining . . . I wonder if you could rig up the televisor? No, I forgot. We don't even have one yet. And I suspect you couldn't do it. That light switch business was a fluke."

He looked out at the rain and thought of Veronica. Then she was there before him, dark and slender, smiling a little.

"Wha—" Fowler said throatily.

He blinked. Hallucinations? He looked again, and she was still there, three-dimensionally, outside the window—

Norman smiled and nodded. He pointed to the apparition.

"Do you see it too?" Fowler asked madly. "It can't be. She's outside. She'll get wet. What in the name of—"

But it was only Fowler who got wet, dashing out bareheaded in the drenching rain. There was no one outside. He looked through the window and saw the familiar room, and Norman.

He came back. "Did you paint her on the window?" he asked. "But you've never seen Veronica. Besides, she's moving—three-dimensional. Oh, it can't be. My mind's snapping. I need peace and quiet. A green thought in a green shade." He focused on a green thought, and Veronica faded out slowly. A cool, quiet, woodland glade was visible through the window.

After a while Fowler figured it out. His window made thoughts visible.

It wasn't as simple as that, naturally. He had to experiment and brood for quite some time. Norman was no help. But the fact finally emerged that whenever Fowler looked at the window and visualized something with strong emphasis, an image of that thought appeared—a projective screen, so to speak.

It was like throwing a stone into calm water. The ripples moved out for a while, and then slowly quieted. The woodland scene wasn't static; there was a breeze there, and the leaves glittered and the branches swayed. Clouds moved softly across a blue sky. It was a scene Fowler finally recognized, a Vermont woodland he had seen years ago. Yet when did sequoias ever grow in Vermont?

A composite, then. And the original impetus of his thoughts set the scene into action along normal lines. When he visualized the forest, he had known that there would be a wind, and that the branches would move. So they moved. But slower and slower—though it took a long while for the action to run down.

He tried again. This time Chicago's lake shore. Cars rushed along the drive. He tried to make them run backwards, but got a sharp headache and a sense of watching a jerky film. Possibly he could reverse the normal course of events, but his mind wasn't geared to handle film running backward. Then he thought hard and watched a seascape appear through the glass. This time he waited to see how long it would take the image to vanish. The action stopped in an hour, but the picture did not face completely for another hour.

Only then did the possibilities strike him with an impact as violent as lightning.

Considerable poetry has been written about what happens when love rejected turns to hate. Psychology could explain the cause as well as the effect—the mechanism of displacement. Energy has to go somewhere, and if one channel is blocked, another will be found. Not that Veronica had definitely rejected Fowler, and certainly his emotion for the girl had not suffered an alchemic transformation, unless one wishes to delve into the abysses of psychology in which love is merely the other face of hatred—but on those levels of semantic confusion you can easily prove anything.

Call it reorientation. Fowler had never quite let himself believe that Veronica wouldn't fall into his arms. His ego was damaged. Consequently it had to find some other justification, some assurance—and it was unfortunate for Norman that the displacement had to occur when he was available as scapegoat. For the moment Fowler began to see the commercial possibilities of the magic windowpane, Norman was doomed.

Not at once; in the beginning, Fowler would have been shocked and horrified had he seen the end result of his plan. He was no villain, for there are no villains. There is a check-and-balance system, as inevitable in nature and mind as in politics, and the balance was beginning to tip when Fowler locked Norman in the windowless room for safekeeping and drove to New York to see a patent attorney. He was careful at first. He knew the formula for the telepathically-receptive window paint by now, but he merely arranged to patent the light-switch gadget that was operated by a gesture. Afterwards, he regretted his ignorance, for clever infringements appeared on the heels of his own device. He hadn't known enough about the matter to protect himself thoroughly in the patent.

By a miracle, he had kept the secret of the telepathic paint to himself. All this took time, naturally, and meanwhile Norman, urged on by his host, had made little repairs and improvements around the house. Some of them were impractical, but others were decidedly worth using—short-cuts, conveniences, clever methods of bridging difficulties that would be worth money in the open market. Norman's way of thinking seemed curiously alien. Given a problem, he could solve it, but he had no initiative on his own. He seemed satisfied to stay in the house—

Well, satisfied was scarcely the word. He was satisfied in the same sense that a jellyfish is satisfied to remain in its pool. If there were quivers of volition, slight directional stirrings, they were very feeble indeed. There were times when Fowler, studying his guest, decided that Norman was in a psychotic state—catatonic stupor seemed the most appropriate label. The man's will was submerged, if, indeed, he had ever had any.

No one has ever detailed the probable reactions of the man who owned the goose who laid the golden eggs. He brooded over a mystery, and presently took empirical steps, afterwards regretted. Fowler had a more analytical mind, and suspected that Norman might be poised at a precarious state of balance, during which—and only during which—he laid golden eggs. Metal can be pliable until pressure is used, after which it may become work-hardened and inflexible. Fowler was afraid of applying too much pressure. But he was equally afraid of not finding out all he could about the goose's unusual oviparity.

So he studied Norman. It was like watching a shadow. Norman seemed to have none of the higher reflexes; his activities were little more than tropism. Ego-consciousness was present, certainly, but—where had he come from? What sort of place or time had it been? Or was Norman simply a freak, a lunatic, a mutation? All that seemed certain was that part of his brain didn't know its own function. Without conscious will or volition, it was useless. Fowler had to supply the volition; he had to give orders. Between orders, Norman simply sat, occasionally quivering slightly.

It was bewildering. It was fascinating.

Also, it might be a little dangerous. Fowler had no intention of letting his captive escape if he could help it, but vague recollections of peonage disturbed him sometimes. Probably this was illegal. Norman ought to be in an institution, under medical care. But then, Norman had such unusual talents!

Fowler, to salve his uneasiness, ceased to lock the door of the windowless room. By now he had discovered it was unnecessary, anyhow. Norman was like a subject in deep hypnosis. He would obey when told not to leave the room. Fowler, with a layman's knowledge of law, thought that probably gave him an out. He pictured himself in the dock blandly stating that Norman had never been a prisoner, had always been free to leave the house if he chose.

Actually, only hunger would rouse Norman to disobey Fowler's commands to stay in his room. He would have to be almost famished, even then, before he would go to the kitchen and eat whatever he found, without discrimination and apparently without taste.

Time went by. Fowler was reorienting, though he scarcely knew it yet, toward a whole new set of values. He let his illustrating dwindle away until he almost ceased to accept orders. This was after an abortive experiment with Norman in which he tried to work out on paper an equivalent of the telepathic pictures on glass. If he could simply sit and *think* his drawings onto bristol board—

That was, however, one of Norman's failures.

It wasn't easy to refrain from sharing this wonderful new secret with Veronica. Fowler found himself time and again shutting his lips over the information just in time. He didn't invite her out to the house any more; Norman was too often working at odd jobs around the premises. Beautiful visions of the future were building up elaborately in Fowler's mind—Veronica wrapped in mink and pearls, himself commanding financial empires all based on Norman's extraordinary talents and Norman's truly extraordinary willingness to obey.

That was because of his physical weakness, Fowler felt sure. It seemed to take so much of Norman's energy simply to breathe and eat that nothing remained. And after the solution of a problem, a complete fatigue overcame him. He was useless for a day or two between jobs, recovering from the utter exhaustion that work seemed to induce. Fowler was quite willing to accept that. It made him even surer of his—guest. The worst thing that could happen, of course, would be Norman's recovery, his return to normal—

* * *

Money began to come in very satisfactorily, although Fowler wasn't really a good business man. In fact, he was a remarkably poor one. It didn't matter much. There was always more where the first had come from.

With some of the money Fowler started cautious inquiries about missing persons. He wanted to be sure no indignant relatives would turn up and demand an accounting of all this money. He questioned Norman futilely.

Norman simply could not talk. His mind was too empty for coherence. He could produce words, but he could not connect them. And this was a thing that seemed to give him his only real trouble. For he wanted desperately sometimes to speak. There was something he seemed frantic to tell Fowler, in the intervals when his strength was at its peak.

Fowler didn't want to know it. Usually when Norman reached this pitch he set him another exhausting problem. Fowler wondered for awhile just why he dreaded hearing the message. Presently he faced the answer.

Norman might be trying to explain how he could be cured.

Eventually, Fowler had to face an even more unwelcome truth. Norman did seem in spite of everything to be growing stronger.

He was working one day on a vibratory headset gimmick later to be known as a Hed-D-Acher, when suddenly he threw down his tools and faced Fowler over the table with a look that bordered on animation—for Norman.

"Sick—" he said painfully. "I . . . know . . . *work!*" It was an anathema. He made a defiant gesture and pushed the tools away.

Fowler, with a sinking sensation, frowned at the rebellious nonentity.

"All right, Norman," he said soothingly. "All right. You can rest when you finish this job. You must finish it first, though. You must finish this job, Norman. Do you understand that? You must finish—"

It was sheer accident, of course—or almost accident—that the job turned out to be much more complicated than Fowler had expected. Norman, obedient to the slow, repeated commands, worked very late and very hard.

The end of the job found him so completely exhausted he couldn't speak or move for three days.

As a matter of fact it was the Hed-D-Acher that turned out to be an important milestone in Fowler's progress. He couldn't recognize it at the time, but when he looked back, years later, he saw the occasion of his first serious mistake. His first, that is, unless you count the moment when he lifted Norman across his threshold at the very start of the thing.

Fowler had to go to Washington to defend himself in some question of patent infringement. A large firm had found out about the Hed-D-Acher and jumped in on the grounds of similar wiring—at least that was Fowler's impression. He was no technician. The main point was that the Hed-D-Acher couldn't be patented in its present form, and Fowler's rivals were trying to squeeze through a similar—and stolen—Hed-D-Acher of their own.

Fowler phoned the Korys Agency. Long distance television was not on the market yet and he was not able to see Veronica's face, but he knew what expression must be visible on it when he told her what he wanted.

"But I'm going out on a job, John. I can't just drop everything and rush out to your house."

"Listen, Veronica, there may be a hundred thousand bucks in it. I . . . there's no one else I can trust." He didn't add his chief reason for trusting her—the fact that she wasn't over-bright.

In the end, she went. Dramatic situations appealed to her, and he dropped dark hints of corporation espionage and bloody doings on Capitol Hill. He told her where to find the key and she hung up, leaving Fowler to gnaw his nails intermittently and try to limit himself to one whiskey-soda every half hour. He was paged, it seemed to him, some years later.

"Hello, Veronica?"

"Right. I'm at the house. The key was where you said. Now what?"

Fowler had had time to work out a plan. He put pencil and note pad on the jutting shelf before him and frowned slightly. This might be a risk, but—

But he intended to marry Veronica, so it was no great risk. And she wasn't smart enough to figure out the real answers.

He told her about the windowless room. "That's my houseboy's—Norman. He's slightly half-witted, but a good boy on mechanical stuff. Only he's a little deaf, and you've got to tell him a thing three times before he understands it."

"I think I'd better get out of here," Veronica remarked. "Next you'll be telling me he's a homicidal maniac."

Fowler laughed heartily. "There's a box in the kitchen—it's in that red cupboard with the blue handle. It's pretty heavy. But see if you can manage it. Take it in to Norman and tell him to make another Hed-D-Acher with a different wiring circuit.''

"Are you drunk?"

Fowler repressed an impulse to bite the mouthpiece off the telephone. His nerves were crawling under his skin. "This isn't a gag, Veronica. I told you how important it is. A hundred thousand bucks isn't funny. Look, got a pencil? Write this down.'' He dictated some technical instructions he had gleaned by asking the right questions. "Tell that to Norman. He'll find all the materials and tools he needs in the box.''

"If this is a gag—" Veronica said, and there was a pause. "Well, hang on.''

Silence drew on. Fowler tried to hear what was happening so many miles away. He caught a few vague sounds, but they were meaningless. Then voices rose in loud debate.

"Veronica!" Fowler shouted. "Veronica!" There was no answer.

After that, voices again, but softer. And presently:

"Johnny," Veronica said, "if you ever pull a trick like that on me again—"

"What happened?"

"Hiding a gibbering idiot in your house—" She was breathing fast.

"He's . . . what did he do? *What happened?*"

"Oh, nothing. Nothing at all. Except when I opened the door your houseboy walked out and began running around the house like a . . . a bat. He was trying to talk—Johnny, he scared me!" She was plaintive.

"Where is he now?"

"Back in his room. I . . . I was afraid of him. But I was trying not to show it. I thought if I could get him back in and lock the door—I spoke to him, and he swung around at me so fast I guess I let out a yell. And then he kept trying to say something—"

"What?"

"How should I know? He's in his room, but I couldn't find a key to it. I'm not staying here a minute longer. I . . . *here he comes!*"

"Veronica! Tell him to go back to his room. Loud and—like you mean it!''

She obeyed. Fowler could hear her saying it. She said it several times.

"It doesn't work. He's going out—"

"Stop him!"

"I won't! I had enough trouble coaxing him back the first time—"

"Let me talk to him," Fowler said suddenly. "He'll obey me. Hold the phone to his ear. Get him to listen to me." He raised his voice to a shout. "*Norman! Come here! Listen to me!*" Outside the booth people were turning to stare, but he ignored them.

He heard a faint mumble and recognized it.

"Norman," he said, more quietly but with equal firmness. "Do exactly what I tell you to do. Don't leave the house. Don't leave the house. *Don't leave the house.* Do you understand?"

Mumble. Then words: "Can't get out . . . can't—"

"Don't leave the house. Build another Hed-D-Acher. Do it now. Get the equipment you need and build it in the living room, on the table where the telephone is. Do it now."

A pause, and then Veronica said shakily: "He's gone back to his room. Johnny, I . . . he's coming back! With that box of stuff—"

"Let me talk to him again. Get yourself a drink. A couple of 'em." He needed Veronica as his interpreter, and the best way to keep her there would be with the aid of Dutch courage.

"Well—here he is."

Norman mumbled.

Fowler referred to his notes. He gave firm, incisive, detailed directions. He told Norman exactly what he wanted. He repeated his orders several times.

And it ended with Norman building a Hed-D-Acher, with a different type of circuit, while Veronica watched, made measurements as Fowler commanded, and relayed the information across the wire. By the time she got slightly high, matters were progressing more smoothly. There was the danger that she might make inaccurate measurements, but Fowler insisted on check and double-check of each detail.

Occasionally he spoke to Norman. Each time the man's voice was weaker. The dangerous surge of initiative was passing as energy drained out of Norman while his swift fingers flew.

In the end, Fowler had his information, and Norman, completely exhausted, was ordered back to his room. According to Veronica, he went there obediently and fell flat on the floor.

"I'll buy you a mink coat," Fowler said. "See you later."

"But—"

"I've got to hurry. Tell you all about it when I see you."

*   *   *

He got the patent, by the skin of his teeth. There was instant litigation, which was why he didn't clean up on the gadget immediately. He was willing to wait. The goose still laid golden eggs.

But he was fully aware of the danger now. He had to keep Norman busy. For unless the man's strength remained at a minimum, initiative would return. And there would be nothing to stop Norman from walking out of the house, or—

Or even worse. For Fowler could, after all, keep the doors locked. But he knew that locks wouldn't imprison Norman long once the man discovered how to pose a problem to himself. Once Norman thought: *Problem how to escape*—then his clever hands would construct a wall-melter or a matter-transmitter, and that would be the end for Fowler.

Norman had one specialized talent. To keep that operating efficiently—for Fowler's purpose—all Norman's other faculties had to be cut down to minimum operation speed.

The rosy light in the high-backed booth fell flatteringly upon Veronica's face. She twirled her martini glass on the table and said: "But John, I don't think I want to marry you." The martini glass shot pinpoints of soft light in his face as she turned it. She looked remarkably pretty, even for a Korys model. Fowler felt like strangling her.

"Why not?" he demanded.

She shrugged. She had been blowing hot and cold, so far as Fowler was concerned, ever since the day she had seen Norman. Fowler had been able to buy her back, at intervals, with gifts or moods that appealed to her, but the general drift had been toward estrangement. She wasn't intelligent, but she did have sensitivity of a sort, and it served its purpose. It was stopping her from marrying John Fowler.

"Maybe we're too much alike, Johnny," she said reflectively. "I don't know. I . . . how's that miserable house-boy of yours?"

"Is *that* still bothering you?" His voice was impatient. She had been showing too much concern over Norman. It had probably been a mistake to call her in at all, but what else could he have done? "I wish you'd forget about Norman. He's all right."

"Johnny, I honestly do think he ought to be under a doctor's care. He didn't look at all well that day. Are you sure—"

"Of course I'm sure! What do you take me for? As a matter of fact, he is under a doctor's care. Norman's just feeble-minded. "I've told you that a dozen times, Veronica. I wish you'd take my word for it. He . . . he sees a doctor regularly. It was just having you there that upset him. Strangers throw him off his balance. He's fine now. Let's forget about Norman. We were talking about getting married, remember?''

"You were. Not me. No, Johnny, I'm afraid it wouldn't work.'' She looked at him in the soft light, her face clouded with doubt and—was it suspicion? With a woman of Veronica's mentality, you never knew just where you stood. Fowler could reason her out of every objection she offered to him, but because reason meant so little to her, the solid substratum of her convictions remained unchanged.

"You'll marry me,'' he said, his voice confident.

"No.'' She gave him an uneasy look and then drew a deep breath and said: "You may as well know this now, Johnny—I've just about decided to marry somebody else.''

"Who?'' He wanted to shout the question, but he forced himself to be calm.

"No one you know. Ray Barnaby. I . . . I've pretty well made up my mind about it, John.''

"I don't know the man,'' Fowler told her evenly, "but I'll make it my business to find out all I can.''

"Now John, let's not quarrel. I—''

"You're going to marry me or nobody, Veronica.'' Fowler was astonished at the sudden violence of his own reaction. "Do you understand that?''

"Don't be silly, John. You don't own me.''

"I'm not being silly! I'm just telling you.''

"John, I'll do exactly as I please. Now, let's not quarrel about it.''

Until now, until this moment of icy rage, he had never quite realized what an obsession Veronica had become. Fowler had got out of the habit of being thwarted. His absolute power over one individual and one unchanging situation was giving him a taste for tyranny. He sat looking at Veronica in the pink dimness of the booth, grinding his teeth together in an effort not to shout at her.

"If you go through with this, Veronica, I'll make it my business to see you regret it as long as you live,'' he told her in a harsh, low voice.

She pushed her half-emptied glass aside with sudden violence that matched his. "Don't get me started, John Fowler!'' she said angrily. "I've got a temper, too! I've always known there was something I didn't like about you.''

"There'll be a lot more you don't like if you—''

"That's enough, John!'' She got up abruptly, clutching at her slipping handbag. Even in this soft light he could see the sudden hardening of her face, the lines of anger pinching downward along her nose and mouth. A perverse triumph filled him because at this moment she was ugly in her rage, but it did not swerve his determination.

"You're going to marry me," he told her harshly. "Sit down. You're going to marry me if I have to—" He paused.

"To what?" Her voice was goading. He shook his head. He couldn't finish the threat aloud.

Norman will help me, he was thinking in cold triumph. *Norman will find a way.*

He smiled thinly after her as she stalked in a fury out of the bar.

For a week Fowler heard no more from her. He made inquiries about the man Barnaby and was not surprised to learn that Veronica's intended—if she had really been serious about the fellow, after all—was a young broker of adequate income and average stupidity. A nonentity. Fowler told himself savagely that they were two of a kind and no doubt deserved each other. But his obsession still ruled him, and he was determined that no one but himself should marry Veronica.

Short of hypnosis, there seemed no immediate way to change her mind. But perhaps he could change Barnaby's. He believed he could, given enough time. Norman was at work on a rather ingenious little device involving the use of a trick lighting system. Fowler had been impressed, on consideration, by the effect of a rosy light in the bar on Veronica's appearance.

Another week passed, with no news about Veronica. Fowler told himself he could afford to remain aloof. He had the means to control her very nearly within his grasp. He would watch her, and wait his time in patience.

He was very busy, too, with other things. Two more devices were ready for patenting—the Magic Latch keyed to fingerprint patterns, and the Haircut Helmet that could be set for any sort of hair trimming and would probably wreak havoc among barbers. But litigation on the Hed-D-Acher was threatening to be expensive, and Fowler had learned already to live beyond his means. Far beyond. It seemed ridiculous to spend only what he took in each day, when such fortunes in royalties were just around the corner.

Twice he had to take Norman off the lighting device to perform small tasks in other directions. And Norman was in himself a problem.

The work exhausted him. It had to exhaust him. That was

necessary. An unpleasant necessity, of course, but there it was. Sometimes the exhaustion in Norman's eyes made one uncomfortable. Certainly Norman suffered. But because he was seldom able to show it plainly, Fowler could tell himself that perhaps he imagined the worst part of it. Casuistry, used to good purpose, helped him to ignore what he preferred not to see.

By the end of the second week, Fowler decided not to wait on Veronica any longer. He bought a dazzling solitaire diamond whose cost faintly alarmed even himself, and a wedding band that was a full circle of emerald-cut diamonds to complement it. With ten thousand dollars worth of jewelry in his pocket, he went into the city to pay her a call.

Barnaby answered the door.

Stupidly Fowler heard himself saying: "Miss Wood here?"

Barnaby, grinning, shook his head and started to answer. Fowler knew perfectly well what he was about to say. The fatuous grin would have told him even if some accurate sixth sense had not already made it clear. But he wouldn't let Barnaby say it. He thrust the startled bridegroom aside and shouldered angrily into the apartment, calling: "Veronica! Veronica, where are you?"

She came out of the kitchen in a ruffled apron, apprehension and defiance on her face.

"You can just get right out of here, John Fowler," she said firmly. Barnaby came up from behind him and began a blustering remonstrance, but she slipped past Fowler and linked her arm with Barnaby's, quieting him with a touch.

"We were married day before yesterday, John," she said.

Fowler was astonished to discover that the cliché about a red swimming maze of rage was perfectly true. The room and the bridal couple shimmered before him for an instant. He could hardly breathe in the suffocating fury that swam in his brain.

He took out the white velvet box, snapped it open and waved it under Veronica's nose. Liquid fire quivered in the myriad cut surfaces of the jewels and for an instant pure greed made Veronica's face as hard as the diamonds.

Barnaby said: "I think you'd better go, Fowler."

In silence, Fowler went.

The little light-device wouldn't do now. He would need something more powerful for his revenge. Norman put the completed gadget aside and began to work on something new. There would be a use for the thing later. Already plans were spinning themselves out in Fowler's mind.

They would be expensive plans. Fowler took council with himself and decided that the moment had come to put the magic window on the market.

Until now he had held this in reserve. Perhaps he had even been a little afraid of possible repercussions. He was artist enough to know that a whole new art-form might result from a practical telepathic projector. There were so many possibilities—

But the magic window failed.

Not wholly, of course. It was a miracle, and men always will buy miracles. But it wasn't the instant, overwhelming financial success Fowler had felt certain it would be. For one thing, perhaps this was too much of a miracle. Inventions can't become popular until the culture is ready for them. Talking films were made in Paris by Méliès around 1890, but perhaps because that was a double miracle, nobody took to the idea. As for a telepathic screen—

It was a specialized luxury item. And it wasn't as easy or as safe to enjoy as one might suppose. For one thing, few minds turned out to be disciplined enough to maintain a picture they deliberately set out to evoke. As a mass entertaining medium it suffered from the same faults as family motion pictures—other peoples' memories and dreams are notoriously boring unless one sees oneself in them.

Besides, this was too close to pure telepathy to be safe. Fowler had lived alone too long to remember the perils of exposing one's thoughts to a group. Whatever he wanted to project on his private window, he projected. But in the average family it wouldn't do. It simply wouldn't do.

Some Hollywood companies and some millionaires leased windows—Fowler refused to sell them outright. A film studio photographed a batch of projected ideations and cut them into a dream sequence for a modern Cinderella story. But trick photography had already done work so similar that it made no sensation whatever. Even Disney had done some of the stuff better. Until trained imaginative projective artists could be developed, the windows were simply not going to be a commercial success.

One ethnological group tried to use a window to project the memories of oldsters in an attempt to recapture everyday living customs of the recent past, but the results were blurred and inaccurate, full of anachronisms. They all had to be winnowed and checked so completely that little of value remained. The fact stood out that the ordinary mind is too undisciplined to be worth anything as a projector. Except as a toy, the window was useless.

It was useless commercially. But for Fowler it had one intrinsic usefulness more valuable than money—

One of the wedding presents Vernonica and Barnaby received was a telepathic window. It came anonymously. Their suspicions should have been roused. Perhaps they were, but they kept the window. After all, in her modeling work Veronica had met many wealthy people, and Barnaby also had moneyed friends, any of whom might in a generous mood have taken a window-lease for them as a goodwill gesture. Also, possession of a magic window was a social distinction. They did not allow themselves to look the gift-horse too closely in the mouth. They kept the window.

They could not have known—though they might have guessed— that this was a rather special sort of window. Norman had been at work on it through long, exhausting hours, while Fowler stood over him with the goading repetitious commands that kept him at his labor.

Fowler was not too disappointed at the commercial failure of the thing. There were other ways of making money. So long as Norman remained his to command the natural laws of supply and demand did not really affect him. He had by now almost entirely ceased to think in terms of the conventional mores. Why should he? They no longer applied to him. His supply of money and resources was limitless. He never really had to suffer for a failure. It would always be Norman, not Fowler, who suffered.

There was unfortunately no immediate way in which he could check how well his magic window was working. To do that you would have to be an invisible third person in the honeymoon apartment. But Fowler, knowing Veronica as he did, could guess.

The window was based on the principle that if you give a child a jackknife he'll probably cut himself.

Fowler's first thought had been to create a window on which he could project his own thoughts, disguised as those of the bride or groom. But he had realized almost immediately that a far more dangerous tool lay ready-made in the minds of the two whose marriage he meant to undermine.

"It isn't as if they wouldn't break up anyhow, in a year or two," he told himself as he speculated on the possibilities of his magic window. He was not justifying his intent. He didn't need to, any more. He was simply considering possibilities. "They're both stupid, they're both selfish. They're not material you could make a good marriage of. This ought to be almost too easy—"

Every man, he reasoned, has a lawless devil in his head. What filters through the censor-band from the unconscious mind is controllable. But the lower levels of the brain are utterly without morals.

Norman produced a telepathic window that would at times project images from the unconscious mind.

It was remotely controlled, of course; most of the time it operated on the usual principles of the magic window. But whenever Fowler chose he could throw a switch that made the glass twenty miles away hypersensitive.

Before he threw it for the first time, he televised Veronica. It was evening. When the picture dawned in the television he could see the magic window set up in its elegant frame within range of the televisor, so that everyone who called might be aware of the Barnaby's distinction.

Luckily it was Veronica who answered, though Barnaby was visible in the background, turning toward the 'visor an interested glance that darkened when Fowler's face dawned upon the screen. Veronica's politely expectant look turned sullen as she recognized the caller.

"Well?"

Fowler grinned. "Oh, nothing. Just wondered how you were getting along."

"Beautifully, thanks. Is that all?"

Fowler shrugged. "If that's the way you feel, yes."

"Good-by," Veronica said firmly, and flicked the switch. The screen before Fowler went blank. He grinned. All he had wanted to do was remind her of himself. He touched the stud that would activate that magic window he had just seen, and settled down to wait.

What would happen now he didn't know. Something would. He hoped the sight of him had reminded Veronica of the dazzling jewelry he had carried when they last met. He hoped that upon the window now would be dawning a covetous image of those diamonds, clear as dark water and quivering with fiery light. The sight should be enough to rouse resentment in Barnaby's mind, and when two people quarrel wholeheartedly, there are impulses toward mayhem in even the most civilized mind. It should shock the bride and groom to see on a window that reflected their innermost thoughts a picture of hatred and wishful violence. Would Veronica see herself being strangled in effigy in the big wall-frame? Would Barnaby see himself bleeding from the deep scratches his bride would be yearning to score across his face?

Fowler sat back comfortably, luxuriating in speculation.

It might take a long time. It might take years. He was willing to wait.

It took even longer than Fowler had expected. Slowly the poison built up in the Barnaby household, very slowly. And in that time a different sort of toxicity developed in Fowler's. He scarcely realized it. He was too close.

He never recognized the moment when his emotional balance shifted and he began actively to hate Norman.

The owner of the golden goose must have lived under considerable strain. Every day when he went out to look in the nest he must have felt a quaking wonder whether this time the egg would be white, and valuable only for omelets or hatching. Also, he must have had to stay very close to home, living daily with the nightmare of losing his treasure—

Norman was a prisoner—but a prisoner handcuffed to his jailer. Both men were chained. If Fowler left him alone for too long, Norman might recover. It was the inevitable menace that made travel impossible. Fowler could keep no servants; he lived alone with his prisoner. Occasionally he thought of Norman as a venomous snake whose poison fangs had to be removed each time they were renewed. He dared not cut out the poison sacs themselves, for there was no way to do that without killing the golden goose. The mixed metaphors were indicative of the state of Fowler's mind by then.

And he was almost as much a prisoner in the house as Norman was.

Constantly now he had to set Norman problems to solve simply as a safety measure, whether or not they had commercial value. For Norman was slowly regaining his strength. He was never completely coherent, but he could talk a little more, and he managed to put across quite definitely his tremendous urge to give Fowler certain obscure information.

Fowler knew, of course, what it probably was. The cure. And Norman seemed to have a strangely touching confidence that if he could only frame his message intelligibly, Fowler would make arrangements for the mysterious cure.

Once Fowler might have been touched by the confidence. Not now. Because he was exploiting Norman so ruthlessly, he had to hate either Norman or himself. By a familiar process he was projecting his own fault upon his prisoner and punishing Norman for it. He no longer speculated upon Norman's mysterious origin or the source of his equally mysterious powers. There was obviously something in that clouded mind that gave forth flashes of a certain peculiar genius. Fowler accepted the fact and used it.

There was probably some set of rules that would govern what Norman could and could not do, but Fowler did not discover—until it was too late—what the rules were. Norman could produce inconceivably intricate successes, and then fail dismally at the simplest tasks.

Curiously, he turned out to be an almost infallible finder of lost articles, so long as they were lost in the confines of the house. Fowler discovered this by accident, and was gratified to learn that for some reason that kind of search was the most exhausting task he could set for his prisoner. When all else failed, and Norman still seemed too coherent or too strong for safekeeping, Fowler had only to remember that he had misplaced his wristwatch or a book or screwdriver, and to send Norman after it.

Then something very odd happened, and after that he stopped the practice, feeling bewildered and insecure. He had ordered Norman to find a lost folder of rather important papers. Norman had gone into his own room and closed the door. He was missing for a long time. Eventually Fowler's impatience built up enough to make him call off the search, and he shouted to Norman to come out.

There was no answer. When he had called a third time in vain, Fowler opened the door and looked in. The room was empty. There were no windows. The door was the only exit, and Fowler could have sworn Norman had not come out of it.

In a rising panic he ransacked the room, calling futilely. He went through the rest of the house in a fury of haste and growing terror. Norman was not in the kitchen or the living room or the cellar or anywhere in sight outside.

Fowler was on the verge of a nervous collapse when Norman's door opened and the missing man emerged, staggering a little, his face white and blank with exhaustion, and the folder of papers in his hand.

He slept for three days afterward. And Fowler never again used that method of keeping his prisoner in check.

After six uneventful months had passed Fowler put Norman to work on a supplementary device that might augment the Barnaby magic window. He was receiving reports from a bribed daily maid, and he took pains to hear all the gossip mutual friends were happy to pass on. The Barnaby marriage appeared to suffer from a higher than normal percentage of spats and disagreements, but so far it still held. The magic window was not enough.

Norman turned out a little gadget that produced supersonics guaranteed to evoke irritability and nervous tension. The maid smuggled it into the apartment. Thereafter, the reports Fowler received were more satisfactory, from his point of view.

All in all, it took three years.

And the thing that finally turned the trick was the lighting gadget which Fowler had conceived in that bar interlude when Veronica first told him about Barnaby.

Norman worked on the fixtures for some time. They were subtle. The exact tinting involved a careful study of Veronica's skin tones, the colors of the apartment, the window placement. Norman had a scale model of the rooms where the Barnabys were working out their squabbles toward divorce. He took a long time to choose just what angles of lighting he would need to produce the worst possible result. And of course it all had to be done with considerable care because the existing light fixtures couldn't be changed noticeably.

With the help of the maid, the job was finally done. And thereafter, Veronica in her own home was—ugly.

The lights made her look haggard. They brought out every line of fatigue and ill-nature that lurked anywhere in her face. They made her sallow. They caused Barnaby increasingly to wonder why he had ever thought the girl attractive.

"It's your fault!" Veronica said hysterically. "It's all your fault and you know it!"

"How could it be my fault?" Fowler demanded in a smug voice, trying hard to iron out the smile that kept pulling up the corners of his mouth.

The television screen was between them like a window. Veronica leaned toward it, the cords in her neck standing out as she shouted at him. He had never seen that particular phenomenon before. Probably she had acquired much practice in angry shouting in the past three years. There were thin vertical creases between her brows that were new to him, too. He had seen her face to face only a few times in the years of her marriage. It had been safer and pleasanter to create her in the magic window when he felt the need of seeing her.

This was a different face, almost a different woman. He wondered briefly if he was watching the effect of his own disenchanting lighting system, but a glimpse beyond her head of a crowded drugstore assured him that he was not. This was real, not illusory. This was a Veronica he and Norman had, in effect, created.

"You did it!" Veronica said accusingly. "I don't know how, but you did it."

Fowler glanced down at the morning paper he had just been reading, folded back to the gossip column that announced last night's spectacular public quarrel between a popular Korys model and her broker husband.

"What really happened?" Fowler asked mildly.

"None of your business," Veronica told him with fine illogic. "You ought to know! You were behind it—you know you were! You and that half-wit of yours, that Norman. You think I don't know? With all those fool inventions you two work out, I know perfectly well you must have done *something*—"

"Veronica, you're raving."

She was, of course. It was sheer hysteria, plus her normal conviction that no unpleasant thing that happened to her could possibly be her own fault. By pure accident she had hit upon the truth, but that was beside the point.

"Has he left you? Is that it?" Fowler demanded.

She gave him a look of hatred. But she nodded. "It's your fault and you've got to help me. I need money. I—"

"All right, all right! You're hysterical, but I'll help you. Where are you? I'll pick you up and we'll have a drink and talk things over. You're better off than you know, baby. He never was the man for you. You haven't got a thing to worry about. I'll be there in half an hour and we can pick up where we left off three years ago."

Part of what he implied was true enough, he reflected as he switched off the television screen. Curiously, he still meant to marry her. The changed face with its querulous lines and corded throat repelled him, but you don't argue with an obsession. He had worked three years toward this moment, and he still meant to marry Veronica Barnaby as he had originally meant to marry Veronica Wood. Afterward—well, things might be different.

One thing frightened him. She was not quite as stupid as he had gambled on that day years ago when he had been forced to call on her for help with Norman. She had seen too much, deduced too much—remembered much too much. She might be dangerous. He would have to find out just what she thought she knew about him and Norman.

It might be necessary to silence her, in one way or another.

*   *   *

Norman said with painful distinctness: "Must tell you . . .
must—"

"No, Norman." Fowler spoke hastily. "We have a job to do.
There isn't time now to discuss—"

"Can't work," Norman said. "No . . . *must* tell you—" He
paused, lifted a shaking hand to his eyes, grimacing against his
own palm with a look of terrible effort and entreaty. The strength
that was mysteriously returning to him at intervals now had made
him almost a human being again. The blankness of his face
flooded sometimes with almost recognizable individuality.

"Not yet, Norman!" Fowler heard the alarm in his own voice.
"I need you. Later we'll work out whatever it is you're trying to
say. Not now. I . . . look, we've got to reverse that lighting
system we made for Veronica. I want a set of lights that will
flatter her. I need it in a hurry, Norman. You'll have to get to
work on it right away."

Norman looked at him with hollow eyes. Fowler didn't like it.
He would not meet the look. He focused on Norman's forehead
as he repeated his instructions in a patient voice.

Behind that colorless forehead the being that was Norman
must be hammering against its prison walls of bone, striving
hard to escape. Fowler shook off the fanciful idea in distaste,
repeated his orders once more and left the house in some haste.
Veronica would be waiting.

But the look in Norman's eyes haunted him all the way into
the city. Dark, hollow, desperate. The prisoner in the skull, shut
into a claustrophobic cell out of which no sound could carry. He
was getting dangerously strong, that prisoner. It would be a mercy
in the long run if some task were set to exhaust him, throw him
back into that catatonic state in which he no longer knew he was
in prison.

Veronica was not there. He waited for an hour in the bar.
Then he called her apartment, and got no answer. He tried his
own house, and no one seemed to be there either. With unreasonably mounting uneasiness, he went home at last.

She met him at the door.

"Veronica! I waited for an hour! What's the idea?"

She only smiled at him. There was an almost frightening
triumph in the smile, but she did not speak a word.

Fowler pushed past her, fighting his own sinking sensation of
alarm. He called for Norman almost automatically, as if his
unconscious mind recognized before the conscious knew just
what the worst danger might be. For Veronica might be stupid

but he had perhaps forgotten how cunning the stupid sometimes are. Veronica could put two and two together very well. She could reason from cause to effect quite efficiently, when her own welfare was at stake.

She had reasoned extremely well today.

Norman lay on the bed in his windowless room, his face as blank as paper. Some effort of the mind and will had exhausted him out of all semblance to a rational being. Some new, some overwhelming task, set him by—Veronica? Not by Fowler. The job he had been working on an hour ago was no such killing job as this.

But would Norman obey anyone except Fowler? He had defied Veronica on that other occasion when she tried to give him orders. He had almost escaped before Fowler's commanding voice ordered him back. Wait, though—she had coaxed him. Fowler remembered now. She could not command, but she had coaxed the blank creature into obedience. So there was a way. And she knew it.

But what had the task been?

With long strides Fowler went back into the drop-shaped living room. Veronica stood in the doorway where he had left her. She was waiting.

"What did you do?" he demanded.

She smiled. She said nothing at all.

"What happened?" Fowler cried urgently. "Veronica, answer me! What did you do?"

"I talked to Norman," she said. "I . . . got him to do a little job for me. That was all. Good-by, John."

"Wait! You can't leave like that. I've got to know what happened. I—"

"You'll find out," Veronica said. She gave him that thin smile again and then the door closed behind her. He heard her heels click once or twice on the walk and she was gone. There was nothing he could do about it.

He didn't know what she had accomplished. That was the terrifying thing. She had talked to Norman— And Norman had been in an almost coherent mood today. If she asked the right questions, she could have learned—almost anything. About the magic window and the supersonics and the lighting. About Norman himself. About—even about a weapon she could use against Fowler. Norman would make one if he were told to. He was an automaton. He could not reason; he could only comply.

Perhaps she had a weapon, then. But what? Fowler knew nothing at all of Veronica's mind. He had no idea what sort of revenge she might take if she had a field as limitless as Norman's talents offered her. Fowler had never been interested in Veronica's mind at all. He had no idea what sort of being crouched there behind her forehead as the prisoner crouched behind Norman's. He only knew that it would have a thin smile and that it hated him.

"You'll find out," Veronica had said. But it was several days before he did, and even then he could not be sure. So many things could have been accidental. Although he tried desperately he could not find Veronica anywhere in the city. But he kept thinking her eyes were on him, that if he could turn quickly enough he would catch her staring.

"That's what makes voodoo magic work," he told himself savagely. "A man can scare himself to death, once he knows he's been threatened—"

Death, of course, had nothing to do with it. Clearly it was no part of her plan that her enemy should die—and escape her. She knew what Fowler would hate most—ridicule.

Perhaps the things that kept happening were accidents. The time he tripped over nothing and did a foolishly clownish fall for the amusement of a long line of people waiting before a ticket window. His ears burned whenever he remembered that. Or the time he had three embarrassing slips of the tongue in a row when he was trying to make a good impression on a congressman and his pompous wife in connection with a patent. Or the time in the Biltmore dining room when he dropped every dish or glass he touched, until the whole room was staring at him and the head-waiter was clearly of two minds about throwing him out.

It was like a perpetual time bomb. He never knew what would happen next, or when or where. And it was certainly sheer imagination that made him think he could hear Veronica's clear, high, ironic laughter whenever his own body betrayed him into one of these ridiculous series of slips.

He tried shaking the truth out of Norman.

"What did you do?" he demanded of the blank, speechless face. "What did she make you do? Is there something wrong with my synapses now? Did you rig up something that would throw me out of control whenever she wants me to? *What did you do, Norman?*"

But Norman could not tell him.

On the third day she televised the house. Fowler went limp with relief when he saw her features taking shape in the screen. But before he could speak she said sharply: "All right, John. I only have a minute to waste on you. I just wanted you to know I'm *really* going to start to work on you beginning next week. That's all, John. Good-by.''

The screen would not make her face form again no matter how sharply he rapped on it, no matter how furiously he jabbed the buttons to call her back. After awhile he relaxed limply in his chair and sat staring blankly at the wall. And now he began to be afraid—

It had been a long time since Fowler faced a crisis in which he could not turn to Norman for help. And Norman was no use to him now. He could not or would not produce a device that Fowler could use as protection against the nameless threat. He could give him no inkling of what weapon he had put in Veronica's hand.

It might be a bluff. Fowler could not risk it. He had changed a great deal in three years, far more than he had realized until this crisis arose. There had been a time when his mind was flexible enough to assess dangers coolly and resourceful enough to produce alternative measures to meet them. But not any more. He had depended too long on Norman to solve all his problems for him. Now he was helpless. Unless—

He glanced again at that stunning alternative and then glanced mentally away, impatient, knowing it for an impossibility. He had thought of it often in the past week, but of course it couldn't be done. Of course—

He got up and went into the windowless room where Norman sat quietly, staring at nothing. He leaned against the door frame and looked at Norman. There in that shuttered skull lay a secret more precious than any miracle Norman had yet produced. The brain, the mind, the source. The mysterious quirk that brought forth golden eggs.

"There's a part of your brain in use that normal brains don't have," Fowler said thoughtfully aloud. Norman did not stir. "Maybe you're a freak. Maybe you're a mutation. But there's something like a thermostat in your head. When it's activated, your mind's activated, too. You don't use the same brain-centers I do. You're an idling motor. When the supercharger cuts in *something* begins to work along lines of logic I don't understand. I see the result, but I don't know what the method is. If I could know that—''

He paused and stared piercingly at the bent head. "If I could only get that secret out of you, Norman! It's no good to you. But there isn't any limit to what *I* could do with it if I had your secret and my own brain.''

If Norman heard he made no motion to show it. But some impulse suddenly goaded Fowler to action. "I'll do it!" he declared. "I'll try it! What have I got to lose, anyhow? I'm a prisoner here as long as this goes on, and Norman's no good to me the way things stand. It's worth a try."

He shook the silent man by the shoulder. "Norman, wake up. Wake up, wake up, wake up. Norman, do you hear me? Wake up, Norman, we have work to do."

Slowly, out of infinite distances, the prisoner returned to his cell, crept forward in the bone cage of the skull and looked dully at Fowler out of deep sockets.

And Fowler was seized with a sudden, immense astonishment that until now he had never really considered this most obvious of courses. Norman could do it. He was quite confident of that, suddenly. Norman could and must do it. This was the point toward which they had both been moving ever since Norman first rang the doorbell years ago. It had taken Veronica and a crisis to make the thing real. But now was the time—time and past time for the final miracle.

Fowler was going to become sufficient unto himself.

"You're going to get a nice long rest, Norman," he said kindly. "You're going to help me learn to . . . to think the way you think. Do you understand, Norman? Do you know what it is that makes your brain work the way it does? I want you to help my brain think that way, too. Afterward, you can rest, Norman. A nice, long rest. I won't be needing you any more after that, Norman."

Norman worked for twenty-four hours without a break. Watching him, forcing down the rising excitement in his mind, Fowler thought the blank man too seemed overwrought at this last and perhaps greatest of all his tasks. He mumbled a good deal over the intricate wiring of the thing he was twisting together. It looked rather like a tesseract, an open, interlocking framework which Norman handled with great care. From time to time he looked up and seemed to want to talk, to protest. Fowler ordered him sternly back to his task.

When it was finished it looked a little like the sort of turban a sultan might wear. It even had a jewel set in the front, like a headlight, except that this jewel really was light. All the wires came together there, and out of nowhere the bluish radiance sprang, shimmering softly in its little nest of wiring just above the forehead. It made Fowler think of an eye gently opening and closing. A thoughtful eye that looked up at him from between Norman's hands.

At the last moment Norman hesitated. His face was gray with exhaustion as he bent above Fowler, holding out the turban. Like Charlemagne, Fowler reached impatiently for the thing and set it on his own head. Norman bent reluctantly to adjust it.

There was a singing moment of anticipation—

The turban was feather-light on his head, but wherever it touched it made his scalp ache a bit, as if every hair had been pulled the wrong way. The aching grew. It wasn't only the hair that was going the wrong way, he realized suddenly—

It wasn't only his hair, but his mind—

It wasn't only—

Out of the wrenching blur that swallowed up the room he saw Norman's anxious face take shape, leaning close. He felt the crown of wire lifted from his head. Through a violent, blinding ache he watched Norman grimace with bewilderment.

"No," Norman said. "No . . . wrong . . . *you* . . . wrong—"

"I'm wrong?" Fowler shook his head a little and the pain subsided, but not the feeling of singing anticipation, nor the impatient disappointment at this delay. Any moment now might bring some interruption, might even bring some new, unguessable threat from Veronica that could ruin everything.

"What's wrong?" he asked, schooling himself to patience. "Me? How am I wrong, Norman? Didn't anything happen?"

"No. Wrong . . . *you*—"

"Wait, now." Fowler had had to help work out problems like this before. "O.K., I'm wrong. How?" He glanced around the room. "Wrong room?" he suggested at random. "Wrong chair? Wrong wiring? Do I have to co-operate somehow?" The last question seemed to strike a response. "Co-operate how? Do you need help with the wiring? Do I have to do something after the helmet's on?"

"Think!" Norman said violently.

"I have to think?"

"No. Wrong, wrong. Think wrong."

"I'm thinking wrong?"

Norman made a gesture of despair and turned away toward his room, carrying the wire turban with him.

Fowler, rubbing his forehead where the wires had pressed, wondered dizzily what had happened. *Think wrong.* It didn't make sense. He looked at himself in the television screen, which was a mirror when not in use, fingered the red line of the turban's pressure, and murmured, "Thinking, something to do with thinking. What?" Apparently the turban was designed to alter his patterns of thought, to open up some dazzling door through which he could perceive the new causalities that guided Norman's mind.

He thought that in some way it was probably connected with that moment when the helmet had seemed to wrench first his hair and then his skull and then his innermost thoughts in the wrong direction. But he couldn't work it out. He was too tired. All the emotional strain of the past days, the menace still hanging over him, the tremulous excitement of what lay in the immediate future—no, he couldn't be expected to reason things through very clearly just now. It was Norman's job. Norman would have to solve that problem for them both.

Norman did. He came out of his room in a few minutes, carrying the turban, twisted now into a higher, rounder shape, the gem of light glowing bluer than before. He approached Fowler with a firm step.

"You . . . thinking wrong," he said with great distinctness. "Too . . . too old. Can't change. Think wrong!"

He stared anxiously at Fowler and Fowler stared back, searching the deep-set eyes for some clue to the meaning hidden in the locked chambers of the skull behind them.

"Thinking wrong." Fowler echoed. "Too . . . old? I don't understand. Or—do I? You mean my mind isn't flexible enough any more?" He remembered the wrenching moment when every mental process had tried vainly to turn sidewise in his head. "But then it won't work at all!"

"Oh, yes," Norman said confidently.

"But if I'm too old—" It wasn't age, really. Fowler was not old in years. But the grooves of his thinking had worn themselves deep in the past years since Norman came. He had fixed inflexibly in the paths of his own self-indulgence and now his mind could not accept the answer the wire turban offered. "I can't change," he told Norman despairingly. "If I'd only made you do this when you first came, before my mind set in its pattern—"

Norman held out the turban, reversed so that the blue light bathed his face in blinking radiance. "This—will work," he said confidently.

Belated caution made Fowler dodge back a little. "Now wait. I want to know more before we . . . how *can* it work? You can't make me any younger, and I don't want any random tampering with my brain. I—"

Norman was not listening. With a swift, sure gesture he pressed the wired wreath down on Fowler's head.

There was the wrenching of hair and scalp, skull and brain. This first—and then very swiftly the shadows moved upon the floor, the sun gleamed for one moment through the eastern windows and the world darkened outside. The darkness winked and was purple, was dull red, was daylight—

Fowler could not stir. He tried furiously to snatch the turban from his head, but no impulse from his brain made any connection with the motionless limbs. He still stood facing the mirror, the blue light still winked thoughtfully back at him, but everything moved so fast he had no time to comprehend light or dark for what they were, or the blurred motions reflected in the glass, or what was happening to him.

This was yesterday, and the week before, and the year before, but he did not clearly know it. *You can't make me any younger*. Very dimly he remembered having said that to Norman at some remote interval of time. His thoughts moved sluggishly somewhere at the very core of his brain, whose outer layers were being peeled off one by one, hour by hour, day by day. But Norman could make him younger. Norman *was* making him younger. Norman was whisking him back and back toward the moment when his brain would regain flexibility enough for the magical turban to open that door to genius.

Those blurs in the mirror were people moving at normal time-speed—himself, Norman, Veronica going forward in time as he slipped backward through it, neither perceiving the other. But twice he saw Norman moving through the room at a speed that matched his own, walking slowly and looking for something. He saw him search behind a chair-cushion and pull out a creased folder, legal size—the folder he had last sent Norman to find, on that day when he vanished from his closed room!

Norman, then, had traveled in time before. Norman's powers must be more far-reaching, more dazzling, than he had ever guessed. As his own powers would be, when his mind cleared again and this blinding flicker stopped.

Night and day went by like the flapping of a black wing. That was the way Wells had put it. That was the way it looked. A hypnotic flapping. It left him dazed and dull—

Norman, holding the folder, lifted his head and for one instant looked Fowler in the face in the glass. Then he turned and went away through time to another meeting in another interval that would lead backward again to this meeting, and on and on around a closing spiral which no mind could fully comprehend.

It didn't matter. Only one thing really mattered. Fowler stood there shocked for an instant into almost total wakefulness, staring at his own face in the mirror, remembering Norman's face.

For one timeless moment, while night and day flapped around him, he stood helpless, motionless, staring appalled at his reflection in the gray that was the blending of time—and he knew who Norman was.

Then mercifully the hypnosis took over again and he knew nothing at all.

There are centers in the brain never meant for man's use today. Not until the race has evolved the strength to handle them. A man of today might learn the secret that would unlock those centers, and if he were a fool he might even turn the key that would let the door swing open.

But after that he would do nothing at all of his own volition.

For modern man is still too weak to handle the terrible energy that must pour forth to activate those centers. The grossly overloaded physical and mental connections could hold for only a fraction of a second. Then the energy flooding into the newly unlocked brain-center never meant for use until perhaps a thousand more years have remodeled mankind, would collapse the channels, fuse the connections, make every synapse falter in the moment when the gates of the mind swing wide.

On Fowler's head the turban of wires glowed incandescent and vanished. The thing that had once happened to Norman happened now to him. The dazzling revelation—the draining, the atrophy—

He had recognized Norman's face reflected in the mirror beside his own, both white with exhaustion, both stunned and empty. He knew who Norman was, what motives moved him, what corroding irony had made his punishing of Norman just. But by the time he knew, it was already far too late to alter the future or the past.

Time flapped its wings more slowly. That moment of times gone swung round again as the circle came to its close. Memories flickered more and more dimly in Fowler's mind, like day and night, like the vague, shapeless world which was all he could perceive now. He felt cold and weak, strangely, intolerably, inhumanly weak with a weakness of the blood and bone, of the mind and soul. He saw his surroundings dimly, but he saw—other things—with a swimming clarity that had no meaning to him. He saw causes and effects as tangible before him as he had once seen trees and grass. But remote, indifferent, part of another world.

Help was what he needed. There was something he must remember. Something of terrible import. He must find help, to focus his mind upon the things that would work his cure. Cure was possible; he knew it—he knew it. But he needed help.

Somehow there was a door before him. He reached vaguely, moving his hand almost by reflex toward his pocket. But he had no pocket. This was a suit of the new fashion, sleek in fabric, cut without pockets. He would have to knock, to ring. He remembered—

The face he had seen in the mirror. His own face? But even then it had been changing, as a cloud before the sun drains life and color and soul from a landscape. The expunging amnesia wiped across its mind had had its parallel physically, too; the traumatic shock of moving through time—*the dark wing flapping*—had sponged the recognizable characteristics from his face, leaving the matrix, the characterless basic. This was not his face. He had no face; he had no memory. He knew only that this familiar door before him was the door to the help he must have to save himself from a circling eternity.

It was almost wholly a reflex gesture that moved his finger toward the doorbell. The last dregs of memory and initiative drained from him with the motion.

Again the chimes played three soft notes. Again the circle closed.

Again the blank man waited for John Fowler to open the door.

ALIEN EARTH

by Edmond Hamilton (1904—1977)

Thrilling Wonder Stories, **April**

Isaac mentions that Edmond Hamilton was known as the "Universe-saver," but he was also known to "wreck" a few in his day. Indeed, he was (and is, thank goodness) so well known for his space opera that his fine work in other areas of science fiction is not nearly as famous as it ought to be.

"Alien Earth" is an excellent example of this relative obscurity, a wonderful, moody story that is science fiction at its finest. Amazingly, it has only been reprinted twice—in The Best of Edmond Hamilton *(1977) and in the anthology* Alien Earth and Other Stories *(1969). It is a pleasure to reprint it again.—M.H.G.*

(There are "great dyings" in the course of biological evolution, periods when in a comparatively short interval of time, a large fraction of the species of living things on Earth die. The most recent example was the period at the end of the Cretaceous, 65,000,000 years ago.

I have often thought there are also "great dyings" in the history of science fiction, periods when large percentages of the established science fiction writers stopped appearing. The most dramatic example came in 1938, when John Campbell became editor of Astounding *and introduced an entirely new stable of writers, replacing the old.*

Some old-timers survived, of course (even as some species always survived the biological "great dyings"). To me, one of the most remarkable survivors was Edmond Hamilton. He was one of the great stars of the pre-Campbell era, so grandiose in his plots that he was known as the "Universe-saver." And yet he was able to narrow his focus and survive,

135

whereas many others who seemed to require a smaller re-adaptation could not do so. In "Alien Earth" there is no Universe being saved; there is only a close look at the world of plants.—I.A.)

CHAPTER 1

SLOWED-DOWN LIFE

The dead man was standing in a little moonlit clearing in the jungle when Farris found him.

He was a small swart man in white cotton, a typical Laos tribesman of this Indo-China hinterland. He stood without support, eyes open, staring unwinkingly ahead, one foot slightly raised. And he was not breathing.

"But he can't be dead!" Farris exclaimed. "Dead men don't stand around in the jungle."

He was interrupted by Piang, his guide. That cocksure little Annamese had been losing his impudent self-sufficiency ever since they had wandered off the trail. And the motionless, standing dead man had completed his demoralization.

Ever since the two of them had stumbled into this grove of silk-cotton trees and almost run into the dead man, Piang had been goggling in a scared way at the still unmoving figure. Now he burst out volubly:

"The man is *hunati!* Don't touch him! We must leave here—we have strayed into a bad part of the jungle!"

Farris didn't budge. He had been a teak-hunter for too many years to be entirely skeptical of the superstitions of Southeast Asia. But, on the other hand, he felt a certain responsibility.

"If this man isn't really dead, then he's in bad shape somehow and needs help," he declared.

"No, no!" Piang insisted. "He is *hunati!* Let us leave here quickly!"

Pale with fright, he looked around the moonlit grove. They were on a low plateau where the jungle was monsoon-forest rather than rain-forest. The big silk-cotton and ficus trees were less choked with brush and creepers here, and they could see along dim forest aisles to gigantic distant banyans that loomed like dark lords of the silver silence.

Silence. There was too much of it to be quite natural. They could faintly hear the usual clatter of birds and monkeys from down in the lowland thickets, and the cough of a tiger echoed from the Laos foothills. But the thick forest here on the plateau was hushed.

Farris went to the motionless, staring tribesman and gently touched his thin brown wrist. For a few moments, he felt no pulse. Then he caught its throb—an incredibly slow beating.

"About one beat every two minutes," Farris muttered. "How the devil can he keep living?"

He watched the man's bare chest. It rose—but so slowly that his eye could hardly detect the motion. It remained expanded for minutes. Then, as slowly, it fell again.

He took his pocket-light and flashed it into the tribesman's eyes.

There was no reaction to the light, not at first. Then, slowly, the eyelids crept down and closed, and stayed closed, and finally crept open again.

"A wink—but a hundred times slower than normal!" Farris exclaimed. "Pulse, respiration, reactions—they're all a hundred times slower. The man has either suffered a shock, or been drugged."

Then he noticed something that gave him a little chill.

The tribesman's eyeball seemed to be turning with infinite slowness toward him. And the man's raised foot was a little higher now. As though he were walking—but walking at a pace a hundred times slower than normal.

The thing was eery. There came something more eery. A sound—the sound of a small stick cracking.

Piang exhaled breath in a sound of pure fright, and pointed off into the grove. In the moonlight Farris saw.

There was another tribesman standing a hundred feet away. He, too, was motionless. But his body was bent forward in the attitude of a runner suddenly frozen. And beneath his foot, the stick had cracked.

"They worship the great ones, by the Change!" said the Annamese in a hoarse undertone. "We must not interfere!"

That decided Farris. He had, apparently, stumbled on some sort of weird jungle rite. And he had had too much experience with Asiatic natives to want to blunder into their private religious mysteries.

His business here in easternmost Indo-China was teak-hunting. It would be difficult enough back in this wild hinterland without antagonizing the tribes. These strangely dead-alive men, whatever drug or compulsion they were suffering from, could not be in danger if others were near.

"We'll go on," Farris said shortly.

Piang led hastily down the slope of the forested plateau. He went through the brush like a scared deer, till they hit the trail again.

"This is it—the path to the Government station," he said, in great relief. "We must have lost it back at the ravine. I have not been this far back in Laos, many times."

Farris asked, "Piang, what is *hunati?* This Change that you were talking about?"

The guide became instantly less voluble. "It is a rite of worship." He added, with some return of his cocksureness, "These tribesmen are very ignorant. They have not been to mission school, as I have."

"Worship of what?" Farris asked. "The great ones, you said. Who are they?"

Piang shrugged and lied readily. "I do not know. In all the great forest, there are men who can become *hunati,* it is said. How, I do not know."

Farris pondered, as he tramped onward. There had been something uncanny about those tribesmen. It had been almost a suspension of animation—but not quite. Only an incredible slowing down.

What could have caused it? And what, possibly, could be the purpose of it?

"I should think," he said, "that a tiger or snake would make short work of a man in that frozen condition."

Piang shook his head vigorously. "No. A man who is *hunati* is safe—at least, from beasts. No beast would touch him."

Farris wondered. Was that because the extreme motionlessness made the beasts ignore them? He supposed that it was some kind of fear-ridden nature-worship. Such animistic beliefs were common in this part of the world. And it was small wonder, Farris thought a little grimly. Nature, here in the tropical forest, wasn't the smiling goddess of temperate lands. It was something, not to be loved, but to be feared.

He ought to know! He had had two days of the Laos jungle since leaving the upper Mekong, when he had expected that one would take him to the French Government botanic survey station that was his goal.

He brushed stinging winged ants from his sweating neck, and wished that they had stopped at sunset. But the map had showed them but a few miles from the Station. He had not counted on

Piang losing the trail. But he should have, for it was only a wretched track that wound along the forested slope of the plateau.

The hundred-foot ficus, dyewood and silk-cotton trees smothered the moonlight. The track twisted constantly to avoid impenetrable bamboo-hells or to ford small streams, and the tangle of creepers and vines had a devilish deftness at tripping one in the dark.

Farris wondered if they had lost their way again. And he wondered not for the first time, why he had ever left America to go into teak.

"That is the Station," said Piang suddenly, in obvious relief.

Just ahead of them on the jungled slope was a flat ledge. Light shone there, from the windows of a rambling bamboo bungalow.

Farris became conscious of all his accumulated weariness, as he went the last few yards. He wondered whether he could get a decent bed here, and what kind of chap this Berreau might be who had chosen to bury himself in such a Godforsaken post of the botanical survey.

The bamboo house was surrounded by tall, graceful dyewoods. But the moonlight showed a garden around it, enclosed by a low sappan hedge.

A voice from the dark veranda reached Farris and startled him. It startled him because it was a girl's voice, speaking in French.

"Please, Andre! Don't go again! It is madness!"

A man's voice rapped harsh answer, *"Lys, tais-toi! Je reviendrai—"*

Farris coughed diplomatically and then said up to the darkness of the veranda, "Monsieur Berreau?"

There was a dead silence. Then the door of the house was swung open so that light spilled out on Farris and his guide.

By the light, Farris saw a man of thirty, bareheaded, in whites—a thin, rigid figure. The girl was only a white blur in the gloom.

He climbed the steps. "I suppose you don't get many visitors. My name is Hugh Farris. I have a letter for you, from the Bureau at Saigon."

There was a pause. Then, "If you will come inside, M'sieu Farris—"

In the lamplit, bamboo-walled living room, Farris glanced quickly at the two.

Berreau looked to his experienced eye like a man who had stayed too long in the tropics—his blond handsomeness tarnished by a corroding climate, his eyes too feverishly restless.

"My sister, Lys," he said, as he took the letter Farris handed.

Farris' surprise increased. A wife, he had supposed until now. Why should a girl under thirty bury herself in this wilderness?

He wasn't surprised that she looked unhappy. She might have been a decently pretty girl, he thought, if she didn't have that woebegone anxious look.

"Will you have a drink?" she asked him. And then, glancing with swift anxiety at her brother, "You'll not be going now, Andre?"

Berreau looked out at the moonlit forest, and a queer, hungry tautness showed his cheekbones in a way Farris didn't like. But the Frenchman turned back.

"No, Lys. And drinks, please. Then tell Ahra to care for his guide."

He read the letter swiftly, as Farris sank with a sigh into a rattan chair. He looked up from it with troubled eyes.

"So you come for teak?"

Farris nodded. "Only to spot and girdle trees. They have to stand a few years then before cutting, you know."

Berreau said, "The Commissioner writes that I am to give you every assistance. He explains the necessity of opening up new teak cuttings."

He slowly folded the letter. It was obvious, Farris thought, that the man did not like it, but had to make the best of orders.

"I shall do everything possible to help," Berreau promised. "You'll want a native crew, I suppose. I can get one for you." Then a queer look filmed his eyes. "But there are some forests here that are impracticable for lumbering. I'll go into that later."

Farris, feeling every moment more exhausted by the long tramp, was grateful for the rum and soda Lys handed him.

"We have a small extra room—I think it will be comfortable," she murmured.

He thanked her. "I could sleep on a log, I'm so tired. My muscles are as stiff as though I were *hunati* myself."

Berreau's glass dropped with a sudden crash.

CHAPTER 2

SORCERY OF SCIENCE

Ignoring the shattered glass, the young Frenchman strode quickly toward Farris.

"What do you know of *huanti?*" he asked harshly.

Farris saw with astonishment that the man's hands were shaking.

"I don't know anything except what we saw in the forest. We came upon a man standing in the moonlight who looked dead, and wasn't. He just seemed incredibly slowed down. Piang said he was *hunati*."

A flash crossed Berreau's eyes. He exclaimed, "I knew the Rite would be called! And the others are there—"

He checked himself. It was as though the unaccustomedness of strangers had made him for a moment forget Farris' presence.

Lys' blonde head drooped. She looked away from Farris.

"You were saying?" the American prompted.

But Berreau had tightened up. He chose his words now. "The Laos tribes have some queer beliefs, M'sieu Farris. They're a little hard to understand."

Farris shrugged. "I've seen some queer Asian witchcraft, in my time. But this is unbelievable!"

"It is science, not witchcraft," Berreau corrected. "Primitive science, born long ago and transmitted by tradition. That man you saw in the forest was under the influence of a chemical not found in our pharmacopeia, but nonetheless potent."

"You mean that these tribesmen have a drug that can slow the life-process to that incredibly slow tempo?" Farris asked skeptically. "One that modern science doesn't know about?"

"Is that so strange? Remember, M'sieu Farris, that a century ago an old peasant woman in England was curing heart-disease with foxglove, before a physician studied her cure and discovered digitalis."

"But why on earth would even a Laos tribesman want to live so much *slower?*" Farris demanded.

"Because," Berreau answered, "they believe that in that state they can commune with something vastly greater than themselves."

Lys interrupted. "M'sieu Farris must be very weary. And his bed is ready."

Farris saw the nervous fear in her face, and realized that she wanted to end this conversation.

He wondered about Berreau, before he dropped off to sleep. There was something odd about the chap. He had been too excited about this *hunati* business.

Yet that was weird enough to upset anyone, that incredible and uncanny slowing-down of a human being's life-tempo. "To commune with something vastly greater than themselves," Berreau had said.

What gods were so strange that a man must live a hundred times slower than normal, to commune with them?

Next morning, he breakfasted with Lys on the broad veranda. The girl told him that her brother had already gone out.

"He will take you later today to the tribal village down in the valley, to arrange for your workers," she said.

Farris noted the faint unhappiness still in her face. She looked silently at the great, green ocean of forest that stretched away below this plateau on whose slope they were.

"You don't like the forest?" he ventured.

"I hate it," she said. "It smothers one, here."

Why, he asked, didn't she leave? The girl shrugged.

"I shall, soon. It is useless to stay. Andre will not go back with me."

She explained. "He has been here five years too long. When he didn't return to France, I came out to bring him. But he won't go. He has ties here now."

Again, she became abruptly silent. Farris discreetly refrained from asking her what ties she meant. There might be an Annamese woman in the background—though Berreau didn't look that type.

The day settled down to the job of being stickily tropical, and the hot still hours of the morning wore on. Farris, sprawling in a chair and getting a welcome rest, waited for Berreau to return.

He didn't return. And as the afternoon waned, Lys looked more and more worried.

An hour before sunset, she came out onto the veranda, dressed in slacks and jacket.

"I am going down to the village—I'll be back soon," she told Farris.

She was a poor liar. Farris got to his feet. "You're going after your brother. Where is he?"

Distress and doubt struggled in her face. She remained silent.

"Believe me, I want to be a friend," Farris said quietly. "Your brother is mixed up in something here, isn't he?"

She nodded, white-faced. "It's why he wouldn't go back to France with me. He can't bring himself to leave. It's like a horrible fascinating vice."

"What is?"

She shook her head. "I can't tell you. Please wait here."

He watched her leave, and then realized she was not going down the slope but up it—up toward the top of the forested plateau.

He caught up to her in quick strides. "You can't go up into that forest alone, in a blind search for him."

"It's not a blind search. I think I know where he is," Lys whispered. "But you should not go there. The tribesmen wouldn't like it!"

Farris instantly understood. "That big grove up on top of the plateau, where we found the *hunati* natives?"

Her unhappy silence was answer enough. "Go back to the bungalow," he told her. "I'll find him."

She would not do that. Farris shrugged, and started forward. "Then we'll go together."

She hesitated, then came on. They went up the slope of the plateau, through the forest.

The westering sun sent spears and arrows of burning gold through chinks in the vast canopy of foliage under which they walked. The solid green of the forest breathed a rank, hot exhalation. Even the birds and monkeys were stifledly quiet at this hour.

"Is Berreau mixed up in that queer *hunati* rite?" Farris asked.

Lys looked up as though to utter a quick denial, but then dropped her eyes.

"Yes, in a way. His passion for botany got him interested in it. Now he's involved."

Farris was puzzled. "Why should botanical interest draw a man to that crazy drug-rite or whatever it is?"

She wouldn't answer that. She walked in silence until they reached the top of the forested plateau. Then she spoke in a whisper.

"We must be quiet now. It will be bad if we are seen here."

The grove that covered the plateau was pierced by horizontal bars of red sunset light. The great silk-cottons and ficus trees were pillars supporting a vast cathedral-nave of darkening green.

A little way ahead loomed up those huge, monster banyans he had glimpsed before in the moonlight. They dwarfed all the rest, towering bulks that were infinitely ancient and infinitely majestic.

Farris suddenly saw a Laos tribesman, a small brown figure, in the brush ten yards ahead of him. There were two others, farther in the distance. And they were all standing quite still, facing away from him.

They were *hunati*, he knew. In that queer state of slowed-down life, that incredible retardation of the vital processes.

Farris felt a chill. He muttered over his shoulder, "You had better go back down and wait."

"No," she whispered. "There is Andre."

He turned, startled. Then he too saw Berreau.

His blond head bare, his face set and white and masklike,

standing frozenly beneath a big wild-fig a hundred feet to the right.

Hunati!

Farris had expected it, but that didn't make it less shocking. It wasn't that the tribesmen mattered less as human beings. It was just that he had talked with a normal Berreau only a few hours before. And now, to see him like this!

Berreau stood in a position ludicrously reminiscent of the old-time "living statues." One foot was slightly raised, his body bent a little forward, his arms raised a little.

Like the frozen tribesmen ahead, Berreau was facing toward the inner recesses of the grove, where the giant banyans loomed.

Farris touched his arm. "Berreau, you have to snap out of this."

"It's no use to speak to him," whispered the girl. "He can't hear."

No, he couldn't hear. He was living at a tempo so low that no ordinary sound could make sense to his ears. His face was a rigid mask, lips slightly parted to breathe, eyes fixed ahead. Slowly, slowly, the lids crept down and veiled those staring eyes and then crept open again in the infinitely slow wink. Slowly, slowly, his slightly raised left foot moved down toward the ground.

Movement, pulse, breathing—all a hundred times slower than normal. Living, but not in a human way—not in a human way at all.

Lys was not so stunned as Farris was. He realized later that she must have seen her brother like this, before.

"We must take him back to the bungalow, somehow," she murmured. "I *can't* let him stay out here for many days and nights, again!"

Farris welcomed the small practical problem that took his thoughts for a moment away from this frozen, standing horror.

"We can rig a stretcher, from our jackets," he said. "I'll cut a couple of poles."

The two bamboos, through the sleeves of the two jackets, made a makeshift stretcher which they laid upon the ground.

Farris lifted Berreau. The man's body was rigid, muscles locked in an effort no less strong because it was infinitely slow.

He got the young Frenchman down on the stretcher, and then looked at the girl. "Can you help carry him? Or will you get a native?"

She shook her head. "The tribesmen mustn't know of this. Andre isn't heavy."

He wasn't. He was light as though wasted by fever, though the sickened Farris knew that it wasn't any fever that had done it.

Why should a civilized young botanist go out into the forest and partake of a filthy primitive drug of some kind that slowed him down to a frozen stupor? It didn't make sense.

Lys bore her share of their living burden through the gathering twilight, in stolid silence. Even when they put Berreau down at intervals to rest, she did not speak.

It was not until they reached the dark bungalow and had put him down on his bed, that the girl sank into a chair and buried her face in her hands.

Farris spoke with a rough encouragement he did not feel. "Don't get upset. He'll be all right now. I'll soon bring him out of this."

She shook her head. "No, you must not attempt that! He must come out of it by himself. And it will take many days."

The devil it would, Farris thought. He had teak to find, and he needed Berreau to arrange for workers.

Then the dejection of the girl's small figure got him. He patted her shoulder.

"All right, I'll help you take care of him. And together, we'll pound some sense into him and make him go back home. Now you see about dinner."

She lit a gasoline lamp, and went out. He heard her calling the servants.

He looked down at Berreau. He felt a little sick, again. The Frenchman lay, eyes staring toward the ceiling. He was living, breathing—and yet his retarded life-tempo cut him off from Farris as effectually as death would.

No, not quite. Slowly, so slowly that he could hardly detect the movement, Berreau's eyes turned toward Farris' figure.

Lys came back into the room. She was quiet, but he knew her better, and he knew by her face that she was startled.

"The servants are gone! Ahra, and the girls—and your guide. They must have seen us bring Andre in."

Farris understood. "They left because we brought back a man who's *hunati?*"

She nodded. "All the tribespeople fear the rite. It's said there's only a few who belong to it, but they're dreaded."

Farris spared a moment to curse softly the vanished Annamese. "Piang would bolt like a scared rabbit, from something like this. A sweet beginning for my job here."

"Perhaps you had better leave," Lys said uncertainly. Then she added contradictorily, "No, I can't be heroic about it! Please stay!"

"That's for sure," he told her. "I can't go back down river and report that I shirked my job because of—"

He stopped, for she wasn't listening to him. She was looking past him, toward the bed.

Farris swung around. While they two had been talking, Berreau had been moving. Infinitely slowly—but moving.

His feet were on the floor now. He was getting up. His body straightened with a painful, dragging slowness, for many minutes.

Then his right foot began to rise almost imperceptibly from the floor. He was starting to walk, only a hundred times slower than normal.

He was starting to walk toward the door.

Lys' eyes had a yearning pity in them. "He is trying to go back up to the forest. He will try so long as he is *hunati*."

Farris gently lifted Berreau back to the bed. He felt a cold dampness on his forehead.

What was there up there that drew worshippers in a strange trance of slowed-down life?

CHAPTER 3

UNHOLY LURE

He turned to the girl and asked, "How long will he stay in this condition?"

"A long time," she answered heavily. "It may take weeks for the *hunati* to wear off."

Farris didn't like the prospect, but there was nothing he could do about it.

"All right, we'll take care of him. You and I."

Lys said, "One of us will have to watch him, all the time. He will keep trying to go back to the forest."

"You've had enough for a while," Farris told her. "I'll watch him tonight."

Farris watched. Not only that night but for many nights. The days went into weeks, and the natives still shunned the house, and he saw nobody except the pale girl and the man who was living in a different way than other humans lived.

Berreau didn't change. He didn't seem to sleep, nor did he

seem to need food or drink. His eyes never closed, except in that infinitely slow blinking.

He didn't sleep, and he did not quit moving. He was always moving, only it was in that weird, utterly slow-motion tempo that one could hardly see.

Lys had been right. Berreau wanted to go back to the forest. He might be living a hundred times slower than normal, but he was obviously still conscious in some weird way, and still trying to go back to the hushed, forbidden forest up there where they had found him.

Farris wearied of lifting the statue-like figure back into bed, and with the girl's permission tied Berreau's ankles. It did not make things much better. It was even more upsetting, in a way, to sit in the lamplit bedroom and watch Berreau's slow struggles for freedom.

The dragging slowness of each tiny movement made Farris' nerves twitch to see. He wished he could give Berreau some sedative to keep him asleep, but he did not dare to do that.

He had found, on Berreau's forearm, a tiny incision stained with sticky green. There were scars of other, old incisions near it. Whatever crazy drug had been injected into the man to make him *hunati* was unknown. Farris did not dare try to counteract its effect.

Finally, Farris glanced up one night from his bored perusal of an old *L'Illustration* and then jumped to his feet.

Berreau still lay on the bed, but he had just winked. Had winked with normal quickness, and not that slow, dragging blink.

"Berreau!" Farris said quickly. "Are you all right now? Can you hear me?"

Berreau looked up at him with a level, unfriendly gaze. "I can hear you. May I ask why you meddled?"

It took Farris aback. He had been playing nurse so long that he had unconsciously come to think of the other as a sick man who would be grateful to him. He realized now that Berreau was coldly angry, not grateful.

The Frenchman was untying his ankles. His movements were shaky, his hands trembling, but he stood up normally.

"Well?" he asked.

Farris shrugged. "Your sister was going up there after you. helped her bring you back. That's all."

Berreau looked a little startled. "Lys did that? P
breaking of the Rite! It can mean trouble for her!"

Resentment and raw nerves made Farris sud

should you worry about Lys now, when you've made her wretched for months by your dabbing in native wizardries?"

Berreau didn't retort angrily, as he had expected. The young Frenchman answered heavily.

"It's true. I've done that to Lys."

Farris exclaimed, "Berreau, why do you do it? Why this unholy business of going *hunati*, of living a hundred times slower? What can you gain by it?"

The other man looked at him with haggard eyes. "By doing it, I've entered an alien world. A world that exists around us all our lives, but that we never live in or understand at all."

"What world?"

"The world of green leaf and root and branch," Berreau answered. "The world of plant life, which we can never comprehend because of the difference between its life-tempo and our life-tempo."

Farris began dimly to understand. "You mean, this *hunati* change makes you live at the same tempo as plants?"

Berreau nodded. "Yes. And that simple difference in life-tempo is the doorway into an unknown, incredible world."

"But how?"

The Frenchman pointed to the half-healed incision on his bare arm. "The drug does it. A native drug, that slows down metabolism, heart-action, respiration, nerve-messages, everything.

"Chlorophyll is its basis. The green blood of plant-life, the complex chemical that enables plants to take their energy direct from sunlight. The natives prepare it directly from grasses, by some method of their own."

"I shouldn't think," Farris said incredulously, "that chlorophyll could have any effect on an animal organism."

"Your saying that," Berreau retorted, "shows that your biochemical knowledge is out of date. Back in March of Nineteen Forty-Eight, two Chicago chemists engaged in mass production or extraction of chlorophyll, announced that their injection of it into dogs and rats seemed to prolong life greatly by altering the oxidation capacity of the cells.

"Prolong life greatly—yes! But it prolongs it, by slowing it
p̲ tree lives longer than a man, because it doesn't live so
Be⟍n make a man live as long—*and as slowly*—as a
⟍ the right chlorophyll compound into his blood."
ˊs what you meant, by saying that primitive
ˊcipate modern scientific discoveries?"
ˊs chlorophyll *hunati* solution may be an

age-old secret. I believe it's always been known to a few among the primitive forest-folk of the world."

He looked somberly past the American. "Tree-worship is as old as the human race. The Sacred Tree of Sumeria, the groves of Dodona, the oaks of the Druids, the tree Ygdrasil of the Norse, even our own Christmas Tree—they all stem from primitive worship of that other, alien kind of life with which we share Earth.

"I think that a few secret worshippers have always known how to prepare the chlorophyll drug that enabled them to attain complete communion with that other kind of life, by living at the same slow rate for a time."

Farris stared. "But how did *you* get taken into this queer secret worship?"

The other man shrugged. "The worshippers were grateful to me, because I had saved the forests here from possible death."

He walked across to the corner of the room that was fitted as a botanical laboratory, and took down a test-tube. It was filled with dusty, tiny spores of a leprous, gray-green color.

"This is the Burmese Blight, that's withered whole great forests down south of the Mekong. A deadly thing, to tropical trees. It was starting to work up into this Laos country, but I showed the tribes how to stop it. The secret *hunati* sect made me one of them, in reward."

"But I still can't understand why an educated man like you would want to join such a crazy mumbo-jumbo," Farris said.

"*Dieu*, I'm trying to make you understand why! To show you that it was my curiosity as a botanist that made me join the Rite and take the drug!"

Berreau rushed on. "But you can't understand, any more than Lys could! You can't comprehend the wonder and strangeness and beauty of living that other kind of life!"

Something in Berreau's white, rapt face, in his haunted eyes, made Farris' skin crawl. His words seemed momentarily to lift a veil, to make the familiar vaguely strange and terrifying.

"Berreau, listen! You've got to cut this and leave here at once."

The Frenchman smiled mirthlessly. "I know. Many times, I have told myself so. But I do not go. How can I leave something that is a botanist's heaven?"

Lys had come into the room, was looking wanly at her brother's face.

"Andre, won't you give it up and go home with me?" she appealed.

"Or are you too sunken in this uncanny habit to care whether your sister breaks her heart?" Farris demanded.

Berreau flared. "You're a smug pair! You treat me like a drug addict, without knowing the wonder of the experience I've had! I've gone into another world, an alien Earth that is around us every day of our lives and that we can't even see. And I'm going back again, and again."

"Use that chlorophyll drug and go *hunati* again?" Farris said grimly.

Berreau nodded defiantly.

"No," said Farris. "You're not. For if you do, we'll just go out there and bring you in again. You'll be quite helpless to prevent us, once you're *hunati*."

The other man raged. "There's a way I can stop you from doing that! Your threats are dangerous!"

"There's no way," Farris said flatly. "Once you've frozen yourself into that slower life-tempo, you're helpless against normal people. And I'm not threatening. I'm trying to save your sanity, man!"

Berreau flung out of the room without answer. Lys looked at the American, with tears glimmering in her eyes.

"Don't worry about it," he reassured her. "He'll get over it, in time."

"I fear not," the girl whispered. "It has become a madness in his brain."

Inwardly, Farris agreed. Whatever the lure of the unknown world that Berreau had entered by that change in life-tempo, it had caught him beyond all redemption.

A chill swept Farris when he thought of it—men out there, living at the same tempo as plants, stepping clear out of the plane of animal life to a strangely different kind of life and world.

The bungalow was oppressively silent that day—the servants gone, Berreau sulking in his laboratory, Lys moving about with misery in her eyes.

But Berreau didn't try to go out, though Farris had been expecting that and had been prepared for a clash. And by evening, Berreau seemed to have got over his sulks. He helped prepare dinner.

He was almost gay, at the meal—a febrile good humor that Farris didn't quite like. By common consent, none of the three spoke of what was uppermost in their minds.

Berreau retired, and Farris told Lys, "Go to bed—you've lost so much sleep lately you're half asleep now. I'll keep watch."

In his own room, Farris found drowsiness assailing him too.

He sank back in a chair, fighting the heaviness that weighed down his eyelids.

Then, suddenly, he understood. "Drugged!" he exclaimed, and found his voice little more than a whisper. "Something in the dinner!"

"Yes," said a remote voice. "Yes, Farris."

Berreau had come in. He loomed gigantic to Farris' blurred eyes. He came closer, and Farris saw in his hand a needle that dripped sticky green.

"I'm sorry, Farris." He was rolling up Farris' sleeve, and Farris could not resist. "I'm sorry to do this to you and Lys. But you *would* interfere. And this is the only way I can keep you from bringing me back."

Farris felt the sting of the needle. He felt nothing more, before drugged unconsciousness claimed him.

CHAPTER 4

INCREDIBLE WORLD

Farris awoke, and for a dazed moment wondered what it was that so bewildered him. Then he realized.

It was the daylight. It came and went, every few minutes. There was the darkness of night in the bedroom, and then a sudden burst of dawn, a little period of brilliant sunlight, and then night again.

It came and went, as he watched numbly, like the slow, steady beating of a great pulse—a systole and diastole of light and darkness.

Days shortened to minutes? But how could that be? And then, as he awakened fully, he remembered.

"*Hunati!* He injected the chlorophyll drug into my bloodstream!"

Yes. He was *hunati*, now. Living at a tempo a hundred times slower than normal.

And that was why day and night seemed a hundred times faster than normal, to him. He had, already, lived through several days!

Farris stumbled to his feet. As he did so, he knocked his pipe from the arm of the chair.

It did not fall to the floor. It just disappeared instantly, and the next instant was lying on the floor.

"It fell. But it fell so fast I couldn't see it."

Farris felt his brain reel to the impact of the unearthly. He found that he was trembling violently.

He fought to get a grip on himself. This wasn't witchcraft. It was a secret and devilish science, but it wasn't supernatural.

He, himself, felt as normal as ever. It was his surroundings, the swift rush of day and night especially, that alone told him he was changed.

He heard a scream, and stumbled out to the living-room of the bungalow. Lys came running toward him.

She still wore her jacket and slacks, having obviously been too worried about her brother to retire completely. And there was terror in her face.

"What's happened?" she cried. "The light—"

He took her by the shoulders. "Lys, don't lose your nerve. What's happened is that we're *hunati* now. Your brother did it—drugged us at dinner, then injected the chlorophyll compound into us."

"But why?" she cried.

"Don't you see? He was going *hunati* himself again, going back up to the forest. And we could easily overtake and bring him back, if we remained normal. So he changed us too, to prevent that."

Farris went into Berreau's room. It was as he had expected. The Frenchman was gone.

"I'll go after him," he said tightly. "He's got to come back, for he may have an antidote to that hellish stuff. You wait here."

Lys clung to him. "No! I'd go mad, here by myself, like this."

She was, he saw, on the brink of hysterics. He didn't wonder. The slow, pulsing beat of day and night alone was enough to unseat one's reason.

He acceded. "All right. But wait till I get something."

He went back to Berreau's room and took a big bolo-knife he had seen leaning in a corner. Then he saw something else, something glittering in the pulsing light, on the botanist's laboratory-table.

Farris stuffed that into his pocket. If force couldn't bring Berreau back, the threat of this other thing might influence him.

He and Lys hurried out onto the veranda and down the steps. And then they stopped, appalled.

The great forest that loomed before them was now a nightmare sight. It seethed and stirred with unearthly life—great branches clawing and whipping at each other as they fought for the light,

vines writhing through them at incredible speed, a rustling uproar of tossing, living plant-life.

Lys shrank back. "The forest is *alive* now!"

"It's just the same as always," Farris reassured. "It's we who
have changed—who are living so slowly now that the plants
seem to live faster."

"And Andre is out in that!" Lys shuddered. Then courage
came back into her pale face. "But I'm not afraid."

They started up through the forest toward the plateau of giant
trees. And now there was an awful unreality about this incredible
world.

Farris felt no difference in himself. There was no sensation of
slowing down. His own motions and perceptions appeared normal.
It was simply that all around him the vegetation had now a
savage motility that was animal in its swiftness.

Grasses sprang up beneath his feet, tiny green spears climbing
toward the light. Buds swelled, burst, spread their bright petals
on the air, breathed out their fragrance—and died.

New leaves leaped joyously up from every twig, lived out
their brief and vital moment, withered and fell. The forest was a
constantly shifting kaleidoscope of colors, from pale green to
yellowed brown, that rippled as the swift tides of growth and
death washed over it.

But it was not peaceful nor serene, that life of the forest.
Before, it had seemed to Farris that the plants of the earth existed
in a placid inertia utterly different from the beasts, who must
constantly hunt or be hunted. Now he saw how mistaken he had
been.

Close by, a tropical nettle crawled up beside a giant fern.
Octopus-like, its tendrils flashed around and through the plant.
The fern writhed. Its fronds tossed wildly, its stalks strove to be
free. But the stinging death conquered it.

Lianas crawled like great serpents among the trees, encircling
the trunks, twining themselves swiftly along the branches, striking their hungry parasitic roots into the living bark.

And the trees fought them. Farris could see how the branches
lashed and struck against the killer vines. It was like watching a
man struggle against the crushing coils of the python.

Very likely. Because the trees, the plants, knew. In their own
strange, alien fashion, they were as sentient as their swifter
brothers.

Hunter and hunted. The strangling lianas, the deadly, beautiful
orchid that was like a cancer eating a healthy trunk, the leprous,

crawling fungi—they were the wolves and the jackals of this leafy world.

Even among the trees, Farris saw, existence was a grim and never-ending struggle. Silk-cotton and bamboo and ficus trees—they too knew pain and fear and the dread of death.

He could hear them. Now, with his aural nerves slowed to an incredible receptivity, he heard the voice of the forest, the true voice that had nothing to do with the familiar sounds of wind in the branches.

The primal voice of birth and death that spoke before ever man appeared on Earth, and would continue to speak after he was gone.

At first he had been conscious only of that vast, rustling uproar. Now he could distinguish separate sounds—the thin screams of grass blades and bamboo-shoots thrusting and surging out of the earth, the lash and groan of enmeshed and dying branches, the laughter of young leaves high in the sky, the stealthy whisper of the coiling vines.

And almost, he could hear thoughts, speaking in his mind. The age-old thoughts of the trees.

Farris felt a freezing dread. He did not want to listen to the thoughts of the trees.

And the slow, steady pulsing of darkness and light went on. Days and nights, rushing with terrible speed over the *hunati*.

Lys, stumbling along the trail beside him, uttered a little cry of terror. A snaky black vine had darted out of the bush at her with cobra swiftness, looping swiftly to encircle her body.

Farris swung his bolo, slashed through the vine. But it struck out again, growing with that appalling speed, its tip groping for him.

He slashed again with sick horror, and pulled the girl onward, on up the side of the plateau.

"I am afraid!" she gasped. "I can hear the thoughts—the thoughts of the forest!"

"It's your own imagination!" he told her. "Don't listen!"

But he too could hear them! Very faintly, like sounds just below the threshold of hearing. It seemed to him that every minute—or every minute-long day—he was able to get more clearly the telepathic impulses of these organisms that lived an undreamed-of life of their own, side by side with man, yet forever barred from him, except when man was *hunati*.

It seemed to him that the temper of the forest had changed, that his slaying of the vine had made it aware of them. Like a crowd aroused to anger, the massed trees around them grew wrathful. A tossing and moaning rose among them.

Branches struck at Farris and the girl, lianas groped with blind heads and snakelike grace toward them. Brush and bramble clawed them spitefully, reaching out thorny arms to rake their flesh. The slender saplings lashed them like leafy whips, the swift-growing bamboo spears sought to block their path, canes clattering together as if in rage.

"It's only in our own minds!" he said to the girl. "Because the forest is living at the same rate as we, we imagine it's aware of us."

He had to believe that, he knew. He had to, because when he quit believing it there was only black madness.

"No!" cried Lys. "No! The forest knows we are here."

Panic fear threatened Farris' self-control, as the mad uproar of the forest increased. He ran, dragging the girl with him, sheltering her with his body from the lashing of the raging forest.

They ran on, deeper into the mighty grove upon the plateau, under the pulsing rush of day and darkness. And now the trees about them were brawling giants, great silk-cotton and ficus that struck crashing blows at each other as their branches fought for clear sky—contending and terrible leafy giants beneath which the two humans were pigmies.

But the lesser forest beneath them still tossed and surged with wrath, still plucked and tore at the two running humans. And still, and clearer, stronger, Farris' reeling mind caught the dim impact of unguessable telepathic impulses.

Then, drowning all those dim and raging thoughts, came vast and dominating impulses of greater majesty, thought-voices deep and strong and alien as the voice of primal Earth.

"Stop them!" they seemed to echo in Farris' mind. "Stop them! Slay them! For they are our enemies!"

Lys uttered a trembling cry. "Andre!"

Farris saw him, then. Saw Berreau ahead, standing in the shadow of the monster banyans there. His arms were upraised toward those looming colossi, as though in worship. Over him towered the leafy giants, dominating all the forest.

"Stop them! Slay them!"

They thundered, now, those majestic thought-voices that Farris' mind could barely hear. He was closer to them—closer—

He knew, then, even though his mind refused to admit the knowledge. Knew whence those mighty voices came, and why Berreau worshipped the banyans.

And surely they were godlike, these green colossi who had

lived for ages, whose arms reached skyward and whose aerial roots drooped and stirred and groped like hundreds of hands!

Farris forced that thought violently away. He was a man, of the world of men, and he must not worship alien lords.

Berreau had turned toward them. The man's eyes were hot and raging, and Farris knew even before Berreau spoke that he was no longer altogether sane.

"Go, both of you!" he ordered. "You were fools, to come here after me! You killed as you came through the forest, and the forest knows!"

"Berreau, listen!" Farris appealed. "You've got to go back with us, forget this madness!"

Berreau laughed shrilly. "Is it madness that the Lords even now voice their wrath against you? You hear it in your mind, but you are afraid to listen! Be afraid, Farris! There is reason! You have slain trees, for many years, as you have just slain here— and the forest knows you for a foe."

"Andre!" Lys was sobbing, her face half-buried in her hands.

Farris felt his mind cracking under the impact of the crazy scene. The ceaseless, rushing pulse of light and darkness, the rustling uproar of the seething forest around them, the vines creeping snakelike and branches whipping at them and giant banyans rocking angrily overhead.

"*This* is the world that man lives in all his life, and never sees or senses!" Berreau was shouting. "I've come into it, again and again. And each time, I've heard more clearly the voices of the Great Ones!

"The oldest and mightiest creatures on our planet! Long ago, men knew that and worshipped them for the wisdom they could teach. Yes, worshipped them as Ygdrasil and the Druid Oak and the Sacred Tree! But modern men have forgotten this other Earth. Except me, Farris—except me! I've found wisdom in this world such as you never dreamed. And your stupid blindness is not going to drag me out of it!"

Farris realized then that it was too late to reason with Berreau. The man had come too often and too far into this other Earth that was as alien to humanity as thought it lay across the universe.

It was because he had feared that, that he had brought the little thing in his jacket pocket. The one thing with which he might force Berreau to obey.

Farris took it out of his pocket. He held it up so that the other could see it.

"You know what it is, Berreau! And you know what I can do with it, if you force me to!"

Wild dread leaped into Berreau's eyes as he recognized that glittering little vial from his own laboratory.

"The Burmese Blight! You wouldn't, Farris! You wouldn't turn that loose *here!*"

"I will!" Farris said hoarsely. "I will, unless you come out of here with us, now!"

Raging hate and fear were in Berreau's eyes as he stared at that innocent corked glass vial of gray-green dust.

He said thickly, "For this, I will kill!"

Lys screamed. Black lianas had crept upon her as she stood with her face hidden in her hands. They had writhed around her legs like twining serpents, they were pulling her down.

The forest seemed to roar with triumph. Vine and branch and bramble and creeper surged toward them. Dimly thunderous throbbed the strange telepathic voices.

"Slay them!" said the trees.

Farris leaped into that coiling mass of vines, his bolo slashing. He cut loose the twining lianas that held the girl, sliced fiercely at the branches that whipped wildly at them.

Then, from behind, Berreau's savage blow on his elbow knocked the bolo from his hand.

"I told you not to kill, Farris! I told you!"

"Slay them!" pulsed the alien thought.

Berreau spoke, his eyes not leaving Farris. "Run, Lys. Leave the forest. This—murderer must die."

He lunged as he spoke, and there was death in his white face and clutching hands.

Farris was knocked back, against one of the giant banyan trunks. They rolled, grappling. And already the vines were sliding around them—looping and enmeshing them, tightening upon them!

It was then that the forest shrieked.

A cry telepathic and auditory at the same time—and dreadful. An utterance of alien agony beyond anything human.

Berreau's hands fell away from Farris. The Frenchman, enmeshed with him by the coiling vines, looked up in horror.

Then Farris saw what had happened. The little vial, the vial of the blight, had smashed against the banyan trunk as Berreau charged.

And that little splash of gray-green mould was rushing through the forest faster than flame! The blight, the gray-green killer from far away, propagating itself with appalling rapidity! *"Dieu!"* screamed Berreau. *"Non—non—"*

Even normally, a blight seems to spread swiftly. And to Farris and the other two, slowed down as they were, this blight was a raging cold fire of death.

It flashed up trunks and limbs and aerial roots of the majestic banyans, eating leaf and spore and bud. It ran triumphantly across the ground, over vine and grass and shrub, bursting up other trees, leaping along the airy bridges of lianas.

And it leaped among the vines that enmeshed the two men! In mad death-agonies the creepers writhed and tightened.

Farris felt the musty mould in his mouth and nostrils, felt the construction as of steel cables crushing the life from him. The world seemed to darken—

Then a steel blade hissed and flashed, and the pressure loosened. Lys' voice was in his ears, Lys' hand trying to drag him from the dying, tightening creepers that she had partly slashed through. He wrenched free. "My brother!" she gasped.

With the bolo he sliced clumsily through the mass of dying writhing snake-vines that still enmeshed Berreau.

Berreau's face appeared, as he tore away the slashed creepers. It was dark purple, rigid, his eyes staring and dead. The tightening vines had caught him around the throat, strangling him.

Lys knelt beside him, crying wildly. But Farris dragged her to her feet.

"We have to get out of here! He's dead—but I'll carry his body!"

"No, leave it," she sobbed. "Leave it here, in the forest."

Dead eyes, looking up at the death of the alien world of life into which he had now crossed, forever! Yes, it was fitting.

Farris' heart quailed as he stumbled away with Lys through the forest that was rocking and raging in its death-throes.

Far away around them, the gray-green death was leaping on. And fainter, fainter, came the strange telepathic cries that he would never be sure he had really heard.

"We die, brothers! We die!"

And then, when it seemed to Farris that sanity must give way beneath the weight of alien agony, there came a sudden change.

The pulsing rush of alternate day and night lengthened in tempo. Each period of light and darkness was longer now, and longer—

Out of a period of dizzying semi-consciousness, Farris came

back to awareness. They were standing unsteadily in the blighted forest, in bright sunlight.

And they were no longer *hunati*.

The chlorophyll drug had spent its force in their bodies, and they had come back to the normal tempo of human life.

Lys looked up dazedly, at the forest that now seemed static, peaceful, immobile—and in which the gray-green blight now crept so slowly they could not see it move.

"The same forest, and it's still writhing in death!" Farris said huskily. "But now that we're living at normal speed again, we can't see it!"

"Please, let us go!" choked the girl. "Away from here, at once!"

It took but an hour to return to the bungalow and pack what they could carry, before they took the trail toward the Mekong.

Sunset saw them out of the blighted area of the forest, well on their way toward the river.

"Will it kill all the forest?" whispered the girl.

"No. The forest will fight back, come back, conquer the blight, in time. A long time, by our reckoning—years, decades. But to *them,* that fierce struggle is raging on even now."

And as they walked on, it seemed to Farris that still in his mind there pulsed faintly from far behind that alien, throbbing cry.

"We die, brothers!"

He did not look back. But he knew that he would not come back to this or any other forest, and that his profession was ended, and that he would never kill a tree again.

HISTORY LESSON

by Arthur C. Clarke (1917–   )

Startling Stories, May

Trivia contests have become quite popular at science fiction conventions large and small. Sf fans pride themselves on their knowledge of the field and don't hesitate to engage in determined contests to show off their ability to retrieve information. One exciting category of question involves identifying the author and title of a work based on the opening sentence; more rarely, closing lines are used in a similar fashion. "History Lesson" contains one of the most famous closing lines in science fiction—but if you are approaching the story for the first time, don't you dare take a peek!

Arthur C. Clarke's "The Forgotten Enemy" (New Worlds, England, May) just missed inclusion in this volume.—M.H.G.

(During the New York World's Fair of 1939, a "time capsule" was buried and the plan was to have it dug up five thousand years later so that our long-distant descendants could see what life was like in the United States in the 20th Century. For that reason, a wide variety of objects were included, all sealed under an inert atmosphere to preserve them, as far as possible, from deterioration.

Among the objects included was a copy of Amazing Stories so that our descendants might be amused by our primitive science fictional speculations. —And I was devastated. The issue they included was that of February, 1939. Had they waited one more month for the March, 1939 issue they would have had the one with my first published story. By that much did I miss immortality! (Or at least so it seemed to me at the time, since I had no way of knowing then that I would become

so prolific that I might survive—for some time, at least—
without the help of a time capsule.)

But that is personal and unimportant. What do we have left
over to tell us about daily life in ancient Sumeria, Egypt, or
Rome? What trivia just happens to survive? What laundry
bills? What letters written home by students in need of money?

In "History Lesson," Arthur Clarke tackles that subject for
Earth as a whole.—I.A.)

No one could remember when the tribe had begun its long
journey. The land of great rolling plains that had been its first
home was now no more than a half-forgotten dream.

For many years Shann and his people had been fleeing through
a country of low hills and sparkling lakes, and now the mountains lay ahead. This summer they must cross them to the
southern lands. There was little time to lose. The white terror
that had come down from the Poles, grinding continents to dust
and freezing the very air before it, was less than a day's march
behind.

Shann wondered if the glaciers could climb the mountains
ahead, and within his heart he dared to kindle a little flame of
hope. This might prove a barrier against which even the remorse-
less ice would batter in vain. In the southern lands of which the
legends spoke, his people might find refuge at last.

It took weeks to discover a pass through which the tribe and
the animals could travel. When midsummer came, they had
camped in a lonely valley where the air was thin and the stars
shone with a brilliance no one had ever seen before.

The summer was waning when Shann took his two sons and
went ahead to explore the way. For three days they climbed, and
for three nights slept as best they could on the freezing rocks.
And on the fourth morning there was nothing ahead but a gentle
rise to a cairn of gray stones built by other travelers, centuries
ago.

Shann felt himself trembling, and not with cold, as they
walked toward the little pyramid of stones. His sons had fallen
behind. No one spoke, for too much was at stake. In a little
while they would know if all their hopes had been betrayed.

To east and west, the wall of mountains curved away as if
embracing the land beneath. Below lay endless miles of undulat-
ing plain, with a great river swinging across it in tremendous
loops. It was a fertile land, one in which the tribe could raise

crops knowing that there would be no need to flee before the harvest came.

Then Shann lifted his eyes to the south, and saw the doom of all his hopes. For there at the edge of the world glimmered that deadly light he had seen so often to the north—the glint of ice below the horizon.

There was no way forward. Through all the years of flight, the glaciers from the south had been advancing to meet them. Soon they would be crushed beneath the moving walls of ice. . . .

Southern glaciers did not reach the mountains until a generation later. In the last summer the sons of Shann carried the sacred treasures of the tribe to the lonely cairn overlooking the plain. The ice that had once gleamed below the horizon was now almost at their feet. By spring it would be splintering against the mountain walls.

No one understood the treasures now. They were from a past too distant for the understanding of any man alive. Their origins were lost in the mists that surrounded the Golden Age, and how they had come at last into the possession of this wandering tribe was a story that now would never be told. For it was the story of a civilization that had passed beyond recall.

Once, all these pitiful relics had been treasured for some good reason and now they had become sacred though their meaning had long been lost. The print in the old books had faded centuries ago though much of the lettering was still visible—if there had been any to read it. But many generations had passed since anyone had had a use for a set of seven-figure logarithms, an atlas of the world, and the score of Sibelius' Seventh Symphony, printed, according to the flyleaf, by H. K. Chu and Sons. At the City of Pekin in the year A.D. 2371.

The old books were placed reverently in the little crypt that had been made to receive them. There followed a motley collection of fragments—gold and platinum coins, a broken telephoto lens, a watch, a cold-light lamp, a microphone, the cutter from an electric shaver, some midget radio tubes, the flotsam that had been left behind when the great tide of civilization had ebbed forever.

All these treasures were carefully stowed away in their resting place. Then came three more relics, the most sacred of all because the least understood.

The first was a strangely shaped piece of metal, showing the coloration of intense heat. It was, in its way, the most pathetic of all these symbols from the past, for it told of man's greatest achievement and of the future he might have known. The mahogany stand on which it was mounted bore a silver plate with the inscription:

Auxiliary igniter from Starboard Jet
Spaceship *Morning Star*
Earth-Moon, A.D. 1985

Next followed another miracle of the ancient science—a sphere of transparent plastic with strangely shaped pieces of metal embedded in it. At its center was a tiny capsule of synthetic radio-element, surrounded by the converting screens that shifted its radiation far down the spectrum. As long as the material remained active, the sphere would be a tiny radio transmitter, broadcasting power in all directions. Only a few of these spheres had ever been made. They had been designed as perpetual beacons to mark the orbits of the asteroids. But man had never reached the asteroids and the beacons had never been used.

Last of all was a flat, circular tin, wide in comparison with its depth. It was heavily sealed, and rattled when shaken. The tribal lore predicted that disaster would follow if it were ever opened, and no one knew that it held one of the great works of art of nearly a thousand years before.

The work was finished. The two men rolled the stones back into place and slowly began to descend the mountainside. Even to the last, man had given some thought to the future and had tried to preserve something for posterity.

That winter the great waves of ice began their first assault on the mountains, attacking from north and south. The foothills were overwhelmed in the first onslaught, and the glaciers ground them into dust. But the mountains stood firm, and when the summer came the ice retreated for a while.

So, winter after winter, the battle continued, and the roar of the avalanches, the grinding of rock and the explosions of splintering ice filled the air with tumult. No war of man's had been fiercer than this, and even man's battles had not quite engulfed the globe as this had done.

At last the tidal waves of ice began to subside and to creep slowly down the flanks of the mountains they had never quite subdued. The valleys and passes were still firmly in their grip. It was stalemate. The glaciers had met their match, but their defeat was too late to be of any use to Man.

So the centuries passed, and presently there happened something that must occur once at least in the history of every world in the universe, no matter how remote and lonely it may be.

The ship from Venus came five thousand years too late, but its crew knew nothing of this. While still many millions of miles away, the telescopes had seen the great shroud of ice that made Earth the most brilliant object in the sky next to the sun itself.

Here and there the dazzling sheet was marred by black specks that revealed the presence of almost buried mountains. That was all. The rolling oceans, the plains and forests, the deserts and lakes—all that had been the world of Man was sealed beneath the ice, perhaps forever.

The ship closed in to Earth and established an orbit less than a thousand miles away. For five days it circled the planet, while cameras recorded all that was left to see and a hundred instruments gathered information that would give the Venusian scientists many years of work.

An actual landing was not intended. There seemed little purpose in it. But on the sixth day the picture changed. A panoramic monitor, driven to the limit of its amplification, detected the dying radiation of the five-thousand-year-old beacon. Through all the centuries, it had been sending out its signals with ever-failing strength as its radioactive heart steadily weakened.

The monitor locked on the beacon frequency. In the control room, a bell clamored for attention. A little later, the Venusian ship broke free from its orbit and slanted down toward Earth, toward a range of mountains that still towered proudly above the ice, and to a cairn of gray stones that the years had scarcely touched. . . .

The great disc of the Sun blazed fiercely in a sky no longer veiled with mist, for the clouds that had once hidden Venus had now completely gone. Whatever force had caused the change in the Sun's radiation had doomed one civilization, but had given birth to another. Less than five thousand years before, the half-savage people of Venus had seen Sun and stars for the first time. Just as the science of Earth had begun with astronomy, so had that of Venus, and on the warm, rich world that man had never seen progress had been incredibly rapid.

Perhaps the Venusians had been lucky. They never knew the Dark Ages that held Man enchained for a thousand years. They missed the long detour into chemistry and mechanics but came at once to the more fundamental laws of radiation physics. In the time that man had taken to progress from the Pyramids to the rocket-propelled spaceship, the Venusians had passed from the discovery of agriculture to antigravity itself—the ultimate secret that Man had never learned.

The warm ocean that still bore most of the young planet's life rolled its breakers languidly against the sandy shore. So new was this continent that the very sands were coarse and gritty. There had not yet been time enough for the sea to wear them smooth.

The scientists lay half in the water, their beautiful reptilian bodies gleaming in the sunlight. The greatest minds of Venus had gathered on this shore from all the islands of the planet. What they were going to hear they did not yet know, except that it concerned the Third World and the mysterious race that had peopled it before the coming of the ice.

The Historian was standing on the land, for the instruments he wished to use had no love of water. By his side was a large machine which attracted many curious glances from his colleagues. It was clearly concerned with optics, for a lens system projected from it toward a screen of white material a dozen yards away.

The Historian began to speak. Briefly he recapitulated what little had been discovered concerning the third planet and its people.

He mentioned the centuries of fruitless research that had failed to interpret a single word of the writings of Earth. The planet had been inhabited by a race of great technical ability. That, at least, was proved by the few pieces of machinery that had been found in the cairn upon the mountain.

"We do not know why so advanced a civilization came to an end," he observed. "Almost certainly, it had sufficient knowledge to survive an Ice Age. There must have been some factor of which we know nothing. Possibly disease or racial degeneration may have been responsible. It has even been suggested that the tribal conflicts endemic to our own species in prehistoric times may have continued on the third planet after the coming of technology.

"Some philosophers maintain that knowledge of machinery does not necessarily imply a high degree of civilization, and it is theoretically possible to have wars in a society possessing mechanical power, flight, and even radio. Such a conception is alien to our thoughts, but we must admit its possibility. It would certainly account for the downfall of the lost race.

"It has always been assumed that we should never know anything of the physical form of the creatures who lived in Planet Three. For centuries our artists have been depicting scenes from the history of the dead world, peopling it with all manner

of fantastic beings. Most of the creations have resembled us
more or less closely, though it has often been pointed out that
because *we* are reptiles it does not follow that all intelligent life
must necessarily be reptilian.

"We now know the answer to one of the most baffling
problems of history. At last, after a hundred years of research,
we have discovered the exact form and nature of the ruling life
on the Third Planet."

There was a murmur of astonishment from the assembled
scientists. Some were so taken aback that they disappeared for a
while into the comfort of the ocean, as all Venusians were apt to
do in moments of stress. The Historian waited until his colleagues reemerged into the element they so disliked. He himself
was quite comfortable, thanks to the tiny sprays that were continually playing over his body. With their help he could live on
land for many hours before having to return to the ocean.

The excitement slowly subsided and the lecturer continued:

"One of the most puzzling of the objects found on Planet
Three was a flat metal container holding a great length of
transparent plastic material, perforated at the edges and wound
tightly into a spool. This transparent tape at first seemed quite
featureless, but an examination with the new subelectronic micro-
scope has shown that this is not the case. Along the surface of
the material, invisible to our eyes but perfectly clear under the
correct radiation, are literally thousands of tiny pictures. It is
believed that they were imprinted on the material by some
chemical means, and have faded with the passage of time.

"These pictures apparently form a record of life as it was on
the Third Planet at the height of its civilization. They are not
independent. Consecutive pictures are almost identical, differing
only in the detail of movement. The purpose of such a record is
obvious. It is only necessary to project the scenes in rapid
succession to give an illusion of continuous movement. We have
made a machine to do this, and I have here an exact reproduction
of the picture sequence.

"The scenes you are now going to witness take us back many
thousands of years, to the great days of our sister planet. They
show a complex civilization, many of whose activities we can
only dimly understand. Life seems to have been very violent and
energetic, and much that you will see is quite baffling.

"It is clear that the Third Planet was inhabited by a number of
different species, none of them reptilian. That is a blow to our
pride, but the conclusion is inescapable. The dominant type of
life appears to have been a two-armed biped. It walked upright

and covered its body with some flexible material, possibly for protection against the cold, since even before the Ice Age the planet was at a much lower temperature than our own world. But I will not try your patience any further. You will now see the record of which I have been speaking."

A brilliant light flashed from the projector. There was a gentle whirring, and on the screen appeared hundreds of strange beings moving rather jerkily to and fro. The picture expanded to embrace one of the creatures, and the scientists could see that the Historian's description had been correct.

The creature possessed two eyes, set rather close together, but the other facial adornaments were a little obscure. There was a large orifice in the lower portion of the head that was continually opening and closing. Possibly it had something to do with the creature's breathing.

The scientists watched spellbound as the strange being became involved in a series of fantastic adventures. There was an incredibly violent conflict with another, slightly different creature. It seemed certain that they must both be killed, but when it was all over neither seemed any the worse.

Then came a furious drive over miles of country in a four-wheeled mechanical device which was capable of extraordinary feats of locomotion. The ride ended in a city packed with other vehicles moving in all directions at breathtaking speeds. No one was surprised to see two of the machines meet head on with devastating results.

After that, events became even more complicated. It was now quite obvious that it would take many years of research to analyze and understand all that was happening. It was also clear that the record was a work of art, somewhat stylized, rather than an exact reproduction of life as it actually had been on the Third Planet.

Most of the scientists felt themselves completely dazed when the sequence of pictures came to an end. There was a final flurry of motion, in which the creature that had been the center of interest became involved in some tremendous but incomprehensible catastrophe. The picture contracted to a circle, centered on the creature's head.

The last scene of all was an expanded view of its face, obviously expressing some powerful emotion. But whether it was rage, grief, defiance, resignation or some other feeling could not be guessed. The picture vanished. For a moment some lettering appeared on the screen, then it was all over.

For several minutes there was complete silence, save the

lapping of the waves upon the sand. The scientists were too stunned to speak. The fleeting glimpse of Earth's civilization had had a shattering effect on their minds. Then little groups began to start talking together, first in whispers and then more and more loudly as the implications of what they had seen became clearer. Presently the Historian called for attention and addressed the meeting again.

"We are now planning," he said, "a vast program of research to extract all available knowledge from this record. Thousands of copies are being made for distribution to all workers. You will appreciate the problems involved. The psychologists in particular have an immense task confronting them.

"But I do not doubt that we shall succeed. In another generation, who can say what we many not have learned of this wonderful race? Before we leave, let us look again at our remote cousins, whose wisdom may have surpassed our own but of whom so little has survived."

Once more the final picture flashed on the screen, motionless this time, for the projector had been stopped. With something like awe, the scientists gazed at the still figure from the past, while in turn the little biped stared back at them with its characteristic expression of arrogant bad temper.

For the rest of time it would symbolize the human race. The psychologists of Venus would analyze its actions and watch its every movement until they could reconstruct its mind. Thousands of books would be written about it. Intricate philosophies would be contrived to account for its behavior.

But all this labor, all this research, would be utterly in vain. Perhaps the proud and lonely figure on the screen was smiling sardonically at the scientists who were starting on their agelong fruitless quest.

Its secret would be safe as long as the universe endured, for no one now would ever read the lost language of Earth. Millions of times in the ages to come those last few words would flash across the screen, and none could ever guess their meaning:

A Walt Disney Production.

ETERNITY LOST

by Clifford D. Simak (1904–   )

Astounding Science Fiction, **July**

As Isaac points out, this fine story is about immortality, one of the most important themes in modern science fiction. However, it is also about personal and political corruption, which in modern science fiction is a common assumption, if not a theme. The corruptibility of human beings in positions of power in sf stories is the rule, not the exception, and directly parallels attitudes in American society, which views politicians with great distrust, ranking them last out of twenty occupational types in a recent poll (used car salesman was nineteenth). However, it should be pointed out that these attitudes are almost universal across human cultures.

We have discussed the impressive career of Clifford D. Simak in earlier volumes of this series, but for the record let it be stated again that he has been working productively in this field for some fifty-five years, and is still near the top of his form.—M.H.G.

(Immortality is the oldest dream of human beings. Death is the ultimate outrage; the ultimate disappointment. Why should people die?

Surely, that was not the original plan. Human beings were meant to live forever and it was only through some small miscalculation or misstep that death entered the world. In Gilgamesh, *the oldest surviving epic in the world, Gilgamesh searched for immortality and attained it and then lost it when, while he was asleep, a snake filched the plant that contained the secret.*

In the story of Adam and Eve, with which the Bible begins, Adam and Eve had immortality, until a snake— But you know that one.

And even today, so many people, so many people [even that supreme rationalist, Martin Gardner, to my astonishment] can't accept death but believe that something about us must remain eternal. Personally, I don't know why. Considering how few people find any happiness in this wonderful world of ours, why should human beings, generally, feel anything but relief at the thought that life is only temporary?

Science fiction writers sometimes play with the possibility of physical immortality attained through technological advance, but you can't cheat drama. The excitement comes, as with Gilgamesh and Adam, with the chance that immortality may be lost, as in "Eternity Lost," by Clifford D. Simak.—I.A.)

Mr. Reeves: *The situation, as I see it, calls for well defined safeguards which would prevent continuation of life from falling under the patronage of political parties or other groups in power.*

Chairman Leonard: *You mean you are afraid it might become a political football?*

Mr. Reeves: *Not only that, sir, I am afraid that political parties might use it to continue beyond normal usefulness the lives of certain so-called elder statesmen who are needed by the party to maintain prestige and dignity in the public eye.*

From the Records of a hearing before the science subcommittee of the public policy committee of the World House of Representatives.

Senator Homer Leonard's visitors had something on their minds. They fidgeted mentally as they sat in the senator's office and drank the senator's good whiskey. They talked, quite importantly, as was their wont, but they talked around the thing they had come to say. They circled it like a hound dog circling a coon, waiting for an opening, circling the subject to catch an opportunity that might make the message sound just a bit offhanded—as if they had just thought of it in passing and had not called purposely on the senator to say it.

It was queer, the senator told himself. For he had known these two for a good while now. And they had known him equally as long. There should be nothing they should hesitate to tell him.

They had, in the past, been brutally frank about many things in his political career.

It might be, he thought, more bad news from North America, but he was as well acquainted with that bad news as they. After all, he told himself philosophically, a man cannot reasonably expect to stay in office forever. The voters, from sheer boredom if nothing else, would finally reach the day when they would vote against a man who had served them faithfully and well. And the senator was candid enough to admit, at least to himself, that there had been times when he had served the voters of North America neither faithfully nor well.

Even at that, he thought, he had not been beaten yet. It was still several months until election time and there was a trick or two that he had never tried, political dodges that even at this late date might save the senatorial hide. Given the proper time and the proper place and he would win out yet. Timing, he told himself—proper timing is the thing that counts.

He sat quietly in his chair, a great hulk of a man, and for a single instant he closed his eyes to shut out the room and the sunlight in the window. Timing, he thought. Yes, timing and a feeling for the public, a finger on the public pulse, the ability to know ahead of time what the voter eventually will come to think—those were the ingredients of good strategy. To know ahead of time, to be ahead in thinking, so that in a week or a month or year, the voters would say to one another: "You know, Bill, old Senator Leonard had it right. Remember what he said last week—or month or year—over there in Geneva. Yes, sir, he laid it on the line. There ain't much that gets past that old fox of a Leonard."

He opened his eyes a slit, keeping them still half closed so his visitors might think he'd only had them half closed all the time. For it was impolite and a political mistake to close one's eyes when one had visitors. They might get the idea one wasn't interested. Or they might seize the opportunity to cut one's throat.

It's because I'm getting old again, the senator told himself. Getting old and drowsy. But just as smart as ever. Yes, sir, said the senator, talking to himself, just as smart and slippery as I ever was.

He saw by the tight expressions on the faces of the two that they finally were set to tell him the thing they had come to tell. All their circling and sniffing had been of no avail. Now they had to come out with it, on the line, cold turkey.

"There has been a certain matter," said Alexander Gibbs,

"which has been quite a problem for the party for a long time now. We had hoped that matters would so arrange themselves that we wouldn't need to call it to your attention, senator. But the executive committee held a meeting in New York the other night and it seemed to be the consensus that we communicate it to you."

It's bad, thought the senator, even worse than I thought it might be—for Gibbs is talking in his best double-crossing manner.

The senator gave them no help. He sat quietly in his chair and held the whiskey glass in a steady hand and did not ask what it was all about, acting as if he didn't really care.

Gibbs floundered slightly. "It's a rather personal matter, senator," he said.

"It's this life continuation business," blurted Andrew Scott.

They sat in shocked silence, all three of them, for Scott should not have said it in that way. In politics, one is not blunt and forthright, but devious and slick.

"I see," the senator said finally. "The party thinks the voters would like it better if I were a normal man who would die a normal death."

Gibbs smoothed his face of shocked surprise.

"The common people resent men living beyond their normal time," he said. "Especially—"

"Especially," said the senator, "those who have done nothing to deserve it."

"I wouldn't put it exactly that way," Gibbs protested.

"Perhaps not," said the senator. "But no matter how you say it, that is what you mean."

They sat uncomfortably in the office chairs, with the bright Geneva sunlight pouring through the windows.

"I presume," said the senator, "that the party, having found I am no longer an outstanding asset, will not renew my application for life continuation. I suppose that is what you were sent to tell me."

Might as well get it over with, he told himself grimly. Now that it's out in the open, there's no sense in beating around the bush.

"That's just about it, senator," said Scott.

"That's exactly it," said Gibbs.

The senator heaved his great body from the chair, picked up the whiskey bottle, filled their glasses and his own.

"You delivered the death sentence very deftly," he told them. "It deserves a drink."

He wondered what they had thought that he would do. Plead

with them, perhaps. Or storm around the office. Or denounce the party.

Puppets, he thought. Errand boys. Poor, scared errand boys.

They drank, their eyes on him, and silent laughter shook inside him from knowing that the liquor tasted very bitter in their mouths.

Chairman Leonard: *You are agreed then, Mr. Chapman, with the other witnesses, that no person should be allowed to seek continuation of life for himself, that it should be granted only upon application by someone else, that—*

Mr. Chapman: *It should be a gift of society to those persons who are in the unique position of being able to materially benefit the human race.*

Chairman Leonard: *That is very aptly stated, sir.*

From the Records of a hearing before the science subcommittee of the public policy committee of the World House of Representatives.

The senator settled himself carefully and comfortably into a chair in the reception room of the Life Continuation Institute and unfolded his copy of the *North American Tribune*.

Column one said that system trade was normal, according to a report by the World Secretary of Commerce. The story went on at length to quote the secretary's report. Column two was headed by an impish box that said a new life form may have been found on Mars, but since the discoverer was a spaceman who had been more than ordinarily drunk, the report was being viewed with some skepticism. Under the box was a story reporting a list of boy and girl health champions selected by the state of Finland to be entered later in the year in the world health contest. The story in column three gave the latest information on the unstable love life of the world's richest woman.

Column four asked a question:

WHAT HAPPENED TO DR. CARSON:
NO RECORD OF REPORTED DEATH

The story, the senator saw, was by-lined Anson Lee and the senator chuckled dryly. Lee was up to something. He was always up to something, always ferreting out some fact that eventually was sure to prove embarrassing to someone. Smart as a steel trap, that Lee, but a bad man to get into one's hair.

There had been, for example, that matter of the spaceship contract.

Anson Lee, said the senator underneath his breath, is a pest. Nothing but a pest.

But Dr. Carson? Who was Dr. Carson?

The senator played a little mental game with himself, trying to remember, trying to identify the name before he read the story.

Dr. Carson?

Why, said the senator, I remember now. Long time ago. A biochemist or something of the sort. A very brilliant man. Did something with colonies of soil bacteria, breeding the things for therapeutic work.

Yes, said the senator, a very brilliant man. I remember that I met him once. Didn't understand half the things he said. But that was long ago. A hundred years or more.

A hundred years ago—maybe more than that.

Why, bless me, said the senator, he must be one of us.

The senator nodded and the paper slipped from his hands and fell upon the floor. He jerked himself erect. There I go again, he told himself. Dozing. It's old age creeping up again.

He sat in his chair, very erect and quiet, like a small scared child that won't admit it's scared, and the old, old fear came tugging at his brain. Too long, he thought. I've already waited longer than I should. Waiting for the party to renew my application and now the party won't. They've thrown me overboard. They've deserted me just when I needed them the most.

Death sentence, he had said back in the office, and that was what it was—for he couldn't last much longer. He didn't have much time. It would take a while to engineer whatever must be done. One would have to move most carefully and never tip one's hand. For there was a penalty—a terrible penalty.

The girl said to him: "Dr. Smith will see you now."

"Eh?" said the senator.

"You asked to see Dr. Dana Smith," the girl reminded him. "He will see you now."

"Thank you, miss," said the senator. "I was sitting here half dozing."

He lumbered to his feet.

"That door," said the girl.

"I know," the senator mumbled testily. "I know. I've been here many times before."

Dr. Smith was waiting.

"Have a chair, senator," he said. "Have a drink? Well, then, a cigar, maybe. What is on your mind?"

The senator took his time, getting himself adjusted to the chair. Grunting comfortably, he clipped the end off the cigar, rolled it in his mouth.

"Nothing particular on my mind," he said. "Just dropped around to pass the time of day. Have a great and abiding interest in your work here. Always have had. Associated with it from the very start."

The director nodded. "I know. You conducted the original hearings on life continuation."

The senator chuckled. "Seemed fairly simple then. There were problems, of course, and we recognized them and we tried the best we could to meet them."

"You did amazingly well," the director told him. "The code you drew up five hundred years ago has never been questioned for its fairness and the few modifications which have been necessary have dealt with minor points which no one could have anticipated."

"But it's taken too long," said the senator.

The director stiffened. "I don't understand," he said.

The senator lighted the cigar, applying his whole attention to it, flaming the end carefully so it caught even fire.

He settled himself more solidly in the chair. "It was like this," he said. "We recognized life continuation as a first step only, a rather blundering first step toward immortality. We devised the code as an interim instrument to take care of the period before immortality was available—not to a selected few, but to everyone. We viewed the few who could be given life continuation as stewards, persons who would help to advance the day when the race could be granted immortality."

"That still is the concept," Dr. Smith said, coldly.

"But the people grow impatient."

"That is just too bad," Smith told him. "The people will simply have to wait."

"As a race, they may be willing to," explained the senator. "As individuals, they're not."

"I fail to see your point, senator."

"There may not be a point," said the senator. "In late years I've often debated with myself the wisdom of the whole procedure. Life continuation is a keg of dynamite if it fails of immortality. It will breed, system-wide revolt if the people wait too long."

"Have you a solution, senator?"

"No," confessed the senator. "No, I'm afraid I haven't. I've often thought that it might have been better if we had taken the people into our confidence, let them know all that was going on. Kept them up with all developments. An informed people are a rational people.''

The director did not answer and the senator felt the cold weight of certainty seep into his brain.

He knows, he told himself. He knows the party has decided not to ask that I be continued. He knows that I'm a dead man. He knows I'm almost through and can't help him any more—and he's crossed me out. He won't tell me a thing. Not the thing I want to know.

But he did not allow his face to change. He knew his face would not betray him. His face was too well trained.

''I know there is an answer,'' said the senator. ''There's always been an answer to any question about immortality. You can't have it until there's living space. Living space to throw away, more than we ever think we'll need, and a fair chance to find more of it if it's ever needed.''

Dr. Smith nodded. ''That's the answer, senator. The only answer I can give.''

He sat silent for a moment, then he said: ''Let me assure you on one point, senator. When Extrasolar Research finds the living space, we'll have the immortality.''

The senator heaved himself out of the chair, stood planted solidly on his feet.

''It's good to hear you say that, doctor,'' he said. ''It is very heartening. I thank you for the time you gave me.''

Out on the street, the senator thought bitterly:

They have it now. They have immortality. All they're waiting for is the living space and another hundred years will find that. Another hundred years will simply have to find it.

Another hundred years, he told himself, just one more continuation, and I would be in for good and all.

Mr. Andrews: *We must be sure there is a divorcement of life continuation from economics. A man who has money must not be allowed to purchase additional life, either through the payment of money or the pressure of influence, while another man is doomed to die a natural death simply because he happens to be poor.*

Chairman Leonard: *I don't believe that situation has ever been in question.*

Mr. Andrews: *Nevertheless, it is a matter which must be emphasized again and again. Life continuation must not be a*

*commodity to be sold across the counter at so many dollars
for each added year of life.*

> From the Records of a hearing before the science subcom-
> mittee of the public policy committee of the World House
> of Representatives.

The senator sat before the chessboard and idly worked at the
problem. Idly, since his mind was on other things than chess.

So they had immortality, had it and were waiting, holding it a
secret until there was assurance of sufficient living space. Holding it a secret from the people and from the government and
from the men and women who had spent many lifetimes working
for the thing which already had been found.

For Smith had spoken, not as a man who was merely confident,
but as a man who knew. When Extrasolar Research finds the
living space, he'd said, we'll have immortality. Which meant
they had it now. Immortality was not predictable. You would not
know you'd have it; you would only know if and when you had
it.

The senator moved a bishop and saw that he was wrong. He
slowly pulled it back.

Living space was the key, and not living space alone, but
economic living space, self-supporting in terms of food and other
raw materials, but particularly in food. For if living space had
been all that mattered, Man had it in Mars and Venus and the
moons of Jupiter. But not one of those worlds was self-supporting.
They did not solve the problem.

Living space was all they needed and in a hundred years
they'd have that. Another hundred years was all that anyone
would need to come into possession of the common human
heritage of immortality.

Another continuation would give me that hundred years, said
the senator, talking to himself. A hundred years and some to
spare, for this time I'll be careful of myself. I'll lead a cleaner
life. Eat sensibly and cut out liquor and tobacco and the
woman-chasing.

There were ways and means, of course. There always were.
And he would find them, for he knew all the dodges. After five
hundred years in world government, you got to know them all. If
you didn't know them, you simply didn't last.

Mentally he listed the possibilities as they occurred to him.

ONE: A person could engineer a continuation for someone

else and then have that person assign the continuation to him. It would be costly, of course, but it might be done.

You'd have to find someone you could trust and maybe you couldn't find anyone you could trust that far—for life continuation was something hard to come by. Most people, once they got it, wouldn't give it back.

Although on second thought, it probably wouldn't work. For there'd be legal angles. A continuation was a gift of society to one specific person to be used by him alone. It would not be transferable. It would not be legal property. It would not be something that one owned. It could not be bought or sold, it could not be assigned.

If the person who had been granted a continuation died before he got to use it—died of natural causes, of course, of wholly natural causes that could be provable—why, maybe, then— But still it wouldn't work. Not being property, the continuation would not be part of one's estate. It could not be bequeathed. It most likely would revert to the issuing agency.

Cross that one off, the senator told himself.

TWO: He might travel to New York and talk to the party's executive secretary. After all, Gibbs and Scott were mere messengers. They had their orders to carry out the dictates of the party and that was all. Maybe if he saw someone in authority—

But, the senator scolded himself, that is wishful thinking. The party's through with me. They've pushed their continuation racket as far as they dare push it and they have wrangled about all they figure they can get. They don't dare ask for more and they need my continuation for someone else most likely—someone who's a comer; someone who has vote appeal.

And I, said the senator, am an old has-been.

Although I'm a tricky old rascal, and ornery if I have to be, and slippery as five hundred years of public life can make one.

After that long, said the senator, parenthetically, you have no more illusions, not even of yourself.

I couldn't stomach it, he decided. I couldn't live with myself if I went crawling to New York—and a thing has to be pretty bad to make me feel like that. I've never crawled before and I'm not crawling now, not even for an extra hundred years and a shot at immortality.

Cross that one off, too, said the senator.

THREE: Maybe someone could be bribed.

Of all the possibilities, that sounded the most reasonable. There always was someone who had a certain price and always someone else who could act as intermediary. Naturally, a world senator could not get mixed up directly in a deal of that sort.

It might come a little high, but what was money for? After all, he reconciled himself, he'd been a frugal man of sorts and had been able to lay away a wad against such a day as this.

The senator moved a rook and it seemed to be all right, so he left it there.

Of course, once he managed the continuation, he would have to disappear. He couldn't flaunt his triumph in the party's face. He couldn't take a chance of someone asking how he'd been continuated. He'd have to become one of the people, seek to be forgotten, live in some obscure place and keep out of the public eye.

Norton was the man to see. No matter what one wanted, Norton was the man to see. An appointment to be secured, someone to be killed, a concession on Venus or a spaceship contract—Norton did the job. All quietly and discreetly and no questions asked. That is, if you had the money. If you didn't have the money, there was no use of seeing Norton.

Otto came into the room on silent feet.

"A gentleman to see you, sir," he said.

The senator stiffened upright in his chair.

"What do you mean by sneaking up on me?" he shouted. "Always pussyfooting. Trying to startle me. After this you cough or fall over a chair or something so I'll know that you're around."

"Sorry, sir," said Otto. "There's a gentleman here. And there are those letters on the desk to read."

"I'll read the letters later," said the senator.

"Be sure you don't forget," Otto told him, stiffly.

"I never forget," said the senator. "You'd think I was getting senile, the way you keep reminding me."

"There's a gentleman to see you," Otto said patiently. "A Mr. Lee."

"Anson Lee, perhaps."

Otto sniffed. "I believe that was his name. A newspaper person, sir."

"Show him in," said the senator.

He sat stolidly in his chair and thought: Lee's found out about it. Somehow he's ferreted out the fact the party's thrown me over. And he's here to crucify me.

He may suspect, but he cannot know. He may have heard a rumor, but he can't be sure. The party would keep mum, must necessarily keep mum, since it can't openly admit its traffic in life continuation. So Lee, having heard a rumor, had come to blast it out of me, to catch me by surprise and trip me up with words.

I must not let him do it, for once the thing is known, the wolves will come in packs knee deep.

Lee was walking into the room and the senator rose and shook his hand.

"Sorry to disturb you, senator," Lee told him, "but I thought maybe you could help me."

"Anything at all," the senator said, affably. "Anything I can. Sit down, Mr. Lee."

"Perhaps you read my story in the morning paper," said Lee. "The one on Dr. Carson's disappearance."

"No," said the senator. "No, I'm afraid I—"

He rumbled to a stop, astounded.

He hadn't read the paper!

He had forgotten to read the paper!

He always read the paper. He never failed to read it. It was a solemn rite, starting at the front and reading straight through to the back, skipping only those sections which long ago he'd found not to be worth the reading.

He'd had the paper at the institute and he had been interrupted when the girl told him that Dr. Smith would see him. He had come out of the office and he'd left the paper in the reception room.

It was a terrible thing. Nothing, absolutely nothing, should so upset him that he forgot to read the paper.

"I'm afraid I didn't read the story," the senator said lamely. He simply couldn't force himself to admit that he hadn't read the paper.

"Dr. Carson," said Lee, "was a biochemist, a fairly famous one. He died ten years or so ago, according to an announcement from a little village in Spain, where he had gone to live. But I have reason to believe, senator, that he never died at all, that he may still be living."

"Hiding?" asked the senator.

"Perhaps," said Lee. "Although there seems no reason that he should. His record is entirely spotless."

"Why do you doubt he died, then?"

"Because there's no death certificate. And he's not the only one who died without benefit of certificate."

"Hm-m-m," said the senator.

"Galloway, the anthropologist, died five years ago. There's no certificate. Henderson, the agricultural expert, died six years ago. There's no certificate. There are a dozen more I know of and probably many that I don't."

"Anything in common?" asked the senator. "Any circumstances that might link these people?"

"Just one thing," said Lee. "They were all continuators."

"I see," said the senator. He clasped the arms of his chair with a fierce grip to keep his hands from shaking.

"Most interesting," he said. "Very interesting."

"I know you can't tell me anything officially," said Lee, "but I thought you might give me a fill-in, an off-the-record background. You wouldn't let me quote you, of course, but any clues you might give me, any hint at all—"

He waited hopefully.

"Because I've been close to the Life Continuation people?" asked the senator.

Lee nodded. "If there's anything to know, you know it, senator. You headed the committee that held the original hearings on life continuation. Since then you've held various other congressional posts in connection with it. Only this morning you saw Dr. Smith."

"I can't tell you anything," mumbled the senator. "I don't know anything. You see, it's a matter of policy—"

"I had hoped you would help me, senator."

"I can't," said the senator. "You'll never believe it, of course, but I really can't."

He sat silently for a moment and then he asked a question: "You say all these people you mention were continuators. You checked, of course, to see if their applications had been renewed?"

"I did," said Lee. "There are no renewals for any one of them—at least no records of renewals. Some of them were approaching death limit and they actually may be dead by now, although I doubt that any of them died at the time or place announced."

"Interesting," said the senator. "And quite a mystery, too."

Lee deliberately terminated the discussion. He gestured at the chessboard. "Are you an expert, senator?"

The senator shook his head. "The game appeals to me. I fool around with it. It's a game of logic and also a game of ethics. You are perforce a gentleman when you play it. You observe certain rules of correctness of behavior."

"Like life, senator?"

"Like life should be," said the senator. "When the odds are

too terrific, you resign. You do not force your opponent to play out to the bitter end. That's ethics. When you see that you can't win, but that you have a fighting chance, you try for the next best thing—a draw. That's logic.''

Lee laughed, a bit uncomfortably. "You've lived according to those rules, senator?"

"I've done my best," said the senator, trying to sound humble.

Lee rose. "I must be going, senator."

"Stay and have a drink."

Lee shook his head. "Thanks, but I have work to do."

"I owe you a drink," said the senator. "Remind me of it sometime."

For a long time after Lee left, Senator Homer Leonard sat unmoving in his chair.

Then he reached out a hand and picked up a knight to move it, but his fingers shook so that he dropped it and it clattered on the board.

Any person who gains the gift of life continuation by illegal or extralegal means, without bona fide recommendation or proper authorization through recognized channels, shall be, in effect, excommunicated from the human race. The facts of that person's guilt, once proved, shall be published by every means at humanity's command throughout the Earth and to every corner of the Earth so that all persons may know and recognize him. To further insure such recognition and identification, said convicted person must wear at all times, conspicuously displayed upon his person, a certain badge which shall advertise his guilt. While he may not be denied the ordinary basic requirements of life, such as food, adequate clothing, a minimum of shelter and medical care, he shall not be allowed to partake of or participate in any of the other refinements of civilization. He will not be allowed to purchase any item in excess of the barest necessities for the preservation of life, health and decency; he shall be barred from all endeavors and normal associations of humankind; he shall not have access to nor benefit of any library, lecture hall, amusement place or other facility, either private or public, designed for instruction, recreation or entertainment. Nor may any person, under certain penalties hereinafter set forth, knowingly converse with him or establish any human relationship whatsoever with him. He will be suffered to live out his life within the framework of the human community, but to all intent and purpose he will be denied all the privileges and obligations of a human being. And the same provisions as are listed above

*shall apply in full and equal force to any person or persons who
shall in any way knowingly aid such a person to obtain life
continuation by other than legal means.*

From The Code of Life Continuation.

"What you mean," said J. Barker Norton, "is that the party
all these years has been engineering renewals of life continuation
for you. Paying you off for services well rendered."

The senator nodded miserably.

"And now that you're on the verge of losing an election, they
figure you aren't worth it any longer and have refused to ask for
a renewal."

"In curbstone language," said the senator, "that sums it up
quite neatly."

"And you come running to me," said Norton. "What in the
world do you think I can do about it?"

The senator leaned forward. "Let's put it on a business basis,
Norton. You and I have worked together before."

"That's right," said Norton. "Both of us cleaned up on that
spaceship deal."

The senator said: "I want another hundred years and I'm
willing to pay for it. I have no doubt you can arrange it for me."

"How?"

"I wouldn't know," said the senator. "I'm leaving that to
you. I don't care how you do it."

Norton leaned back in his chair and made a tent out of his
fingers.

"You figure I could bribe someone to recommend you. Or
bribe some continuation technician to give you a renewal without
authorization."

"Those are a pair of excellent ideas," agreed the senator.

"And face excommunication if I were found out," said Norton.
"Thanks, senator, I'm having none of it."

The senator sat impassively, watching the face of the man
across the desk.

"A hundred thousand," the senator said quietly.

Norton laughed at him.

"A half million, then."

"Remember that excommunication, senator. It's got to be
worth my while to take a chance like that."

"A million," said the senator. "And that's absolutely final."

"A million now," said Norton. "Cold cash. No receipt. No
record of the transaction. Another million when and if I can
deliver."

The senator rose slowly to his feet, his face a mask to hide the excitement that was stirring in him. The excitement and the naked surge of exultation. He kept his voice level.

"I'll deliver that million before the week is over."

Norton said: "I'll start looking into things."

On the street outside, the senator's step took on a jauntiness it had not known in years. He walked along briskly, flipping his cane.

Those others, Carson and Galloway and Henderson, had disappeared, exactly as he would have to disappear once he got his extra hundred years. They had arranged to have their own deaths announced and then had dropped from sight, living against the day when immortality would be a thing to be had for the simple asking.

Somewhere, somehow, they had got a new continuation, an unauthorized continuation, since a renewal was not listed in the records. Someone had arranged it for them. More than likely Norton.

But they had bungled. They had tried to cover up their tracks and had done no more than call attention to their absence.

In a thing like this, a man could not afford to blunder. A wise man, a man who took the time to think things out, would not make a blunder.

The senator pursed his flabby lips and whistled a snatch of music.

Norton was a gouger, of course. Pretending that he couldn't make arrangements, pretending he was afraid of excommunication, jacking up the price.

The senator grinned wryly. It would take almost every dime he had, but it was worth the price.

He'd have to be careful, getting together that much money. Some from one bank, some from another, collecting it piecemeal by withdrawals and by cashing bonds, floating a few judicious loans so there'd not be too many questions asked.

He bought a paper at the corner and hailed a cab. Settling back in the seat, he creased the paper down its length and startd in on column one. Another health contest. This time in Australia.

Health, thought the senator, they're crazy on this health business. Health centers. Health cults. Health clinics.

He skipped the story, moved on to column two.

The head said:

SIX SENATORS POOR BETS FOR RE-ELECTION

The senator snorted in disgust. One of the senators, of course, would be himself.

He wadded up the paper and jammed it in his pocket.

Why should he care? Why knock himself out to retain a senate seat he could never fill? He was going to grow young again, get another chance at life. He would move to some far part of the earth and be another man.

Another man. He thought about it and it was refreshing. Dropping all the old dead wood of past association, all the ancient accumulation of responsibilities.

Norton had taken on the job. Norton would deliver.

Mr. Miller: *What I want to know is this: Where do we stop? You give this life continuation to a man and he'll want his wife and kids to have it. And his wife will want her Aunt Minnie to have it and the kids will want the family dog to have it and the dog will want—*

Chairman Leonard: *You're facetious, Mr. Miller.*

Mr. Miller: *I don't know what that big word means, mister. You guys here in Geneva talk fancy with them six-bit words and you get the people all balled up. It's time the common people got in a word of common sense.*

From the Records of a hearing before the science sub-committee of the public policy committee of the World House of Representatives.

"Frankly," Norton told him, "it's the first time I ever ran across a thing I couldn't fix. Ask me anything else you want to, senator, and I'll rig it up for you."

The senator sat stricken. "You mean you couldn't— But, Norton, there was Dr. Carson and Galloway and Henderson. Someone took care of them."

Norton shook his head. "Not I. I never heard of them."

"But someone did," said the senator. "They disappeared—"

His voice trailed off and he slumped deeper in the chair and the truth suddenly was plain—the truth he had failed to see.

A blind spot, he told himself. A blind spot!

They had disappeared and that was all he knew. They had published their own deaths and had not died, but had disappeared.

He had assumed they had disappeared because they had got an illegal continuation. But that was sheer wishful thinking. There was no foundation for it, no fact that would support it.

There could be other reasons, he told himself, many other

reasons why a man would disappear and seek to cover up his tracks with a death report.

But it had tied in so neatly!

They were continuators whose applications had not been renewed. Exactly as he was a continuator whose application would not be renewed.

They had dropped out of sight. Exactly as he would have to drop from sight once he gained another lease on life.

It had tied in so neatly—and it had been all wrong.

"I tried every way I knew," said Norton. "I canvassed every source that might advance your name for continuation and they laughed at me. It's been tried before, you see, and there's not a chance of getting it put through. Once your original sponsor drops you, you're automatically cancelled out.

"I tried to sound out technicians who might take a chance, but they're incorruptible. They get paid off in added years for loyalty and they're not taking any chance of trading years for dollars."

"I guess that settles it," the senator said wearily. "I should have known."

He heaved himself to his feet and faced Norton squarely. "You are telling me the truth," he pleaded. "You aren't just trying to jack up the price a bit."

Norton stared up at him, almost unbelieving. "Jack up the price! Senator, if I had put this through, I'd have taken your last penny. Want to know how much you're worth? I can tell you within a thousand dollars."

He waved a hand at a row of filing cases ranged along the wall.

"It's all there, senator. You and all the other big shots. Complete files on every one of you. When a man comes to me with a deal like yours, I look in the files and strip him to the bone."

"I don't suppose there's any use of asking for some of my money back?"

Norton shook his head. "Not a ghost. You took your gamble, senator. You can't even prove you paid me. And, beside, you still have plenty left to last you the few years you have to live."

The senator took a step toward the door, then turned back.

"Look, Norton, I can't die! Not now. Just one more continuation and I'd be—"

The look on Norton's face stopped him in his tracks. The look he'd glimpsed on other faces at other times, but only glimpsed. Now he stared at it—at the naked hatred of a man whose life is short for the man whose life is long.

"Sure, you can die," said Norton. "You're going to. You can't live forever. Who do you think you are!"

The senator reached out a hand and clutched the desk.

"But you don't understand."

"You've already lived ten times as long as I have lived," said Norton, coldly, measuring each word, "and I hate your guts for it. Get out of here, you sniveling old fool, before I throw you out."

Dr. Barton: *You may think that you would confer a boon on humanity with life continuation, but I tell you, sir, that it would be a curse. Life would lose its value and its meaning if it went on forever, and if you have life continuation now, you eventually must stumble on immortality. And when that happens, sir, you will be compelled to set up boards of review to grant the boon of death. The people, tired of life, will storm your hearing rooms to plead for death.*

Chairman Leonard: *It would banish uncertainty and fear.*

Dr. Barton: *You are talking of the fear of death. The fear of death, sir, is infantile.*

Chairman Leonard: *But there are benefits—*

Dr. Barton: *Benefits, yes. The benefit of allowing a scientist the extra years he needs to complete a piece of research; a composer an additional lifetime to complete a symphony. Once the novelty wore off, men in general would accept added life only under protest, only as a duty.*

Chairman Leonard: *You're not very practical-minded, doctor.*

Dr. Barton: *But I am. Extremely practical and down to earth. Man must have newness. Man cannot be bored and live. How much do you think there would be left to look forward to after the millionth woman, the billionth piece of pumpkin pie?*

From the Records of the hearing before the science subcommittee of the public policy committee of the World House of Representatives.

So Norton hated him.

As all people of normal lives must hate, deep within their souls, the lucky ones whose lives went on and on.

A hatred deep and buried, most of the time buried. But sometimes breaking out, as it had broken out of Norton.

Resentment, tolerated because of the gently, skillfully fostered hope that those whose lives went on might some day make it possible that the lives of all, barring violence or accident or incurable disease, might go on as long as one would wish.

I can understand it now, thought the senator, for I am one of them. I am one of those whose lives will not continue to go on, and I have even fewer years than the most of them.

He stood before the window in the deepening dusk and saw the lights come out and the day die above the unbelievably blue waters of the far-famed lake.

Beauty came to him as he stood there watching, beauty that had gone unnoticed through all the later years. A beauty and a softness and a feeling of being one with the city lights and the last faint gleam of day above the darkening waters.

Fear? The senator admitted it.

Bitterness? Of course.

Yet, despite the fear and bitterness, the window held him with the scene it framed.

Earth and sky and water, he thought. I am one with them. Death has made me one with them. For death brings one back to the elementals, to the soil and trees, to the clouds and sky and the sun dying in the welter of its blood in the crimson west.

This is the price we pay, he thought, that the race must pay, for its life eternal—that we may not be able to assess in their true value the things that should be dearest to us; for a thing that has no ending, a thing that goes on forever, must have decreasing value.

Rationalization, he accused himself. Of course, you're rationalizing. You want another hundred years as badly as you ever did. You want a chance at immortality. But you can't have it and you trade eternal life for a sunset seen across a lake and it is well you can. It is a blessing that you can.

The senator made a rasping sound within his throat.

Behind him the telephone came to sudden life and he swung around. It chirred at him again. Feet pattered down the hall and the senator called out: "I'll get it, Otto."

He lifted the receiver. "New York calling," said the operator. "Senator Leonard, please."

"This is Leonard."

Another voice broke in. "Senator, this is Gibbs."

"Yes," said the senator. "The executioner."

"I called you," said Gibbs, "to talk about the election."

"What election?"

"The one here in North America. The one you're running in. Remember?"

"I am an old man," said the senator, "and I'm about to die. I'm not interested in elections."

Gibbs practically chattered. "But you have to be. What's the matter with you, senator? You have to do something. Make some speeches, make a statement, come home and stump the country. The party can't do it all alone. You have to do some of it yourself."

"I will do something," declared the senator. "Yes, I think that finally I'll do something."

He hung up and walked to the writing desk, snapped on the light. He got paper out of a drawer and took a pen out of his pocket.

The telephone went insane and he paid it no attention. It rang on and on and finally Otto came and answered.

"New York calling, sir," he said.

The senator shook his head and he heard Otto talking softly and the phone did not ring again.

The senator wrote:

To Whom It May Concern:

Then crossed it out.

He wrote:

A Statement to the World:

And crossed it out.

He wrote:

A Statement by Senator Homer Leonard:

He crossed that out, too.

He wrote:

Five centuries ago the people of the world gave into the hands of a few trusted men and women the gift of continued life in the hope and belief that they would work to advance the day when longer life spans might be made possible for the entire population.

From time to time, life continuation has been granted additional men and women, always with the implied understanding that the gift was made under the same conditions—that the persons so favored should work against the day when each inhabitant of the entire world might enter upon a heritage of near-eternity.

Through the years some of us have carried that trust forward and have lived with it and cherished it and bent every effort toward its fulfillment.

Some of us have not.

Upon due consideration and searching examination of my own status in this regard, I have at length decided that I no longer can accept further extension of the gift.

Human dignity requires that I be able to meet my fellow man upon the street or in the byways of the world without flinching from him. This I could not do should I continue to accept a gift to which I have no claim and which is denied to other men.

The senator signed his name, neatly, carefully, without the usual flourish.

"There," he said, speaking aloud in the silence of the night-filled room, "that will hold them for a while."

Feet padded and he turned around.

"It's long past your usual bedtime, sir," said Otto.

The senator rose clumsily and his aching bones protested. Old, he thought. Growing old again. And it would be so easy to start over, to regain his youth and live another lifetime. Just the nod of someone's head, just a single pen stroke and he would be young again.

"This statement, Otto," he said. "Please give it to the press."

"Yes, sir," said Otto. He took the paper, held it gingerly.

"Tonight," said the senator.

"Tonight, sir? It is rather late."

"Nevertheless, I want to issue it tonight."

"It must be important, sir."

"It's my resignation," said the senator.

"Your resignation! From the senate, sir!"

"No," said the senator. "From life."

Mr. Michaelson: *As a churchman, I cannot think otherwise than that the proposal now before you gentlemen constitutes a perversion of God's law. It is not within the province of man to say a man may live beyond his allotted time.*

Chairman Leonard: *I might ask you this: How is one to know when a man's allotted time has come to an end? Medicine has prolonged the lives of many persons. Would you call a physician a perverter of God's law?*

Mr. Michaelson: *It has become apparent through the testimony given here that the eventual aim of continuing research is immortality. Surely you can see that physical immortality does not square with the Christian concept. I tell you this, sir: You can't fool God and get away with it.*

From the Records of a hearing before the science subcommittee of the public policy committee of the World House of Representatives.

Chess is a game of logic.

But likewise a game of ethics.

You do not shout and you do not whistle, nor bang the pieces on the board, nor twiddle your thumbs, nor move a piece then take it back again. When you're beaten, you admit it. You do not force your opponent to carry on the game to absurd lengths. You resign and start another game if there is time to play one. Otherwise, you just resign and you do it with all the good grace possible. You do not knock all the pieces to the floor in anger. You do not get up abruptly and stalk out of the room. You do not reach across the board and punch your opponent in the nose.

When you play chess you are, or you are supposed to be, a gentleman.

The senator lay wide-awake, staring at the ceiling.

You do not reach across the board and punch your opponent in the nose. You do not knock the pieces to the floor.

But this isn't chess, he told himself, arguing with himself. This isn't chess; this is life and death. A dying thing is not a gentleman. It does not curl up quietly and die of the hurt inflicted. It backs into a corner and it fights, it lashes back and does all the hurt it can.

And I am hurt. I am hurt to death.

And I have lashed back. I have lashed back, most horribly.

They'll not be able to walk down the street again, not ever again, those gentlemen who passed the sentence on me. For they have no more claim to continued life than I and the people now will know it. And the people will see to it that they do not get it.

I will die, but when I go down I'll pull the others with me. They'll know I pulled them down, down with me into the pit of death. That's the sweetest part of all—they'll know who pulled them down and they won't be able to say a word about it. They can't even contradict the noble things I said.

Someone in the corner said, some voice from some other time and place: *You're no gentleman, senator. You fight a dirty fight.*

Sure I do, said the senator. They fought dirty first. And politics always was a dirty game.

Remember all that fine talk you dished out to Lee the other day?

That was the other day, snapped the senator.

You'll never be able to look a chessman in the face again, said the voice in the corner.

I'll be able to look my fellow men in the face, however, said the senator.

Will you? asked the voice.

And that, of course, was the question. Would he?

I don't care, the senator cried desperately. I don't care what happens. They played a lousy trick on me. They can't get away with it. I'll fix their clocks for them. I'll—

Sure, you will, said the voice, mocking.

Go away, shrieked the senator. Go away and leave me. Let me be alone.

You are alone, said the thing in the corner. *You are more alone than any man has ever been before.*

Chairman Leonard: *You represent an insurance company, do you not, Mr. Markely? A big insurance company.*

Mr. Markely: *That is correct.*

Chairman Leonard: *And every time a person dies, it costs your company money?*

Mr. Markely: *Well, you might put it that way if you wished, although it is scarcely the case—*

Chairman Leonard: *You do have to pay out benefits on deaths, don't you?*

Mr. Markely: *Why, yes, of course we do.*

Chairman Leonard: *Then I can't understand your opposition to life continuation. If there were fewer deaths, you'd have to pay fewer benefits.*

Mr. Markely: *All very true, sir. But if people had reason to believe they would live virtually forever, they'd buy no life insurance.*

Chairman Leonard: *Oh, I see. So that's the way it is*

> From the Records of a hearing before the science subcommittee of the public policy committee of the World House of Representatives.

The senator awoke. He had not been dreaming, but it was almost as if he had awakened from a bad dream—or awakened to a bad dream—and he struggled to go back to sleep again, to gain the Nirvana of unawareness, to shut out the harsh reality of existence, to dodge the shame of knowing who and what he was.

But there was someone stirring in the room, and someone spoke to him and he sat upright in bed, stung to wakefulness by the happiness and something else that was almost worship which the voice held.

"It's wonderful, sir," said Otto. "There have been phone calls all night long. And the telegrams and radiograms still are stacking up."

The senator rubbed his eyes with pudgy fists.

"Phone calls, Otto? People sore at me?"

"Some of them were, sir. Terribly angry, sir. But not too many of them. Most of them were happy and wanted to tell you what a great thing you'd done. But I told them you were tired and I could not waken you."

"Great thing?" said the senator. "What great thing have I done?"

"Why, sir, giving up life continuation. One man said to tell you it was the greatest example of moral courage the world had ever known. He said all the common people would bless you for it. Those were his very words. He was very solemn, sir."

The senator swung his feet to the floor, sat on the edge of the bed, scratching at his ribs.

It was strange, he told himself, how a thing would turn out sometimes. A heel at bedtime and a hero in the morning.

"Don't you see, sir," said Otto, "you have made yourself one of the common people, one of the short-lived people. No one has ever done a thing like that before."

"I was one of the common people," said the senator, "long before I wrote that statement. And I didn't make myself one of them. I was forced to become one of them, much against my will."

But Otto, in his excitement, didn't seem to hear.

He rattled on: "The newspapers are full of it, sir. It's the biggest news in years. The political writers are chuckling over it. They're calling it the smartest political move that was ever pulled. They say that before you made the announcement you didn't have a chance of being re-elected senator and now, they say, you can be elected president if you just say the word."

The senator sighed. "Otto," he said, "please hand me my pants. It is cold in here."

Otto handed him his trousers. "There's a newspaperman waiting in the study, sir. I held all the others off, but this one sneaked in the back way. You know him, sir, so I let him wait. He is Mr. Lee."

"I'll see him," said the senator.

So it was a smart political move, was it? Well, maybe so, but after a day or so, even the surprised political experts would begin to wonder about the logic of a man literally giving up his life to be re-elected to a senate seat.

Of course the common herd would love it, but he had not done it for applause. Although, so long as the people insisted upon thinking of him as great and noble, it was all right to let them go on thinking so.

The senator jerked his tie straight and buttoned his coat. He went into the study and Lee was waiting for him.

"I suppose you want an interview," said the senator. "Want to know why I did this thing."

Lee shook his head. "No, senator, I have something else. Something you should know about. Remember our talk last week? About the disappearances."

The senator nodded.

"Well, I have something else. You wouldn't tell me anything last week, but maybe now you will. I've checked, senator, and I've found this—the health winners are disappearing, too. More than eighty percent of those who participated in the finals of the last ten years have disappeared."

"I don't understand," said the senator.

"They're going somewhere," said Lee. "Something's happening to them. Something's happening to two classes of our people—the continuators and the healthiest youngsters."

"Wait a minute," gasped the senator. "Wait a minute, Mr. Lee."

He groped his way to the desk, grasped its edge and lowered himself into a chair.

"There is something wrong, senator?" asked Lee.

"Wrong?" mumbled the senator. "Yes, there must be something wrong."

"They've found living space," said Lee, triumphantly. "That's it, isn't it? They've found living space and they're sending out the pioneers."

The senator shook his head. "I don't know, Lee. I have not been informed. Check Extrasolar Research. They're the only ones who know—and they wouldn't tell you."

Lee grinned at him. "Good day, senator," he said. "Thanks so much for helping."

Dully, the senator watched him go.

Living space? Of course, that was it.

They had found living space and Extrasolar Research was sending out handpicked pioneers to prepare the way. It would take years of work and planning before the discovery could be announced. For once announced, world government must be ready to confer immortality on a mass production basis, must have ships available to carry out the hordes to the far, new worlds. A premature announcement would bring psychological and economic disruption that would make the government a shambles. So they would work very quietly, for they must work quietly.

His eyes found the little stack of letters on one corner of the desk and he remembered, with a shock of guilt, that he had meant to read them. He had promised Otto that he would and then he had forgotten.

I keep forgetting all the time, said the senator. I forget to read my paper and I forget to read my letters and I forget that some men are loyal and morally honest instead of slippery and slick. And I indulge in wishful thinking and that's the worst of all.

Continuators and health champions disappearing. Sure, they're disappearing. They're headed for new worlds and immortality.

And I . . . I . . . if only I had kept my big mouth shut—

The phone chirped and he picked it up.

"This is Sutton at Extrasolar Research," said an angry voice.

"Yes, Dr. Sutton," said the senator. "It's nice of you to call."

"I'm calling in regard to the invitation that we sent you last week," said Sutton. "In view of your statement last night, which we feel very keenly is an unjust criticism, we are withdrawing it."

"Invitation," said the senator. "Why, I didn't—"

"What I can't understand," said Sutton, "is why, with the invitation in your pocket, you should have acted as you did."

"But," said the senator, "but, doctor—"

"Good-by, senator," said Sutton.

Slowly the senator hung up. With a fumbling hand, he reached out and picked up the stack of letters.

It was the third one down. The return address was Extrasolar Research and it had been registered and sent special delivery and it was marked both PERSONAL and IMPORTANT.

The letter slipped out of the senator's trembling fingers and fluttered to the floor. He did not pick it up.

It was too late now, he knew, to do anything about it.

THE ONLY THING WE LEARN

by C.M. Kornbluth (1923-1958)

Startling Stories, July

One of the great things about Cyril Kornbluth is that his stories stand the test of time, and this little gem is a perfect example of this virtue. It also conveys the essence of the attitude he brought to almost all his fiction—an intense cynicism that was an extension of himself. When he died at the age of thirty-five he had been a professional writer for nearly twenty years. What would he have said about the 1960s and beyond? It is a tragedy that we will never know. However, he left us a great deal, and will begin to appear frequently in future volumes in this series.—M.H.G.

(I like to use quotations or well-known phrases, or parts of them, for titles, and so do others.

In Philosophy of History, published in 1832, and written by the German philosopher, Georg W. F. Hegel, it is stated, "What experience and history teach is this—that people and governments never have learned anything from history, or acted on principles deduced from it."

And in 1903, George Bernard Shaw, in The Revolutionist's Handbook, deliberately paraphrasing Hegel, said, "We learn from history that we learn nothing from history." The usual form the quotation takes today is "The only thing we learn from history is that we don't learn anything from history."

This is just a little bit of pedantry on my part. Now go ahead and read "The Only Thing We Learn" by C. M. Kornbluth.—I.A.)

The Professor, though he did not know the actor's phrase for it, was counting the house—peering through a spyhole in the door through which he would in a moment appear before the class. He was pleased with what he saw. Tier after tier of young people, ready with notebooks and styli, chattering tentatively, glancing at the door against which his nose was flattened, waiting for the pleasant interlude known as "Archaeo-Literature 203" to begin.

The professor stepped back, smoothed his tunic, crooked four books in his left elbow and made his entrance. Four swift strides brought him to the lectern and, for the thousandth-odd time, he impassively swept the lecture hall with his gaze. Then he gave a wry little smile. Inside, for the thousandth-odd time, he was nagged by the irritable little thought that the lectern really ought to be a foot or so higher.

The irritation did not show. He was out to win the audience, and he did. A dead silence, the supreme tribute, gratified him. Imperceptibly, the lights of the lecture hall began to dim and the light on the lectern to brighten.

He spoke.

"Young gentlemen of the Empire, I ought to warn you that this and the succeeding lectures will be most subversive."

There was a little rustle of incomprehension from the audience—but by then the lectern light was strong enough to show the twinkling smile about his eyes that belied his stern mouth, and agreeable chuckles sounded in the gathering darkness of the tiered seats. Glow-lights grew bright gradually at the students' tables, and they adjusted their notebooks in the narrow ribbons of illumination. He waited for the small commotion to subside.

"Subversive—" He gave them a link to cling to. "Subversive because I shall make every effort to tell both sides of our ancient beginnings with every resource of archaeology and with every clue my diligence has discovered in our epic literature.

"There *were* two sides, you know—difficult though it may be to believe that if we judge by the Old Epic alone—such epics as the noble and tempestuous *Chant of Remd*, the remaining fragments of *Krall's Voyage*, or the gory and rather out-of-date *Battle for the Ten Suns*." He paused while styli scribbled across the notebook pages.

"The Middle Epic is marked, however, by what I might call the rediscovered ethos." From his voice, every student knew that that phrase, surer than death and taxes, would appear on an examination paper. The styli scribbled. "By this I mean an awakening of fellow-feeling with the Home Suns People, which had once been filial loyalty to them when our ancestors were few and pioneers, but which turned into contempt when their numbers grew.

"The Middle Epic writers did not despise the Home Suns People, as did the bards of the Old Epic. Perhaps this was because they did not have to—since their long war against the Home Suns was drawing to a victorious close.

"Of the New Epic I shall have little to say. It was a literary fad, a pose, and a silly one. Written within historic times, the some two score pseudo-epics now moulder in their cylinders, where they belong. Our ripening civilization could not with integrity work in the epic form, and the artistic failures produced so indicate. Our genius turned to the lyric and to the unabashedly romantic novel.

"So much, for the moment, of literature. What contribution, you must wonder, have archaeological studies to make in an investigation of the wars from which our ancestry emerged?

"Archaeology offers—one—a check in historical matter in the epics—confirming or denying. Two—it provides evidence glossed over in the epics—for artistic or patriotic reasons. Three—it provides evidence which has been lost, owing to the fragmentary nature of some of the early epics."

All this he fired at them crisply, enjoying himself. Let them not think him a dreamy litterateur, nor, worse, a flat precisionist, but let them be always a little off-balance before him, never knowing what came next, and often wondering, in class and out. The styli paused after heading Three.

"We shall examine first, by our archaeo-literary technique, the second book of the *Chant of Remd.* As the selected youth of the Empire, you know much about it, of course—much that is false, some that is true and a great deal that is irrelevant. You know that Book One hurls us into the middle of things, aboard ship with Algan and his great captain, Remd, on their way from the triumph over a Home Suns stronghold, the planet Telse. We watch Remd on his diversionary action that splits the Ten Suns Fleet into two halves. But before we see the destruction of those halves by the Horde of Algan, we are told in Book Two of the battle for Telse."

He opened one of his books on the lectern, swept the amphitheater again and read sonorously.

> "Then battle broke
> And high the blinding blast
> Sight-searing leaped
> While folk in fear below
> Cowered in caverns
> From the wrath of Remd—

"Or, in less sumptuous language, one fission bomb—or a stick of time-on-target bombs—was dropped. An unprepared and disorganized populace did not take the standard measure of dispersing, but huddled foolishly to await Algan's gunfighters and the death they brought.

"One of the things you believe because you have seen them in notes to elementary-school editions of *Remd* is that Telse was the fourth planet of the star, Sol. Archaeology denies it by establishing that the fourth planet—actually called Marse, by the way—was in those days weather-roofed at least, and possibly atmosphere-roofed as well. As potential warriors, you know that one does not waste fissionable material on a roof, and there is no mention of chemical explosives being used to crack the roof. Marse, therefore, was not the locale of *Remd*, Book Two.

"Which planet was? The answer to that has been established by X-radar, differential decay analyses, video-coring and every other resource of those scientists still quaintly called 'diggers.' We know and can prove that Telse was the *third* planet of Sol. So much for the opening of the attack. Let us jump to Canto Three, the Storming of the Dynastic Palace.

> "Imperial purple wore they
> Fresh from the feast
> Grossly gorged
> They sought to slay—

"And so on. Now, as I warned you, Remd is of the Old Epic, and makes no pretense at fairness. The unorganized huddling of Telse's population was read as cowardice instead of poor A.R.P. The same is true of the Third Canto. Video-cores show on the site of the palace a hecatomb of dead in once-purple livery, but also shows impartially that they were not particularly gorged and that digestion of their last meals had been well advanced. They didn't give such a bad accounting of themselves, either. I hesitate to guess, but perhaps they accounted for one of our ancestors apiece and were simply outnumbered. The study is not complete.

"That much we know." The professor saw they were tiring of the terse scientist and shifted gears. "But if the veil of time were rent that shrouds the years between us and the Home Suns People, how much more would we learn? Would we despise the Home Suns People as our frontiersman ancestors did, or would we cry: '*This* is our spiritual home—this world of rank and order, this world of formal verse and exquisitely patterned arts'?''

If the veil of time were rent—?

We can try to rend it . . .

Wing Commander Arris heard the clear jangle of the radar net alarm as he was dreaming about a fish. Struggling out of his too-deep, too-soft bed, he stepped into a purple singlet, buckled on his Sam Browne belt with its holstered .45 automatic and tried to read the radar screen. Whatever had set it off was either too small or too distant to register on the five-inch C.R.T.

He rang for his aide, and checked his appearance in a wall-mirror while waiting. His space tan was beginning to fade, he saw, and made a mental note to get it renewed at the parlor. He stepped into the corridor as Evan, his aide, trotted up—younger, browner, thinner, but the same officer type that made the Service what it was, Arris thought with satisfaction.

Evan gave him a bone-cracking salute, which he returned. They set off for the elevator that whisked them down to a large, chilly, dark underground room where faces were greenly lit by radar screens and the lights of plotting tables. Somebody yelled ''Attention!'' and the tecks snapped. He gave them ''At ease'' and took the brisk salute of the senior teck, who reported to him in flat, machine-gun delivery:

''Object-becoming-visible-on-primary-screen-sir.''

He studied the sixty-inch disk for several seconds before he spotted the intercepted particle. It was coming in fast from zenith, growing while he watched.

''Assuming it's now traveling at maximum, how long will it be before it's within striking range?'' he asked the teck.

''Seven hours, sir.''

''The interceptors at Idlewild alerted?''

''Yessir.''

Arris turned on a phone that connected with Interception. The boy at Interception knew the face that appeared on its screen, and was already capped with a crash helmet.

''Go ahead and take him, Efrid,'' said the wing commander.

''Yessir!'' and a punctilious salute, the boy's pleasure plain at being known by name and a great deal more at being on the way to a fight that might be first-class.

Arris cut him off before the boy could detect a smile that was forming on his face. He turned from the pale lunar glow of the sixty-incher to enjoy it. Those kids—when every meteor was an invading dreadnaught, when every ragged scouting ship from the rebels was an armada!

He watched Efrid's squadron soar off on the screen and then he retreated to a darker corner. This was his post until the meteor or scout or whatever it was got taken care of. Evan joined him, and they silently studied the smooth, disciplined functioning of the plot room, Arris with satisfaction and Evan doubtless with the same. The aide broke silence, asking:

"Do you suppose it's a Frontier ship, sir?" He caught the wing commander's look and hastily corrected himself: "I mean rebel ship, sir, of course."

"Then you should have said so. Is that what the junior officers generally call those scoundrels?"

Evan conscientiously cast his mind back over the last few junior messes and reported unhappily: "I'm afraid we do, sir. We seem to have got into the habit."

"I shall write a memorandum about it. How do you account for that very peculiar habit?"

"Well, sir, they do have something like a fleet, and they did take over the Regulus Cluster, didn't they?"

What had got into this incredible fellow, Arris wondered in amazement. Why, the thing was self-evident! They had a few ships—accounts differed as to how many—and they had, doubtless by raw sedition, taken over some systems temporarily.

He turned from his aide, who sensibly became interested in a screen and left with a murmured excuse to study it very closely.

The brigands had certainly knocked together some ramshackle league or other, but— The wing commander wondered briefly if it could last, shut the horrid thought from his head, and set himself to composing mentally a stiff memorandum that would be posted in the junior officer's mess and put an end to this absurd talk.

His eyes wandered to the sixty-incher, where he saw the interceptor squadron climbing nicely toward the particle—which, he noticed, had become three particles. A low crooning distracted him. Was one of the tecks singing at work? It couldn't be!

It wasn't. An unsteady shape wandered up in the darkness, murmuring a song and exhaling alcohol. He recognized the Chief Archivist, Glen.

"This is Service country, mister," he told Glen.

"Hullo, Arris," the round little civilian said, peering at him.

"I come down here regularly—regularly against regulations—to wear off my regular irregularities with the wine bottle. That's all right, isn't it?"

He was drunk and argumentative. Arris felt hemmed in. Glen couldn't be talked into leaving without loss of dignity to the wing commander, and he couldn't be chucked out because he was writing a biography of the chamberlain and could, for the time being, have any head in the palace for the asking. Arris sat down unhappily, and Glen plumped down beside him.

The little man asked him.

"Is that a fleet from the Frontier League?" He pointed to the big screen. Arris didn't look at his face, but felt that Glen was grinning maliciously.

"I know of no organization called the Frontier League," Arris said. "If you are referring to the brigands who have recently been operating in Galactic East, you could at least call them by their proper names." Really, he thought—civilians!

"So sorry. But the brigands should have the Regulus Cluster by now, shouldn't they?" he asked, insinuatingly.

This was serious—a grave breach of security. Arris turned to the little man.

"Mister, I have no authority to command you," he said measuredly. "Furthermore, I understand you are enjoying a temporary eminence in the non-service world which would make it very difficult for me to—ah—tangle with you. I shall therefore refer only to your altruism. How did you find out about the Regulus Cluster?"

"Eloquent!" murmured the little man, smiling happily. "I got it from Rome."

Arris searched his memory. "You mean Squadron Commander Romo broke security? I can't believe it!"

"No, commander. I mean Rome—a place—a time—a civilization. I got it also from Babylon, Assyria, the Mogul Raj—every one of them. You don't understand me, of course."

"I understand that you're trifling with Service security and that you're a fat little, malevolent, worthless drone and scribbler!"

"Oh, commander!" protested the archivist. "I'm not so little!" He wandered away, chuckling.

Arris wished he had the shooting of him, and tried to explore the chain of secrecy for a weak link. He was tired and bored by this harping on the Fron—on the brigands.

His aide tentatively approached him. "Interceptors in striking range, sir," he murmured.

"Thank you," said the wing commander, genuinely grateful to be back in the clean, etched-line world of the Service and out of that blurred, water-color, civilian land where long-dead Syrians apparently retailed classified matter to nasty little drunken warts who had no business with it. Arris confronted the sixty-incher. The particle that had become three particles was now—he counted—eighteen particles. Big ones. Getting bigger.

He did not allow himself emotion, but turned to the plot on the interceptor squadron.

"Set up Lunar relay," he ordered.

"Yessir."

Half the plot room crew bustled silently and efficiently about the delicate job of applied relativistic physics that was 'lunar relay.' He knew that the palace power plant could take it for a few minutes, and he wanted to *see*. If he could not believe radar pips, he might believe a video screen.

On the great, green circle, the eighteen—now twenty-four—particles neared the thirty-six smaller particles that were interceptors, led by the eager young Efrid.

"Testing Lunar relay, sir," said the chief teck.

The wing commander turned to a twelve-inch screen. Unobtrusively, behind him, tecks jockeyed for position. The picture on the screen was something to see. The chief let mercury fill a thick-walled, ceramic tank. There was a sputtering and contact was made.

"Well done," said Arris. "Perfect seeing."

He saw, upper left, a globe of ships—what ships! Some were Service jobs, with extra turrets plastered on them wherever there was room. Some were orthodox freighters, with the same porcupine-bristle of weapons. Some were obviously home-made crates, hideously ugly—and as heavily armed as the others.

Next to him, Arris heard his aide murmur, "It's all wrong, sir. They haven't got any pick-up boats. They haven't got any hospital ships. What happens when one of them gets shot up?"

"Just what ought to happen, Evan," snapped the wing commander. "They float in space until they desiccate in their suits. Or if they get grappled inboard with a boat hook, they don't get any medical care. As I told you, they're brigands, without decency even to care for their own." He enlarged on the theme. "Their morale must be insignificant compared with our men's. When the Service goes into action, every rating and teck knows he'll be cared for if he's hurt. Why, if we didn't have pick-up boats and hospital ships the men wouldn't—'' He almost finished it with "fight," but thought, and lamely ended—"wouldn't like it."

Evan nodded, wonderingly, and crowded his chief a little as he craned his neck for a look at the screen.

"Get the hell away from here!" said the wing commander in a restrained yell, and Evan got.

The interceptor squadron swam into the field—a sleek, deadly needle of vessels in perfect alignment, with its little cloud of pick-ups trailing, and farther astern a white hospital ship with the ancient red cross.

The contact was immediate and shocking. One of the rebel ships lumbered into the path of the interceptors, spraying fire from what seemed to be as many points as a man has pores. The Service ships promptly riddled it and it should have drifted away—but it didn't. It kept on fighting. It rammed an interceptor with a crunch that must have killed every man before the first bulwark, but aft of the bulwark the ship kept fighting.

It took a torpedo portside and its plumbing drifted through space in a tangle. Still the starboard side kept squirting fire. Isolated weapon blisters fought on while they were obviously cut off from the rest of the ship. It was a pounded tangle of wreckage, and it had destroyed two interceptors, crippled two more, and kept fighting.

Finally, it drifted away, under feeble jets of power. Two more of the fantastic rebel fleet wandered into action, but the wing commander's horrified eyes were on the first pile of scrap. It was going *somewhere*—

The ship neared the thin-skinned, unarmored, gleaming hospital vessel, rammed it amidships, square in one of the red crosses, and then blew itself up, apparently with everything left in its powder magazine, taking the hospital ship with it.

The sickened wing commander would never have recognized what he had seen as it was told in a later version, thus:

> "The crushing course they took
> And nobly knew
> Their death undaunted
> By heroic blast
> The hospital's host
> They dragged to doom
> Hail! Men without mercy
> From the far frontier!"

Lunar relay flickered out as overloaded fuses flashed into vapor. Arris distractedly paced back to the dark corner and sank into a chair.

"I'm sorry," said the voice of Glen next to him, sounding quite sincere. "No doubt it was quite a shock to you."

"Not to you?" asked Arris bitterly.

"Not to me."

"Then how did they do it?" the wing commander asked the civilian in a low, desperate whisper. "They don't even wear .45's. Intelligence says their enlisted men have hit their officers and got away with it. They *elect* ship captains! Glen, what does it all mean?"

"It means," said the fat little man with a timbre of doom in his voice, "that they've returned. They always have. They always will. You see, commander, there is always somewhere a wealthy, powerful city, or nation, or world. In it are those whose blood is not right for a wealthy, powerful place. They must seek danger and overcome it. So they go out—on the marshes, in the desert, on the tundra, the planets, or the stars. Being strong, they grow stronger by fighting the tundra, the planets or the stars. They—they change. They sing new songs. They know new heroes. And then, one day, they return to their old home.

"They return to the wealthy, powerful city, or nation or world. They fight its guardians as they fought the tundra, the planets or the stars—a way that strikes terror to the heart. Then they sack the city, nation or world and sing great, ringing sagas of their deeds. They always have. Doubtless they always will."

"But what shall we do?"

"We shall cower, I suppose, beneath the bombs they drop on us, and we shall die, some bravely, some not, defending the palace within a very few hours. But you will have your revenge."

"How?" asked the wing commander, with haunted eyes.

The fat little man giggled and whispered in the officer's ear. Arris irritably shrugged it off as a bad joke. He didn't believe it. As he died, drilled through the chest a few hours later by one of Algan's gunfighters he believed it even less.

The professor's lecture was drawing to a close. There was time for only one more joke to send his students away happy. He was about to spring it when a messenger handed him two slips of paper. He raged inwardly at his ruined exit and poisonously read from them:

"I have been asked to make two announcements. One, a bulletin from General Sleg's force. He reports that the so-called Outland Insurrection is being brought under control and that there is no cause for alarm. Two, the gentlemen who are members of the S.O.T.C. will please report to the armory at 1375 hours—whatever that may mean—for blaster inspection. The class is dismissed.''

Petulantly, he swept from the lectern and through the door.

PRIVATE—KEEP OUT

by Philip MacDonald (1896–1981?)

The Magazine of Fantasy, Fall later known
as *The Magazine of Fantasy and Science Fiction*

The late Philip MacDonald was the grandson of the famous Scottish poet George MacDonald and a highly regarded
Hollywood screenwriter and detective novelist. Perhaps his
most famous film work was his script for Daphne du Maurier's
Rebecca (1940), but he also wrote a number of Mr. Moto and
Charlie Chan films. His detective character Anthony Gethryn,
introduced in 1924, appeared in some ten novels.

MacDonald's work was partially lost in the large shadows
of the two other great writers with the same last name—John
D. and Ross MacDonald—which is a shame, because he was
a major talent. Mystery critics maintain that his short stories
are even better than his novels; "Private—Keep Out", was
unfortunately one of only a handful of works he published
in the sf field.

And we can't allow another moment to go by without
welcoming The Magazine of Fantasy and Science Fiction to
this series. Few realized it at the time, but Anthony Boucher
and J. Francis McComas had launched what many* believe
to be the finest sf magazine of all time, one that is happily
still with us today. —M.H.G.

*Not *all*, Marty. (I.A.)

(They say that earthquakes are extremely terrifying, even if
you are in no immediate danger of having anything fall on
you; even if you are in an open field and no fissures form;
even if it only lasts for a minute or so.

I have never experienced an earthquake, but I think I can
imagine the sensation and can appreciate what it is that is so

terrifying. It is the fact that the solid earth is moving, shaking, vibrating. We are so used to the ground we walk upon being the motionless substratum on which all exists, we take it so for granted, that when that basic assumption is negated for even a short time, we feel the terror of chaos.

And yet there are assumptions that are more basic still, and if we were to get the notion that these, too, might vanish, our terror would be past description. "Private—Keep Out" by Philip MacDonald deals with such a disruption and you will not be human if you don't feel a frisson of horror at the last sentence.

Marty, by the way, wondered if this story was really science fiction. My response was that it most certainly was; and not only that but that I liked it better than I did any other story in the book—including mine.—I.A.)

The world goes mad—and people tend to put the cause of its sickness down to Man; sometimes even to one particular little man. Perhaps, only a few months ago, I would have thought like this myself about the existing outbreak of virulent insanity—but now I can't.

I can't because of something which happened to me a little while ago. I was in Southern California, working at Paramount. Most days, I used to get to the studio about ten and leave at five forty-five, but on this particular evening—it was Wednesday, the 18th of June—I was a little late getting away.

I went out through the front hall and hurried across the street to the garage. The entrance is a tunnelled archway. It was fairly dark in there—and I bumped square into a man who'd either been on his way out or standing there in the deepest part of the shadow. The latter didn't seem probable, but I had an odd sort of feeling that that was just what he had been doing.

"Sorry," I said. "I was . . ." I cut myself off short and stared. I recognized him, but what with the semi-darkness and the funny, stiff way he was standing and looking at me, I couldn't place him. It wasn't one of those half-memories of having once met someone somewhere. It was a definite, full-fledged memory which told me this man had been a friend closely knit into my particular life-pattern, and not so long ago.

He turned away—and something about the movement slipped the loose memory-cog back into place. It was Charles Moffat—Charles who'd been a friend for fifteen years; Charles whom I hadn't seen or heard about since he'd gone east in a mysterious hurry two years ago; Charles whom I was delighted to see again; Charles who'd changed amazingly; Charles, as I realized with a shock, who must have been very ill.

I shouted his name and leapt after him and grabbed him by the arm and swung him around to face me.

"You old sucker!" I said. "Don't you know me?"

He smiled with his mouth but nothing happened to his eyes. He said:

"How are you? I thought you'd forgotten me."

It should have been a jest—but it wasn't. I felt . . . *uncomfortable*.

"It's so damn' dark in here!" I said, and dragged him out into the sunshine of the street. His arm felt very thin.

"Straight over to Lucey's for a drink!" I was prattling and knew it. "We can talk there. Listen, Charles; you've been ill, haven't you? I can see it. Why didn't you let me know?"

He didn't answer, and I went on babbling rubbish; trying to talk myself out of the . . . the *apprehensiveness* which seemed to be oozing out of him and wrapping itself around the pair of us like a grey fog. I kept looking at him as we walked past the barber's and reached the corner and turned towards Melrose and its rushing river of traffic. He was looking straight ahead of him. He was extraordinarily thin: he must have lost twenty pounds— and he'd never been fat. I kept wishing I could see his eyes again, and then being glad I couldn't.

We stood on the curb by the auto-park and waited a chance to cross Melrose. The sun was low now, and I was shading my eyes from it when Charles spoke for the first time.

"I can use that drink," he said, but he still didn't look at me.

I half-turned, to get the sun out of my eyes—and noticed the briefcase for the first time. It was tucked firmly under his left arm and clamped tightly to his side. Even beneath his sleeve I could see an unusual tensing of the wasted muscles. I was going to say something, but a break came in the traffic and Charles plunged out into the road ahead of me.

It was cool in Lucey's bar, and almost empty. I wondered if the barman would remember Charles, then recalled that he'd only been here a couple of months. We ordered—a gin-and-tonic for me and a whiskey-sour for Charles which he put down in a couple of gulps.

"Another?" he said. He was looking at the pack of cigarettes in his hand.

"Mine's long," I said. "Miss me this time."

While I finished my tall glass, he had two more whiskey-sours, the second with an absinthe float. I chatted, heavily. Charles didn't help: with the briefcase tucked under his arm and clamped against his side, he looked like a starving bird with one wing.

I bought another round—and began to exchange my uneasiness for a sort of anger. I said:

"Look here! This is damn ridiculous!" I swivelled around on my stool and stared at him.

He gave a small barking sound which I suppose was meant to be a laugh. He said:

"*Ridiculous!* . . . Maybe that's not *quite* the word, my boy."

He barked again—and I remembered his old laugh, a Gargantuan affair which would make strangers smile at thirty paces. My anger went and the other feeling came back.

"Look," I said, dropping my voice. "Tell me what's wrong, Charles. There's something awfully wrong. What *is* it?"

He stood up suddenly and clicked his fingers at the barman. "Two more," he said. "And don't forget the absinthe on mine."

He looked at me fully. His eyes were brighter now, but that didn't alter the look in them. I couldn't kid myself any more: it was fear—and, even to me who have seen many varieties of this unpleasant ailment, a new mixture. Not, in fact, as before, but a *new* fear; a fear which transcended all known variations upon the fear theme.

I supposed I sat there gaping at him. But he didn't look at me any more. He clamped the briefcase under his arm and turned away.

" 'Phone," he said. "Back in a minute."

He took a step and then halted, turning his head to speak to me over his shoulder. He said:

"Seen the Archers lately?" and then was gone.

That's exactly what he said, but at the time, I thought I must have mis-heard him—because I didn't know any Archers. Twenty-five years before, there'd been a John Archer at school with me but I hadn't known him well and hadn't liked what I did know.

I puzzled over this for a moment; then went back to my problem. What was the matter with Charles? Where had he been all this time? Why didn't anyone hear from or about him? Above all, what was he afraid of? And why should I be feeling, in the most extraordinary way, that life was a thin crust upon which we all moved perilously?

The barman, a placid crust-walker, set a new drink down in front of me and said something about the weather. I answered him eagerly, diving into a sunny sanctuary of platitude.

It did me good—until Charles came back. I watched him cross the room—and didn't like it. His clothes hung loose about him, with room for another Charles inside them. He picked up his drink and drained it. He drank with his left hand, because the briefcase was under his right arm now. I said:

"Why don't you put that thing down? What's in it, anyway—nuggets?"

He shifted it under the other arm and looked at me for a moment. He said:

"Just some papers. Where're you dining?"

"With you." I made a quick mental cancellation. "Or you are with me, rather."

"Good!" He nodded jerkily. "Let's get a booth now. One of the end ones."

I stood up. "Okay. But if we're going to drink any more, I'll switch to a martini."

He gave the order and we left the bar and in a minute were facing each other in a far corner booth. Charles looked right at me now, and I couldn't get away from his eyes and what was in them. A waiter came with the drinks and put them in front of us and went away. I looked down at mine and began to fool with the toothpick which speared the olive.

"You're not a moron," he said suddenly. "Nor a cabbage. Ever wake up in the morning and know you know the Key—but when you reach for it, you can't remember it? It was just *there* . . ." He made a vague, sharp gesture in the air, close to his head. "But it's gone the minute your waking mind reaches for it. Ever do that? Ever feel that? Not only when you wake maybe; perhaps at some other sort of time?"

He was looking down at the table now and I didn't have to see his eyes. He was looking down at his hands, claw-like as they fiddled with brass locks on the briefcase. I said:

"What're you talking about? What key?" I was deliberately dense.

His eyes blazed at me with some of the old Carolian fire.

"Listen, numbskull!" He spoke without opening his teeth. "Have you, at any moment in your wretched existence, ever felt that you knew, only a moment before, the answer to . . . to *everything?* To the colossal WHY of the Universe? To the myriad questions entailed by the elaborate creation of Man? To . . . to *Everything,* you damned fool!"

I stopped pretending. "Once or twice," I said. "Maybe more than that. You mean that awful sensation that you're on the verge of knowing the . . . the Universal Answer: and know it's amazingly simple and you wonder why you never thought of it before—and then you find you don't know it at all. It's gone; snatched away. And you go practically out of your mind trying to get it back but you never succeed. That's it, isn't it? I've had the feeling several times, notably coming out of ether. Everyone has. Why?''

He was fiddling with the briefcase again. "Why what?" he said dully. The momentary flash of the old fire had died away.

But I kept at him. I said:

"You can't start something like that and then throw it away. Why did you bring the subject up? Did you finally grab the Key this morning—or did it bite you—or what?"

He still didn't look up. He went on fiddling with the brass locks on the case.

"For God's sake, leave that thing alone!" My irritation was genuine enough. "It's getting on my nerves. Sit on it or something, if it's so precious. But quit *fiddling!*"

He stood up suddenly. He didn't seem to hear me.

" 'Phone again," he said. "Sorry. Forgot something. Won't be long." He started away; then turned and slapped the case down in front of me. "Have a look through it. Might interest you."

And he was gone. I put my hands on the case and was just going to slip the locks back with my thumbs, when a most extraordinary sensation . . . *permeated* me is the only word I can think of. I was suddenly extremely loath to open the thing. I pushed it away from me with a quick involuntary gesture, as if it were hot to the touch.

And immediately I was ashamed of this childish behavior and took myself in hand and in a moment had it open and the contents spread in front of me.

They were mostly papers, and all completely innocuous and unrelated. If you tried for a year you couldn't get together a less alarming collection.

There was a program from the Frohman Theatre, New York, for a play called "Every Other Friday" which I remembered seeing in '31. There was a letter from the Secretary to the Dean of Harvard, with several pages of names attached to it, saying that in answer to Mr. Moffat's letter he would find attached the list he had requested of the Alumni of 1925. There was a letter from the Manager of a Fifth Avenue apartment house, courteously replying to Mr. Moffat's request for a list of the tenants of his penthouse during the years 1933 to 1935. There were several old bills from a strange miscellany of stores, a folded page from an old school magazine containing the photograph of the football team of C.M.I. in the year 1919, and a page torn from "Who's Who" around one entry of which heavy blue pencil lines had been drawn.

And that finished the papers. There were only three other things—an empty, much-worn photograph frame of leather, a small silver plate (obviously unscrewed from the base of some trophy) with the names *Charles Moffat* and *T. Perry Devonshire* inscribed upon it, and an old briar pipe with a charred bowl and broken mouthpiece but a shiny new silver band.

The photograph frame stared up at me from the white tablecloth. I picked it up—and, as I did so, was struck by a sudden but undefinable familiarity. I turned it over in my hands, struggling with the elusive memory-shape, and I saw that, although the front of it bore every sign of considerable age and usage, it had never in fact been used. It was one of those frames which you undo at the back to insert the photograph, and pasted across the joint between the body of the frame and the movable part was the original price tag, very old and very dirty, but still bearing the dim figures $5.86.

I was still looking at it when Charles came back.

"Remember it?" he said.

I twisted the thing about, trying to find a new angle to look at it from. He said:

"It used to be on my desk. You've seen it hundreds of times."

I began to remember. I could see it sitting beside a horseshoe inkpot—but I couldn't see what was inside it. I said:

"I can't think what was in it." And then I remembered. "But there can't have been anything." I turned the thing over and showed him the price tag. I was suddenly conscious of personal fear.

"Charles!" I said. "What the hell *is* all this?"

He spoke—but he didn't answer me. He picked up the collection of nonsense and put it back into the briefcase.

"Did you look at all the stuff?" he said.

I nodded, watching him. It seemed that we never looked at each other squarely, for his eyes were upon his hands.

"Did it suggest anything?" he said.

"Not a thing. How could it?" I saw that the knuckles of his interlocked fingers were white. "Look here, Charles, if you don't tell me what all this is about I'll go out of my mind."

And then the head waiter came. He smiled at me and bowed gravely to Charles and asked whether we wished to order.

I was going to tell him to wait, but Charles took the menu and looked at it and ordered something, so I did the same.

It was nearly dark outside now and they'd put on the lights. People were beginning to come in and there was quite a murmur of talk from the bar. I held my tongue: the moment had passed—I must wait for another.

They brought cocktails and we sipped them and smoked and didn't speak until Charles broke the silence. He said then, much too casually:

"So you haven't been seeing much of the Archers?"

"Charles," I said carefully, "I don't know anyone called Archer. I never have—except an unpleasant little tick at school."

Our eyes met now, and he didn't look away. But a waiter came with hors d'oeuvres. I refused them, but Charles heaped his plate and began to eat with strange voracity.

"These Archers?" I said at last. "Who are they? Anything to do with this . . . this . . . trouble you seem to have?"

He looked at me momentarily; then down at his plate again. He finished what was on it and leaned back and gazed at the wall over my right shoulder. He said:

"Adrian Archer was a great friend of mine." He took a cigarette from the pack on the table and lit it. "He was also a friend of yours."

The waiter came again and took away my full plate and Charles's empty one.

"*What* did you say?" I wasn't trusting my ears.

He took the briefcase from the seat beside him and groped in it and brought his hand out holding the extract from "Who's Who."

"Look at this." He handed me the sheet. "That's Adrian's father."

I took the paper, but went on staring at him. His eyes were glittering.

"Go on!" he said. "Read it."

The marked entry was short and prosaic. It was the history, in seven lines, of an Episcopalian minister named William Archibald Archer.

I read it carefully. I ought to have been feeling, I suppose, that Charles was a sick man. But I wasn't feeling anything of the sort. I can't describe what I was feeling.

I read the thing again.

"Look here, Charles," I said. "This man had three daughters. There's no mention of a son."

"Yes," said Charles. "I know."

He twiched the paper out of my hand and fished in the briefcase again and brought out the little silver plate. He said:

"In '29 I won the doubles in the Lakeside tennis tournament. Adrian Archer was my partner." His voice was flat, and the words without any emphasis. He handed the piece of metal across to me and once more I read *Charles Moffet—T. Perry Devonshire*. . . .

And then the waiter was with us again and for the longest half hour of my life I watched Charles devour his food while I pushed mine aside and drank a glass of wine. I watched him eat. I couldn't help myself. He ate with a sort of desperate determination; like a man clutching at the one reality.

Then, at last, the meal was over, with even the coffee gone and just brandy glasses before us. He began to talk. Not in the guarded, jerky way he had been using, but with words pouring out of him. He said:

"I'm going to tell you the story of Adrian Archer—straight. He was a contemporary of ours—in fact, I was at C.M.I. and Harvard with him. It was settled he should be a lawyer, but a year after he left Harvard he suddenly went on the stage. His father and all his friends—*you* included—advised him not to. But Adrian didn't pay attention. He just smiled, with that odd, *secret* smile he'd use sometimes. He just smiled—and his rise to what they call fame was what they call meteoric. In three years he was a big name on Broadway. In four he was another in London. In six they were billing his name before the title of the play—and in the eighth Hollywood grabbed him and made what they call a star out of him in a period they call overnight. That was four years ago—same year that you and I first came out here. We were both at RKO when he made his terrific hit in *Judgment Day*, playing the blind man. . . ."

For the first time I interrupted.

"Charles!" I said. "Charles! I saw *Judgment Day*. Spencer Tracy played . . ."

"Yes," said Charles. "I know. . . . When Adrian came to Hollywood, you and I were awfully glad to see him—and when Margaret came to join him and brought the kid and we'd installed them comfortably in a house on the Santa Monica Palisades, everything was fine."

He drained the brandy in his glass and tipped some more into it from the bottle. The single lamp on the table threw sharp-angled shadows across his face. He said:

"Well, there they were. Adrian went from success to success

in things like *The Key Above the Door, Fit for Heroes* and *Sunday's Children.*"

He stopped again—and looked directly at me.

"I'm sorry for you," he said suddenly. "It's a bad spot to be in—meeting an old friend and finding he's gone out of his mind. And pretending to listen while your mind's busy with doctors' names and 'phone numbers."

I said: "I don't know what I think—except that I'm not doubting your sanity. And I can't understand why I'm not."

I wished he'd stop looking at me now. But his eyes didn't leave my face. He said:

"Seen the Mortimers lately?"

I jumped as if he'd hit me. But I answered in a minute.

"Of course I have," I said. "I see 'em all the time. Frank and I have been working together. Matter of fact, I had dinner there only last night."

His mouth twisted into the shape of a smile. "Still living on the Palisades, are they? 107 Paloma Drive?"

"Yes." I tried to keep my voice steady. "They bought that place, you know."

"Yes," said Charles, "I know. The Archers had the next house, 109. You found it actually. Adrian liked it all right and Margaret and the boy were crazy about it, especially the pool."

He drank some more brandy—and there was a long, sharp-edged silence. But I wouldn't say anything, and he began again. He said:

"D'you remember when you were at MGM two years ago? You were revamping that *Richard The Lion-Heart* job and you had to go to Del Monte on location?"

I nodded. I remembered very well.

"That," said Charles, "was when it happened. The Mortimers gave a cocktail party. At least, that's what it started out to be, but it was after midnight when I left—with the Archers. I'd parked my car at the corner of Paloma and Palisade, right outside their house, so I walked along with them and went in for a nightcap. It was pretty hot, and we sat on the patio, looking over the swimming pool. There weren't any servants up and Adrian went into the house for the drinks. He'd been very quiet all night and not, I thought, looking particularly fit. I said something casual about this to Margaret—and then was surprised when she took me up, very seriously. She said: 'Charles: he's worried—and so am I!'' I remember looking at her and finding that her eyes were grave and troubled as I'd never seen them. 'Charles,' she said, 'he's . . . *frightened*—and so am I!' ''

Charles broke off again. He pulled out a handkerchief and I saw that sweat was glistening on his forehead. He said:

"Before I could say anything Adrian came out with a tray and put it down and began mixing drinks. He looked at Margaret— and asked what we'd been talking about and wouldn't be put off. She looked apprehensive when I told him, but he didn't seem to mind. He gave us both drinks and took one himself—and suddenly asked me a question I asked you earlier this evening."

"About the Key?" My voice surprised me: I hadn't told it to say anything.

Charles nodded. But he didn't go on.

"Then what?" said my voice. "Then what?"

"It's funny," he said. "But this is the first time I've told all this—and I've just realized I should've begun at the other end and said *I* was worried and frightened. Because I was—had been for weeks. . . ."

A frightful feeling of verification swept over me. I said excitedly:

"By God, I remember. About the time I went on location you were sort of down. You'd had a polo spill. I was a bit worried about you, but you said you were O.K. . . ."

For a moment I thought he was going to break. He looked— *Charles Moffat* looked—as if he were going to weep. But he took hold of himself, and the jaw-muscles in his face stood out like wire rope. He said:

"The doctor said I was all right. But I wasn't. Not by a mile! There was only one thing wrong with me—but that was plenty. I wasn't sleeping. It may have been something to do with the crack on the head or it may not. But, whatever it was, it was bad. Very bad. And dope made no difference—except, perhaps, for the worse. I'd *go* to sleep all right—but then I'd keep waking up. And that was the bad part. Because every time I'd wake, that God-damned Key would be a little nearer. . . . At first, it wasn't so worrying—merely an irritation. But as it went on, stronger and stronger, three and four and six times a night—well, it was *bad*!"

He stopped abruptly. His tongue seemed to be trying to moisten his lips. He took a swallow of brandy and then, incredibly, a long draught of water. The film of sweat was over his forehead again, and he mopped at it absentmindedly, with the back of his hand. He said:

"So there you are: and we're back again—half in moonlight, half in shadow—on Adrian's patio, and he's just asked me the question and Margaret is leaning forward, her chin cupped in her hands and I can feel her eyes on my face and I'm staring at Adrian in amazement that *he* should ask *me* whether *I* know what it's like to feel that you're coming nearer and nearer to the Answer—that simple, A.B.C. *answer* which has always eluded Man; the Answer which is forbidden to Man but which, when it's dangled in front of his nose like a donkey's carrot, he's bound to clutch for desperately. . . .

"We were pretty full of drink—you know what the Mortimer hospitality's like—and once I'd got over the awful shock of egotistical surprise at finding that another man, and my greatest friend to boot, was being ridden by a demon I'd considered my own personal property, we began to talk thirty to the dozen, while Margaret turned those great dark eyes upon us in turn. There was fear in them, but we went on, theorizing to reduce *our* fear, and traced the *Key-awareness* back to our adolescence and wondered why we'd never told each other about it at school and gradually—with the decanter getting lower and lower and the impossible California moon beginning to pale—began to strive to put into words what we *thought* might be the *shape* of the Key. . . .

"We didn't get very far and we didn't make much sense: who can when they're talking about things for which there are no words. But we frightened ourselves badly—and Margaret. We began to talk—or Adrian did, rather because he was much *nearer* than I'd ever been—we began to talk about the feeling that made it all the more essential to grasp the thing; the feeling that the knowledge wasn't *allowed*. And Margaret suddenly jumped to her feet, and a glass fell from the wicker table and smashed on the tiles with a thin, shivering ring. I can remember what she said. I can hear her say it any time I want to and many times when I don't. She looked down at us—and she seemed, I remember, to look very tall although she was a little woman. She said: 'Look at it all! *Look!*' and she made a great sweeping gesture with her arms towards everything in the world outside this little brick place where we were sitting. And then she said: "Leave it there—*leave* it! . . .'"

Charles shivered—like a man with ague. And then he took hold of himself. I could see the jaw-muscles again, and the shine of the sweat on his forehead. He said at last:

"Margaret sort of crumpled up and fell back into her chair. She looked small again, and tears were rolling slowly down her cheeks. I know she didn't know there were any tears. She sat with her head up and her arms on the edge of the table and stared out at the world beyond the swimming pool; the world which was turning from solid, moon-shot darkness to vague and nebu-

lous and unhappy grey. Adrian got up. He sat on the arm of her
chair and put an arm around her shoulders and laid his cheek
against her hair. They were very still and absolutely silent. I
couldn't stand it and went into the house and found Adrian's
cellar and a couple of bottles of Perrier Jouet—it was '28, I
remember—and put some ice in a pail and found some glasses
and took my loot back to the patio. They were still exactly as I'd
left them and I shouted at them to break that immobility: I didn't
like it. . . .

"It broke all right—and I fooled around with the pail and the
bottles and began talking a streak and at last shoved some wine
down their throats and put away half a pint at a swallow myself
and started in to be very funny. . . .

"Adrian began to help me—and we played the fool and drank
the second bottle and he found a third and at last we got
Margaret laughing and then he stole the curtain with a very nice
swan dive from the patio-wall into the pool, ruining a good
dinner-jacket in the process. . . .

"It was nearly dawn when I left—and they both came around
to the front of the house to see me off. And Margaret asked me
to come to lunch. And I said I would and waved at them and
started the car. And . . . that was all."

He didn't stop abruptly this time. His voice and words just
trailed softly into silence. He sat looking straight at me, absolutely still. I wanted to get away from his eyes—but I couldn't.
The silence went on too long. I said:

"Go on! I don't understand. What d'you *mean*—'that was
all'?"

He said: "I didn't see the Archers any more. They weren't
there. They . . . weren't. I heard Margaret's voice again—but it
only said one word."

And then more silence. I said, finding some words:

"I don't understand. Tell me."

He dropped his eyes while he found a cigarette and lit it. He
said:

"There's a lot in slang. As Chesterton once pointed out, the
greatest poet of 'em all is Demos. The gag-man or gangster or
rewrite man who first used the phrase *'rub him out'*, said a
whole lot more than he knew. . . . Because that's what happened to Adrian. He was *rubbed out*—erased—deleted in all
three dimensions of Time—cancelled—made not!"

"You can't stop in the middle like that! Tell me what you're
talking about. What d'you mean?"

He still looked at me. "I mean what I said. After that morning,

there was no more Adrian. . . . He was—*rubbed out*. Remember
the things in the briefcase? Well, they'll help to explain. After
. . . it happened, I was—sort of ill. I've no idea for how
long—but when I could *think* again, I set out on a sort of crusade:
to prove to myself that I was the only living thing which
remembered—which knew there'd ever been such an entity as
Adrian Archer. Mind you, I hoped to *disprove* it, though I felt
all the time I never would. And I haven't. You saw those papers
and things—they're just an infinitesimal fraction of my proof.
There *was* an Adrian Archer—but now there never has been.
That photograph frame used to have his and Margaret's picture
in it—but now there's the old price-tag to show it's never been
opened. That pipe: Adrian gave it to me and my initials were on
it in facsimile of his writing—but now the band's plain and bare
and new. . . . Adrian Archer was at school and college with me—
but no records show the name and no contemporary mind
remembers. I've known his father since I was a pup—but his
father *knows* he never had a son. There were pictures—photographs—in which Adrian and I both were, sometimes together—
and now those same pictures show me with someone whom
every one knows but me. On the programmes of all his plays
there's another man listed for his part—and that man is a known
and living man in every case; a man who *knows* he played the
part and remembers doing it as well as other people—you, for
instance—remember his playing it. The pictures he made are all
available to be seen—but there's no Adrian in them: there's
some other star—who remembers everything about playing the
part and has the weeks he took in shooting intricately woven into
his life-pattern. Adrian—and everything that was Adrian's—have
been removed and replaced: he *isn't* and *won't be* and *never has
been;* he was cancelled in *esse* and *posse;* taken out of our little
life and time and being like a speck out of yeast. And over the
hole which the speck made the yeast has bubbled and seethed
and closed—and there never was any speck—except to the knowledge of another speck; a speck who was almost as near to the
danger-point of accidental knowledge as the one which was
removed; a speck whose punishment and warning are memory!''

"Tell me!'' I said. "Tell me what *happened*—after you drove
away. . . .''

"My God!'' said Charles, and there seemed to be tears in his
eyes. "My God! You're believing me! . . . I'll tell you: I drove
home. I was so tired I thought I might really sleep. I tore off my
clothes and rolled into bed after I'd pulled the blinds tight down
against the sun which would be up in a few minutes. And I *did*

sleep. I'd put a note on the door for my servant not to wake me, and he didn't. But the telephone did—and I cursed and rolled over and groped for it without opening my eyes. . . .

"And then I heard Margaret's voice, calling my name. I knew it was her voice—though it was shrill and harsh with wild, incredible terror. It called my name, over and over again. And then, when I answered, it said 'Adrian's . . .' And then, without any other sound—without any click or noise or any sound at all—she wasn't there.

"I didn't waste any time. I slammed the phone down—and in nothing flat I was in the car and racing up Sunset, past the Riviera.

"I took the turn into Paloma Drive on two wheels and went on, around those endless curves, at well over sixty. And I came, past the Mortimers' house, to the corner of Paloma and Palisade. . . ."

I interrupted again, in that voice which didn't feel like mine.

"Wait! I've remembered something. You say this house was on the corner of Palisade Avenue and Paloma Drive, next the Mortimers'? Well, *there isn't any house there!* There's a little park-place there—a garden. . . .''

"Yes," said Charles, "I know. That's what *you* know; what everyone knows; what the Urban records would prove. . . . But there, right on that corner, *had been* a white colonial house, which *you* got for the Archers, and out of which I had come only a few hours before. . . .

"It was glaring, monstrous impossibility—and a brutal, inescapable fact! The green grass and the red flowers blazed at me with appalling reality, flaunting neat and well-tended and matured beauty—and the little white railings and the odd-shaped green seats and the yellow gravel paths and the spraying fountain all stared at me with smug actuality. . . .

"I stopped the car somehow. I knew I was on the right road because I'd seen Mary Mortimer talking to a gardener in front of their house. I was shaking all over—and Fear had me by the guts with a cold claw which twisted. I fumbled at the car door. I had to have air. The sunshine was bright and golden but it was . . . *filthy* somehow; it was like the light which might be shed by some huge, undreamt-of reptile. I had to have air, though. I stumbled out onto the sidewalk and staggered across it towards one of the seats by the fountain. And my foot caught against something and there was a sharp pain in my leg and I looked down. I'd run my shin onto one of those little metal signs they stick up on lawns, and the plate was bent back so that the white printing on the green background was staring up at me. It said: 'KEEP OFF THE GRASS'!''

The crust felt thin beneath my feet. I knew he wasn't going to say any more—but I kept expecting him to. We sat for a long time, while a waiter came and cleared away and spread a clean cloth and finally went.

"Just a minute," said Charles suddenly. "Have to 'phone again."

He walked away—and I went on sitting.

In half an hour, the waiter came back. I asked him where Mr. Moffat was; surely not still in the 'phone-booth?

He stared. "Mr. Who, sir?"

I said after a long pause but very sharply:

"Mr. Moffat. The gentleman who was dining with me."

He didn't seem to know what I was talking about.

I wonder how much longer there is for me.

THE HURKLE IS A HAPPY BEAST

by Theodore Sturgeon (1918–   )

The Magazine of Fantasy and Science Fiction,
Fall

Alien beings are one of the staples of modern science fiction, appearing in countless stories and novels. They come in all sizes, shapes and colors; they are sometimes very intelligent, sometimes not; some can handle our atmosphere and some cannot; sometimes we visit them and on occasion they visit us—the variations are endless. However, in the early history of American genre sf, aliens were mean—they wanted our planet because their own was dying or because it was overpopulated; they wanted our resources; and they frequently (beyond all biological possibility) seemed to want our women (there were very few stories in which they wanted our men in the same way). Sometimes they wanted all of us for dinner.

Things did change after a time, thanks to writers like Stanley G. Weinbaum, and friendly aliens began to appear and then humans often mistreated them or took advantage of them and they became surrogates for colonized native peoples, American Indians, and minority group members. Currently another type of alien appears frequently—the cuddly, cutesy aliens of Close Encounters of the Third Kind *and especially* E.T. *Personally, I like my aliens without many redeeming qualities, but I have an open mind and I know a great cutesy alien story when I read one.*

So here is "The Hurkle is a Happy Beast," one of the best of its sub-type, and also one (it's only fair to warn you) that's not all that it appears to be.—M.H.G.

(A woman, recently, told me that she never read science fiction because it frightened her so. I realized that she was

*thinking of science fiction purely in terms of horror stories
such as those written by Stephen King. Seeing a chance to
educate her and, at the same time, do myself a bit of good, I
said, "Buy one of my science fiction books. It won't frighten
you. If it does, let me know, and I'll refund your money."*

*After a few days, she wrote me, quite enthusiastically, that
my book had not frightened her at all, but had greatly interested her, and that she had now discovered a new and particularly suitable sort of reading material. I was delighted.*

*As a matter of fact, science fiction can not only be non-
frightening; it can be downright light and happy. "The Hurkle
Is a Happy Beast" by Theodore Sturgeon is an example. It is
a very pleasant story involving a very pleasant alien beast
whom any one of us would gladly hug to his (or her) bosom.*

*And if that makes you happy, then perhaps you had better
not read the last eight lines.—I.A.)*

Lirht is either in a different universal plane or in another island
galaxy. Perhaps these terms mean the same thing. The fact
remains that Lirht is a planet with three moons (one of which is
unknown) and a sun, which is as important in its universe as is
ours.

Lirht is inhabited by gwik, its dominant race, and by several
less highly developed species which, for purposes of this narrative,
can be ignored. Except, of course, for the hurkle. The hurkle are
highly regarded by the gwik as pets, in spite of the fact that a
hurkle is so affectionate that it can have no loyalty.

The prettiest of the hurkle are blue.

Now, on Lirht, in its greatest city, there was trouble, the
nature of which does not matter to us, and a gwik named Hvov,
whom you may immediately forget, blew up a building which
was important for reasons we cannot understand. This event
caused great excitement, and gwik left their homes and factories
and strubles and streamed toward the center of town, which is
how a certain laboratory door was left open.

In times of such huge confusion, the little things go on.
During the "Ten Days that Shook the World" the cafes and
theaters of Moscow and Petrograd remained open, people fell in
love, sued each other, died, shed sweat and tears; and some of
these were tears of laughter. So on Lirht, while the decisions on
the fate of the miserable Hvov were being formulated, gwik still
fardled, funted, and fupped. The great central hewton still beat
out its mighty pulse, and in the anams the corsons grew . . .

Into the above-mentioned laboratory, which had been left open through the circumstances described, wandered a hurkle kitten. It was very happy to find itself there; but then, the hurkle is a happy beast. It prowled about fearlessly—it could become invisible if frightened—and it glowed at the legs of the tables and at the glittering, racked walls. It moved sinuously, humping its back and arching along on the floor. Its front and rear legs were stiff and straight as the legs of a chair; the middle pair had two sets of knees, one bending forward, one back. It was engineered as ingeniously as a scorpion, and it was exceedingly blue.

Occupying almost a quarter of the laboratory was a huge and intricate machine, unhoused, showing the signs of development projects the galaxies over—temporary hookups from one component to another, cables terminating in spring clips, measuring devices standing about on small tables near the main work. The kitten regarded the machine with curiosity and friendly intent, sending a wave of radiations outward which were its glow or purr. It arched daintily around to the other side, stepping delicately but firmly on a floor switch.

Immediately there was a rushing, humming sound, like small birds chasing large mosquitoes, and parts of the machine began to get warm. The kitten watched curiously, and saw, high up inside the clutter of coils and wires, the most entrancing muzziness it had ever seen. It was like heat-flicker over a fallow field; it was like a smoke-vortex; it was like red neon lights on a wet pavement. To the hurkle kitten's senses, that red-orange flicker was also like the smell of catnip to a cat, or anise to a terrestrial terrier.

It reared up toward the glow, hooked its forelegs over a busbar—fortunately there was no ground potential—and drew itself upward. It climbed from transformer to powerpack, skittered up a variable condenser—the setting of which was changed thereby—disappeared momentarily as it felt the bite of a hot tube, and finally teetered on the edge of the glow.

The glow hovered in midair in a sort of cabinet, which was surrounded by heavy coils embodying tens of thousands of turns of small wire and great loops of bus. One side, the front, of the cabinet was open, and the kitten hung there fascinated, rocking back and forth to the rhythm of some unheard music it made to contrast this sourceless flame. Back and forth, back and forth it rocked and wove, riding a wave of delicious, compelling sensation. And once, just once, it moved its center of gravity too far from its point of support. Too far—far enough. It tumbled into the cabinet, into the flame.

* * *

One muggy, mid-June day a teacher, whose name was Stott and whose duties were to teach seven subjects to forty moppets in a very small town, was writing on a blackboard. He was writing the word Madagascar, and the air was so sticky and warm that he could feel his undershirt pasting and unpasting itself on his shoulder blade with each round "a" he wrote.

Behind him there was a sudden rustle from the moist seventh-graders. His schooled reflexes kept him from turning from the board until he had finished what he was doing, by which time the room was in a young uproar. Stott about-faced, opened his mouth, closed it again. A thing like this would require more than a routine reprimand.

His forty-odd charges were writhing and squirming in an extraordinary fashion, and the sound they made, a sort of whimpering giggle, was unique. He looked at one pupil after another. Here a hand was busily scratching a nape; there a boy was digging guiltily under his shirt; yonder a scrubbed and shining damsel violently worried her scalp.

Knowing the value of individual attack, Stott intoned, "Hubert, what seems to be the trouble?"

The room immediately quieted, though diminished scrabblings continued. "Nothin', Mister Stott," quavered Hubert.

Stott flicked his gaze from side to side. Wherever it rested, the scratching stopped and was replaced by agonized control. In its wake was rubbing and twitching. Stott glared, and idly thumbed a lower left rib. Someone snickered. Before he could identify the source, Stott was suddenly aware of an intense itching. He checked the impulse to go after it, knotted his jaw, and swore to himself that he wouldn't scratch as long as he was out there, front and center. "The class will—" he began tautly, and then stopped.

There was a—a *something* on the sill of the open window. He blinked and looked again. It was a translucent, bluish cloud which was almost nothing at all. It was less than a something should be, but it was indeed more than a nothing. If he stretched his imagination just a little, he might make out the outlines of an arched creature with too many legs; but of course that was ridiculous.

He looked away from it and scowled at his class. He had had two unfortunate experiences with stink bombs, and in the back of his mind was the thought of having seen once, in a trick-store window, a product called "itching powder." Could this be it, this terrible itch? He knew better, however, than to accuse anyone yet; if he were wrong, there was no point in giving the little geniuses any extracurricular notions.

He tried again. "The cl—" He swallowed. This itch was . . . "The class will—" He noticed that one head, then another and another, were turning toward the window. He realized that if the class got too interested in what he thought he saw on the window sill, he'd have a panic on his hands. He fumbled for his ruler and rapped twice on the desk. His control was not what it should have been at the moment; he struck far too hard, and the reports were like gunshots. The class turned to him as one; and behind them the thing on the window sill appeared with great distinctness.

It was blue—a truly beautiful blue. It had a small spherical head and an almost identical knob at the other end. There were four stiff, straight legs, a long sinuous body, and two central limbs with a boneless look about them. On the side of the head were four pairs of eyes, of graduated sizes. It teetered there for perhaps ten seconds, and then, without a sound, leapt through the window and was gone.

Mr. Stott, pale and shaking, closed his eyes. His knees trembled and weakened, and a delicate, dewy mustache of perspiration appeared on his upper lip. He clutched at the desk and forced his eyes open; and then, flooding him with relief, pealing into his terror, swinging his control back to him, the bell rang to end the class and the school day.

"Dismissed," he mumbled, and sat down. The class picked up and left, changing itself from a twittering pattern of rows to a rowdy kaleidoscope around the bottleneck doorway. Mr. Stott slumped down in his chair, noticing that the dreadful itch was gone, had been gone since he had made that thunderclap with the ruler.

Now, Mr. Stott was a man of method. Mr. Stott prided himself on his ability to teach his charges to use their powers of observation and all the machinery of logic at their command. Perhaps, then, he had more of both at his command—after he recovered himself—than could be expected of an ordinary man.

He sat and stared at the open window, not seeing the sunswept lawns outside. And after going over these events a halfdozen times, he fixed on two important facts:

First, that the animal he had seen, or thought he had seen, had six legs.

Second, that the animal was of such nature as to make anyone who had not seen it believe he was out of his mind.

These two thoughts had their corollaries:

First, that every animal he had ever seen which had six legs was an insect, and

Second, that if anything were to be done about this fantastic creature, he had better do it by himself. And whatever action he took must be taken immediately. He imagined the windows being kept shut to keep the thing out—in this heat—and he cowered away from the thought. He imagined the effect of such a monstrosity if it bounded into the midst of a classroom full of children in their early teens, and he recoiled. No; there could be no delay in this matter.

He went to the window and examined the sill. Nothing. There was nothing to be seen outside, either. He stood thoughtfully for a moment, pulling on his lower lip and thinking hard. Then he went downstairs to borrow five pounds of DDT powder from the janitor for an "experiment." He got a wide, flat wooden box and an electric fan, and set them up on a table he pushed close to the window. Then he sat down to wait, in case, just in case the blue beast returned.

When the hurkle kitten fell into the flame, it braced itself for a fall at least as far as the floor of the cabinet. Its shock was tremendous, then, when it found itself so braced and already resting on a surface. It looked around, panting with fright, its invisibility reflex in full operation.

The cabinet was gone. The flame was gone. The laboratory with its windows, lit by the orange Lirhtian sky, its ranks of shining equipment, its hulking, complex machine—all were gone.

The hurkle kitten sprawled in an open area, a sort of lawn. No colors were right; everything seemed half-lit, filmy, out-of-focus. There were trees, but not low and flat and bushy like honest Lirhtian trees, but with straight naked trunks and leaves like a portle's tooth. The different atomospheric gases had colors; clouds of fading, changing faint colors obscured and revealed everything. The kitten twitched its cafmors and ruddled its kump, right there where it stood; for no amount of early training could overcome a shock like this.

It gathered itself together and tried to move; and then it got its second shock. Instead of arching over inchwormwise, it floated into the air and came down three times as far as it had ever jumped in its life.

It cowered on the dreamlike grass, darting glances all about, under, and up. It was lonely and terrified and felt very much put upon. It saw its shadow through the shifting haze, and the sight terrified it even more, for it had no shadow when it was fright-

ened on Lirht. Everything here was all backwards and wrong
way up; it got more visible, instead of less, when it was frightened;
its legs didn't work right, it couldn't see properly, and there
wasn't a single, solitary malapek to be throdded anywhere. It
thought it heard some music; happily, that sounded all right
inside its round head, though somehow it didn't resonate as well
as it had.

It tried, with extreme caution, to move again. This time its
trajectory was shorter and more controlled. It tried a small,
grounded pace, and was quite successful. Then it bobbed for a
moment, seesawing on its flexible middle pair of legs, and, with
utter abandon, flung itself skyward. It went up perhaps fifteen
feet, turning end over end, and landed with its stiff forefeet in
the turf.

It was completely delighted with this sensation. It gathered
itself together, gryting with joy, and leapt up again. This time it
made more distance than altitude, and bounced two long, happy
bounces as it landed.

Its fears were gone in the exploration of this delicious new
freedom of motion. The hurkle, as has been said before, is a
happy beast. It curvetted and sailed, soared and somersaulted,
and at last brought up against a brick wall with stunning and
unpleasant results. It was learning, the hard way, a distinction
between weight and mass. The effect was slight but painful. It
drew back and stared forlornly at the bricks. Just when it was
beginning to feel friendly again . . .

It looked upward, and saw what appeared to be an opening in
the wall some eight feet above the ground. Overcome by a spirit
of high adventure, it sprang upward and came to rest on a
window sill—a feat of which it was very proud. It crouched
there, preening itself, and looked inside.

It saw a most pleasing vista. More than forty amusingly ugly
animals, apparently imprisoned by their lower extremities in
individual stalls, bowed and nodded and mumbled. At the far
end of the room stood a taller, more slender monster with a
naked head—naked compared with those of the trapped ones,
which were covered with hair like a mawson's egg. A few
moments' study showed the kitten that in reality only one side of
the heads was hairy; the tall one turned around and began
making tracks in the end wall, and its head proved to be hairy on
the other side too.

The hurkle kitten found this vastly entertaining. It began to
radiate what was, on Lirht, a purr, or glow. In this fantastic
place it was not visible; instead, the trapped animals began to

respond with most curious writhings and squirmings and susurrant rubbings of their hides with their claws. This pleased the kitten even more, for it loved to be noticed, and it redoubled the glow. The receptive motions of the animals became almost frantic.

Then the tall one turned around again. It made a curious sound or two. Then it picked up a stick from the platform before it and brought it down with a horrible crash.

The sudden noise frightened the hurkle kitten half out of its wits. It went invisible; but its visibility system was reversed here, and it was suddenly outstandingly evident. It turned and leapt outside, and before it reached the ground, a loud metallic shrilling pursued it. There were gabblings and shufflings from the room which added force to the kitten's consuming terror. It scrambled to a low growth of shrubbery and concealed itself among the leaves.

Very soon, however, its irrepressible good nature returned. It lay relaxed, watching the slight movement of the stems and leaves—some of them may have been flowers—in a slight breeze. A winged creature came humming and dancing about one of the blossoms. The kitten rested on one of its middle legs, shot the other out and caught the creature in flight. The thing promptly jabbed the kitten's foot with a sharp black probe. This the kitten ignored. It ate the thing, and belched. It lay still for a few minutes, savoring the sensation of the bee in its clarfel. The experiment was suddenly not a success. It ate the bee twice more and then gave it up as a bad job.

It turned its attention again to the window, wondering what those racks of animals might be up to now. It seemed very quiet up there . . . Boldly the kitten came from hiding and launched itself at the window again. It was pleased with itself; it was getting quite proficient at precision leaps in this mad place. Preening itself, it balanced on the window sill and looked inside.

Surprisingly, all the smaller animals were gone. The larger one was huddled behind the shelf at the end of the room. The kitten and the animal watched each other for a long moment. The animal leaned down and stuck something into the wall.

Immediately there was a mechanical humming sound and something on a platform near the window began to revolve. The next thing the kitten knew it was enveloped in a cloud of pungent dust.

It choked and became as visible as it was frightened, which was very. For a long moment it was incapable of motion; gradually, however, it became conscious of a poignant, painfully

penetrating sensation which thrilled it to the core. It gave itself
up to the feeling. Wave after wave of agonized ecstasy rolled
over it, and it began to dance to the waves. It glowed brilliantly,
though the emanation served only to make the animal in the
room scratch hysterically.

The hurkle felt strange, transported. It turned and leapt high
into the air, out from the building.

Mr. Stott stopped scratching. Disheveled indeed, he went to
the window and watched the odd sight of the blue beast, quite
invisible now, but coated with dust, so that it was like a bubble
in a fog. It bounced across the lawn in huge floating leaps,
leaving behind it diminishing patches of white powder in the
grass. He smacked his hands, one on the other, and smirking,
withdrew to straighten up. He had saved the earth from battle,
murder, and bloodshed, forever, but he did not know that. No
one ever found out what he had done. So he lived a long and
happy life.

And the hurkle kitten?

It bounded off through the long shadows, and vanished in a
copse of bushes. There it dug itself a shallow pit, working
drowsily, more and more slowly. And at last it sank down and
lay motionless, thinking strange thoughts, making strange music,
and racked by strange sensations. Soon even its slightest movements ceased, and it stretched out stiffly, motionless . . .

For about two weeks. At the end of that time, the hurkle, no
longer a kitten, was possessed of a fine, healthy litter of just
under two hundred young. Perhaps it was the DDT, and perhaps
it was the new variety of radiation that the hurkle received from
the terrestrial sky, but they were all parthenogenetic females,
even as you and I.

And the humans? Oh, we *bred* so! And how happy we were!

But the humans had the slidy itch, and the scratchy itch, and
the prickly or tingly or titillative paraesthetic formication. And
there wasn't a thing they could do about it.

So they left.

Isn't this a lovely place?

KALEIDOSCOPE

by Ray Bradbury (1920–   )

Thrilling Wonder Stories, October

Thrilling Wonder Stories, *like its sister magazine,* Startling Stories, *was one of the Standard Magazines group of publications. From 1945 to 1951 both magazines were edited by Sam Merwin (1910–   ), who has to be one of the most criminally neglected editors in the history of science fiction.* Thrilling *and* Startling *existed in the shadow of* Astounding, *which in many cases was the preferred market for sf writers. However, under Merwin and then under Samuel Mines they achieved a high level of excellence, providing badly needed alternatives for writers who would not submit to John W. Campbell, Jr., or for whatever reason would not be published by him. The Kuttners were regulars (although they also published heavily in ASF), as was Ray Bradbury, for whom they, along with* Planet Stories, *were major markets in the late 1940s. Fully one-third of the stories in this book first appeared in the pages of those two magazines.*

The late 1940s were very productive years for Ray Bradbury, and two other stories, "The Naming of Names" (Thrilling, August) and "The Man" (Thrilling, February), just missed inclusion in this volume.—M.H.G.

(I've never been able to figure out Ray Bradbury's writing. If I were to describe the plot of one of his stories, I think it would seem to you to be impossible to make a story out of it that would be any good at all, let alone memorable. And you would be right!

—Unless the story was written by Ray Bradbury.

He can write vignettes in which he creates a powerful

*emotion out of the simplest situation, and "Kaleidoscope" is
an example.*

   *It is unrelievedly grim, yet it reads quickly, matter-of-
factly, and is unforgettable. And, at the end, there is one
quick sub-vignette only four lines long that makes it seem—*

   *But I'll let you figure out the "moral." Yours may be
different from mine.*

   *I've only met Ray Bradbury twice in my life. He lives on
the west coast; I live on the east coast; and neither of us flies.
That makes the process of life-intersection a difficult one·for
us.—I.A.)*

The first concussion cut the ship up the side like a giant can
opener. The men were thrown into space like a dozen wriggling
silverfish. They were scattered into a dark sea; and the ship, in a
million pieces, went on like a meteor swarm seeking a lost sun.

   'Barkley, Barkley, where are you?'

   The sound of voices calling like lost children on a cold night.

   'Woode, Woode!'

   'Captain!'

   'Hollis, Hollis, this is Stone.'

   'Stone, this is Hollis. Where are you?'

   'I don't know, how can I? Which way is up? I'm falling.
Good gosh, I'm falling.'

   They fell. They fell as pebbles fall in the long autumns of
childhood, silver and thin. They were scattered as jack-stones are
scattered from a gigantic throw. And now instead of men there
were only voices—all kinds of voices, disembodied and im-
passioned, in varying degrees of terror and resignation.

   'We're going away from each other.'

   This was true. Hollis, swinging head over heels, knew this
was true. He knew it with a vague acceptance. They were
parting to go their separate ways, and nothing could bring them
back. They were wearing their sealed-tight space suits with the
glass tubes over their pale faces, but they hadn't had time to lock
on their force units. With them, they could be small lifeboats in
space, saving themselves, saving others, collecting together,
finding each other until they were an island of men with some
plan. But without the force units snapped to their shoulders they
were meteors, senseless, each going to a separate and irrecover-
able fate.

   A period of perhaps ten minutes elapsed while the first terror
died and a metallic calm took its place. Space began to weave

their strange voices in and out, on a great dark loom, crossing, recrossing, making a final pattern.

'Stone to Hollis. How long can we talk by phone?'

'It depends on how fast you're going your way and I'm going mine.'

'An hour, I make it.'

'That should do it,' said Hollis, abstracted and quiet.

'What happened?' said Hollis, a minute later.

'The rocket blew up, that's all. Rockets do blow up.'

'Which way are you going?'

'It looks like I'll hit the sun.'

'It's Earth for me. Back to old Mother Earth at ten thousand miles per hour. I'll burn like a match.' Hollis thought of it with a queer abstraction of mind. He seemed to be removed from his body, watching it fall down and down through space, as objective as he had been in regard to the first falling snowflakes of a winter season long gone.

The others were silent, thinking of the destiny that had brought them to this, falling, falling, and nothing they could do to change it. Even the captain was quiet, for there was no command or plan he knew that could put things back together again.

'Oh, it's a long way down, oh it's a long way down, a long, long, long, way down,' said a voice. 'I don't want to die. I don't want to die, it's a long way down.'

'Who's that?'

'I don't know.'

'Stimson, I think. Stimson, is that you?'

'It's a long long way and I don't like it, oh God, I don't like it.'

'Stimson, this is Hollis, Stimson, you hear me?'

A pause while they fell separate from one another.

'Stimson?'

'Yes.'' He replied at last.

'Stimson, take it easy, we're all in the same fix.'

'I don't want to be here, I want to be somewhere else.'

'There's a chance we'll be found.'

'I must be, I must be,' said Stimson. 'I don't believe this, I don't believe any of this is happening.'

'It's a bad dream,' said someone.

'Shut up!' said Hollis.

'Come and make me,' said the voice. It was Applegate. He laughed easily, with a similar objectivity. 'Come and shut me up.'

Hollis for the first time felt the impossibility of his position. A great anger filled him, for he wanted more than anything in existence at this moment to be able to do something to Applegate. He had wanted for many years to do something and now it was too late. Applegate was only a telephonic voice.

Falling, falling, falling!

Now, as if they had discovered the horror, two of the men began to scream. In a nightmare, Hollis saw one of them float by, very near, screaming and screaming.

'Stop it!' The man was almost at his fingertips, screaming insanely. He would never stop. He would go on screaming for a million miles, as long as he was in radio range, disturbing all of them, making it impossible for them to talk to one another.

Hollis reached out. It was best this way. He made the extra effort and touched the man. He grasped the man's ankle and pulled himself up along the body until he reached the head. The man screamed and clawed frantically, like a drowning swimmer. The screaming filled the universe.

One way or the other, thought Hollis. The sun or Earth or meteors will kill him, so why not now?

He smashed the man's glass mask with his iron fist. The screaming stopped. He pushed off from the body and let it spin away on its own course, falling, falling.

Falling, falling down space went Hollis and the rest of them in the long, endless dropping and whirling of silent terror.

'Hollis, you still there?'

Hollis did not speak, but felt the rush of heat in his face.

'This is Applegate again.'

'All right, Applegate.'

'Let's talk. We haven't anything else to do.'

The captain cut in. 'That's enough of that. We've got to figure a way out of this.'

'Captain, why don't you shut up?' said Applegate.

'What!'

'You heard me, Captain. Don't pull your rank on me, you're ten thousand miles away by now, and let's not kid ourselves. As Stimson puts it, it's a long way down.'

'See here, Applegate!'

'Can it. This a mutiny of one. I haven't a damn thing to lose. Your ship was a bad ship and you were a bad captain and I hope you roast when you hit the sun.'

'I'm ordering you to stop!'

'Go on, order me again.' Applegate smiled across ten thousand miles. The captain was silent. Applegate continued, 'Where were we, Hollis? Oh, yes, I remember. I hate you, too. But you know that. You've known it for a long time.'

Hollis clenched his fists, helplessly.

'I want to tell something,' said Applegate. 'Make you happy. I was the one who blackballed you with the Rocket Company five years ago.'

A meteor flashed by. Hollis looked down and his left hand was gone. Blood spurted. Suddenly there was no air in his suit. He had enough air in his lungs to move his right hand over and twist a knob at his left elbow, tightening the joint and sealing the leak. It had happened so quickly that he was not surprised. Nothing surprised him any more. The air in the suit came back to normal in an instant now that the leak was sealed. And the blood that had flowed so swiftly was pressured as he fastened the knob yet tighter, until it made a tourniquet.

All of this took place in a terrible silence on his part. And the other men chatted. That one man, Lespere, went on and on with his talk about his wife on Mars, his wife on Venus, his wife on Jupiter, his money, his wondrous times, his drunkenness, his gambling, his happiness. On and on, while they all fell, fell. Lespere reminisced on the past, happy, while he fell to his death.

It was so very odd. Space, thousands of miles of space, and these voices vibrating in the center of it. No one visible at all, and only the radio waves quivering and trying to quicken other men into emotion.

'Are you angry, Hollis?'

'No.' And he was not. The abstraction had returned and he was a thing of dull concrete, forever falling nowhere.

'You wanted to get to the top all your life, Hollis. And I ruined it for you. You always wondered what happened. I put the black mark on you just before I was tossed out myself.'

'That isn't important,' said Hollis. And it was not. It was gone. When life is over it is like a flicker of bright film, an instant on the screen, all of its prejudices and passions condensed and illumined for an instant on space, and before you could cry out. There was a happy day, there a bad one, there an evil face, there a good one, the film burned to a cinder, the screen went dark.

From this outer edge of his life, looking back, there was only one remorse, and that was only that he wished to go on living. Did all dying people feel this way, as if they had never lived? Does life seem that short, indeed, over and down before you took a breath? Did it seem this abrupt and impossible to everyone, or only to himself, here, now, with a few hours left to him for thought and deliberation?

One of the other men was talking. 'Well, I had me a good life. I had a wife on Mars and one on Venus and one on Earth and one on Jupiter. Each of them had money and they treated me swell. I had a wonderful time. I got drunk and once I gambled away twenty thousand dollars.'

But you're here now, thought Hollis. I didn't have any of those things. When I was living I was jealous of you, Lespere, when I had another day ahead of me I envied you your women and your good times. Women frightened me and I went into space, always wanting them, and jealous of you for having them, and money, and as much happiness as you could have in your own wild way. But now, falling here, with everything over, I'm not jealous of you any more, because it's over for you as it is over for me, and right now it's like it never was. Hollis craned his face forward and shouted into the telephone.

'It's all over, Lespere!'

Silence.

'It's just as if it never was, Lespere!'

'Who's that?' Lespere's faltering voice.

'This is Hollis.'

He was being mean. He felt the meanness, the senseless meanness of dying. Applegate had hurt him, now he wanted to hurt another. Applegate and space had both wounded him.

'You're out here, Lespere. It's all over. It's just as if it had never happened, isn't it?'

'No.'

'When anything's over, it's just like it never happened. Where's your life any better than mine, now? While it was happening, yes, but now? Now is what counts. Is it any better, is it?'

'Yes, it's better!'

'How!'

'Because I got my thoughts; I remember!' cried Lespere, far away, indignant, holding his memories to his chest with both hands.

And he was right. With a feeling of cold water gushing through his head and his body, Hollis knew he was right. There were differences between memories and dreams. He had only dreams of things he had wanted to do, while Lespere had memories of things done and accomplished. And this knowledge began to pull Hollis apart, with a slow, quivering precision.

'What good does it do you?' he cried to Lespere. 'Now? When a thing's over it's not good any more. You're no better off than me.'

'I'm resting easy,' said Lespere. 'I've had my turn. I'm not getting mean at the end, like you.'

'Mean?' Hollis turned the word on his tongue. He had never been mean, as long as he could remember, in his life. He had never dared to be mean. He must have saved it all of these years for such a time as this. 'Mean.' He rolled the word into the back of his mind. He felt tears start into his eyes and roll down his face. Someone must have heard his gasping voice.

'Take it easy, Hollis.'

It was, of course, ridiculous. Only a minute before he had been giving advice to others, to Stimson, he had felt a braveness which he had thought to be the genuine thing, and now he knew that it had been nothing but shock and the objectivity possible in shock. Now he was trying to pack a lifetime of suppressed emotion into an interval of minutes.

'I know how you feel, Hollis,' said Lespere, now twenty thousand miles away, his voice fading. 'I don't take it personally.'

But aren't we equal, his wild mind wondered. Lespere and I? Here, now? If a thing's over it's done, and what good is it? You die anyway. But he knew he was rationalizing, for it was like trying to tell the difference between a live man and a corpse. There was a spark in one, and not in the other, an aura, a mysterious element.

So it was with Lespere and himself; Lespere had lived a good full life, and it made him a different man now, and he, Hollis, had been as good as dead for many years. They came to death by separate paths and, in all likelihood, if there were kinds of deaths, their kinds would be as different as night from day. The quality of death, like that of life, must be of infinite variety, and if one has already died once, then what is there to look for in dying for once and all, as he was now?

It was a second later that he discovered his right foot was cut sheer away. It almost made him laugh. The air was gone from his suit again, he bent quickly, and there was blood, and the meteor had taken flesh and suit away to the ankle. Oh, death in space was most humorous, it cut you away, piece by piece, like a black and invisible butcher. He tightened the valve at the knee, his head whirling into pain, fighting to remain aware, and with the valve tightened, the blood retained, the air kept, he straightened up and went on falling, falling, for that was all there was left to do.

'Hollis?'

Hollis nodded sleepily, tired of waiting for death.

'This is Applegate again,' said the voice.

'Yes.'

'I've had time to think. I listened to you. This isn't good. It makes us mean. This is a bad way to die. It brings all the bile out. You listening, Hollis?'

'Yes.'

'I lied. A minute ago. I lied. I didn't blackball you. I don't know why I said that. Guess I wanted to hurt you. You seemed the one to hurt. We've always fought. Guess I'm getting old fast and repenting fast, I guess listening to you be mean made me ashamed. Whatever the reason, I want you to know I was an idiot, too. There's not an ounce of truth in what I said. To heck with you.'

Hollis felt his heart begin to work again. It seemed as if it hadn't worked for five minutes, but now all of his limbs began to take color and warmth. The shock was over, and the successive shocks of anger and terror and loneliness were passing. He felt like a man emerging from a cold shower in the morning, ready for breakfast and a new day.

'Thanks, Applegate.'

'Don't mention it. Up your nose, you slob.'

'Where's Stimson, how is he?'

'Stimson?'

They listened.

No answer.

'He must be gone.'

'I don't think so. Stimson!'

They listened again.

They could hear a long, slow, hard breathing in their phones.

'That's him. Listen.'

'Stimson!'

No reply.

Only the slow, hard breathing.

'He won't answer.'

'He's gone insane, God help him.'

'That's it. Listen.'

The silent breathing, the quiet.

'He's closed up like a clam. He's in himself, making a pearl. Listen to the poet, will you. He's happier than us now, anyway.'

They listened to Stimson float away.

'Hey,' said Stone.

'What?' Hollis called across space, for Stone, of all of them, was a good friend.

'I've got myself into a meteor swarm, some little asteroids.'

'Meteors?'

'I think it's the Myrmidone cluster that goes out past Mars and in toward Earth once every five years. I'm right in the middle. It's like a big kaleidoscope. You get all kinds of colors and shapes and sizes. God, it's beautiful, all the metal.'

Silence.

'I'm going with them,' said Stone. 'They're taking me off with them. I'll be damned.' He laughed tightly.

Hollis looked to see, but saw nothing. There were only the great jewelries of space, the diamonds and sapphires and emerald mists and velvet inks of space, with God's voice mingling among the crystal fires. There was a kind of wonder and imagination in the thought of Stone going off in the meteor swarm, out past Mars for years and coming in toward Earth every five years, passing in and out of the planet's ken for the next million years, Stone and the Myrmidone cluster eternal and unending, shifting and shaping like the kaleidoscope colours when you were a child and held the long tube to the sun and gave it a twirl.

'So long, Hollis.' Stone's voice, very faint now. 'So long.'

'Good luck,' shouted Hollis across thirty thousand miles.

'Don't be funny,' said Stone, and was gone.

The stars closed in.

Now all the voices were fading, each on their own trajectories, some to the sun, others into farthest space. And Hollis himself. He looked down. He, of all the others, was going back to Earth alone.

'So long.'

'Take it easy.'

'So long, Hollis.' That was Applegate.

The many goodbyes. The short farewells. And now the great loose brain was disintegrating. The components of the brain which had worked so beautifully and efficiently in the skull case of the rocket ship racing through space, were dying one by one, the meaning of their life together was falling apart. And as a body dies when the brain ceases functioning, so the spirit of the ship and their long time together and what they meant to one another was dying. Applegate was now no more than a finger blown from the parent body, no longer to be despised and worked against. The brain was exploded, and the senseless, useless fragments of it were far-scattered. The voices faded and now all of space was silent. Hollis was alone, falling.

They were all alone. Their voices had died like echoes of the words of God spoken and vibrating in the starred space. There went the captain to the sun; there Stone with the meteor swarm; there Stimson, tightened and unto himself; there Applegate toward Pluto; there Smith and Turner and Underwood and all the rest, the shards of the kaleidoscope that had formed a thinking pattern for so long, now hurled apart.

And I? thought Hollis. What can I do? Is there anything I can do now to make up for a terrible and empty life? If I could do one good thing to make up for the meanness I collected all these years and didn't even know was in me? But there's no one here, but myself, and how can you do good all alone? You can't. Tomorrow night I'll hit Earth's atmosphere.

I'll burn, he thought, and be scattered in ashes all over the continental lands. I'll be put to use. Just a little bit, but ashes are ashes and they'll add to the land.

He fell swiftly, like a bullet, like a pebble, like an iron weight, objective, objective all of the time now, not sad or happy or anything, but only wishing he could do a good thing now that everyone was gone, a good thing for just himself to know about.

When I hit the atmosphere, I'll burn like a meteor.

'I wonder,' he said. 'If anyone'll see me?'

The small boy on the country road looked up and screamed. 'Look, Mom, look! A falling star!'

The blazing white star fell down the sky of dusk in Illinois.

'Make a wish,' said his mother. 'Make a wish.'

DEFENSE MECHANISM

by Katherine MacLean (1925–   )

Astounding Science Fiction, October

The number of notable first stories in the history of science
fiction is truly impressive. In fact, at least two anthologies of
these stories have been published, First Flight *(1963)*, and
First Voyages *(greatly expanded version of the previous book,
1981), and one could easily fill up several additional volumes.
"Defense Mechanism" was Katharine MacLean's first published story, and began a career that, while filled with excellent stories and some recognition, never attained the heights
she was capable of. Like Ray Bradbury and Harlan Ellison,
she is primarily a short story writer, but unlike them she is
not very prolific. She won a Nebula Award for "The Missing
Man" (1971), a part of her novel* Missing Man *(1975). The
best of her early stories can be found in* The Diploids *(1962),
while* Cosmic Checkmate *(1962, written with Charles de Vet)
is an interesting first, and so far, only novel (Missing Man
consists of previously published linked stories).—M.H.G.*

*(Telepathy is something we all apparently have a hankering
for. At least, any report of the existence of telepathy is
eagerly accepted, and any story dealing with telepathy has a
great big point in its favor from the start.*

*Why this interest? I suppose an obvious answer is that it
would be so convenient to be able to communicate as easily
as we think.*

*Isn't talking almost as convenient and easy as thinking?
Well, maybe, but the possibility of lying turns speech sour. As
the saying goes, "Speech was invented so that we might
conceal our thoughts."*

In that case, might it not be very convenient to be tele-

pathic and to see beyond the lies? Convenient for whom? Not for the liar, certainly. —And that means all of us.

If you're not a liar, tell the truth! Do you want all your thoughts out in the open? Isn't it convenient, even necessary, to let your words mismatch the facts now and then?

Actually, there are all sorts of quirks to telepathy and, in "Defense Mechanism," Katherine Maclean thinks up a nice one. And if her speculation were correct, to how many of us might something like this have happened?—I.A.)

The article was coming along smoothly, words flowing from the typewriter in pleasant simple sequence, swinging to their prede-termined conclusion like a good tune. Ted typed contentedly, adding pages to the stack at his elbow.

A thought, a subtle modification of the logic of the article began to glow in his mind; but he brushed it aside impatiently. This was to be a short article, and there was no room for subtlety. His articles sold, not for depth, but for an oddly individual quirk that he could give to commonplaces.

While he typed a little faster, faintly in the echoes of his thought the theme began to elaborate itself richly with correlations, modifying qualifications, and humorous parenthetical remarks. An eddy of especially interesting conclusions tried to insert itself into the main stream of his thoughts. Furiously he typed along the dissolving thread of his argument.

"Shut up," he snarled. "Can't I have any privacy around here?"

The answer was not a remark, it was merely a concept; two electro-chemical calculators pictured with the larger in use as a control mech, taking a dangerously high inflow, and controlling it with high resistance and blocs, while the smaller one lay empty and unblocked, its unresistant circuits ramifying any im-pulses received along the easy channels of pure calculation. Ted recognized the diagram from his amateur concepts of radio and psychology.

"All right. So I'm doing it myself. So you can't help it!" He grinned grudgingly. "Answering back at your age!"

Under the impact of a directed thought the small circuits of the idea came in strongly, scorching their reception and rapport diagram into his mind in flashing repetitions, bright as small lightning strokes. Then it spread and the small other brain flashed into brightness, reporting and repeating from every center. Ted even received a brief kinesthetic sensation of lying down, before it was all cut off in a hard bark of thought that came back in exact echo of his own irritation.

"Tune down!" It ordered furiously. "You're blasting in too loud and jamming everything up! What do you want, an idiot child?"

Ted blanketed down desperately, cutting off all thoughts, relaxing every muscle; but the angry thoughts continued coming in strongly a moment before fading.

"Even when I take a nap," they said, "he starts thinking at me! Can't I get any peace and privacy around here?"

Ted grinned. The kid's last remark sounded like something a little better than an attitude echo. It would be hard to tell when the kid's mind grew past a mere selective echoing of outside thoughts and became true personality, but that last remark was a convincing counterfeit of a sincere kick in the shin. Conditioned reactions can be efficient.

All the luminescent streaks of thought faded and merged with the calm meaningless ebb and flow of waves in the small sleeping mind. Ted moved quietly into the next room and looked down into the blue-and-white crib. The kid lay sleeping, his thumb in his mouth and his chubby face innocent of thought. Junior—Jake.

It was an odd stroke of luck that Jake was born with this particular talent. Because of it they would have to spend the winter in Connecticut, away from the mental blare of crowded places. Because of it Ted was doing free lance in the kitchen, instead of minor editing behind a New York desk. The winter countryside was wide and windswept, as it had been in Ted's own childhood, and the warm contacts with the stolid personalities of animals through Jake's mind were already a pleasure. Old acquaintances—Ted stopped himself skeptically. He was no telepath. He decided that it reminded him of Ernest Thompson Seton's animal biographies, and went back to typing, dismissing the question.

It was pleasant to eavesdrop on things through Jake, as long as the subject was not close enough to the article to interfere with it.

Five small boys let out of kindergarten came trooping by on the road, chattering and throwing pebbles. Their thoughts came in jumbled together in distracting cross currents, but Ted stopped typing for a moment, smiling, waiting for Jake to show his latest trick. Babies are hypersensitive to conditioning. The burnt hand learns to yank back from fire, the unresisting mind learns automatically to evade too many clashing echoes of other minds.

Abruptly the discordant jumble of small boy thoughts and sensations delicately untangled into five compartmented strands of thoughts, then one strand of little boy thoughts shoved the others out, monopolizing and flowing easily through the blank baby mind, as a dream flows by without awareness, leaving no imprint of memory, fading as the children passed over the hill. Ted resumed typing, smiling. Jake had done the trick a shade faster than he had yesterday. He was learning reflexes easily enough to demonstrate normal intelligences. At least he was to be more than a gifted moron.

A half hour later, Jake had grown tired of sleeping and was standing up in his crib, shouting and shaking the bars. Martha hurried in with a double armload of groceries.

"Does he want something?"

"Nope. Just exercising his lungs." Ted stubbed out his cigarette and tapped the finished stack of manuscript contentedly. "Got something here for you to proofread."

"Dinner first," she said cheerfully, unpacking food from the bags. "Better move the typewriter and give us some elbow room."

Sunlight came in the windows and shone on the yellow table top, and glinted on her dark hair as she opened packages.

"What's the local gossip?" he asked, clearing off the table. "Anything new?"

"Meat's going up again," she said, unwrapping peas and fillets of mackerel. "Mrs. Watkins' boy, Tom, is back from the clinic. He can see fine now, she says."

He put water on to boil and began greasing a skillet while she rolled the fillets in cracker crumbs. "If I'd had to run a flame thrower during the war, I'd have worked up a nice case of hysteric blindness myself," he said. "I call that a legitimate defense mechanism. Sometimes it's better to be blind."

"But not all the time," Martha protested, putting baby food in the double boiler. In five minutes lunch was cooking.

"Whaaaa—" wailed Jake.

Martha went into the baby's room, and brought him out, cuddling him and crooning. "What do you want, Lovekins? Baby just wants to be cuddled, doesn't baby."

"Yes," said Ted.

She looked up, startled, and her expression changed, became withdrawn and troubled, her dark eyes clouded in difficult thought.

Concerned, he asked: "What is it, Honey?"

"Ted, you shouldn't—" She struggled with words. "I know, it is handy to know what he wants, whenever he cries. It's handy having you tell me, but I don't— It isn't right somehow. It isn't *right*."

Jake waved an arm and squeaked randomly. He looked unhappy. Ted took him and laughed, making an effort to sound confident and persuasive. It would be impossible to raise the kid in a healthy way if Martha began to feel he was a freak. "Why isn't it right? It's normal enough. Look at E. S. P. Everybody has that according to Rhine."

"E. S. P. is different," she protested feebly, but Jake chortled and Ted knew he had her. He grinned, bouncing Jake up and down in his arms.

"Sure it's different," he said cheerfully. "E. S. P. is queer. E. S. P. comes in those weird accidental little flashes that contradict time and space. With clairvoyance you can see through walls, and read pages from a closed book in France. E. S. P., when it comes, is so ghastly precise it seems like tips from old Omniscience himself. It's enough to drive a logical man insane, trying to explain it. It's illogical, incredible, and random. But what Jake has is limited telepathy. It is starting out fuzzy and muddled and developing towards accuracy by plenty of trial and error—like sight, or any other normal sense. You don't mind communicating by English, so why mind communicating by telepathy?"

She smiled wanly. "But he doesn't weigh much, Ted. He's not growing as fast as it says he should in the baby book."

"That's all right. I didn't really start growing myself until I was about two. My parents thought I was sickly."

"And look at you now." She smiled genuinely. "All right, you win. But when does he start talking English? I'd like to understand him, too. After all, I'm his mother."

"Maybe this year, maybe next year," Ted said teasingly. "I didn't start talking until I was three."

"You mean that you don't want him to learn," she told him indignantly, and then smiled coaxingly at Jake. "You'll learn English soon for Mommy, won't you, Lovekins?"

Ted laughed annoyingly. "Try coaxing him next month or the month after. Right now he's not listening to all these thoughts. He's just collecting associations and reflexes. His cortex might organize impressions on a logic pattern he picked up from me, but it doesn't know what it is doing any more than this fist knows that it is in his mouth. That right, bud?" There was no demanding thought behind the question, but instead, very delicately, Ted introspected to the small world of impression and sensation that flickered in what seemed a dreaming corner of his own mind. Right then it was a fragmentary world of green and brown that murmured with the wind.

"He's out eating grass with the rabbit," Ted told her.

Not answering, Martha started putting out plates. "I like animal stories for children," she said determinedly. "Rabbits are nicer than people."

Putting Jake in his pen, Ted began to help. He kissed the back of her neck in passing. "Some people are nicer than rabbits."

Wind rustled tall grass and tangled vines where the rabbit snuffled and nibbled among the sun-dried herbs, moving on habit, ignoring the abstract meaningless contact of minds, with no thought but deep comfort.

Then for a while Jake's stomach became aware that lunch was coming, and the vivid business of crying and being fed drowned the gentler distant neural flow of the rabbit.

Ted ate with enjoyment, toying with an idea fantastic enough to keep him grinning, as Martha anxiously spooned food into Jake's mouth. She caught him grinning and indignantly began justifying herself. "But he only gained four pounds, Ted. I have to make sure he eats something."

"Only!" he grinned. "At that rate he'd be thirty feet high by the time he reaches college."

"So would any baby." But she smiled at the idea, and gave Jake his next spoonful still smiling. Ted did not tell his real thought, that if Jake's abilities kept growing in a straight-line growth curve, by the time he was old enough to vote he would be God; but he laughed again, and was rewarded by an answering smile from both of them.

The idea was impossible, of course. Ted knew enough biology to know that there could be no sudden smooth jumps in evolution. Smooth changes had to be worked out gradually through generations of trial and selection. Sudden changes were not smooth, they crippled and destroyed. Mutants were usually monstrosities.

Jake was no sickly freak, so it was certain that he would not turn out very different from his parents. He could be only a little better. But the contrary idea had tickled Ted and he laughed again. "Boom food," he told Martha. "Remember those straight-line growth curves in the story?"

Martha remembered, smiling, "Redfern's dream—sweet little man, dreaming about a growth curve that went straight up." She chuckled, and fed Jake more spoonfuls of strained spinach, saying, "Open wide. Eat your boom food, darling. Don't you want to grow up like King Kong?"

Ted watched vaguely, toying now with a feeling that these months of his life had happened before, somewhere. He had felt it before, but now it came back with a sense of expectancy, as if something were going to happen.

It was while drying the dishes that Ted began to feel sick. Somewhere in the far distance at the back of his mind a tiny phantom of terror cried and danced and gibbered. He glimpsed it close in a flash that entered and was cut off abruptly in a vanishing fragment of delirium. It had some-thing to do with a tangle of brambles in a field, and it was urgent.

Jake grimaced, his face wrinkled as if ready either to smile or cry. Carefully Ted hung up the dish towel and went out the back door, picking up a billet of wood as he passed the woodpile. He could hear Jake whimpering, beginning to wail.

"Where to?" Martha asked, coming out the back door.

"Dunno," Ted answered. "Gotta go rescue Jake's rabbit. It's in trouble."

Feeling numb, he went across the fields through an outgrowth of small trees, climbed a fence into a field of deep grass and thorny tangles of raspberry vines, and started across.

A few hundred feet into the field there was a hunter sitting on an outcrop of rock, smoking, with a successful bag of two rabbits dangling near him. He turned an inquiring face to Ted.

"Sorry," the hunter said. He was quiet-looking man with a sagging, middle-aged face. "It can't understand being upside down with its legs tied." Moving with shaky urgency he took his penknife and cut the small animal's pulsing throat, then threw the wet knife out of his hand into the grass. The rabbit kicked once more, staring still at the tangled vines of refuge. Then its nearsighted baby eyes lost their glazed bright stare and became meaningless.

"That's all right," Ted replied, "but be a little more careful next time, will you? You're out of season anyhow." He looked up from the grass to smile stiffly at the hunter. It was difficult.

There was a crowded feeling in his head, like a coming head-ache, or a stuffy cold. It was difficult to breathe, difficult to think.

It occurred to Ted then to wonder why Jake had never put him in touch with the mind of an adult. After a frozen stoppage of thought he laboriously started the wheels again and realized that something had put him in touch with the mind of the hunter, and that was what was wrong. His stomach began to rise. In another minute he would retch.

Ted stepped forward and swung the billet of wood in a clumsy sidewise sweep. The hunter's rifle went off and missed as the middle-aged man tumbled face first into the grass.

Wind rustled the long grass and stirred the leafless branches of trees. Ted could hear and think again, standing still and breathing in deep, shuddering breaths of air to clean his lungs. Briefly he planned what to do. He would call the sheriff and say that a hunter hunting out of season had shot at him and he had been forced to knock the man out. The sheriff would take the man away, out of thought range.

Before he started back to telephone he looked again at the peaceful, simple scene of field and trees and sky. It was safe to let himself think now. He took a deep breath and let himself think. The memory of horror came into clarity.

The hunter had been psychotic.

Thinking back, Ted recognized parts of it, like faces glimpsed in writhing smoke. The evil symbols of psychiatry, the bloody poetry of the Golden Bough, that had been the law of mankind in the five hundred thousand lost years before history. Torture and sacrifice, lust and death, a mechanism in perfect balance, a short circuit of conditioning through a glowing channel of symbols, an irreversible and perfect integration of traumas. It is easy to go mad, but it is not easy to go sane.

"Shut up!" Ted had been screaming inside his mind as he struck. "Shut up."

It had stopped. It had shut up. The symbols were fading without having found root in his mind. The sheriff would take the man away out of thought reach, and there would be no danger. It had stopped.

The burned hand avoids the fire. Something else had stopped. Ted's mind was queerly silent, queerly calm and empty, as he walked home across the winter fields, wondering how it had happened at all, kicking himself with humor for a suggestible fool, not yet missing—Jake.

And Jake lay awake in his pen, waving his rattle in random motions, and crowing "glaglagla gla—" in a motor sensory cycle, closed and locked against outside thoughts.

He would be a normal baby, as Ted had been, and as Ted's father before him.

And as all mankind was "normal."

COLD WAR

by Henry Kuttner (1914—1958)

Thrilling Wonder Stories, October

The third selection by the terrific Kuttners (and to some extent all they published under whatever name after their marriage owed something to both) is this charming tale about "just plain folks" who happen to be mutants. "Cold War" is the last of a series of four stories about the Hogbens, all of which appeared in Thrilling Wonder Stories—*"Exit the Professor" (October, 1947), "Pile of Trouble" (April, 1948), and "See You Later" (June, 1949). It's a shame that they didn't write a few more, because they would have made a fine collection.—M.H.G.*

(When I first started to write, I attempted, in a few stories, to present a dialect by means of specialized spelling. No doubt I wasn't skillful enough to carry it off, so that I found the stories embarrassing to reread when I was done, and even more embarrassing to reread if they happened to get published (as a few did.) Quite early in the game I therefore stopped and had every character I dealt with speak cultured English or, at least, correctly spelled English.

There are advantages to dialect, however. If you tell a story in the first person and in dialect, you make it plain to the reader that you are dealing with a culture quite distinct from that of the American establishment. It gives odd events and odd outlooks a greater verisimilitude, and it also serves as a source of humor. Of two narratives, all things being otherwise equal, the one in dialect is funnier.

If, that is, it is done right. Henry Kuttner does it right in Cold War *as I'm sure you will very quickly decide for yourself. I couldn't do it.—I.A.)*

Chapter I. Last of the Pughs

I'll never have a cold in the haid again without I think of little Junior Pugh. Now there was a repulsive brat if ever I saw one. Built like a little gorilla, he was. Fat, pasty face, mean look, eyes so close together you could poke 'em both out at once with one finger. His paw thought the world of him though. Maybe that was natural, seeing as how little Junior was the image of his pappy.

"The last of the Pughs," the old man used to say stickin' his chest out and beamin' down at the little gorilla. "Finest little lad that ever stepped."

It made my blood run cold sometimes to look at the two of 'em together. Kinda sad, now, to think back to those happy days when I didn't know either of 'em. You may not believe it but them two Pughs, father and son, between 'em came within *that* much of conquerin' the world.

Us Hogbens is quiet folks. We like to keep our heads down and lead quiet lives in our own little valley, where nobody comes near withouten we say so. Our neighbors and the folks in the village are used to us by now. They know we try hard not to act conspicuous. They make allowances.

If Paw gets drunk, like last week, and flies down the middle of Main Street in his red underwear most people make out they don't notice, so's not to embarrass Maw. They know he'd walk like a decent Christian if he was sober.

The thing that druv Paw to drink that time was Little Sam, which is our baby we keep in a tank down-cellar, startin' to teethe again. First time since the War Between the States. We'd figgered he was through teething, but with Little Sam you never can tell. He was mighty restless, too.

A perfesser we keep in a bottle told us once Little Sam e-mitted subsonic somethings when he yells but that's just his way of talking. Don't mean a thing. It makes your nerves twiddle, that's all. Paw can't stand it. This time it even woke up Grandpaw in the attic and he hadn't stirred since Christmas. First thing after he got his eyes open he bust out madder'n a wet hen at Paw.

"I see ye, wittold knave that ye are!" he howled. "Flying again, is it? Oh, sic a reowfule sigte! I'll ground ye, ywis!" There was a far-away thump.

"You made me fall a good ten feet!" Paw hollered from away down the valley. "It ain't fair. I could of busted something!"

"Ye'll bust us all, with your dronken carelessness," Grandpaw said. "Flying in full sight of the neighbors! People get burned at the stake for less. You want mankind to find out all about us? Now shut up and let me tend to Baby."

Grandpaw can always quiet the baby if nobody else can. This time he sung him a little song in Sanskrit and after a bit they was snoring a duet.

I was fixing up a dingus for Maw to sour up some cream for sour-cream biscuits. I didn't have much to work with but an old sled and some pieces of wire but I didn't need much. I was trying to point the top end of the wire north-northeast when I seen a pair of checked pants rush by in the woods.

It was Uncle Lem. I could hear him thinking. "It *ain't* me!" he was saying, real loud, inside his haid. "Git back to yer work, Saunk. I ain't within a mile of you. Yer Uncle Lem's a fine old feller and never tells lies. Think I'd fool ye, Saunkie boy?"

"You shore would," I thunk back. "If you could. What's up, Uncle Lem?"

At that he slowed down and started to saunter back in a wide circle.

"Oh, I just had an idy yer Maw might like a mess of blackberries," he thunk, kicking a pebble very nonchalant. "If anybody asks you say you ain't seen me. It's no lie. You ain't."

"Uncle Lem," I thunk, real loud, "I gave Maw my bounden word I wouldn't let you out of range without me along, account of the last time you got away—"

"Now, now, my boy," Uncle Lem thunk fast. "Let bygones be bygones."

"You just can't say no to a friend, Uncle Lem," I reminded him, taking a last turn of the wire around the runner. "So you wait a shake till I get this cream soured and we'll both go together, wherever it is you have in mind."

I saw the checked pants among the bushes and he come out in the open and give me a guilty smile. Uncle Lem's a fat little feller. He means well, I guess, but he can be talked into most anything by most anybody, which is why we have to keep a close eye on him.

"How you gonna do it?" he asked me, looking at the creamjug. "Make the little critters work faster?"

"Uncle Lem!" I said. "You know better'n that. Cruelty to dumb animals is something I can't abide. Them there little critters work hard enough souring milk the way it is. They're such teentsy-weentsy fellers I kinda feel sorry for 'em. Why, you can't even see 'em without you go kinda crosseyed when you look. Paw says they're enzymes. But they can't be. They're too teeny.''

"Teeny is as teeny does," Uncle Lem said. "How you gonna do it, then?"

"This here gadget," I told him, kinda proud, "will send Maw's cream-jug ahead into next week some time. This weather, don't take cream more'n a couple of days but I'm giving it plenty of time. When I bring it back—bingo, it's sour.'' I set the jug on the sled.

"I never seen such a do-lass brat," Uncle Lem said, stepping forward and bending a wire crosswise. "You better do it thataway, on account of the thunderstorm next Tuesday. All right now, shoot her off."

So I shot her off. When she come back, sure enough, the cream was sour enough to walk a mouse. Crawling up the can there was a hornet from next week, which I squashed. Now that was a mistake. I knowed it the minute I touched the jug. Dang Uncle Lem, anyhow.

He jumped back into the underbrush, squealing real happy.

"Fooled you that time, you young stinker," he yelled back. "Let's see you get your thumb outa the middle of next week!"

It was the time-lag done it. I mighta knowed. When he crossed that wire he didn't have no thunderstorm in mind at all. Took me nigh onto ten minutes to work myself loose, account of some feller called Inertia, who mixes in if you ain't careful when you fiddle around with time. I don't understand much about it myself. I ain't got my growth yet. Uncle Lem says he's already forgot more'n I'll ever know.

With that head start I almost lost him. Didn't even have time to change into my store-bought clothes and I knowed by the way he was all dressed up fit to kill he was headed for somewheres fancy.

He was worried, too. I kept running into little stray worrisome thoughts he'd left behind him, hanging like teeny little mites of clouds on the bushes. Couldn't make out much on account of they was shredding away by the time I got there but he'd shore done something he shouldn't. That much *anybody* coulda told. They went something like this:

"Worry, worry—wish I hadn't done it—oh, heaven help me if Grandpaw ever finds out—oh, them nasty Pughs, how could I a-been such a fool? Worry, worry—pore ole feller, such a good soul, too, never done nobody no harm and look at me now.

"That Saunk, too big for his britches, teach him a thing or two, ha-ha. Oh, worry, worry—never mind, brace up, you good ole boy, everything's bound to turn out right in the end. You deserve the best, bless you, Lemuel. Grandpaw'll never find out."

Well, I seen his checkered britches high-tailing through the woods after a bit, but I didn't catch up to him until he was down the hill, across the picnic grounds at the edge of town and pounding on the sill of the ticket-window at the railroad station with a Spanish dubloon he snitched from Paw's seachest.

It didn't surprise me none to hear him asking for a ticket to State Center. I let him think I hadn't caught up. He argued something turrible with the man behind the window but finally he dug down in his britches and fetched up a silver dollar, and the man calmed down.

The train was already puffing up smoke behind the station when Uncle Lem darted around the corner. Didn't leave me much time but I made it too—just. I had to fly a little over the last half-dozen yards but I don't think anybody noticed.

Once when I was just a little shaver there was a Great Plague in London, where we were living at the time, and all us Hogbens had to clear out. I remember the hullabaloo in the city but looking back now it don't seem a patch on the hullabaloo in State Center station when the train pulled in. Times have changed, I guess.

Whistles blowing, horns honking, radios yelling bloody murder—seems like every invention in the last two hundred years had been noisier than the one before it. Made my head ache until I fixed up something Paw once called a raised decibel threshold, which was pure showing-off.

Uncle Lem didn't know I was anywhere around. I took care to think real quiet but he was so wrapped up in his worries he wasn't paying no mind to nothing. I followed him through the crowds in the station and out onto a wide street full of traffic. It was a relief to get away from the trains.

I always hate to think what's going on inside the boiler, with all the little bitty critters so small you can't hardly see 'em, pore things, flying around all hot and excited and bashing their heads together. It seems plumb pitiable.

Of course, it just don't do to think what's happening inside the automobiles that go by.

Uncle Lem knowed right where he was headed. He took off down the street so fast I had to keep reminding myself not to fly, trying to keep up. I kept thinking I ought to get in touch with the folks at home, in case this turned into something I couldn't handle, but I was plumb stopped everywhere I turned. Maw was at the church social that afternoon and she whopped me the last time I spoke to her outa thin air right in front of the Reverend Jones. He ain't used to us Hogbens yet.

Paw was daid drunk. No good trying to wake him up. And I was scared to death I *would* wake the baby if I tried to call on Grandpaw.

Uncle Lem scuttled right along, his checkered legs a-twinkling. He was worrying at the top of his mind, too. He'd caught sight of a crowd in a side-street gathered around a big truck, looking up at a man standing on it and waving bottles in both hands.

He seemed to be making a speech about headaches. I could hear him all the way to the corner. There was big banners tacked along the sides of the truck that said, PUGH HEADACHE CURE.

"Oh, worry, worry!" Uncle Lem thunk. "Oh, bless my toes, what *am* I going to do? I never *dreamed* anybody'd marry Lily Lou Mutz. Oh, worry!"

Well, I reckon we'd all been surprised when Lily Lou Mutz up and got herself a husband awhile back—around ten years ago, I figgered. But what it had to do with Uncle Lem I couldn't think. Lily Lou was just about the ugliest female that ever walked. Ugly ain't no word for her, pore gal.

Grandpaw said once she put him in mind of a family name of Gorgon he used to know. Not that she wasn't a goodhearted critter. Being so ugly, she put up with a lot in the way of rough acting-up from the folks in the village—the riff-raff lot, I mean.

She lived by herself in a little shack up the mountain and she musta been close onto forty when some feller from the other side of the river come along one day and rocked the whole valley back on its heels by asking her to marry up with him. Never saw the feller myself but I heard tell he wasn't no beauty-prize winner neither.

Come to think of it, I told myself right then, looking at the truck—come to think of it, feller's name was Pugh.

Chapter 2. A Fine Old Feller

Next thing I knowed, Uncle Lem had spotted somebody under a lamp-post on the sidewalk, at the edge of the crowd. He trotted over. It seemed to be a big gorilla and a little gorilla, standing there watching the feller on the truck selling bottles with both hands.

"Come and get it," he was yelling. "Come and get your bottle of Pugh's Old Reliable Headache Cure while they last!"

"Well, Pugh, here I am," Uncle Lem said, looking up at the big gorilla. "Hello, Junior," he said right afterward, glancing down at the little gorilla. I seen him shudder a little.

You shore couldn't blame him for that. Two nastier specimens of the human race I never did see in all my born days. If they hadn't been *quite* so pasty-faced or just the least mite slimmer, maybe they wouldn't have put me so much in mind of two well-fed slugs, one growed-up and one baby-sized. The paw was all dressed up in a Sunday-meeting suit with a big gold watch-chain across his front and the way he strutted you'd a thought he'd never had a good look in a mirror.

"Howdy, Lem," he said, casual-like. "Right on time, I see. Junior, say howdy to Mister Lem Hogben. You owe Mister Hogben a lot, sonny." And he laughed a mighty nasty laugh.

Junior paid him no mind. He had his beady little eyes fixed on the crowd across the street. He looked about seven years old and mean as they come.

"Shall I do it now, paw?" he asked in a squeaky voice. "Can I let 'em have it now, paw? Huh, paw?" From the tone he used, I looked to see if he'd got a machine-gun handy. I didn't see none but if looks was ever mean enough to kill Junior Pugh could of mowed the crowd right down.

"Manly little feller, ain't he, Lem?" Paw Pugh said, real smug. "I tell you, I'm mighty proud of this youngster. Wish his dear grandpaw coulda lived to see him. A fine old family line, the Pughs is. Nothing like it anywhere. Only trouble is, Junior's the last of his race. You see why I got in touch with you, Lem."

Uncle Lem shuddered again. "Yep," he said. "I see, all right. But you're wasting your breath, Pugh. I ain't a-gonna do it."

Young Pugh spun around in his tracks.

"Shall I let him have it, paw?" he squeaked, real eager. "Shall I, paw? Now, paw? Huh?"

"Shaddup, sonny," the big feller said and he whammed the little feller across the side of the haid. Pugh's hands was like hams. He shore was built like a gorilla.

The way his great big arms swung down from them big hunched shoulders, you'd of thought the kid would go flying across the street when his paw whopped him one. But he was a burly little feller. He just staggered a mite and then shook his haid and went red in the face.

He yelled out, loud and squeaky, "Paw, I warned you! The

last time you whammed me I warned you! Now I'm gonna let
you have it!''

He drew a deep breath and his two little teeny eyes got so
bright I coulda sworn they was gonna touch each other across the
middle of his nose. His pasty face got bright red.

"Okay, Junior," Paw Pugh said, real hasty. "The crowd's
ready for you. Don't waste your strength on me, sonny. Let the
crowd have it!''

Now all this time I was standing at the edge of the crowd,
listening and watching Uncle Lem. But just then somebody
jiggled my arm and a thin kinda voice said to me, real polite,
"Excuse me, but may I ask a question?''

I looked down. It was a skinny man with a kind-hearted face.
He had a notebook in his hand.

"It's all right with me," I told him, polite. "Ask away,
mister.''

"I just wondered how you feel, that's all," the skinny man
said, holding his pencil over the notebook ready to write down
something.

"Why, peart," I said. "Right kind of you to inquire. Hope
you're feeling well too, mister.''

He shook his head, kind of dazed. "That's the trouble," he
said. "I just don't understand it. I feel fine.''

"Why not?" I asked. "Fine day.''

"Everybody here feels fine," he went right on, just like I
hadn't spoke. "Barring normal odds, everybody's in average
good health in this crowd. But in about five minutes or less, as I
figure it—'' He looked at his wristwatch.

Just then somebody hit me right on top of the haid with a
red-hot sledge-hammer.

Now you shore can't hurt a Hogben by hitting him on the
haid. Anybody's a fool to try. I felt my knees buckle a little but I
was all right in a couple of seconds and I looked around to see
who'd whammed me.

Wasn't a soul there. But oh my, the moaning and groaning
that was going up from that there crowd! People was a-clutching
at their foreheads and a-staggering around the street, clawing at
each other to get to that truck where the man was handing out the
bottles of headache cure as fast as he could take in the dollar
bills.

The skinny man with the kind face rolled up his eyes like a
duck in thunder.

"Oh, my head!" he groaned. "What did I tell you? Oh, my

head!'' Then he sort of tottered away, fishing in his pocket for money.

Well, the family always did say I was slow-witted but you'd have to be downright feeble-minded if you didn't know there was something mighty peculiar going on around here. I'm no ninny, no matter what Maw says. I turned around and looked for Junior Pugh.

There he stood, the fat-faced little varmint, red as a turkey-gobbler, all swole up and his mean little eyes just a-flashing at the crowd.

"It's a hex," I thought to myself, perfectly calm. "I'd never have believed it but it's a real hex. Now how in the world—"

Then I remembered Lily Lou Mutz and what Uncle Lem had been thinking to himself. And I began to see the light.

The crowd had gone plumb crazy, fighting to get at the headache cure. I purty near had to bash my way over toward Uncle Lem. I figured it was past time I took a hand, on account of him being so soft in the heart and likewise just about as soft in the haid.

"Nosirree," he was saying, firm-like. "I won't do it. Not by no manner of means I won't.''

"Uncle Lem," I said.

I bet he jumped a yard into the air.

"Saunk!" he squeaked. He flushed up and grinned sheepish and then he looked mad, but I could tell he was kinda relieved, too. "I told you not to foller me," he said.

"Maw told me not to let you out of my sight," I said. "I promised Maw and us Hogbens never break a promise. What's going on here, Uncle Lem?"

"Oh, Saunk, everything's gone dead wrong!" Uncle Lem wailed out. "Here I am with a heart of gold and I'd just as soon be dead! Meet Mister Ed Pugh, Saunk. He's trying to get me kilt.''

"Now Lem," Ed Pugh said. "You know that ain't so. I just want my rights, that's all. Pleased to meet you, young fellow. Another Hogben, I take it. Maybe you can talk your uncle into—''

"Excuse me for interrupting, Mister Pugh," I said, real polite. "But maybe you'd better explain. All this is purely a mystery to me.''

He cleared his throat and threw his chest out, important-like. I could tell this was something he liked to talk about. Made him feel pretty big, I could see.

"I don't know if you was acquainted with my dear departed

wife, Lily Lou Mutz that was," he said. "This here's our little child, Junior. A fine little lad he is too. What a pity we didn't have eight or ten more just like him." He sighed real deep.

"Well, that's life. I'd hoped to marry young and be blessed with a whole passel of younguns, being as how I'm the last of a fine old line. I don't mean to let it die out, neither." Here he gave Uncle Lem a mean look. Uncle Lem sorta whimpered.

"I ain't a-gonna do it," he said. "You can't make me do it."

"We'll see about that," Ed Pugh said, threatening. "Maybe your young relative here will be more reasonable. I'll have you know I'm getting to be a power in this state and what I says goes."

"Paw," little Junior squeaked out just then, "Paw, they're kinda slowing down. Kin I give it to 'em double-strength this time, Paw? Betcha I could kill a few if I let myself go. Hey, Paw—"

Ed Pugh made as if he was gonna clonk the little varmint again, but I guess he thought better of it.

"Don't interrupt your elders, sonny," he said. "Paw's busy. Just tend to your job and shut up." He glanced out over the moaning crowd. "Give that bunch over beyond the truck a little more treatment," he said. "They ain't buying fast enough. But no double-strength, Junior. You gotta save your energy. You're a growing boy."

He turned back to me. "Junior's a talented child," he said, very proud. "As you can see. He inherited it from his dear dead-and-gone mother, Lily Lou. I was telling you about Lily Lou. It was my hope to marry young, like I said, but the way things worked out, somehow I just didn't get around to wifin' till I'd got well along into the prime of life."

He blew out his chest like a toadfrog, looking down admiring. I never did see a man that thought better of himself. "Never found a woman who'd look at—I mean, never found the right woman," he went on, "till the day I met Lily Lou Mutz."

"I know what you mean," I said, polite. I did, too. He musta searched a long, long ways before he found somebody ugly enough herself to look twice at him. Even Lily Lou, pore soul, musta thunk a long time afore she said yes.

"And that," Ed Pugh went on, "is where your Uncle Lem comes in. It seems like he'd give Lily Lou a bewitchment quite some while back."

"I never!" Uncle Lem squealed. "And anyway, how'd I know she'd get married and pass it on to her child? Who'd ever think Lily Lou would—"

"He gave her a bewitchment," Ed Pugh went right on talking. "Only she never told me till she was a-layin' on her death-bed a year ago. Lordy, I sure woulda whopped her good if I'd knowed how she held out on me all them years! It was the hex Lemuel gave her and she inherited it on to her little child."

"I only done it to protect her," Uncle Lem said, right quick. "You know I'm speaking the truth, Saunk boy. Pore Lily Lou was so pizon ugly, people used to up and heave a clod at her now and then afore they could help themselves. Just automatic-like. Couldn't blame 'em. I often fought down the impulse myself.

"But pore Lily Lou, I shore felt sorry for her. You'll never know how long I fought down my good impulses, Saunk. But my heart of gold does get me into messes. One day I felt so sorry for the pore hideous critter I gave her the hexpower. Anybody'd have done the same, Saunk."

"How'd you do it?" I asked, real interested, thinking it might come in handy someday to know. I'm young yet, and I got lots to learn.

Well, he started to tell me and it was kinda mixed up. Right at first I got a notion some furrin feller named Gene Chromosome had done it for him and after I got straight on that part he'd gone cantering off into a rigamarole about the alpha waves of the brain.

Shucks, I knowed that much my own self. Everybody musta noticed the way them little waves go a-sweeping over the tops of people's haids when they're thinking. I've watched Grandpaw sometimes when he had as many as six hundred different thoughts follering each other up and down them little paths where his brain is. Hurts my eyes to look too close when Grandpaw's thinking.

"So that's how it is, Saunk," Uncle Lem wound up. "And this here little rattlesnake's inherited the whole shebang."

"Well, why don't you get this here Gene Chromosome feller to unscramble Junior and put him back the way other people are?" I asked. "I can see how easy you could do it. Look here, Uncle Lem." I focused down real sharp on Junior and made my eyes go funny the way you have to when you want to look inside a person.

Sure enough, I seen just what Uncle Lem meant. There was teensy-weensy little chains of fellers, all hanging onto each other for dear life, and skinny little rods jiggling around inside them awful teensy cells everybody's made of—except maybe Little Sam, our baby.

"Look here, Uncle Lem," I said. "All you did when you gave Lily Lou the hex was to twitch these here little rods over *that-away* and patch 'em onto them little chains that wiggle so fast. Now why can't you switch 'em back again and make Junior behave himself? It oughta be easy."

"It would be easy," Uncle Lem kinda sighed at me. "Saunk, you're a scatterbrain. You wasn't listening to what I said. I can't switch 'em back without I kill Junior."

"The world would be a better place," I said.

"I know it would. But you know what we promised Grandpaw? No more killings."

"But Uncle Lem!" I bust out. "This is turrible! You mean this nasty little rattlesnake's gonna go on all his life hexing people?"

"Worse than that, Saunk," pore Uncle Lem said, almost crying. "He's gonna pass the power on to his descendants, just like Lily Lou passed it on to him."

For a minute it sure did look like a dark prospect for the human race. Then I laughed.

"Cheer up, Uncle Lem," I said. "Nothing to worry about. Look at the little toad. There ain't a female critter alive who'd come within a mile of him. Already he's as repulsive as his daddy. And remember, he's Lily Lou Mutz's child, too. Maybe he'll get even horribler as he grows up. One thing's sure—he ain't never gonna get married."

"Now there's where you're wrong," Ed Pugh busted in, talking real loud. He was red in the face and he looked mad. "Don't think I ain't been listening," he said. "And don't think I'm gonna forget what you said about my child. I told you I was a power in this town. Junior and me can go a long way, using his talent to help us.

"Already I've got on to the board of aldermen here and there's gonna be a vacancy in the state senate come next week—unless the old coot I have in mind's a lot tougher than he looks. So I'm warning you, young Hogben, you and your family's gonna pay for them insults."

"Nobody oughta get mad when he hears the gospel truth about himself," I said. "Junior *is* a repulsive specimen."

"He just takes getting used to," his paw said. "All us Pughs is hard to understand. Deep, I guess. But we got our pride. And I'm gonna make sure the family line never dies out. Never, do you hear that, Lemuel?"

Uncle Lem just shut his eyes up tight and shook his head fast.

"Nosirree," he said. "I'll never do it. Never, never, never, never—"

"Lemuel," Ed Pugh said, real sinister. "Lemuel, do you want me to set Junior on you?"

"Oh, there ain't no use in that," I said. "You seen him try to hex me along with the crowd, didn't you? No manner of use, Mister Pugh. Can't hex a Hogben."

"Well—" He looked around, searching his mind. "Hm-m. I'll think of something. I'll—soft-hearted, aren't you? Promised your Grandpappy you wouldn't kill nobody, hey? Lemuel, open your eyes and look over there across the street. See that sweet old lady walking with the cane? How'd you like it if I had Junior drop her dead in her tracks?"

Uncle Lemuel just squeezed his eyes tighter shut.

"I won't look. I don't know the sweet old thing. If she's that old, she ain't got much longer anyhow. Maybe she'd be better off dead. Probably got rheumatiz something fierce."

"All right, then, how about that purty young girl with the baby in her arms? Look, Lemuel. Mighty sweet-looking little baby. Pink ribbon in its bonnet, see? Look at them dimples. Junior, get ready to blight them where they stand. Bubonic plague to start with maybe. And after that—"

"Uncle Lem," I said, feeling uneasy. "I dunno what Grandpaw would say to this. Maybe—"

Uncle Lem popped his eyes wide open for just a second. He glared at me, frantic.

"I can't help it if I've got a heart of gold," he said. "I'm a fine old feller and everybody picks on me. Well, I won't stand for it. You can push me just so far. Now I don't care if Ed Pugh kills off the whole human race. I don't care if Grandpaw *does* find out what I done. I don't care a hoot about nothing no more." He gave a kind of wild laugh.

"I'm gonna get out from under. I won't know nothing about nothing. I'm gonna snatch me a few winks, Saunk."

And with that he went rigid all over and fell flat on his face on the sidewalk, stiff as a poker.

Chapter 3. Over a Barrel

Well, worried as I was, I had to smile. Uncle Lem's kinda cute sometimes. I knowed he'd put hisself to sleep again, the way he always does when trouble catches up with him. Paw says it's catalepsy but cats sleep a lot lighter than that.

Uncle Lem hit the sidewalk flat and kinda bounced a little. Junior give a howl of joy. I guess maybe he figgered he'd had something to do with Uncle Lem falling over. Anyhow, seeing somebody down and helpless, Junior naturally rushed over and pulled his foot back and kicked Uncle Lem in the side of the haid.

Well, like I said, us Hogbens have got pretty tough haids. Junior let out a howl. He started dancing around nursing his foot in both hands.

"I'll hex you good!" he yelled at Uncle Lem. "I'll hex you good, you—you ole Hogben, you!" He drew a deep breath and turned purple in the face and—

And then it happened.

It was like a flash of lightning. I don't take no stock in hexes, and I had a fair idea of what was happening, but it took me by surprise. Paw tried to explain to me later how it worked and he said it just stimulated the latent toxins inherent in the organism. It made Junior into a catalytoxic agent on account of the way the rearrangement of the desoxyribonucleic acid his genes was made of worked on the kappa waves of his nasty little brain, stepping them up as much as thirty microvolts. But shucks, you know Paw. He's too lazy to figger the thing out in English. He just steals them fool words out of other folks' brains when he needs 'em.

What really happened was that all the pizon that little varmint had bottled up in him, ready to let go on the crowd, somehow seemed to r'ar back and smack Uncle Lem right in the face. I never seen such a hex. And the awful part was—it worked.

Because Uncle Lem wasn't resisting a mite now he was asleep. Red-hot pokers wouldn't have waked him up and I wouldn't put red-hot pokers past little Junior Pugh. But he didn't need 'em this time. The hex hit Uncle Lem like a thunderbolt.

He turned pale green right before our eyes.

Somehow it seemed to me a turrible silence fell as Uncle Lem went green. I looked up, surprised. Then I realized what was happening. All that pitiful moaning and groaning from the crowd had stopped.

People was swigging away at their bottles of headache cure, rubbing their foreheads and kinda laughing weak-like with relief. Junior's whole complete hex had gone into Uncle Lem and the crowd's headaches had naturally stopped right off.

"What's happened here?" somebody called out in a kinda familiar voice. "Has that man fainted? Why don't you help him? Here, let me by—I'm a doctor."

It was the skinny man with the kind-looking face. He was still drinking out of the headache bottle as he pushed his way through the crowd toward us but he'd put his notebook away. When he saw Ed Pugh he flushed up angrylike.

"So it's you, is it, Alderman Pugh?" he said. "How is it you're always around when trouble starts? What did you do to this poor man, anyhow? Maybe this time you've gone too far."

"I didn't do a thing," Ed Pugh said. "Never touched him. You watch your tongue, Dr. Brown, or you'll regret it. I'm a powerful man in this here town."

"Look at that!" Dr. Brown yells, his voice going kinda squeaky as he stares down at Uncle Lem. "The man's dying! Call an ambulance, somebody, quick!"

Uncle Lem was changing color again. I had to laugh a little, inside my haid. I knowed what was happening and it was kinda funny. Everybody's got a whole herd of germs and viruses and suchlike critters swarming through them all the time, of course.

When Junior's hex hit Uncle Lem it stimulated the entire herd something turrible, and a flock of little bitty critters Paw calls antibodies had to get to work pronto. They ain't really as sick as they look, being white by nature.

Whenever a pizon starts chawing on you these pale little fellers grab up their shooting-irons and run like crazy to the battlefield in your insides. Such fighting and yelling and swearing you never seen. It's a regular Bull Run.

That was going on right then inside Uncle Lem. Only us Hogbens have got a special militia of our own inside us. And they got called up real fast.

They was swearing and kicking and whopping the enemy so hard Uncle Lem had gone from pale green to a sort of purplish color, and big yeller and blue spots was beginning to bug out all over him where it showed. He looked oncommon sick. Course it didn't do him no real harm. The Hogbens militia can lick any germ that breathes.

But he sure looked revolting.

The skinny doctor crouched down beside Uncle Lem and felt his pulse.

"Now you've done it," he said, looking up at Ed Pugh. "I don't know how you've worked this, but for once you've gone too far. This man seems to have bubonic plague. I'll see you're put under control this time and that young Kallikak of yours, too."

Ed Pugh just laughed a little. But I could see he was mad. "Don't you worry about me, Dr. Brown," he said, mean.

"When I get to be governor—and I got my plans all made—that there hospital you're so proud of ain't gonna operate on state funds no more. A fine thing!

"Folks laying around in hospitals eating their fool heads off! Make 'em get out and plough, that's what I say. Us Pughs never gets sick. I got lots of better uses for state money than paying folks to lay around in bed when I'm governor."

All the doctor said was, "Where's that ambulance?"

"If you mean that big long car making such a noise," I said, "it's about three miles off but coming fast. Uncle Lem don't need no help, though. He's just having an attack. We get 'em in the family all the time. It don't mean nothing."

"Good heavens!" the doc said, staring down at Uncle Lem. "You mean he's had this before and lived?" Then he looked up at me and smiled all of a sudden. "Oh, I see," he said. "Afraid of hospitals, are you? Well, don't worry. We won't hurt him."

That surprised me some. He was a smart man. I'd fibbed a little for just that reason. Hospitals is no place for Hogbens. People in hospitals are too danged nosy. So I called Uncle Lem real loud, inside my head.

"Uncle Lem!" I hollered, only thinking it, not out loud. "Uncle Lem, wake up quick! Grandpaw'll nail your hide to the barn door if'n you let yourself get took to a hospital. You want 'em to find out about them two hearts you got in your chest? And the way your bones are fixed and the shape of your gizzard? Uncle Lem! Wake up!"

It wasn't no manner of use. He never even twitched.

Right then I began to get really scared. Uncle Lem had sure landed me in the soup. There I was with all that responsibility on my shoulders and I didn't have the least idea how to handle it. I'm just a young feller after all. I can hardly remember much farther back than the great fire of London, when Charles II was king, with all them long curls a-hanging on his shoulders. On him, though, they looked good.

"Mister Pugh," I said, "you've got to call off Junior. I can't let Uncle Lem get took to the hospital. You know I can't."

"Junior, pour it on," Mister Pugh said, grinning real nasty. "I want a little talk with young Hogben here." The doctor looked up, puzzled, and Ed Pugh said, "Step over here a mite, Hogben. I want a private word with you. Junior, bear down!"

Uncle Lem's yellow and blue spots got green rings around their outside edges. The doctor sorta gasped and Ed Pugh took my arm and pulled me back. When we was out of earshot he said to me, confidential, fixing me with his tiny little eyes:

"I reckon you know what I want, Hogben. Lem never did say he *couldn't*, he only said he wouldn't, so I know you folks can do it for me."

"Just exactly what is it you want, Mister Pugh?" I asked him.

"You know. I want to make sure our fine old family line goes on. I want there should always be Pughs. I had so much trouble getting married off myself and I know Junior ain't going to be easy to wife. Women don't have no taste nowadays.

"Since Lily Lou went to glory there hasn't been a woman on earth ugly enough to marry a Pugh and I'm skeered Junior'll be the last of a great line. With his talent I can't bear the thought. You just fix it so our family won't never die out and I'll have Junior take the hex off Lemuel."

"If I fixed it so your line didn't die out," I said, "I'd be fixing it so everybody else's line *would* die out, just as soon as there was enough Pughs around."

"What's wrong with that?" Ed Pugh asked, grinning. "Way I see it we're good strong stock." He flexed his gorilla arms. He was taller than me, even. "No harm in populatin' the world with good stock, is there? I figger given time enough us Pughs could conquer the whole danged world. And you're gonna help us do it, young Hogben."

"Oh, no," I said. "Oh, no! Even if I knowed how—"

There was a turrible noise at the end of the street and the crowd scattered to make way for the ambulance, which drawed up at the curb beside Uncle Lem. A couple of fellers in white coats jumped out with a sort of pallet on sticks. Dr. Brown stood up, looking real relieved.

"Thought you'd never get here," he said. "This man's a quarantine case, I think. Heaven knows what kind of results we'll find when we start running tests on him. Hand me my bag out of the back there, will you? I want my stethoscope. There's something funny about this man's heart."

Well, *my* heart sunk right down into my boots. We was goners and I knowed it—the whole Hogben tribe. Once them doctors and scientists find out about us we'll never know a moment's peace again as long as we live. We won't have no more privacy than a corncob.

Ed Pugh was watching me with a nasty grin on his pasty face.

"Worried, huh?" he said. "You gotta right to be worried. I know about you Hogbens. All witches. Once they get Lem in the hospital, no telling what they'll find out. Against the law to be witches, probably. You've got about half a minute to make up your mind, young Hogben. What do you say?''

Well, what could I say? I couldn't give him a promise like he was asking, could I? Not and let the whole world be overrun by hexing Pughs. Us Hogbens live a long time. We've got some pretty important plans for the future when the rest of the world begins to catch up with us. But if by that time the rest of the world is all Pughs, it won't hardly seem worth while, somehow. I couldn't say yes.

But if I said no Uncle Lem was a goner. Us Hogbens was doomed either way, it seemed to me.

Looked like there was only one thing to do. I took a deep breath, shut my eyes, and let out a desperate yell inside my head.

"Grandpaw!" I hollered.

"Yes, my boy?" said a big deep voice in the middle of my brain. You'd athought he'd been right alongside me all the time, just waiting to be called. He was a hundred-odd miles off, and sound asleep. But when a Hogben calls in the tone of voice *I* called in he's got a right to expect an answer—quick. I got it.

Mostly Grandpaw woulda dithered around for fifteen minutes, asking cross questions and not listening to the answers, and talking in all kinds of queer old-fashioned dialects, like Sanskrit, he's picked up through the years. But this time he seen it was serious.

"Yes, my boy?" was all he said.

I flapped my mind wide open like a school-book in front of him. There wasn't no time for questions and answers. The doc was getting out his dingus to listen to Uncle Lem's two hearts beating out of tune and once he heard that the jig would be up for us Hogbens.

"Unless you let me kill 'em, Grandpaw," I added. Because by that time I knowed he'd read the whole situation from start to finish in one fast glance.

It seemed to me he was quiet an awful long time after that. The doc had got the dingus out and he was fitting its little black arms into his ears. Ed Pugh was watching me like a hawk. Junior stood there all swole up with pizon, blinking his mean little eyes around for somebody to shoot it at. I was half hoping he'd pick on me. I'd worked out a way to make it bounce back in his face and there was a chance it might even kill him.

I heard Grandpaw give a sorta sigh in my mind.

"They've got us over a barrel, Saunk," he said. I remember being a little surprised he could speak right plain English when he wanted to. "Tell Pugh we'll do it."

"But Grandpaw—" I said.

"Do as I say!" It gave me a headache, he spoke so firm. "Quick, Saunk! Tell Pugh we'll give him what he wants."

Well, I didn't dare disobey. But this once I really came close to defying Grandpaw.

It stands to reason even a Hogben has got to get senile someday, and I thought maybe old age had finally set in with Grandpaw at last.

What I thunk at him was, "All right, if you say so, but I sure hate to do it. Seems like if they've got us going and coming, the least we can do is take our medicine like Hogbens and keep all that pizon bottled up in Junior stead of spreading it around the world." But out loud I spoke to Mister Pugh.

"All right, Mister Pugh," I said, real humble. "You win. Only, call off your hex. Quick, before it's too late."

Chapter 4. Pughs A-Coming

Mister Pugh had a great big yellow automobile, low-slung, without no top. It went awful fast. And it was sure awful noisy. Once I'm pretty sure we run over a small boy in the road but Mister Pugh paid him no mind and I didn't dare say nothing. Like Grandpaw said, the Pughs had us over a barrel.

It took quite a lot of palaver before I convinced 'em they'd have to come back to the homestead with me. That was part of Grandpaw's orders.

"How do I know you won't murder us in cold blood once you get us out there in the wilderness?" Mister Pugh asked.

"I could kill you right here if I wanted," I told him. "I would too but Grandpaw says no. You're safe if Grandpaw says so, Mister Pugh. The word of a Hogben ain't never been broken yet."

So he agreed, mostly because I said we couldn't work the spells except on home territory. We loaded Uncle Lem into the back of the car and took off for the hills. Had quite an argument with the doc, of course. Uncle Lem sure was stubborn.

He wouldn't wake up nohow but once Junior took the hex off Uncle Lem faded out fast to a good healthy color again. The doc just didn't believe it coulda happened, even when he saw it. Mister Pugh had to threaten quite a lot before we got away. We left the doc sitting on the curb, muttering to himself and rubbing his haid dazed like.

I could feel Grandpaw a-studying the Pughs through my mind all the way home. He seemed to be sighing and kinda shaking his haid—such as it is—and working out problems that didn't make no manner of sense to me.

When we drawed up in front of the house there wasn't a soul in sight. I could hear Grandpaw stirring and muttering on his gunnysack in the attic but Paw seemed to have went invisible and he was too drunk to tell me where he was when I asked. The baby was asleep. Maw was still at the church sociable and Grandpaw said to leave her be.

"We can work this out together, Saunk," he said as soon as I got outa the car. "I've been thinking. You know that sled you fixed up to sour your Maw's cream this morning? Drag it out, son. Drag it out."

I seen in a flash what he had in mind. "Oh, no, Grandpaw!" I said, right out loud.

"Who you talking to?" Ed Pugh asked, lumbering down outa the car. "I don't see nobody. This your homestead? Ratty old dump, ain't it? Stay close to me, Junior. I don't trust these folks any farther'n I can see 'em."

"Get the sled, Saunk," Grandpaw said, very firm. "I got it all worked out. We're gonna send these two gorillas right back through time, to a place they'll really fit."

"But Grandpaw!" I hollered, only inside my head this time. "Let's talk this over. Lemme get Maw in on it anyhow. Paw's right smart when he's sober. Why not wait till he wakes up? I think we oughta get the Baby in on it too. I don't think sending 'em back through time's a good idea at all, Grandpaw."

"The Baby's asleep," Grandpaw said. "You leave him be. He read himself to sleep over his Einstein, bless his little soul."

I think the thing that worried me most was the way Grandpaw was talking plain English. He never does when he's feeling normal. I thought maybe his old age had all caught up with him at one bank, and knocked all the sense outa his—so to speak—haid.

"Grandpaw," I said, trying to keep calm. "Don't you see? If we send 'em back through time and give 'em what we promised it'll make everything a million times worse than before. You gonna strand 'em back there in the year one and break your promise to 'em?"

"Saunk!" Grandpaw said.

"I know. If we promised we'd make sure the Pugh line won't die out, then we gotta make sure. But if we send 'em back to the year one that'll mean all the time before then and now they'll spend spreading out and spreading out. More Pughs every generation.

"Grandpaw, five seconds after they hit the year one, I'm liable to feel my two eyes rush together in my haid and my face go all fat and pasty like Junior. Grandpaw, everybody in the world may be Pughs if we give 'em that much time to spread out in!"

"Cease thy chirming, thou chilce dolt," Grandpaw hollered. "Do my bidding, young fool!"

That made me feel a little better but not much. I went and dragged out the sled. Mister Pugh put up quite a argument about that.

"I ain't rid on a sled since I was so high," he said. "Why should I git on one now? This is some trick. I won't do it."

Junior tried to bite me.

"Now Mister Pugh," I said, "you gotta cooperate or we won't get nowheres. I know what I'm doing. Just step up here and set down. Junior, there's room for you in front. That's fine."

If he hadn't seen how worried I was I don't think he'd a-done it. But I couldn't hide how I was feeling.

"Where's your Grandpaw?" he asked, uneasy. "You're not going to do this whole trick by yourself, are you? Young ignorant feller like you? I don't like it. Suppose you made a mistake?"

"We give our word," I reminded him. "Now just kindly shut up and let me concentrate. Or maybe you don't want the Pugh line to last forever?"

"That was the promise," he says, settling himself down. "You gotta do it. Lemme know when you commence."

"All right, Saunk," Grandpaw says from the attic, right brisk. "Now you watch. Maybe you'll learn a thing or two. Look sharp. Focus your eyes down and pick out a gene. Any gene."

Bad as I felt about the whole thing I couldn't help being interested. When Grandpaw does a thing he does it up brown. Genes are mighty slippery little critters, spindle-shaped and awful teensy. They're partners with some skinny guys called chromosomes, and the two of 'em show up everywhere you look, once you've got your eyes focused just right.

"A good dose of ultraviolet ought to do the trick," Grandpaw muttered. "Saunk, you're closer."

I said, "All right, Grandpaw," and sort of twiddled the light as it sifted down through the pines above the Pughs. Ultraviolet's the color at the *other* end of the line, where the colors stop having names for most people.

Grandpaw said, "Thanks, son. Hold it for a minute."

The genes began to twiddle right in time with the light waves. Junior said, "Paw, something's tickling me."

Ed Pugh said, "Shut up."

Grandpaw was muttering to himself. I'm pretty sure he stole the words from that perfesser we keep in the bottle, but you can't tell, with Grandpaw. Maybe he was the first person to make 'em up in the beginning.

"The euchromatin," he kept muttering. "That ought to fix it. Ultraviolet gives us hereditary mutation and the euchromatin contains the genes that transmit heredity. Now that other stuff's heterochromatin and *that* produces evolutionary change of the cataclysmic variety.

"Very good, very good. We can always use a new species. Hum-m-m. About six bursts of heterochromatinic activity ought to do it." He was quiet for a minute. Then he said, "Ich am eldre and ek magti! Okay, Saunk, take it away."

I let the ultraviolet go back where it came from.

"The year one, Grandpaw?" I asked, very doubtful.

"That's close enough," he said. "Wite thou the way?"

"Oh yes, Grandpaw," I said. And I bent over and give them the necessary push.

The last thing I heard was Mister Pugh's howl.

"What's that you're doin'?" he hollered at me. "What's the idea? Look out, there, young Hogben or—what's this? Where we goin'? Young Saunk, I warn you, if this is some trick I'll set Junior on you! I'll send you such a hex as even you-u . . ."

Then the howl got real thin and small and far away until it wasn't no more than the noise a mosquito makes. After that it was mighty quiet in the dooryard.

I stood there all braced, ready to stop myself from turning into a Pugh if I could. Them little genes is tricky fellers.

I knowed Grandpaw had made a turrible mistake.

The minute them Pughs hit the year one and started to bounce back through time toward now I knowed what would happen.

I ain't sure how long ago the year one was, but there was plenty of time for the Pughs to populate the whole planet. I put two fingers against my nose to keep my eyes from banging each other when they started to rush together in the middle like all us Pughs' eyes do—

"You ain't a Pugh yet, son," Grandpaw said, chuckling. "Kin ye see 'em?"

"No," I said. "What's happening?"

"The sled's starting to slow down," he said. "Now it's

stopped. Yep, it's the year one, all right. Look at all them men and women flockin' outa the caves to greet their new company! My, my, what great big shoulders the men have got. Bigger even than Paw Pugh's.

"An' ugh—just look at the women! I declare, little Junior's positively handsome alongside them folks! He won't have no trouble finding a wife when the time comes."

"But Grandpaw, that's turrible!" I said.

"Don't sass your elders, Saunk," Grandpaw chuckled. "Looka there now. Junior's just pulled a hex. Another little child fell over flat on his ugly face. Now the little child's mother is knocking Junior endwise. Now his pappy's sailing into Paw Pugh. Look at that fight! Just look at it! Oh, I guess the Pugh family's well took care of, Saunk."

"But what about our family?" I said, almost wailing.

"Don't you worry," Grandpaw said. "Time'll take care of that. Wait a minute, let me watch. Hm-m. A generation don't take long when you know how to look. My, my, what ugly little critters the ten baby Pughs was! They was just like their pappy and their grandpappy.

"I wish Lily Lou Mutz could see her grandbabies. I shorely do. Well, now, ain't that cute? Every one of them babies growed up in a flash, seems like, and each of 'em has got ten babies of their own. I like to see my promises working out, Saunk. I said I'd do this, and I done it."

I just moaned.

"All right," Grandpaw said. "Let's jump ahead a couple of centuries. Yep, still there and spreading like crazy. Family likeness is still strong, too. Hum-m. Another thousand years and—well, I declare! If it ain't Ancient Greece! Hasn't changed a bit, neither. What do you know, Saunk!" He cackled right out, tickled pink.

"Remember what I said once about Lily Lou putting me in mind of an old friend of mine named Gorgon? No wonder! Perfectly natural. You ought to see Lily Lou's great-great-great-grandbabies! No, on second thought, it's lucky you can't. Well, well, this is shore interesting."

He was still about three minutes. Then I heard him laugh.

"Bang," he said. "First heterochromatinic burst. Now the changes start."

"What changes, Grandpaw?" I asked, feeling pretty miserable.

"The changes," he said, "that show your old Grandpaw ain't such a fool as you thought. I know what I'm doing. They go

fast, once they start. Look there now, that's the second change.
Look at them little genes mutate!''

"You mean," I said, "I ain't gonna turn into a Pugh after all?
But Grandpaw, I thought we'd promised the Pughs their line
wouldn't die out.''

"I'm keeping my promise," Grandpaw said, dignified. "The
genes will carry the Pugh likeness right on to the toot of the
judgment horn, just like I said. And the hex power goes right
along with it.''

Then he laughed.

"You better brace yourself, Saunk," he said. "When Paw
Pugh went sailing off into the year one seems like he uttered a
hex threat, didn't he? Well, he wasn't fooling. It's a-coming at
you right now.''

"Oh, Lordy!" I said. "There'll be a million of 'em by the
time they get here! Grandpaw! What'll I do?''

"Just brace yourself," Grandpaw said, real unsympathetic.
"A million, you think? Oh, no, lots more than a million.''

"How many?" I asked him.

He started in to tell me. You may not believe it but he's *still*
telling me. It takes that long. There's that many of 'em.

You see, it was like with that there Jukes family that lived
down south of here. The bad ones was always a mite worse than
their children and the same dang thing happened to Gene Chromosome and his kin, so to speak. The Pughs stayed Pughs and
they kept the hex power—and I guess you might say the Pughs
conquered the whole world, after all.

But it could of been worse. The Pughs could of stayed the
same size down through the generations. Instead they got
smaller—a whole lot smaller. When I knowed 'em they was
bigger than most folks—Paw Pugh, anyhow.

But by the time they'd done filtering the generations from the
year one, they'd shrunk so much them little pale fellers in the
blood was about their size. And many a knock-down drag-out
fight they have with 'em, too.

Them Pugh genes took such a beating from the heterochromatinic
bursts Grandpaw told me about that they got whopped all outa
their proper form. You might call 'em a virus now—and of
course a virus is exactly the same thing as a gene, except the
virus is friskier. But heavens above, that's like saying the Jukes
boys is exactly the same as George Washington!

The hex hit me—hard.

I sneezed something turrible. Then I heard Uncle Lem sneez-
ing in his sleep, lying back there in the yaller car. Grandpaw was

still droning on about how many Pughs was a-coming at me right that minute, so there wasn't no use asking questions. I fixed my eyes different and looked right down into the middle of that sneeze to see what had tickled me—

Well, you never seen so many Junior Pughs in all your born days! It was the hex, all right. Likewise, them Pughs is still busy, hexing everybody on earth, off and on. They'll do it for quite a time, too, since the Pugh line has got to go on forever, account of Grandpaw's promise.

They tell me even the microscopes ain't never yet got a good look at certain viruses. The scientists are sure in for a surprise someday when they focus down real close and see all them pasty-faced little devils, ugly as sin, with their eyes set real close together, wiggling around hexing everybody in sight.

It took a long time—since the year one, that is—but Gene Chromosome fixed it up, with Grandpaw's help. So Junior Pugh ain't a pain in the neck no more, so to speak.

But I got to admit he's an awful cold in the haid.

THE WITCHES OF KARRES

by James H. Schmitz (1911–1981)

Astounding Science Fiction, December

The late James Schmitz was the creator of Telzey Amberton, a female secret agent who starred in such exciting novels as The Universe Against Her *(1964) and* The Lion Game *(1973) as well as the story collection* The Telzey Toy *(1973). Telzey was certainly ahead of her time—her adventurous and amorous escapades were fully worthy of male protaganists, and she is frequently referred to in defenses of science fiction's earlier anti-female bias.*

Telzey is also a telepath, like the three Witches of Karres. This was no accident, because John Campbell's postwar Astounding *was a center for "psi" stories of all types, one of several seeming obsessions of this great editor.* Astounding *began to enter a period of slow decline as the 1940s ended, brought on in no small measure by the magazine boom which saw the creation of powerful competition in the form of* Galaxy *and* The Magazine of Fantasy and Science Fiction. *It is also possible that by this time Campbell had done as much for science fiction as he could.*

Astounding *accounts for less than half of the stories in this book.—M.H.G.*

(Witches come in all sorts. During the European witch-hunting mania, witches were unredeemably evil, and in league with the Devil.

It depends on your definition, of course. All through the Christian centuries there was the survival of remnants of pre-Christian ritual which had not been absorbed into Christianity. The practitioners of such archaic rites were members of a competing religion, and the only competing religion that Christian enthusiasts recognized was devil-worship. From which it followed—

For those who don't take witchcraft seriously, but who write stories about witches, witches (and their male counterparts, the wizards or warlocks) are only practitioners of magic. And like the practitioners of technology, they can do so for good or for evil. Thus, in The Wizard of Oz *we have the Wicked Witch of the West, immortalized forever by Margaret Hamilton, while we also have the Good Witch, Glinda, much less convincingly played by Billie Burke.*

In the running, however, for the most charming witches are the three little girls who are "The Witches of Karres" as portrayed by James H. Schmitz.—I.A.)

I.

It was around the hub of the evening on the planet of Porlumma that Captain Pausert, commercial traveler from the Republic of Nikkeldepain, met the first of the witches of Karres.

It was just plain fate, so far as he could see.

He was feeling pretty good as he left a high-priced bar on a cobbly street near the spaceport, with the intention of returning straight to his ship. There hadn't been an argument, exactly. But someone grinned broadly, as usual, when the captain pronounced the name of his native system; and the captain had pointed out then, with considerable wit, how much more ridiculous it was to call a planet Porlumma, for instance, then to call it Nikkeldepain.

He proceeded to collect a gradually increasing number of pained stares by a detailed comparison of the varied, interesting and occasionally brilliant role Nikkeldepain had played in history with Porlumma's obviously dull and dumpy status as a sixth-rate Empire outpost.

In conclusion, he admitted frankly that he wouldn't care to be found dead on Porlumma.

Somebody muttered loudly in Imperial Universum that in that case it might be better if he didn't hang around Porlumma too long. But the captain only smiled politely, paid for his two drinks and left.

There was no point in getting into a rhubarb on one of these border planets. Their citizens still had an innocent notion that they ought to act like frontiersmen—but then the Law always showed up at once.

He felt pretty good. Up to the last four months of his young

life, he had never looked on himself as being particularly patriotic.
But compared to most of the Empire's worlds, Nikkeldepain was
downright attractive in its stuffy way. Besides, he was returning
there solvent—would they ever be surprised!

And awaiting him, fondly and eagerly, was Illyla, the Miss
Onswud, fair daughter of the mighty Councilor Onswud, and the
captain's secretly affianced for almost a year. She alone had
believed in him!

The captain smiled and checked at a dark cross-street to get
his bearings on the spaceport beacon. Less than half a mile
away— He set off again. In about six hours, he'd be beyond the
Empire's space borders and headed straight for Illyla.

Yes, she alone had believed! After the prompt collapse of the
captain's first commercial venture—a miffel-fur farm, largely on
capital borrowed from Councilor Onswud—the future had looked
very black. It had even included a probable ten-year stretch of
penal servitude for "willful and negligent abuse of intrusted
monies." The laws of Nikkeldepain were rough on debtors.

"But you've always been looking for someone to take out the
old *Venture* and get her back into trade!" Illyla reminded her
father tearfully.

"Hm-m-m, yes! But it's in the blood, my dear! His great-
uncle Threbus went the same way! It would be far better to let
the law take its course," Councilor Onswud said, glaring at
Pausert who remained sulkily silent. He had *tried* to explain that
the mysterious epidemic which suddenly wiped out most of the
stock of miffels wasn't his fault. In fact, he more than suspected
the tricky hand of young Councilor Rapport who had been
wagging futilely around Illyla for the last couple of years!

"The *Venture*, now—!" Councilor Onswud mused, stroking
his long, craggy chin. "Pausert can handle a ship, at least," he
admitted.

That was how it happened. Were they ever going to be
surprised! For even the captain realized that Councilor Onswud
was unloading all the dead fish that had gathered the dust of his
warehouses for the past fifty years on him and the *Venture*, in a
last, faint hope of getting *some* return on those half-forgotten
investments. A value of eighty-two thousand maels was placed on
the cargo; but if he'd brought even three-quarters of it back in
cash, all would have been well.

Instead—well, it started with that lucky bet on a legal point
with an Imperial Official at the Imperial capitol itself. Then
came a six-hour race fairly won against a small, fast private
yacht—the old *Venture* 7333 had been a pirate-chaser in the last

century and could still produce twice as much speed as her looks suggested. From there on, the captain was socially accepted as a sporting man and was in on a long string of jovial parties and meets.

Jovial and profitable—the wealthier Imperials just couldn't resist a gamble; and the penalty he always insisted on was that they had to buy!

He got rid of the stuff right and left! Inside of twelve weeks, nothing remained of the original cargo except two score bundles of expensively-built but useless tinklewood fishing poles and one dozen gross bales of useful but unattractive allweather cloaks. Even on a bet, nobody would take them! But the captain had a strong hunch those items had been hopefully added to the cargo from his own stocks by Councilor Rapport; so his failure to sell them didn't break his heart.

He was a neat twenty percent net ahead, at that point—

And finally came this last-minute rush-delivery of medical supplies to Porlumma on the return route. That haul alone would have repaid the miffle-farm losses three times over!

The captain grinned broadly into the darkness. Yes, they'd be surprised—but just where was he now?

He checked again in the narrow street, searching for the port-beacon in the sky. There it was—off to his left and a little behind him. He'd got turned around somehow!

He set off carefully down an excessively dark little alley. It was one of those towns where everybody locked their front doors at night and retired to lit-up, inclosed courtyards at the backs of the houses. There were voices and the rattling of dishes nearby, and occasional whoops of laughter and singing all around him; but it was all beyond high walls which let little or no light into the alley.

It ended abruptly in a cross-alley and another wall. After a moment's debate, the captain turned to his left again. Light spilled out on his new route a few hundred yards ahead, where a courtyard was opened on the alley. From it, as he approached, came the sound of doors being violently slammed, and then a sudden, loud mingling of voices.

"Yeeee-eep!" shrilled a high, childish voice. It could have been mortal agony, terror, or even hysterical laughter. The captain broke into an apprehensive trot.

"Yes, I see you up there!" a man shouted excitedly in Universum. "I caught you now—you get down from those boxes! I'll skin you alive! Fifty-two customers sick of the stomachache—YOW!''

The last exclamation was accompanied by a sound as of a small, loosely-built wooden house collapsing, and was followed by a succession of squeals and an angry bellowing, in which the only distinguishable words were: ''. . . .threw the boxes on me!'' Then more sounds of splintering wood.

''Hey!'' yelled the captain indignantly from the corner of the alley.

All action ceased. The narrow courtyard, brightly illuminated under its single overhead bulb, was half covered with a tumbled litter of what appeared to be empty wooden boxes. Standing with his foot temporarily caught in one of them was a very large, fat man dressed all in white and waving a stick. Momentarily cornered between the wall and two of the boxes, over one of which she was trying to climb, was a smallish, fair-haired girl dressed in a smock of some kind, which was also white. She might be about fourteen, the captain thought—a helpless kid, anyway.

''What *you* want?'' grunted the fat man, pointing the stick with some dignity at the captain.

''Lay off the kid!'' rumbled the captain, edging into the courtyard.

''Mind your own business!'' shouted the fat man, waving his stick like a club. ''I'll take care of her! She—''

''I never did!'' squealed the girl. She burst into tears.

''Try it, Fat and Ugly!'' the captain warned. ''I'll ram the stick down your throat!''

He was very close now. With a sound of grunting exasperation, the fat man pulled his foot free of the box, wheeled suddenly and brought the end of the stick down on the top of the captain's cap. The captain hit him furiously in the middle of the stomach.

There was a short flurry of activity, somewhat hampered by shattering boxes everywhere. Then the captain stood up, scowling and breathing hard. The fat man remained sitting on the ground, gasping about ''. . . the law!''

Somewhat to his surprise, the captain discovered the girl standing just behind him. She caught his eye and smiled.

''My name's Maleen,'' she offered. She pointed at the fat man. ''Is he hurt bad?''

''Huh—no!'' panted the captain. ''But maybe we'd better—''

It was too late! A loud, self-assured voice became audible now at the opening to the alley:

''Here, here, here, here, here!'' it said in the reproachful, situation-under-control tone that always seemed the same to the captain, on whatever world and in whichever language he heard it.

"What's all this about?" it inquired rhetorically.

"You'll all have to come along!" it replied.

Police Court on Porlumma appeared to be a business conducted on a very efficient, around-the-clock basis. They were the next case up.

Nikkeldepain was an odd name, wasn't it, the judge smiled. He then listened attentively to the various charges, countercharges, and denials.

Bruth the Baker was charged with having struck a citizen of a foreign government on the head with a potentially lethal instrument—produced in evidence. Said citizen had admittedly attempted to interfere as Bruth was attempting to punish his slave Maleen—also produced in evidence—whom he suspected of having added something to a batch of cakes she was working on that afternoon, resulting in illness and complaints from fifty-two of Bruth's customers.

Said foreign citizen had also used insulting language—the captain admitted under pressure to "Fat and Ugly."

Some provocation could be conceded for the action taken by Bruth, but not enough. Bruth paled.

Captain Pausert, of the Republic of Nikkeldepain—everybody but the prisoners smiled this time—was charged (a) with said attempted interference, (b) with said insult, (c) with having frequently and severely struck Bruth the Baker in the course of the subsequent dispute.

The blow on the head was conceded to have provided a provocation for charge (c)—but not enough.

Nobody seemed to be charging the slave Maleen with anything. The judge only looked at her curiously, and shook his head.

"As the Court considers this regrettable incident," he remarked, "it looks like two years for you, Bruth; and about three for you, captain. Too bad!"

The captain had an awful sinking feeling. He had seen something and heard a lot of Imperial court methods in the fringe systems. He could probably get out of this three-year rap; but it would be expensive.

He realized that the judge was studying him reflectively.

"The Court wishes to acknowledge," the judge continued, "that the captain's chargeable actions were due largely to a natural feeling of human sympathy for the predicament of the slave Maleen. The Court, therefore, would suggest a settlement as follows—subsequent to which all charges could be dropped:

"That Bruth the Baker resell Maleen of Karres—with whose services he appears to be dissatisfied—for a reasonable sum to Captain Pausert of the Republic of Nikkeldepain."

Bruth the Baker heaved a gusty sigh of relief. But the captain hesitated. The buying of human slaves by private citizens was a very serious offense in Nikkeldepain! Still, he didn't have to make a record of it. If they weren't going to soak him too much—

At just the right moment, Maleen of Karres introduced a barely audible, forlorn, sniffling sound.

"How much are you asking for the kid?" the captain inquired, looking without friendliness at his recent antagonist. A day was coming when he would think less severely of Bruth; but it hadn't come yet.

Bruth scowled back but replied with a certain eagerness: "A hundred and fifty m—" A policeman standing behind him poked him sharply in the side. Bruth shut up.

"Seven hundred maels," the judge said smoothly. "There'll be Court charges, and a fee for recording the transaction—" He appeared to make a swift calculation. "Fifteen hundred and forty-two maels—" He turned to a clerk: "You've looked him up?"

The clerk nodded. "He's right!"

"And we'll take your check," the judge concluded. He gave the captain a friendly smile. "Next case."

The captain felt a little bewildered.

There was something peculiar about this! He was getting out of it much too cheaply. Since the Empire had quit its wars of expansion, young slaves in good health were a high-priced article. Furthermore, he was practically positive that Bruth the Baker had been willing to sell for a tenth of what the captain actually had to pay!

Well, he wouldn't complain. Rapidly, he signed, sealed and thumb-printed various papers shoved at him by a helpful clerk; and made out a check.

"I guess," he told Maleen of Karres, "we'd better get along to the ship."

And now what was he going to do with the kid, he pondered, padding along the unlighted streets with his slave trotting quietly behind him. If he showed up with a pretty girl-slave in Nikkeldepain, even a small one, various good friends there would toss him into ten years or so of penal servitude—immediately after Illyla had personally collected his scalp. They were a moral lot.

Karres—?

"How far off is Karres, Maleen?" he asked into the dark.

"It takes about two weeks," Maleen said tearfully.

Two weeks! The captain's heart sank again.

"What are you blubbering about?" he inquired uncomfortably.

Maleen choked, sniffed, and began sobbing openly.

"I have two little sisters!" she cried.

"Well, well," the captain said encouragingly. "That's nice—you'll be seeing them again soon. I'm taking you home, you know!"

Great Patham—now he'd said it! But after all—

But this piece of good news seemed to be having the wrong effect on his slave! Her sobbing grew much more violent.

"No, I won't," she wailed. "They're here!"

"Huh?" said the captain. He stopped short. "Where?"

"And the people they're with are mean to them, too!" wept Maleen.

The captain's heart dropped clean through his boots. Standing there in the dark, he helplessly watched it coming:

"You could buy them awfully cheap!" she said.

II.

In times of stress, the young life of Karres appeared to take to the heights. It might be a mountainous place.

The Leewit sat on the top shelf of the back wall of the crockery and antiques store, strategically flanked by two expensive-looking vases. She was a doll-sized edition of Maleen; but her eyes were cold and gray instead of blue and tearful. About five or six, the captain vaguely estimated. He wasn't very good at estimating them around that age.

"Good evening," he said, as he came in through the door. The Crockery and Antiques Shop had been easy to find. Like Bruth the Baker's, it was the one spot in the neighborhood that was all lit up.

"Good evening, sir!" said what was presumably the store owner, without looking around. He sat with his back to the door, in a chair approximately at the center of the store and facing the Leewit at a distance of about twenty feet.

". . . and there you can stay without food or drink till the

Holy Man comes in the morning!'' he continued immediately, in the taut voice of a man who has gone through hysteria and is sane again. The captain realized he was addressing the Leewit

"Your other Holy Man didn't stay very long!" the diminutive creature piped, also ignoring the captain. Apparently, she had not yet discovered Maleen behind him.

"This is a stronger denomination—much stronger!" the store owner replied, in a shaking voice but with a sort of relish. "*He'll* exorcise you, all right, little demon—you'll whistle no buttons off him! Your time is up! Go on and whistle all you want! Bust every vase in the place—"

The Leewit blinked her gray eyes thoughtfully at him.

"Might!" she said.

"But if you try to climb down from there," the store owner went on, on a rising note, "I'll chop you into bits—into little, little bits!"

He raised his arm as he spoke and weakly brandished what the captain recognized with a start of horror as a highly ornamented but probably still useful antique battle-ax.

"Ha!" said the Leewit.

"Beg your pardon, sir!" the captain said, clearing his throat.

"Good evening, sir!" the store owner repeated, without looking around. "What can I do for you?"

"I came to inquire," the captain said hesitantly, "about that child."

The store owner shifted about in his chair and squinted at the captain with red-rimmed eyes.

"You're not a Holy Man!" he said.

"Hello, Maleen!" the Leewit said suddenly. "That him?"

"We've come to buy you," Maleen said. "Shut up!"

"Good!" said the Leewit.

"Buy it? Are you mocking me, sir?" the store owner inquired.

"Shut up, Moonell!" A thin, dark, determined-looking woman had appeared in the doorway that led through the back wall of the store. She moved out a step under the shelves; and the Leewit leaned down from the top shelf and hissed. The woman moved hurriedly back into the doorway.

"Maybe he means it," she said in a more subdued voice.

"I can't sell to a citizen of the Empire," the store owner said defeatedly.

"I'm not a citizen," the captain said shortly. This time, he wasn't going to name it.

"No, he's from Nikkel—" Maleen began.

"Shut up, Maleen!" the captain said helplessly in turn.

"I never heard of Nikkel," the store owner muttered doubtfully.

"Maleen!" the woman called shrilly. "That's the name of one of the others—Bruth the Baker got her. He means it, all right! He's buying them—"

"A hundred and fifty maels!" the captain said craftily, remembering Bruth the Baker. "In cash!"

The store owner looked dazed.

"Not enough, Moonell!" the woman called. "Look at all it's broken! Five hundred maels!"

There was a sound then, so thin the captain could hardly hear it. It pierced at his eardrums like two jabs of a delicate needle. To right and left of him, two highly glazed little jugs went "Clink-clink!", showed a sudden veining of cracks, and collapsed.

A brief silence settled on the store. And now that he looked around more closely, the captain could spot here and there other little piles of shattered crockery—and places where similar ruins apparently had been swept up, leaving only traces of colored dust.

The store owner laid the ax down carefully beside his chair, stood up, swaying a little, and came towards the captain.

"You offered me a hundred and fifty maels!" he said rapidly as he approached. "I accept it here, now, see—before witnesses!" He grabbed the captain's right hand in both of his and pumped it up and down vigorously. "Sold!" he yelled.

Then he wheeled around in a leap and pointed a shaking hand at the Leewit.

"And NOW," he howled, "break something! Break anything! You're his! I'll sue him for every mael he ever made and ever will!"

"Oh, do come help me down, Maleen!" the Leewit pleaded prettily.

For a change, the store of Wansing, the jeweler, was dimly lit and very quiet. It was a sleek, fashionable place in a fashionable shopping block near the spaceport. The front door was unlocked, and Wansing was in.

The three of them entered quietly, and the door sighed quietly shut behind them. Beyond a great crystal display-counter, Wansing was moving about among a number of opened shelves, talking softly to himself. Under the crystal of the counter, and in close-packed rows on the satin-covered shelves, reposed a many-colored array gleaming and glittering and shining. Wansing was no piker.

"Good evening, sir!" the captain said across the counter.

"It's morning!" the Leewit remarked from the other side of Maleen.

"Maleen!" said the captain.

"We're keeping out of this," Maleen said to the Leewit.

"All right," said the Leewit.

Wansing had come around jerkily at the captain's greeting, but had made no other move. Like all the slave owners the captain had met on Porlumma so far, Wansing seemed unhappy. Otherwise, he was a large, dark, sleek-looking man with jewels in his ears and a smell of expensive oils and perfumes about him.

"This place is under constant visual guard, of course!" he told the captain gently. "Nothing could possibly happen to me here. Why am I so frightened?"

"Not of me, I'm sure!" the captain said with an uncomfortable attempt at geniality. "I'm glad your store's still open," he went on briskly. "I'm here on business—"

"Oh, yes, it's still open, of course," Wansing said. He gave the captain a slow smile and turned back to his shelves. "I'm making inventory, that's why! I've been making inventory since early yesterday morning. I've counted them all seven times—"

"You're very thorough," the captain said.

"Very, very thorough!" Wansing nodded to the shelves. "The last time I found I had made a million maels. But twice before that, I had lost approximately the same amount. I shall have to count them again, I suppose!" He closed a shelf softly. "I'm sure I counted those before. But they move about constantly. Constantly! It's horrible."

"You've got a slave here called Goth," the captain said, driving to the point.

"Yes, I have!" Wansing said, nodding. "And I'm sure she understands by now I meant no harm! I do, at any rate. It was perhaps a little—but I'm sure she understands now, or will soon!"

"Where is she?" the captain inquired, a trifle uneasily.

"In her room perhaps," Wansing suggested. "It's not so bad when she's there in her room with the door closed. But often she sits in the dark and looks at you as you go past—" He opened another drawer, and closed it quietly again. "Yes, they do move!" he whispered, as if confirming an earlier suspicion. "Constantly—"

"Look, Wansing," the captain said in a loud, firm voice. "I'm not a citizen of the Empire. I want to buy this Goth! I'll pay you a hundred and fifty maels, cash."

Wansing turned around completely again and looked at the

captain. "Oh, you do?" he said. "You're not a citizen?" He walked a few steps to the side of the counter, sat down at a small desk and turned a light on over it. Then he put his face in his hands for a moment.

"I'm a wealthy man," he muttered. "An influential man! The name of Wansing counts for a great deal on Porlumma. When the Empire suggests you buy, you buy, of course—but it need not have been I who bought her! I thought she would be useful in the business—and then, even I could not sell her again within the Empire. She has been here for a week!"

He looked up at the captain and smiled. "One hundred and fifty maels!" he said. "Sold! There are records to be made out—" He reached into a drawer and took out some printed forms. He began to write rapidly. The captain produced identifications.

Maleen said suddenly: "Goth?"

"Right here," a voice murmured. Wansing's hand jerked sharply, but he did not look up. He kept on writing.

Something small and lean and bonelessly supple, dressed in a dark jacket and leggings, came across the thick carpets of Wansing's store and stood behind the captain. This one might be about nine or ten.

"I'll take your check, captain!" Wansing said politely. "You must be an honest man. Besides, I want to frame it."

"And now," the captain heard himself say in the remote voice of one who moves through a strange dream, "I suppose we could go to the ship."

The sky was gray and cloudy; and the streets were lightening. Goth, he noticed, didn't resemble her sisters. She had brown hair cut short a few inches below her ears, and brown eyes with long, black lashes. Her nose was short and her chin was pointed. She made him think of some thin, carnivorous creature, like a weasel.

She looked up at him briefly, grinned, and said: "Thanks!"

"What was wrong with *him*?" chirped the Leewit, walking backwards for a last view of Wansing's store.

"Tough crook," muttered Goth. The Leewit giggled.

"You premoted this just dandy, Maleen!" she stated next.

"Shut up," said Maleen.

"All right," said the Leewit. She glanced up at the captain's face. "You been fighting!" she said virtuously. "Did you win?"

"Of course, the captain won!" said Maleen.

"Good for you!" said the Leewit.

*   *   *

"What about the take-off?" Goth asked the captain. She seemed a little worried.

"Nothing to it!" the captain said stoutly, hardly bothering to wonder how she'd guessed the take-off was the one operation on which he and the old *Venture* consistently failed to co-operate.

"No," said Goth, "I meant when?"

"Right now," said the captain. "They've already cleared us. We'll get the sign any second."

"Good," said Goth. She walked off slowly down the hall towards the back of the ship.

The take-off was pretty bad, but the *Venture* made it again. Half an hour later, with Porlumma dwindling safely behind them, the captain switched to automatic and climbed out of his chair. After considerable experimentation, he got the electric butler adjusted to four breakfasts, hot, with coffee. It was accomplished with a great deal of advice and attempted assistance from the Leewit, rather less from Maleen, and no comments from Goth.

"Everything will be coming along in a few minutes now!" he announced. Afterwards, it struck him there had been a quality of grisly prophecy about the statement.

"If you'd listened to me," said the Leewit, "we'd have been done eating a quarter of an hour ago!" She was perspiring but triumphant—she had been right all along.

"Say, Maleen," she said suddenly, "you premoting again?"

Premoting? The captain looked at Maleen. She seemed pale and troubled.

"Spacesick?" he suggested. "I've got some pills—"

"No, she's premoting," the Leewit said scowling. "What's up, Maleen?"

"Shut up," said Goth.

"All right," said the Leewit. She was silent a moment, and then began to wriggle. "Maybe we'd better—"

"Shut up," said Maleen.

"It's all ready," said Goth.

"What's all ready?" asked the captain.

"All right," said the Leewit. She looked at the captain. "Nothing," she said.

He looked at them then, and they looked at him—one set each of gray eyes, and brown, and blue. They were all sitting around the control room floor in a circle, the fifth side of which was occupied by the electric butler.

What peculiar little waifs, the captain thought. He hadn't

perhaps really realized until now just how *very* peculiar. They were still staring at him.

"Well, well!" he said heartily. "So Maleen 'premotes' and gives people stomach-aches."

Maleen smiled dimly and smoothed back her yellow hair.

"They just thought they were getting them," she murmured.

"Mass history," explained the Leewit, offhandedly.

"Hysteria," said Goth. "The Imperials get their hair up about us every so often."

"I noticed that," the captain nodded. "And little Leewit here—she whistles and busts things."

"It's *the* Leewit," the Leewit said, frowning.

"Oh, I see," said the captain. "Like *the* captain, eh?"

"That's right," said the Leewit. She smiled.

"And what does little Goth do?" the captain addressed the third witch.

Little Goth appeared pained. Maleen answered for her.

"Goth teleports mostly," she said.

"Oh, she does?" said the captain. "I've heard about that trick, too," he added lamely.

"Just small stuff really!" Goth said abruptly. She reached into the top of her jacket and pulled out a cloth-wrapped bundle the size of the captain's two fists. The four ends of the cloth were knotted together. Goth undid the knot. "Like this," she said and poured out the contents on the rug between them. There was a sound like a big bagful of marbles being spilled.

"Great Patham!" the captain swore, staring down at what was a cool quarter-million in jewel stones, or he was still a miffel-farmer.

"Good gosh," said the Leewit, bouncing to her feet. "Maleen, we better get at it right away!"

The two blondes darted from the room. The captain hardly noticed their going. He was staring at Goth.

"Child," he said, "don't you realize they hang you without trial on places like Porlumma, if you're caught with stolen goods?"

"We're not on Porlumma," said Goth. She looked slightly annoyed. "They're for you. You spent money on us, didn't you?"

"Not that kind of money," said the captain. "If Wansing noticed— They're Wansing's, I suppose?"

"Sure!" said Goth. "Pulled them in just before take-off!"

"If he reported, there'll be police ships on our tail any—"

"Goth!" Maleen shrilled.

Goth's head came around and she rolled up on her feet in one motion. "Coming," she shouted. "Excuse me," she murmured to the captain. Then she, too, was out of the room.

But again, the captain scarcely noticed her departure. He had rushed to the control desk with a sudden awful certainty and /itched on all screens.

There they were! Two sleek, black ships coming up fast from hind, and already almost in gun-range! They weren't regular police boats, the captain recognized, but auxiliary craft of the Empire's frontier fleets. He rammed the *Venture*'s drives full on. Immediately, red-and-black fire blossoms began to sprout in space behind him—then a finger of flame stabbed briefly past, not a hundred yards to the right of the ship.

But the communicator stayed dead. Porlumma preferred risking the sacrifice of Wansing's jewels to giving them a chance to surrender! To do the captain justice, his horror was due much more to the fate awaiting his three misguided charges than to the fact that he was going to share it.

He was putting the *Venture* through a wildly erratic and, he hoped, aim-destroying series of sideways hops and forward lunges with one hand, and trying to unlimber the turrets of the nova guns with the other, when suddenly—!

No, he decided at once, there was no use trying to understand it— There were just no more Empire ships around. The screens all blurred and darkened simultaneously; and, for a short while, a darkness went flowing and coiling lazily past the *Venture*. Light jumped out of it at him once, in a cold, ugly glare, and receded again in a twisting, unnatural fashion. The *Venture*'s drives seemed dead.

Then, just as suddenly, the old ship jerked, shivered, roared aggrievedly, and was hurling herself along on her own power again!

But Porlumma's sun was no longer in evidence. Stars gleamed and shifted distantly against the blackness of deep space all about. The patterns seemed familiar, but he wasn't a good enough navigator to be sure.

The captain stood up stiffly, feeling a heavy cloud. And at that moment, with a wild, hilarious clacking like a metallic hen, the electric butler delivered four breakfasts, hot, one after the other, right onto the center of the control room floor.

The first voice said distinctly: "Shall we just leave it on?"

A second voice, considerably more muffled, replied: "Yes, let's! You never know when you need it—"

The third voice, tucked somewhere in between them, said simply: *"Whew!"*

Peering about the dark room in bewilderment, the captain realized suddenly that the voices had come from the speaker of an intership communicator, leading to what had once been the *Venture's* captain's cabin.

He listened; but only a dim murmuring came from it now, and then nothing at all. He started towards the hall, then returned and softly switched off the communicator. He went quietly down the hall until he came to the captain's cabin. Its door was closed.

He listened a moment, and opened it suddenly.

There was a trio of squeals:

"Oh, don't! You spoiled it!"

The captain stood motionless. Just one glimpse had been given him of what seemed to be a bundle of twisted black wires arranged loosely like the frame of a truncated cone on—or was it just above?—a table in the center of the cabin. Where the tip of the cone should have been burned a round, swirling, orange fire. About it, their faces reflecting its glow, stood the three witches.

Then the fire vanished; the wires collapsed. There was only ordinary light in the room. They were looking up at him variously—Maleen with smiling regret, the Leewit in frank annoyance, Goth with no expression at all.

"What out of Great Patham's Seventh Hell was that?" inquired the captain, his hair bristling slowly.

The Leewit looked at Goth; Goth looked at Maleen. Maleen said doubtfully: "We can just tell you its name—"

"That was the Sheewash Drive," said Goth.

"The what-drive?" asked the captain.

"Sheewash," repeated Maleen.

"The one you have to do it with yourself," the Leewit said helpfully.

"Shut up," said Maleen.

There was a long pause. The captain looked down at the handful of thin, black, twelve-inch wires scattered about the table top. He touched one of them. It was dead-cold.

"I see," he said. "I guess we're all going to have a long talk." Another pause. "Where are we now?"

"About three light-years down the way you were going," said Goth. "We only worked it thirty seconds."

"Twenty-eight!" corrected Maleen, with the authority of her years. "The Leewit was getting tired."

"I see," said Captain Pausert carefully. "Well, let's go have some breakfast."

III.

They ate with a silent voraciousness, dainty Maleen, the exquisite Leewit, supple Goth, all alike. The captain, long finished, watched them with amazement and—now at last—with something like awe.

"It's the Sheewash Drive," explained Maleen finally, catching his expression.

"Takes it out of you!" said Goth.

The Leewit grunted affirmatively and stuffed on.

"Can't do too much of it," said Maleen. "Or too often. It kills you sure!"

"What," said the captain, "*is* the Sheewash Drive?"

They became reticent. People did it on Karres, said Maleen, when they had to go somewhere else fast. Everybody knew how there.

"But of course," she added, "we're pretty young to do it right!"

"We did it pretty good!" the Leewit contradicted positively. She seemed to be finished at last.

"But how?" said the captain.

Reticence thickened almost visibly. If you couldn't do it, said Maleen, you couldn't understand it either.

He gave it up, for the time being.

"I guess I'll have to take you home next," he said; and they agreed.

Karres, it developed, was in the Iverdahl System. He couldn't find any planet of that designation listed in his maps of the area, but that meant nothing. The maps were old and often inaccurate, and local names changed a lot.

Barring the use of weird and deadly miracle-drives, that detour was going to cost him almost a month in time—and a good chunk of his profits in power used up. The jewels Goth had illegally teleported must, of course, be returned to their owner, he explained. He'd intended to look severely at the culprit at that point; but she'd meant well, after all! They were extremely peculiar children, but still children—they couldn't really understand.

He would stop off en route to Karres at an Empire planet with banking facilities to take care of that matter, the captain added.

A planet far enough off so the police wouldn't be likely to take any particular interest in the *Venture*.

A dead silence greeted this schedule. It appeared that the representatives of Karres did not think much of his logic.

"Well," Maleen sighed at last, "we'll see you get your money back some other way then!"

The junior witches nodded coldly.

"How did you three happen to get into this fix?" the captain inquired, with the intention of changing the subject.

They'd left Karres together on a jaunt of their own, they explained. No, they hadn't run away—he got the impression that such trips were standard procedure for juveniles in that place. They were on another planet, a civilized one but beyond the borders and law of Empire, when the town they were in was raided by a small fleet of slavers. They were taken along with most of the local youngsters.

"It's a wonder," he said reflectively, "you didn't take over the ship."

"Oh, brother!" exclaimed the Leewit.

"Not that ship!" said Goth.

"That was an Imperial Slaver!" Maleen informed him. "You behave yourself every second on those crates."

Just the same, the captain thought as he settled himself to rest in the control room on a couch he had set up there, it was no longer surprising that the Empire wanted no young slaves from Karres to be transported into the interior! Oddest sort of children— But he ought to be able to get his expenses paid by their relatives. Something very profitable might even be made of this deal—

Have to watch the record-entries though! Nikkeldepain's laws were explicit about the penalties invoked by anything resembling the purchase and sale of slaves.

He'd thoughtfully left the intership communicator adjusted so he could listen in on their conversation in the captain's cabin. However, there had been nothing for some time beyond frequent bursts of childish giggling. Then came a succession of piercing shrieks from the Leewit. It appeared she was being forcibly washed behind the ears by Maleen and obliged to brush her teeth, in preparation for bedtime.

It had been agreed that he was not to enter the cabin, because— for reasons not given—they couldn't keep the Sheewash Drive on in his presence; and they wanted to have it ready, in case of an emergency. Piracy was rife beyond the Imperial borders, and the *Venture* would keep beyond the border for a good part of the trip, to avoid the more pressing danger of police pursuit instigated by Porlumma. The captain had explained the potentialities of the nova guns the *Venture* boasted, or tried to. Possibly, they hadn't understood. At any rate, they seemed unimpressed.

The Sheewash Drive! Boy, he thought in sudden excitement, if he could just get the principles of that. Maybe he would!

He raised his head suddenly. The Leewit's voice had lifted clearly over the communicator:

". . . .not such a bad old dope!" the childish treble remarked.

The captain blinked indignantly.

"He's not so old," Maleen's soft voice returned. "And he's certainly no dope!"

He smiled. Good kid, Maleen.

"Yeah, yeah!" squeaked the Leewit offensively. "Maleen's sweet onthu-ulp!"

A vague commotion continued for a while, indicating, he hoped, that someone he could mention was being smothered under a pillow.

He drifted off to sleep before it was settled.

If you didn't happen to be thinking of what they'd done, they seemed more or less like normal children. Right from the start, they displayed a flattering interest in the captain and his background; and he told them all about everything and everybody in Nikkeldepain. Finally, he even showed them his treasured pocket-sized picture of Illyla—the one with which he'd held many cozy conversations during the earlier part of his trip.

Almost at once, though, he realized that was a mistake. They studied it intently in silence, their heads crowded close together.

"Oh, brother!" the Leewit whispered then, with entirely the wrong kind of inflection.

"Just what did you mean by that?" the captain inquired coldly.

"Sweet!" murmured Goth. But it was the way she closed her eyes briefly, as though gripped by a light spasm of nausea.

"Shut up, Goth!" Maleen said sharply. "I think she's very swee . . . I mean, she looks very nice!" she told the captain.

The captain was disgruntled. Silently, he retrieved the maligned Illyla and returned her to his breast pocket. Silently, he went off and left them standing there.

But afterwards, in private, he took it out again and studied it worriedly. His Illyla! He shifted the picture back and forth under the light. It wasn't really a very good picture of her, he decided.

It had been bungled! From certain angles, one might even say that Illyla did look the least bit insipid.

What was he thinking, he thought, shocked.

He unlimbered the nova gun turrets next and got in a little firing practice. They had been sealed when he took over the *Venture* and weren't supposed to be used, except in absolute emergencies. They were somewhat uncertain weapons, though very effective, and Nikkeldepain had turned to safer forms of armament many decades ago. But on the third day out from Nikkeldepain, the captain made a brief notation in his log:

"Attacked by two pirate craft. Unsealed nova guns. Destroyed one attacker; survivor fled—"

He was rather pleased by that crisp, hard-bitten description of desperate space-adventure, and enjoyed rereading it occasionally. It wasn't true, though. He had put in an interesting four hours at the time pursuing and annihilating large, craggy chunks of substance of a meteorite-cloud he found the *Venture* plowing through. Those nova guns were fascinating stuff! You'd sight the turrets on something; and so long as it didn't move after that, it was all right. If it did move, it got it—unless you relented and deflected the turrets first. They were just the thing for arresting a pirate in midspace.

The *Venture* dipped back into the Empire's borders four days later and headed for the capitol of the local province. Police ships challenged them twice on the way in; and the captain found considerable comfort in the awareness that his passengers foregathered silently in their cabin on these occasions. They didn't tell him they were set to use the Sheewash Drive—somehow it had never been mentioned since that first day; but he knew the queer orange fire was circling over its skimpy framework of twisted wires there and ready to act.

However, the space police waved him on, satisfied with routine identification. Apparently, the *Venture* had not become generally known as a criminal ship, to date.

Maleen accompanied him to the banking institution that was to return Wansing's property to Porlumma. Her sisters, at the captain's definite request, remained on the ship.

The transaction itself went off without a visible hitch. The jewels would reach their destination in Porlumma within a month. But he had to take out a staggering sum in insurance—"Piracy, thieves!" smiled the clerk. "Even summary capital punishment won't keep the rats down." And, of course, he had to register name, ship, home planet, and so on. But since they already had all that information in Porlumma, he gave it without hesitation.

On the way back to the spaceport, he sent off a sealed message by radio-relay to the bereaved jeweler, informing him of the action taken, and regretting the misunderstanding.

He felt a little better after that, though the insurance payment had been a severe blow! If he didn't manage to work out a decent profit on Karres somehow, the losses on the miffel farm would hardly be covered now.

Then he noticed that Maleen was getting uneasy.

"We'd better hurry!" was all she would say, however. Her face grew pale.

The captain understood. She was having another premonition! The hitch to this premoting business was, apparently, that when something was brewing you were informed of the bare fact but had to guess at most of the details. They grabbed an aircab and raced back to the spaceport.

They had just been cleared there when he spotted a small group of uniformed men coming along the dock on the double. They stopped short and then scattered, as the *Venture* lurched drunkenly sideways into the air. Everyone else in sight was scattering, too.

That was a very bad take-off—one of the captain's worst! Once afloat, however, he ran the ship promptly into the nightside of the planet and turned her nose towards the border. The old pirate-chaser had plenty of speed when you gave her the reins; and throughout the entire next sleep-period, he let her use it all.

The Sheewash Drive was not required that time.

Next day, he had a lengthy private talk with Goth on the Golden Rule and the Law, with particular reference to individual property rights. If Councilor Onswud had been monitoring the sentiments expressed by the captain, he could not have failed to rumble surprised approval. The delinquent herself listened impassively; but the captain fancied she showed distinct signs of being rather impressed by his earnestness.

It was two days after that—well beyond the borders again—when they were obliged to make an unscheduled stop at a mining moon. For the captain discovered he had already miscalculated the extent to which the prolonged run on overdrive after leaving the capitol was going to deplete the *Venture*'s reserves. They would have to juice up—

A large, extremely handsome Sirian freighter lay beside them at the Moon station. It was half a battlecraft really, since it dealt regularly beyond the borders. They had to wait while it was

being serviced; and it took a long time. The Sirians turned out to
be as unpleasant as their ship was good-looking—a snooty,
conceited, hairy lot who talked only their own dialect and pretended to be unfamiliar with Imperial Universum.

The captain found himself getting irked by their bad manners—
particularly when he discovered they were laughing over his
argument with the service superintendent about the cost of repow-
ering the *Venture*.

"You're out in deep space, captain!" said the superintendent.
"And you haven't juice enough left even to travel back to the
Border. You can't expect Imperial prices here!"

"It's not what you charged *them*!" The captain angrily jerked
his thumb at the Sirian.

"Regular customers!" the superintendent shrugged. "You start
coming by here every three months like they do, and we can
make an arrangement with you, too."

It was outrageous—it actually put the *Venture* back in the red!
But there was no help for it.

Nor did it improve the captain's temper when he muffed the
take-off once more—and then had to watch the Sirian floating
into space, as sedately as a swan, a little behind him!

An hour later, as he sat glumly before the controls, debating
the chance of recouping his losses before returning to Nikkeldepain,
Maleen and the Leewit hurriedly entered the room. They did
something to a port screen.

"They sure are!" the Leewit exclaimed. She seemed child-
ishly pleased.

"Are what?" the captain inquired absently.

"Following us," said Maleen. She did not sound pleased.
"It's that Sirian ship, Captain Pausert—"

The captain stared bewilderedly at the screen. There *was* a
ship in focus there. It was quite obviously the Sirian and, just as
obviously, it was following them.

"What do they want?" he wondered. "They're stinkers but
they're not pirates. Even if they were, they wouldn't spend an
hour running after a crate like the *Venture*!"

Maleen said nothing. The Leewit observed: "Oh, brother! Got
their bow-turrets out now—better get those nova guns ready!"

"But it's all nonsense!" the captain said, flushing angrily. He
turned suddenly towards the communicators. "What's that Empire general beam-length?"

".0044," said Maleen.

A roaring, abusive voice flooded the control room immediately.

The one word understandable to the captain was *"Venture."* It
was repeated frequently, sometimes as if it were a question.

"Sirian!" said the captain. "Can you understand them?" he
asked Maleen.

She shook her head. "The Leewit can—"

The Leewit nodded, her gray eyes glistening.

"What are they saying?"

"They says you're for stopping," the Leewit translated rapidly,
but apparently retaining much of the original sentence-structure.
"They says you're for skinning alive . . . ha! They says you're
for stopping right now and for only hanging. They says—"

Maleen scuttled from the control room. The Leewit banged the
communicator with one small fist.

"Beak-Wock!" she shrieked. It sounded like that, anyway.
The loud voice paused a moment.

"Beak-Wock?" it returned in an aggrieved, demanding roar.

"Beak-Wock!" the Leewit affirmed with apparent delight.
She rattled off a string of similar-sounding syllables. She paused.

A howl of inarticulate wrath responded.

The captain, in a whirl of outraged emotions, was yelling at
the Leewit to shut up, at the Sirian to go to Great Patham's
Second Hell—the worst—and wrestling with the nova gun adjus-
tors at the same time. He'd had about enough! He'd—

SSS-whoosh!

It was the Sheewash Drive.

"And where are we now?" the captain inquired, in a voice of
unnatural calm.

"Same place, just about," said the Leewit. "Ship's still on
the screen. Way back though—take them an hour again to catch
up." She seemed disappointed; then brightened. "You got lots
of time to get the guns ready!"

The captain didn't answer. He was marching down the hall
towards the rear of the *Venture*. He passed the captain's cabin
and noted the door was shut. He went on without pausing. He
was mad clean through—he knew what had happened!

After all he'd told her, Goth had teleported again.

It was all there, in the storage. Items of half a pound in weight
seemed to be as much as she could handle. But amazing quantities of stuff had met that one requirement—bottles filled with
what might be perfume or liquor or dope, expensive-looking
garments and cloths in a shining variety of colors, small boxes,
odds, ends and, of course, jewelry!

He spent half an hour getting it loaded into a steel space crate.

He wheeled the crate into the rear lock, sealed the inside lock and pulled the switch that activated the automatic launching device.

The outside lock clicked shut. He stalked back to the control room. The Leewit was still in charge, fiddling with the communicators.

"I could try a whistle over them," she suggested, glancing up. She added: "But they'd bust somewheres, sure."

"Get them on again!" the captain said.

"Yes, sir," said the Leewit surprised.

The roaring voice came back faintly.

"SHUT UP!" the captain shouted in Imperial Universum.

The voice shut up.

"Tell them they can pick up their stuff—it's been dumped out in a crate!" the captain told the Leewit. "Tell them I'm proceeding on my course. Tell them if they follow me one light-minute beyond that crate, I'll come back for them, shoot their front end off, shoot their rear end off, and ram 'em in the middle."

"Yes, SIR!" the Leewit sparkled. They proceeded on their course.

Nobody followed.

"Now I want to speak to Goth," the captain announced. He was still at a high boil. "Privately," he added. "Back in the storage—"

Goth followed him expressionlessly into the storage. He closed the door to the hall. He'd broken off a two-foot length from the tip of one of Councilor Rapport's overpriced tinklewood fishing poles. It made a fair switch.

But Goth looked terribly small just now! He cleared his throat. He wished for a moment he were back on Nikkeldepain.

"I warned you," he said.

Goth didn't move. Between one second and the next, however, she seemed to grow remarkably. Her brown eyes focused on the captain's Adam's apple; her lip lifted at one side. A slightly hungry look came into her face.

"Wouldn't try that!" she murmured.

Mad again, the captain reached out quickly and got a handful of leathery cloth. There was a blur of motion, and what felt like a small explosion against his left kneecap. He grunted with anguished surprise and fell back on a bale of Councilor Rapport's all-weather cloaks. But he had retained his grip—Goth fell half on top of him, and that was still a favorable position. Then her head snaked around, her neck seemed to extend itself; and her teeth snapped his wrist.

Weasels don't let go—

*   *   *

"Didn't think he'd have the nerve!" Goth's voice came over the communicator. There was a note of grudging admiration in it. It seemed that she was inspecting her bruises.

All tangled up in the job of bandaging his freely bleeding wrist, the captain hoped she'd find a good plenty to count. His knee felt the size of a sofa pillow and throbbed like a piston engine.

"The captain is a brave man," Maleen was saying reproachfully. "You should have known better—"

"He's not very *smart*, though!" the Leewit remarked suggestively.

There was a short silence.

"Is he? Goth? Eh?" the Leewit urged.

"Perhaps not very," said Goth.

"You two lay off him!" Maleen ordered. "Useless," she added meaningly, "you want to *swim* back to Karres—on the Egger Route!"

"Not me," the Leewit said briefly.

"You could still do it, I guess," said Goth. She seemed to be reflecting. "All right—we'll lay off him. It was a fair fight, anyway."

IV.

They raised Karres the sixteenth day after leaving Porlumma. There had been no more incidents; but then, neither had there been any more stops or other contacts with the defenseless Empire. Maleen had cooked up a poultice which did wonders for his knee. With the end of the trip in sight, all tensions had relaxed; and Maleen, at least, seemed to grow hourly more regretful at the prospect of parting.

After a brief study, Karres could be distinguished easily enough by the fact that it moved counterclockwise to all the other planets of the Iverdahl System.

Well, it would, the captain thought.

They came soaring into its atmosphere on the dayside without arousing any visible interest. No communicator signals reached them; and no other ships showed up to look them over. Karres, in fact, had all the appearance of a completely uninhabited world. There were a larger number of seas, too big to be called lakes and too small to be oceans, scattered over its surface. There was one enormously towering ridge of mountains that ran from pole to pole, and any number of lesser chains. There were two good-sized ice caps; and the southern section of the planet was speckled with intermittent stretches of snow. Almost all of it seemed to be dense forest.

It was a handsome place, in a wild, somber way.

They went gliding over it, from noon through morning and into the dawn fringe—the captain at the controls, Goth and the Leewit flanking him at the screens, and Maleen behind him to do the directing. After a few initial squeals, the Leewit became oddly silent. Suddenly the captain realized she was blubbering.

Somehow, it startled him to discover that her homecoming had affected the Leewit to that extent. He felt Goth reach out behind him and put her hand on the Leewit's shoulder. The smallest witch sniffled happily.

" 'S beautiful!" she growled.

He felt a resurge of the wondering, protective friendliness they had aroused in him at first. They must have been having a rough time of it, at that. He sighed; it seemed a pity they hadn't got along a little better!

"Where's everyone hiding?" he inquired, to break up the mood. So far, there hadn't been a sign of human habitation.

"There aren't many people on Karres," Maleen said from behind his shoulder. "But we're going to The Town—you'll meet about half of them there!"

"What's that place down there?" the captain asked with sudden interest. Something like an enormous lime-white bowl seemed to have been set flush into the floor of the wide valley up which they were moving.

"That's the Theater where . . . ouch!" the Leewit said. She fell silent then but turned to give Maleen a resentful look.

"Something strangers shouldn't be told about, eh?" the captain said tolerantly. Goth glanced at him from the side.

"We've got rules," she said.

He let the ship down a little as they passed over "the Theater where—" It was a sort of large, circular arena, with numerous steep tiers of seats running up around it. But all was bare and deserted now.

On Maleen's direction, they took the next valley fork to the right and dropped lower still. He had his first look at Karres animal life then. A flock of large, creamy-white birds, remarkably Terrestrial in appearance, flapped by just below them, apparently unconcerned about the ship. The forest underneath had opened out into a long stretch of lush meadow land, with small creeks winding down into its center. Here a herd of several

hundred head of beasts was grazing—beasts of mastodonic size
and build, with hairless, shiny black hides. The mouths of their
long, heavy heads were twisted up into sardonic, crocodilian
grins as they blinked up at the passing *Venture.*

"Black Bollems," said Goth, apparently enjoying the captain's
expression. "Lots of them around; they're tame. But the gray
mountain ones are good hunting."

"Good eating, too!" the Leewit said. She licked her lips
daintily. "Breakfast—!" she sighed, her thoughts diverted to a
familiar track. "And we ought to be just in time!"

"There's the field!" Maleen cried, pointing. "Set her down
there, captain!"

The "field" was simply a flat meadow of close-trimmed grass
running smack against the mountainside to their left. One small
vehicle, bright blue in color, was parked on it; and it was
bordered on two sides by very tall, blue-black trees.

That was all.

The captain shook his head. Then he set her down.

The town of Karres was a surprise to him in a good many
ways. For one thing, there was much more of it than you would
have thought possible after flying over the area. It stretched for
miles through the forest, up the flanks of the mountain and
across the valley—little clusters of houses or individual ones,
each group screened from all the rest and from the sky overhead
by the trees.

They liked color on Karres; but then they hid it away! The
houses were bright as flowers, red and white, apple-green, golden-
brown—all spick and span, scrubbed and polished and aired with
that brisk, green forest-smell. At various times of the day, there
was also the smell of remarkably good things to eat. There were
brooks and pools and a great number of shaded vegetable gar-
dens to the town. There were risky-looking treetop playgrounds,
and treetop platforms and galleries which seemed to have no
particular purpose. On the ground was mainly an enormously
confusing maze of paths—narrow trails of sandy soil snaking
about among great brown tree roots and chunks of gray mountain
rock, and half covered with fallen needle leaves. The first six
times the captain set out unaccompanied, he'd lost his way
hopelessly within minutes, and had to be guided back out of the
forest.

But the most hidden of all were the people! About four
thousand of them were supposed to live in the town, with as
many more scattered about the planet. But you never got to see

more than three or four at any one time—except when now and then a pack of children, who seemed to the captain to be uniformly of the Leewit's size, would burst suddenly out of the undergrowth across a path before you, and vanish again.

As for the others, you did hear someone singing occasionally; or there might be a whole muted concert going on all about, on a large variety of wooden musical instruments which they seemed to enjoy tootling with, gently.

But it wasn't a real town at all, the captain thought. They didn't live like people, these Witches of Karres—it was more like a flock of strange forest birds that happened to be nesting in the same general area. Another thing: they appeared to be busy enough—but what was their business?

He discovered he was reluctant to ask Toll too many questions about it. Toll was the mother of his three witches; but only Goth really resembled her. It was difficult to picture Goth becoming smoothly matured and pleasantly rounded; but that was Toll. She had the same murmuring voice, the same air of sideways observation and secret reflection. And she answered all the captain's questions with apparent frankness; but he never seemed to get much real information out of what she said.

It was odd, too! Because he was spending several hours a day in her company, or in one of the next rooms at any rate, while she went about her housework. Toll's daughters had taken him home when they landed; and he was installed in the room that belonged to their father—busy just now, the captain gathered, with some sort of research of a geological nature elsewhere on Karres. The arrangement worried him a little at first, particularly since Toll and he were mostly alone in the house. Maleen was going to some kind of school; she left early in the morning and came back late in the afternoon; and Goth and the Leewit were just plain running wild! They usually got in long after the captain had gone to bed and were off again before he turned out for breakfast.

It hardly seemed like the right way to raise them! One afternoon, he found the Leewit curled up and asleep in the chair he usually occupied on the porch before the house. She slept there for four solid hours, while the captain sat nearby and leafed gradually through a thick book with illuminated pictures called "Histories of Ancient Yarthe." Now and then, he sipped at a cool, green, faintly intoxicating drink Toll had placed quietly beside him some while before, or sucked an aromatic smoke from the enormous pipe with a floor rest, which he understood was a favorite of Toll's husband.

*   *   *

Then the Leewit woke up suddenly, uncoiled, gave him a look between a scowl and a friendly grin, slipped off the porch and vanished among the trees.

He couldn't quite figure that look! It might have meant nothing at all in particular, but—

The captain laid down his book then and worried a little more. It was true, of course, that nobody seemed in the least concerned about his presence. All of Karres appeared to know about him, and he'd met quite a number of people by now in a casual way. But nobody came around to interview him or so much as dropped in for a visit. However, Toll's husband presumably would be returning presently, and—

How long had he been here, anyway?

Great Patham, the captain thought, shocked. He'd lost count of the days!

Or was it weeks?

He went in to find Toll.

"It's been a wonderful visit," he said, "but I'll have to be leaving, I guess. Tomorrow morning, early—"

Toll put some fancy sewing she was working on back in a glass basket, laid her thin, strong witch's hands in her lap, and smiled up at him.

"We thought you'd be thinking that," she said, "and so we— You know, captain, it was quite difficult to find a way to reward you for bringing back the children?"

"It was?" said the captain, suddenly realizing he'd also clean forgotten he was broke! And now the wrath of Onswud lay close ahead.

"Gold and jewel stones would have been just right, of course!" she said, "but unfortunately, while there's no doubt a lot of it on Karres somewhere, we never got around to looking for it. And we haven't money—none that you could use, that is!"

"No, I don't suppose you do," the captain agreed sadly.

"However," said Toll, "we've all been talking about it in the town, and so we've loaded a lot of things aboard your ship that we think you can sell at a fine profit!"

"Well now," the captain said gratefully, "that's fine of—"

"There are furs," said Toll, "the very finest furs we could fix up—two thousand of them!"

"Oh!" said the captain, bravely keeping his smile. "Well, that's wonderful!"

"And essences of perfume!" said Toll. "Everyone brought

one bottle of their own, so that's eight thousand three hundred and twenty-three bottles of perfume essences—all different!"

"Perfume!" said the captain. "Fine, fine—but you really shouldn't—"

"And the rest of it," Toll concluded happily, "is the green Lepti liquor you like so much, and the Wintenberry jellies!" She frowned. "I forgot just how many jugs and jars," she admitted, "but there were a lot. It's all loaded now. And do you think you'll be able to sell all that?" she smiled.

"I certainly can!" the captain said stoutly. "It's wonderful stuff, and there's nothing like it in the Empire."

Which was very true. They wouldn't have considered miffel-furs for lining on Karres. But if he'd been alone he would have felt like he wanted to burst into tears.

The witches couldn't have picked more completely unsalable items if they'd tried! Furs, cosmetics, food and liquor—he'd be shot on sight if he got caught trying to run that kind of merchandise into the Empire. For the same reason that they couldn't use it on Nikkeldepain—they were that scared of contamination by goods that came from uncleared worlds!

He breakfasted alone next morning. Toll had left a note beside his plate, which explained in a large, not too legible script that she had to run off and fetch the Leewit; and that if he was gone before she got back she was wishing him good-by and good luck.

He smeared two more buns with Wintenberry jelly, drank a large mug of cone-seed coffee, finished every scrap of the omelet of swan hawk eggs and then, in a state of pleasant repletion, toyed around with his slice of roasted Bollem liver. Boy, what food! He must have put on fifteen pounds since he landed on Karres.

He wondered how Toll kept that sleek figure.

Regretfully, he pushed himself away from the table, pocketed her note for a souvenir, and went out on the porch. There a tear-stained Maleen hurled herself into his arms.

"Oh, captain!" she sobbed. "You're leaving—"

"Now, now!" the captain murmured, touched and surprised by the lovely child's grief. He patted her shoulders soothingly. "I'll be back," he said rashly.

"Oh, yes, do come back!" cried Maleen. She hesitated and added: "I become marriageable two years from now. Karres time—"

"Well, well," said the captain, dazed. "Well, now—"

He set off down the path a few minutes later, with a strange melody tinkling in his head. Around the first curve, it changed abruptly to a shrill keening which seemed to originate from a spot some two hundred feet before him. Around the next curve, he entered a small, rocky clearing full of pale, misty, early-morning sunlight and what looked like a slow-motion fountain of gleaming rainbow globes. These turned out to be clusters of large, vari-hued soap bubbles which floated up steadily from a wooden tub full of hot water, soap and the Leewit. Toll was bent over the tub; and the Leewit was objecting to a morning bath, with only that minimum of interruptions required to keep her lungs pumped full of a fresh supply of air.

As the captain paused beside the little family group, her red, wrathful face came up over the rim of the tub and looked at him.

"Well, Ugly," she squealed, in a renewed outburst of rage, "who you staring at?" Then a sudden determination came into her eyes. She pursed her lips.

Toll up-ended her promptly and smacked the Leewit's bottom.

"She was going to make some sort of a whistle at you," she explained hurriedly. "Perhaps you'd better get out of range while I can keep her head under. And good luck, captain!"

Karres seemed even more deserted than usual this morning. Of course, it was quite early. Great banks of fog lay here and there among the huge dark trees and the small bright houses. A breeze sighed sadly far overhead. Faint, mournful bird-cries came from still higher up—it could have been swan hawks reproaching him for the omelet.

Somewhere in the distance, somebody tootled on a wood-instrument, very gently.

He had gone halfway up the path to the landing field, when something buzzed past him like an enormous wasp and went *CLUNK*! into the bole of a tree just before him.

It was a long, thin, wicked-looking arrow. On its shaft was a white card; and on the card was printed in red letters:

STOP, MAN OF NIKKELDEPAIN!

The captain stopped and looked around slowly and cautiously. There was no one in sight. What did it mean?

He had a sudden feeling as if all of Karres were rising up silently in one stupendous, cool, foggy trap about him. His skin began to crawl. What was going to happen?

"Ha-ha!" said Goth, suddenly visible on a rock twelve feet to his left and eight feet above him. "You did stop!"

The captain let his breath out slowly.

"What else did you think I'd do?" he inquired. He felt a little faint.

She slid down from the rock like a lizard and stood before him. "Wanted to say good-by!" she told him.

Thin and brown, in jacket, breeches, boots, and cap of gray-green rock-lichen color, Goth looked very much in her element. The brown eyes looked up at him steadily; the mouth smiled faintly; but there was no real expression on her face at all. There was a quiverful of those enormous arrows slung over her shoulder, and some arrow-shooting gadget—not a bow—in her left hand.

She followed his glance.

"Bollem hunting up the mountain," she explained. "The wild ones. They're better meat—"

The captain reflected a moment. That's right, he recalled; they kept the tame Bollem herds mostly for milk, butter, and cheese. He'd learned a lot of important things about Karres, all right!

"Well," he said, "good-by, Goth!"

They shook hands gravely. Goth was the real Witch of Karres, he decided—more so than her sisters, more so even than Toll. But he hadn't actually learned a single thing about any of them.

Peculiar people!

He walked on, rather glumly.

"Captain!" Goth called after him. He turned.

"Better watch those take-offs," Goth called, "or you'll kill yourself yet!"

The captain cussed softly all the way up to the *Venture*.

And the take-off was terrible! A few swan hawks were watching but, he hoped, no one else.

V.

There wasn't the remotest possibility, of course, of resuming direct trade in the Empire with the cargo they'd loaded for him. But the more he thought about it now, the less likely it seemed that Councilor Onswud was going to let a genuine fortune slip through his hands on a mere technicality of embargoes. Nikkeldepain knew all the tricks of interstellar merchandising; and the councilor himself was undoubtedly the slickest unskinned miffel in the Republic.

More hopefully, the captain began to wonder whether some

sort of trade might not be made to develop eventually between Karres and Nikkeldepain. Now and then, he also thought of Maleen growing marriageable two years hence, Karres time. A handful of witch-notes went tinkling through his head whenever that idle reflection occurred.

The calendric chronometer informed him he'd spent three weeks there. He couldn't remember how their year compared with the standard one.

He found he was getting remarkably restless on this homeward run; and it struck him for the first time that space travel could also be nothing much more than a large hollow period of boredom. He made a few attempts to resume his sessions of small-talk with Illyla, via her picture; but the picture remained aloof.

The ship seemed unnaturally quiet now—that was the trouble! The captain's cabin, particularly, and the hall leading past it had become as dismal as a tomb.

But at long last, Nikkeldepain II swam up on the screen ahead. The captain put the *Venture* 7333 on orbit, and broadcast the ship's identification number. Half an hour later, Landing Control called him. He repeated the identification number, and added the ship's name, his name, owner's name, place of origin and nature of cargo.

The cargo had to be described in detail.

"Assume Landing Orbit 21,203 on your instruments," Landing Control instructed him. "A customs ship will come out to inspect."

He went on the assigned orbit and gazed moodily from the vision ports at the flat continents and oceans of Nikkeldepain II as they drifted by below. A sense of equally flat depression overcame him unexpectedly. He shook it off and remembered Illyla.

Three hours later, a ship ran up next to him; and he shut off the orbital drive. The communicator began buzzing. He switched it on.

"Vision, please!" said an official-sounding voice. The captain frowned, located the vision-stud of the communicator screen and pushed it down. Four faces appeared in vague outline on the screen, looking at him.

"Illyla!" the captain said.

"At least," young Councilor Rapport said unpleasantly, "he's brought back the ship, Father Onswud!"

"Illyla!" said the captain.

Councilor Onswud said nothing. Neither did Illyla. They both seemed to be staring at him, but the screen wasn't good enough to permit the study of expression in detail.

The fourth face, an unfamiliar one above a uniform collar, was the one with the official-sounding voice.

"You are instructed to open the forward lock, Captain Pausert," it said, "for an official investigation."

It wasn't till he was releasing the outer lock to the control room that the captain realized it wasn't Customs who had sent a boat out to him, but the police of the Republic.

However, he hesitated for only a moment. Then the outer lock gaped wide.

He tried to explain. They wouldn't listen. They had come on board in contamination-proof repulsor suits, all four of them; and they discussed the captain as if he weren't there. Illyla looked pale and angry and beautiful, and avoided looking at him.

However, he didn't want to speak to her before the others anyway.

They strolled back to the storage and gave the Karres cargo a casual glance.

"Damaged his lifeboat, too!" Councilor Rapport remarked.

They brushed past him down the narrow hallway and went back to the control room. The policeman asked to see the log and commercial records. The captain produced them.

The three men studied them briefly. Illyla gazed stonily out at Nikkeldepain II.

"Not too carefully kept!" the policeman pointed out.

"Surprising he bothered to keep them at all!" said Councilor Rapport.

"But it's all clear enough!" said Councilor Onswud.

They straightened up then and faced him in a line. Councilor Onswud folded his arms and projected his craggy chin. Councilor Rapport stood at ease, smiling faintly. The policeman became officially rigid.

Illyla remained off to one side, looking at the three.

"Captain Pausert," the policeman said, "the following charges—substantiated in part by this preliminary investigation— are made against you—"

"Charges?" said the captain.

"Silence, please!" rumbled Councilor Onswud.

"First: material theft of a quarter-million value of maels of jewels and jeweled items from a citizen of the Imperial Planet of Porlumma—"

"They were returned!" the captain protested.

"Restitution, particularly when inspired by fear of retribution, does not affect the validity of the original charge," Councilor Rapport quoted, gazing at the ceiling.

"Second," continued the policeman. "Purchase of human slaves, permitted under Imperial law but prohibited by penalty of ten years to lifetime penal servitude by the laws of the Republic of Nikkeldepain—"

"I was just taking them back where they belonged!" said the captain.

"We shall get to that point presently," the policeman replied. "Third, material theft of sundry items in the value of one hundred and eighty thousand maels from a ship of the Imperial Planet of Lepper, accompanied by threats of violence to the ship's personnel—"

"I might add in explanation of the significance of this particular charge," added Councilor Rapport, looking at the floor, "that the Regency of Sirius, containing Lepper, is allied to the Republic of Nikkeldepain by commercial and military treaties of considerable value. The Regency has taken the trouble to point out that such hostile conduct by a citizen of the Republic against citizens of the Regency is likely to have an adverse effect on the duration of the treaties. The charge thereby becomes compounded by the additional charge of a treasonable act against the Republic—"

He glanced at the captain. "I believe we can forestall the accused's plea that these pilfered goods also were restored. They were, in the face of superior force!"

"Fourth," the policeman went on patiently, "depraved and licentious conduct while acting as commercial agent, to the detriment of your employer's business and reputation—"

"WHAT?" choked the captain.

"—involving three of the notorious Witches of the Prohibited Planet of Karres—"

"Just like his great-uncle Threbus!" nodded Councilor Onswud gloomily. "It's in the blood, I always say!"

"—and a justifiable suspicion of a prolonged stay on said Prohibited Planet of Karres—"

"I never heard of that place before this trip!" shouted the captain.

"Why don't you read your Instructions and Regulations then?" shouted Councilor Rapport. "It's all there!"

"Silence, please!" shouted Councilor Onswud.

"Fifth," said the policeman quietly, "general willful and

negligent actions resulting in material damage and loss to your employer to the value of eighty-two thousand maels.''

"I've still got fifty-five thousand. And the stuff in the storage," the captain said, also quietly, "is worth half a million, at least!"

"Contraband and hence legally valueless!" the policeman said. Councilor Onswud cleared his throat.

"It will be impounded, of course," he said. "Should a method of resale present itself, the profits, if any, will be applied to the cancellation of your just debts. To some extent, that might reduce your sentence." He paused. "There is another matter—"

"The sixth charge," the policeman said, "is the development *and* public demonstration of a new type of space drive, which should have been brought promptly and secretly to the attention of the Republic of Nikkeldepain!"

They all stared at him—alertly and quite greedily.

So *that* was it—the Sheewash Drive!

"Your sentence may be greatly reduced, Pausert," Councilor Onswud said wheedlingly, "if you decide to be reasonable now. What have you discovered?"

"Look out, father!" Illyla said sharply.

"Pausert," Councilor Onswud inquired in a fading voice, "what is that in your hand?"

"A Blythe gun," the captain said, boiling.

There was a frozen stillness for an instant. Then the policeman's right hand made a convulsive movement.

"Uh-uh!" said the captain warningly.

Councilor Rapport started a slow step backwards.

"Stay where you are!" said the captain.

"Pausert!" Councilor Onswud and Illyla cried out together.

"Shut up!" said the captain.

There was another stillness.

"If you'd looked," the captain said, in an almost normal voice, "you'd have seen I've got the nova gun turrets out. They're fixed on that boat of yours. The boat's lying still and keeping its little yap shut. You do the same—"

He pointed a finger at the policeman. "You got a repulsor suit on," he said. "Open the inner port lock and go squirt yourself back to your boat!"

The inner port lock groaned open. Warm air left the ship in a long, lazy wave, scattering the sheets of the *Venture*'s log and commercial records over the floor. The thin, cold upper atmosphere of Nikkeldepain II came eddying in.

"You next, Onswud!" the captain said.

And a moment later: "Rapport, you just turn around—"

Young Councilor Rapport went through the port at a higher velocity than could be attributed reasonably to his repulsor units. The captain winced and rubbed his foot. But it had been worth it.

"Pausert," said Illyla in justifiable apprehension, "you are stark, staring mad!"

"Not at all, my dear," the captain said cheerfully. "You and I are now going to take off and embark on a life of crime together."

"But, Pausert—"

"You'll get used to it," the captain assured her, "just like I did. It's got Nikkeldepain beat every which way."

"Pausert," Illyla said, whitefaced, "we told them to bring up revolt ships!"

"We'll blow them out through the stratosphere," the captain said belligerently, reaching for the port-control switch. He added, "But they won't shoot anyway while I've got you on board!"

Illyla shook her head. "You just don't understand," she said desperately. "You can't make me stay!"

"Why not?" asked the captain.

"Pausert," said Illyla, "I am Madame Councilor Rapport."

"Oh!" said the captain. There was a silence. He added, crestfallen: "Since when?"

"Five months ago, yesterday," said Illyla.

"Great Patham!" cried the captain, with some indignation. "I'd hardly got off Nikkeldepain then! We were engaged!"

"Secretly . . . and I guess," said Illyla, with a return of spirit, "that I had a right to change my mind!"

There was another silence.

"Guess you had, at that," the captain agreed. "All right—the port's still open, and your husband's waiting in the boat. Beat it!"

He was alone. He let the ports slam shut and banged down the oxygen release switch. The air had become a little thin.

He cussed.

The communicator began rattling for attention. He turned it on.

"Pausert!" Councilor Onswud was calling in a friendly but shaking voice. "May we not depart, Pausert? Your nova guns are still fixed on this boat!"

"Oh, that—" said the captain. He deflected the turrets a trifle. "They won't go off now. Scram!"

The police boat vanished.

There was other company coming, though. Far below him but climbing steadily, a trio of revolt ships darted past on the screen, swung around and came back for the next turn of their spiral. They'd have to get a good deal closer before they started shooting; but they'd try to stay under him so as not to knock any stray chunks out of Nikkeldepain.

He sat a moment, reflecting. The revolt ships went by once more. The captain punched in the *Venture*'s secondary drives, turned her nose towards the planet and let her go. There were some scattered white puffs around as he cut through the revolt ships' plane of flight. Then he was below them, and the *Venture* groaned as he took her out of the dive.

The revolt ships were already scattering and nosing over for a counter-maneuver. He picked the nearest one and swung the nova guns towards it.

"—and ram them in the middle!" he muttered between his teeth.

SSS-whoosh!

It was the Sheewash Drive—but, like a nightmare now, it kept on and on!

VI.

"Maleen!" the captain bawled, pounding at the locked door of the captain's cabin. "Maleen—shut it off! Cut it off! You'll kill yourself, Maleen!"

The *Venture* quivered suddenly throughout her length, then shuddered more violently, jumped and coughed; and commenced sailing along on her secondary drives again. He wondered how many light-years from everything they were by now. It didn't matter!

"Maleen!" he yelled. "Are you all right?"

There was a faint *thump-thump* inside the cabin, and silence. He lost almost a minute finding the right cutting tool in the storage. A few seconds later, a section of door panel sagged inwards; he caught it by one edge and came tumbling into the cabin with it.

He had the briefest glimpse of a ball of orange-colored fire swirling uncertainly over a cone of oddly bent wires. Then the fire vanished, and the wires collapsed with a loose rattling to the table top.

The crumpled small shape lay behind the table, which was

why he didn't discover it at once. He sagged to the floor beside it, all the strength running out of his knees.

Brown eyes opened and blinked at him blearily.

"Sure takes it out of you!" Goth grunted. "Am I hungry?"

"I'll whale the holy, howling tar out of you again," the captain roared, "if you ever—"

"Quit your bawling!" snarled Goth. "I got to eat."

She ate for fifteen minutes straight, before she sank back in her chair, and sighed.

"Have some more Wintenberry jelly," the captain offered anxiously. She looked pretty pale.

Goth shook her head. "Couldn't—and that's about the first thing you've said since you fell through the door, howling for Maleen. Ha-ha! Maleen's *got* a boyfriend!"

"Button your lip, child," the captain said. "I was thinking." He added, after a moment: "Has she really?"

"Picked him out last year," Goth nodded. "Nice boy from town—they get married as soon as she's marriageable. She just told you to come back because she was upset about you. Maleen had a premonition you were headed for awful trouble!"

"She was quite right, little chum," the captain said nastily.

"What were you thinking about?" Goth inquired.

"I was thinking," said the captain, "that as soon as we're sure you're going to be all right, I'm taking you straight back to Karres!"

"I'll be all right now," Goth said. "Except, likely, for a stomach-ache. But you can't take me back to Karres."

"Who will stop me, may I ask?" the captain asked.

"Karres is gone," Goth said.

"Gone?" the captain repeated blankly, with a sensation of not quite definable horror bubbling up in him.

"Not blown up or anything," Goth reassured him. "They just moved it! The Imperialists got their hair up about us again. But this time, they were sending a fleet with the big bombs and stuff, so everybody was called home. But they had to wait then till they found out where we were—me and Maleen and the Leewit. Then you brought us in; and they had to wait again, and decide about you. But right after you'd left . . . *we'd* left, I mean . . . they moved it."

"Where?"

"Great Patham!" Goth shrugged. "How'd I know? There's lots of places!"

*   *   *

There probably were, the captain admitted silently. A scene came suddenly before his eyes—that lime-white, arenalike bowl in the valley, with the steep tiers of seats around it, just before they'd reached the town of Karres—"the Theater where—"

But now there was unnatural night-darkness all over and about that world; and the eight thousand-some Witches of Karres sat in circles around the Theater, their heads bent towards one point in the center, where orange fire washed hugely about the peak of a cone of curiously twisted girders.

And a world went racing off at the speeds of the Sheewash Drive! There'd be lots of places, all right. What peculiar people!

"Anyway," he sighed, "if I've got to start raising you—don't say 'Great Patham' any more. That's a cuss word!"

"I learned it from you!" Goth pointed out.

"So you did, I guess," the captain acknowledged. "I won't say it either. Aren't they going to be worried about you?"

"Not very much," said Goth. "We don't get hurt often—especially when we're young. That's when we can do all that stuff like teleporting, and whistling, like the Leewit. We lose it mostly when we get older—they're working on that now so we won't. About all Maleen can do right now is premote!"

"She premotes just dandy, though," the captain said. "The Sheewash Drive—they can all do that, can't they?"

"Uh-huh!" Goth nodded. "But that's learned stuff. That's one of the things they already studied out." She added, a trace uncomfortably: "I can't tell you about that till you're one yourself."

"Till I'm what myself?" the captain asked, becoming puzzled again.

"A witch, like us," said Goth. "We got our rules. And that won't be for four years, Karres time."

"It won't, eh?" said the captain. "What happens then?"

"That's when I'm marriageable age," said Goth, frowning at the jar of Wintenberry jelly. She pulled it towards her and inspected it carefully. "I got it all fixed," she told the jelly firmly, "as soon as they started saying they ought to pick out a wife for you on Karres, so you could stay. I said it was me, right away; and everyone else said finally that was all right then—even Maleen, because she had this boy friend."

"You mean?" said the captain, stunned, "this was all planned out on Karres?"

"Sure," said Goth. She pushed the jelly back where it had been standing, and glanced up at him again. "For three weeks, that's about all everyone talked about in the town! It set a perceedent—''

She paused doubtfully.

"That would explain it," the captain admitted.

"Uh-huh," Goth nodded relieved, settling back in her chair. "But it was my father who told us how to do it so you'd break up with the people on Nikkeldepain. He said it was in the blood."

"What was in the blood?" the captain said patiently.

"That you'd break up with them. That's Threbus, my father," Goth informed him. "You met him a couple of times in the town. Big man with a blond beard—Maleen and the Leewit take after him."

"You wouldn't mean my great-uncle Threbus?" the captain inquired. He was in a state of strange calm by now.

"That's right," said Goth. "He liked you a lot."

"It's a small Galaxy," said the captain philosophically. "So that's where Threbus wound up! I'd like to meet him again some day."

"We'll start after Karres four years from now, when you learn about those things," Goth said. "We'll catch up with them all right. That's still thirteen hundred and seventy-two Old Sidereal days," she added, "but there's a lot to do in between. You want to pay the money you owe back to those people, don't you? I got some ideas—''

"None of those teleporting tricks now!" the captain warned.

"Kid stuff!" Goth said scornfully. "I'm growing up. This'll be fair swapping. But we'll get rich."

"I wouldn't be surprised," the captain admitted. He thought a moment. "Seeing we've turned out to be distant relatives, I suppose it is all right, too, if I adopt you meanwhile—''

"Sure," said Goth. She stood up.

"Where you going?" the captain asked.

"Bed," said Goth. "I'm tired." She stopped at the hall door. "About all I can tell you about us till then," she said, "you can read in those Regulations, like the one man said—the one you kicked off the ship. There's a lot about us in there. Lots of lies, too, though!"

"And when did you find out about the communicator between here and the captain's cabin?" the captain inquired.

Goth grinned. "A while back," she admitted. "The others never noticed!"

"All right," the captain said. "Good night, witch—if you get a stomach-ache, yell and I'll bring the medicine."

"Good night," Goth yawned. "I will, I think."

"And wash behind your ears!" the captain added, trying to remember the bedtime instructions he'd overheard Maleen giving the junior witches.

"All right," said Goth sleepily. The hall door closed behind her—but half a minute later, it was briskly opened again. The captain looked up startled from the voluminous stack of "General Instructions and Space Regulations of the Republic of Nikkeldepain" he'd just discovered in one of the drawers of the control desk. Goth stood in the doorway, scowling and wide-awake.

"And you wash behind yours!" she said.

"Huh?" said the captain. He reflected a moment. "All right," he said. "We both will, then."

"Right," said Goth, satisfied.

The door closed once more.

The captain began to run his finger down the lengthy index of K's—or could it be under W?

Don't miss the great novels of Dray Prescot on Kregen, world of Antares!

☐ A LIFE FOR KREGEN	(#UE1456—$1.75)
☐ A SWORD FOR KREGEN	(#UJ1485—$1.95)
☐ A FORTUNE FOR KREGEN	(#UJ1505—$1.95)
☐ VICTORY FOR KREGEN	(#UJ1532—$1.95)
☐ BEASTS OF ANTARES	(#UJ1555—$1.95)
☐ REBEL OF ANTARES	(#UJ1582—$1.95)
☐ LEGIONS OF ANTARES	(#UE1648—$2.25)
☐ MANHOUNDS & ARENA OF ANTARES	(#UE1650—$2.75)
☐ ALLIES OF ANTARES	(#UE1671—$2.25)
☐ MAZES OF SCORPIO	(#UE1739—$2.25)
☐ FIRES OF SCORPIO	(#UE1816—$2.50)
☐ DELIA OF VALLIA	(#UE1784—$2.35)
☐ TRANSIT TO SCORPIO	(#UE1820—$2.50)
☐ TALONS OF SCORPIO	(#UE1886—$2.50)

NEW AMERICAN LIBRARY
P.O. Box 999, Bergenfield, New Jersey 07621

Please send me the DAW BOOKS I have checked above. I am enclosing
$_____ (check or money order—no currency or C.O.D.'s).
Please include the list price plus $1.00 per order to cover handling
costs.

Name _____

Address _____

City _____ State _____ Zip Code _____
Please allow at least 4 weeks for delivery

PHILIP K. DICK

"The greatest American novelist of the second half of the 20th Century."

—*Norman Spinrad*

"A genius . . . He writes it the way he sees it and it is the quality, the clarity of his Vision that makes him great."

—*Thomas M. Disch*

"The most consistently brilliant science fiction writer in the world."

—*John Brunner*

PHILIP K. DICK

In print again, in DAW Books' special memorial editions:

- ☐ **WE CAN BUILD YOU** (#UE1793—$2.50)
- ☐ **THE THREE STIGMATA OF PALMER ELDRITCH** (#UE1810—$2.50)
- ☐ **A MAZE OF DEATH** (#UE1830—$2.50)
- ☐ **UBIK** (#UE1859—$2.50)
- ☐ **DEUS IRAE** (#UE1887—$2.50)
- ☐ **NOW WAIT FOR LAST YEAR** (#UE1654—$2.50)
- ☐ **FLOW MY TEARS, THE POLICEMAN SAID** (#UE1624—$2.25)

NEW AMERICAN LIBRARY,
P.O. Box 999, Bergenfield, New Jersey 07621

Please send me the DAW BOOKS I have checked above. I am enclosing $_____ (check or money order—no currency or C.O.D.'s). Please include the list price plus $1.00 per order to cover handling costs.

Name _____

Address _____

City _____ State _____ Zip Code _____

Please allow at least 4 weeks for delivery

Presenting C. J. CHERRYH

- [ ] **DOWNBELOW STATION.** A blockbuster of a novel! Interstellar warfare as humanity's colonies rise in cosmic rebellion. (#UE1594—$2.75)
- [ ] **SERPENT'S REACH.** Two races lived in harmony in a quarantined constellation—until one person broke the truce! (#UE1682—$2.50)
- [ ] **THE PRIDE OF CHANUR.** "Immensely successful . . . *Tour de force* . . . This is quintessential SF. . . ."—Algis Budrys. (#UE1695—$2.95)
- [ ] **HUNTER OF WORLDS.** Triple fetters of the mind served to keep their human prey bondage to this city-sized starship. (#UE1559—$2.25)
- [ ] **BROTHERS OF EARTH.** This in-depth novel of an alien world and a human who had to adjust or die was a Science Fiction Book Club Selection. (#UJ1470—$1.95)
- [ ] **THE FADED SUN: KESRITH.** Universal praise for this novel of the last members of humanity's warrior-enemies . . . and the Earthman who was fated to save them. (#UE1692—$2.50)
- [ ] **THE FADED SUN: SHON'JIR.** Across the untracked stars to the forgotten world of the Mri go the last of that warrior race and the man who had betrayed humanity. (#UE1753—$2.50)
- [ ] **THE FADED SUN: KUTATH.** The final and dramatic conclusion of this bestselling trilogy—with three worlds in militant confrontation. (#UE1743—$2.50)
- [ ] **THE DREAMSTONE.** A marvelous fantasy of the last stronghold of Faerie. (#UE1808—$2.75)
- [ ] **THE TREE OF SWORDS AND JEWELS.** The final showdown between Magick and the Iron Swords. (#UE1850—$2.95)

NEW AMERICAN LIBRARY
P.O. Box 999, Bergenfield, New Jersey 07621

Please send me the DAW BOOKS I have checked above. I am enclosing $_____ (check or money order—no currency or C.O.D.'s). Please include the list price plus $1.00 per order to cover handling costs.

Name _____

Address _____

City _____ State _____ Zip Code _____
Please allow at least 4 weeks for delivery